S.B. Caves

HONEYCOMB

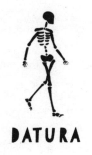

DATURA

DATURA BOOKS
An imprint of Watkins Media Ltd

Unit 11, Shepperton House
89 Shepperton Road
London N1 3DF
UK

daturabooks.com
twitter.com/daturabooks
Everybody loves the queen bee

A Datura Books paperback original, 2024

Cover by Sarah O'Flaherty
Edited by Ella Chappell and Alice Abrams.
Set in Meridien

ISBN 978 1 91552 321 1
Ebook ISBN 978 1 91552 3 228

Printed and bound in the United Kingdom by CPI Group (UK) Ltd, Croydon CR0 4YY.

9 8 7 6 5 4 3 2 1

For my naughty sons, Joobi and Bap-Bap; because I love you more than I could ever put into words.
And for SLB, always.

"In the future, everyone will be world-famous for 15 minutes."
— Andy Warhol

PROLOGUE

James Moshida was becoming obsessed with the rats. Though, if asked, he would have used the word *beguiled*.

He was peering into a large Perspex box, inside of which a black rat sat atop a ledge, nibbling on a cracker. Moshida hadn't seen any adverse physical change in the black rat, whom he now affectionately thought of as Roland, although the rat had grown fatter due to the limitations of his new environment. Roland appeared wary, spooked almost – if a rat *can* be spooked – and lingered on his ledge, skittishly surveying his surroundings. He hadn't trusted the other rats since Day 9.

Below the ledge, five more rats sat single file. They were motionless except for the blinking of their oily black eyes and the odd twitch of their pink noses. Their heads pointed reverently toward Roland. As the days wore on, the rats showed less interest in their food, and Moshida thought he knew why; they didn't want to stray too far from their line for fear of losing rank. He assumed they were playing a waiting game, seeing which of them would survive the hunger strike and earn their coveted place next to Roland.

There had been six rats, but on Day 9, one *deviated*. It had ideas of scuttling up the ramp in an effort to get closer to Roland – an act that sparked outrage among the rest of the mischief.

And then, there were five.

Moshida wondered what they would do tomorrow when he removed Roland from the box. If it was anything like what they did to the offending white rat on Day 9, then he expected a massacre. He had been keeping detailed notes on Roland's congregation, and he estimated they lost their tiny minds somewhere around Day 5. Remembering this made Moshida smile, although the thought of scooping smeared rat gore from the clear walls of the box wasn't exactly his idea of a holiday. Still, it would be interesting to see, and their remains would prove invaluable once he ran his tests. But that came tomorrow.

Roland continued eating his cracker. When he finished the last bite, he waddled to the opposite corner of the box. The other rats' heads turned in unison, watching him go.

CHAPTER 1

Everyone loves a good comeback story, and Amanda Pearson believed this was the beginning of hers. That's why, three hours before the limo arrived, she was already dressed and ready to go. She had not been in a limo in a very long time, and the idea of stepping back into one now filled her with a giddy sense of unease. She could not fully trust herself to resist the lure once she smelled the leather seats and saw the world through tinted windows. The ritual of applying makeup, spritzing herself with perfume, and fussing with her hair in front of the full-length mirror was a sweet cruelty, an indulgence she could too easily get used to again. The feel of the black dress over her skin was exquisite, even if the reflection looking back at her was not. She had not been featured in any of the glossies for months and the dress told her the truth. It might have fit her a year ago, but now it appeared uncomfortably clingy.

So, I've got curves, she thought, and had to quickly remind herself, I look healthy.

Yes, healthy, which was really a media synonym for fat, but of course, it was better than the alternative. There had been a time when this dress would have billowed around her body like a flag at full mast. There had also been a time when her glassy eyes would have rolled around in their sunken sockets, unable to focus.

But those times were gone, and she was thankful.

She turned her face in the mirror, checking her forehead from different angles. The foundation managed to conceal most of the stress bumps that had sprouted in the last day or so, but if someone approached her from the side, it would look like she was growing a horn. There was nothing much that could be done about the crescents of tiredness carved beneath her eyes; she was beyond the gel patches now and would likely need something from a syringe to erase six years of hard living.

She sat down, thought about fixing herself a drink, and then decided against it. She was saving herself for the champagne in the limo, could almost feel the bubbles popping on her tongue. She would pour one glass, make it last for the duration of the journey, and have no more alcohol until she had put away some hors d'oeuvres. She could not afford to turn up tipsy and risk buckling over in her heels, flashing her knickers at the other guests. That was a worst-case scenario, of course, but she had an uncanny knack for humiliating herself.

Tonight was all about new beginnings, leaving the past behind her.

Or was it? She wasn't entirely sure what to make of tonight's event. For all she knew, this whole thing could be a cruel, sadistic prank. There might not be a party at all. She could be sitting here all dolled up waiting for a limousine that would never arrive. As it had a habit of doing, her mind gave flesh to this awful idea, and she envisioned how she would look peeling off the black dress with mascara trailing down her powdery cheeks. She would weep alone in her flat, hating the sound of her hitched breath, and shuffle off to bed seeking refuge beneath the duvet.

Thinking about all that made her face flush with heat. She picked up an envelope from the stack of bills on the coffee table and fanned herself with it, exhaling gently. She didn't want to start sweating this early in the evening, so she closed her eyes and mentally squeezed the thoughts out of her head. The limo would arrive. There was a party in Kensington and she was invited. But just to make sure, she opened her clutch bag, removed her iPhone, and checked the emails again. She scanned the sentences, searching for crossed wires, but it was all very straightforward. In fact, the simplicity scared her. She was used to convoluted contracts, misdirection, paragraphs riddled with ambiguity. Yet, even with her paranoia cranked into fifth gear, she couldn't find any signs of deceit.

Bunny hadn't been in contact for all these years; when Amanda picked up a bad habit, Bunny dropped her like one. Then, completely out of the blue, Amanda received an email from her through her website's generic info address. She usually received about five spam messages a day, ranging from non-surgical ways she could increase the size of her penis, to compensation she was owed from a car crash she had never been involved in. She had not received a lukewarm message from a "fan" or an angry diatribe from a troll in months, but she still checked the inbox daily, hoping for something. Even John Meadows, now a YouTube sensation from his segment on the documentary Super Fans, had gone quiet on her. Meadows was a forty-three year-old cab driver from Birmingham who had seven tattoos of Amanda's face on his body, and lyrics from most of her songs scrawled on his back. She had never replied to any of his rambling love letters, was not even sure what he was saying in most of them, but she appreciated them just the same.

Now, Bunny was apparently her friend again. The message was concise, the clipped sentences reading like bullet points. She was eager to meet Amanda to discuss new opportunities, and suggested they talk over drinks at a private cocktail party.

After rereading the email numerous times, Amanda spent two days wondering whether she should reply at all, and then another two days drafting her response. Despite her eagerness, Amanda didn't want to appear desperate, especially after everything that had transpired between them. There was so much Amanda had wanted to say, and yet, an email couldn't quite convey the complex maelstrom of emotions she felt. Eventually, she had settled for a simple reply, forgoing the filler.

Amanda turned the TV on, hoping it would distract her mind while she waited for the limo, but couldn't seem to settle. She checked her legs for nicks and razor bumps, held out her hands and compared the complexion of her fake tan. She had never been good at painting her own nails but thought she had done a surprisingly good job on this occasion, even though they were already starting to chip.

She was beginning to realize that blue lipstick, no matter how subtle the shade, was a mistake. It looked like something a teenybopper would wear after receiving it free in some gossip mag. What had she been thinking? Well, that was an easy one. Whether deliberately or subliminally, she had been thinking about the video for "Baby, I Can be your Girl," when she wore blue eyeshadow and lipstick, and a luminous green boob-tube that had revealed a bouncing nineteen year-old cleavage and effortless abs.

She stood up with the intention of getting some tissue to wipe her lips when her phone began to ring, startling her. She had the volume up to max just in case. It was a private number. When she answered it, a man's voice said, "Good evening, is that Mrs Pearson?"

No, it was Miss Pearson, not that it mattered. "Uh, yes, hi."

"Hello, I'm your driver. I'm parked up downstairs."

"Great, thank you. I'll be down in two," she said, and hung up. She shuddered, the muscles in her legs turning to sponge. She trotted over to the mirror again, checking her hair, her teeth, the bumps on her forehead, and then began toward the front door. A lump lodged in her throat, making her want to gag every time she swallowed. She whispered, "Please help me tonight, god," and expelled a shaky breath, before leaving the flat.

Her stilettos clicked and clacked in the hallway as she walked, struggling to keep her balance. She was out of practice, and when she thought she had her rhythm nailed and tried to pick up the pace, her ankles wobbled. She had managed less than twenty steps but could already feel the shoes biting painfully into her heels. There would be some nasty blisters before long; she just hoped they didn't burst before she got back to the flat.

Her ears felt hot and full of blood and she knew they would be glowing red. She rummaged around in her bag, found the packet of tissues, and removed one to dab her hairline. When she made it out of the building, the late summer breeze whispered across her skin pleasantly. She craned her head and peered into the car park. In the puddle of dull orange streetlight sat a sleek black limo. She began toward it and saw people on their balconies peering out with phones in hand, recording it as though it were a UFO.

The chauffer saw her approach, got out of the car, and offered her a smile. "Hello Mrs Pearson. Nice to meet you." He opened the back door for her. She thanked him and got inside, sinking down on the plush leather seat. When he closed the door, she could hear her neighbours barking things at the limo, laughing, making jokes.

The hairs prickled on her neck, and her forearms broke out in a rash of gooseflesh. When the limo began to move, her breath caught in her throat and a rapid shutter click of images popped in her mind; memories of pulling up to premiers and exclusive nightclubs, the gasp and commotion from the normal people caught off-guard by her arrival. She let the déjà vu wash over her, drunk on that familiar cocktail of sadness and longing.

"Help yourself to champagne back there," the chauffeur said when he was behind the wheel. He needn't have bothered. She had a flute in hand and was gulping the champagne down like water, her willpower already broken. She had been in the limo for less than five minutes when she realized he was playing "Temper, Temper" – the second single from her debut album. It had gone to number one and stayed there for two weeks, but Amanda knew its charting was only the result of her first single's momentum. The song was putrid and banal, her vocals electronically tweaked until they were almost unrecognizable above the obnoxious reggaeton beat. She hadn't cared at the time of the recording. Her eyes had been so bloodshot from blow it was a miracle she had even been able to read the lyrics, let alone sing them.

"Excuse me driver? Can you turn this off?"

"Sure. Do you want me to put the radio on?"

"No," she said, and poured more champagne.

CHAPTER 2

The limo turned off the high street and cruised down a narrow side road, pulling up to a discreet entrance outside a building. In front of it, two large, suited doormen welcomed in a couple of elegantly dressed women. Amanda wasn't sure who had designed their dresses, but she had enough fashion sense to know that one of them was carrying a genuine crocodile leather handbag. When they turned to enter the building, Amanda saw the red soles of their shoes and analyzed their stride, impressed at the grace with which they navigated the stairs in their heels.

The limo door opened, and the street sounds filtered in, perforating Amanda's protective bubble. Her hands curled over her cheap clutch bag. She looked down at her shoes resentfully, hating them because the soles weren't red, knowing that one misstep and the heels would snap like breadsticks.

"Are you alright, Mrs Pearson?" the chauffeur asked.

"Yeah I'm fine. Sorry, just a second," she said, making no attempt to get out, especially not while another couple were entering the building. She waited until the street seemed empty before struggling out of the car, fearing that her dress would split right down the side as soon as she stood up. The fabric held, thank god, but that counterweight in her brain that balanced her equilibrium rolled to the side. She swayed, grabbed the door for support, surprised at the way the champagne had snuck up on her. She thanked the driver again and started toward the doormen, her teeth chattering with nervousness.

"Good evening," one of the doormen said.

"Hi, I should be on the list. I'm Amanda Pearson?" She hated offering her name. There was always an awkward moment where they had to search the filing cabinet of their minds to dig out the image they remembered. Then, they had to calibrate that image with the person standing before them, looking for similarities.

Without checking a clipboard or referring to a radio, or even asking for ID, the doorman said, "Of course." He gave her a broad smile and lifted the velvet rope.

Clutching the banister, she ascended the broad marble staircase. Dreamy trip-hop music sailed out to her as she reached the first floor and was greeted by a waitress holding a tray of champagne. Amanda took a flute, wanting to occupy her hands more than anything else, and peered into the dimly lit, high-ceilinged room. Clusters of people mingled around, and Amanda thought that more than a few of them were probably famous, though she couldn't have said where she knew them from; it was more the way they dressed and carried themselves, oozing an air of carefree confidence, radiating importance.

She threaded through the room, attempting to admire the artwork that decorated the walls, but between the alcohol and the soft purple glow from the lights, she could barely see much. It was all an act anyway. She just didn't want to look like the lone ranger at a party full of influencers. She watched the DJ for a little while – a young Japanese man with a bleached blonde beard – before exploring another area. Going through a corridor, she came to a room that had a large water fountain in the middle of it. Spotlights beneath the water revealed large, orange- and black-spotted koi carp swimming lazily. She found a space on one of the suede sofas surrounding the fountain and sent a text to Bunny to tell her as much. Within seconds, Bunny replied.

Great, I'll come and find you now.

It sounded to Amanda like the tempo of the music was speeding up and slowing down every few bars, which only disorientated her further. She knew there would be people snorting cocaine off the toilet seats in the bathrooms of this lavish establishment, and could only wonder how they were reacting to the ambience. Paranoia had plagued Amanda for years now, and in her experience, the coke didn't dampen that awful, lurking dread she felt when in a new environment, surrounded by people she didn't know. If she took a bump up the nostril now she would be freaking out within seconds, convinced that someone wanted to hurt her, that they were snapping pictures to put on social media, that they were all in a big conspiracy to point and laugh at the joke she had become. She didn't need drugs to dream up catastrophes; her mind was well attuned to doing that all by itself.

"Amanda?"

The familiar voice jerked her out of her reverie. She looked up and saw Bunny in a tight, shimmering silver dress that made her look like a mermaid. There was a moment of displacement as time and reality clicked out of place, before Amanda shook it off and stood to greet Bunny.

Bunny smiled, her shiny forehead unmoving, and then leaned in for a hug. They fumbled awkwardly into an embrace, smothering the four years of silence between them.

"It's so good to see you again, Mandy."

Nobody had ever called her Mandy except for Bunny. Hearing it again now felt both warm and prickly.

"Thank you for inviting me," Amanda said, still sizing her up. Bunny had to be forty-five now but was better preserved than most of the millennials in here, Amanda included.

"You look great," Bunny said, appraising her.

Amanda touched her hair, self-consciously. "You're still a good liar," she said, unsmiling.

"I mean it," Bunny replied, unruffled by the jab. "You look…"

"Don't say *healthy*."

"…Well. You look well."

Even though it was nothing more than an empty pleasantry, it still made Amanda feel nice. She couldn't remember the last time someone had paid her a compliment that didn't come with a caveat. The magazines hid their brutality with professional insincerity, publishing a picture of her eating a burger while exclaiming how refreshing it was to see women not being so obsessed with their weight.

"Let's get away from this weird music. We have a room upstairs," Bunny said, leading the way back down the corridor to a VIP lift in front of which hung a velvet rope, manned by a guard. Upon seeing Bunny, the guard removed the rope and opened the doors for them. That gesture sent a small, pleasant shiver through Amanda.

They went up to the top floor and into a smaller room that had wall-to-ceiling windows offering a view of the winking city skyline. There were less than two dozen people up here, not including the bar staff or the pianist on the grand piano in the corner.

"This is better, right? We can hear ourselves think. Can I get you another drink or are you happy with champagne?"

"I'm fine with this," Amanda said, tapping the flute.

"I can't drink champagne, it burns right through my stomach. I'm going to grab an Old Fashioned."

Amanda accompanied her to the bar, reading the room as she went. The clientele here was a bit older but undoubtedly still rooted in show business, most likely producers, directors and agents.

"Oh, I needed this," Bunny said, picking the straw out of the glass and raising the drink to her lips. Amanda noticed that her slender fingers were decorated with diamonds. "Look at that view," she said, nodding toward the window. "That's really something, isn't it?"

"Yeah, just like the view from my flat but without the tower blocks."

Bunny gave her a practised PR laugh that ended too abruptly

to be natural. Then, she said, "Do you miss it Amanda? The life, I mean?"

"I miss recording and performing. Some of the other stuff I could do without."

Bunny nodded, stirring the ice in her glass with her straw. "Mandy, I want to ask you something, but I don't want to upset you."

"Oh, come on now, Bunny. That hasn't stopped you in the past."

Bunny took a moment to consider her words before speaking again. "Remember that photo of you at The Butterfly Lounge?"

She let the sentence hang there for Amanda to do the heavy lifting. Amanda felt the muscles tighten in her neck, the low throb of anger working its way up from her stomach. The photo of her leaving The Butterfly Lounge with her nostrils ringed with "suspicious white powder' had made headline news. The bastards had blown the photo up to highlight her watery, bloodshot eyes, giving her an almost demonic appearance. The squeaky-clean girl-next-door image that Bunny and the record label had built was shattered overnight. In a ham-fisted attempt at damage control, Bunny had booked her for an afternoon chat show, to dispel the rumours of drug use. During the interview, Amanda appeared bewildered, giving rambling, incoherent answers to seemingly straightforward questions. She was defensive, gesturing wildly with her hands, and under the harsh studio lights seemed to have aged a decade since the photo was taken.

A week later, her label dropped her, or "parted amicably" as the press release put it. Bunny was the one that had broken the news to her. They hadn't spoken since.

"What about it?" Amanda asked, but thought she already knew where this was going.

"Is that all in the past now?"

"Am I clean, is what you really want to ask me?"

"And what about the YouTube stuff?"

There it was. Bunny had set her up with the Butterfly Lounge jab and now delivered the knockout blow. What she was talking about wasn't really a question, but more of a reminder. Yes, the infamous rant on her now-deleted YouTube channel, or as Amanda thought of it, the single most soul-destroying, embarrassing moment of her life.

"I wasn't very well," Amanda snapped, her fingers curling into a fist. "Everyone wants to talk about mental health these days – well, my mental health was shot to fucking pieces back then, Bunny. If I had been well and not on the verge of a mental breakdown, do you really think I would've made that video?"

It had seemed like such a poignant and powerfully liberating idea at the time. But, if Amanda recalled correctly, she'd been snorting lines and draining vodka for the best part of two days, and the mania culminated in that four-minute-and-fifteen-second tirade. Alone in her flat, paranoid and fidgety, she had stared into the laptop camera and began ranting. Not only did she generally attack her record label, but she dropped names as well – among them, Bunny. If that hadn't been flammable enough to burn the bridge forever, she also started listing off her conspiracy theories, about how the label had spies that were recording her, so she'd had to black out her windows with boot polish. She explained that one of the producers on the album, a reasonably pleasant man named Jeff Corner, had put subliminal messages all through the record, instructing listeners to self-harm, to stab people, and commit suicide. There were some other incoherent ramblings about lizard people, and a random idea accusing a woman who lived two floors above her of being a witch that could astral project into Amanda's living room.

The YouTube video ended up being the most successful thing she'd ever released. It went viral overnight, and by the time she regained her senses and deleted the video, it had already been re-uploaded, and remixed, by a hundred other channels.

Bunny stirred her ice. "I didn't mean to cause any offense–"

"Why don't we cut to the chase." Amanda gulped the last of the champagne and put the flute on the bar. "Why am I here, Bunny? Your email said you wanted to discuss new opportunities with me."

"Of course." Bunny smiled apologetically. "I know it's been a rough road for you. I had no right coming at you like that just now, I apologize."

Amanda inhaled deeply. "I'm clean now," she said. "I have been for almost two years. I know you can't take that on face value, but there's a thing called a hair follicle test you can do to prove it." She had heard about this test on numerous episodes of *Judge Judy*, a show she had become obsessed with in the downtime she had since her career came to a screaming halt.

"There's no need for that," Bunny said. "I believe you. I can see it. I really do mean it, you know; you do look well."

"You don't need to bullshit me. I'm twenty-six and I feel fifty-six. Probably look it too."

"No, you don't. Look." She leaned on the bar, settling in for one of her world-famous pep talks. Déjà vu whispered through Amanda as Bunny looked deep into her eyes. "Everything happened to you so quickly and at such a young age. I mean, nineteen – you were still a baby, and at the risk of sounding like a pretentious old woman, you still are awfully young. Young enough to turn everything around and get back on track. But all that depends."

"On what?"

"On what you want. Sometimes people have a hard time figuring that out. Do you know what you want, Amanda?"

"I don't have a clue what you're trying to say to me, Bunny. I wish you would just get on with it."

"It's warm in here, isn't it? Let's go on the balcony, get some fresh air. Not afraid of heights, are you?"

"No." Amanda shook her head. Now that her temper was settling, she felt vulnerable, with the sudden, unreasonable urge to impress Bunny, to please her. She thought about perhaps finding some way to give her a sample of her voice, to show that she wasn't completely shot. She might've been older and heavier, but Amanda was still the same girl from Croydon that won *Searching for a Star*.

Bunny pushed the fire exit door and held it open for Amanda. "Watch your step there."

Amanda went out onto the balcony and closed the door behind her, muting the melodic piano music.

Inside, the men and women paused their conversations to watch Bunny's progress, their eyes rolling toward the balcony in unison. The pianist's fingers continued to glide over the keys, but even he chanced a look, albeit briefly.

When Amanda turned to check her reflection in the window, the conversation inside the room resumed, and the pantomime continued.

Amanda wasn't aware they had stopped talking at all.

CHAPTER 3

"You have a magic lamp," Bunny began, taking a pull on her cigarette. She exhaled and squinted through a ribbon of smoke. "And you have one wish. What is it?"

"One wish?" Amanda's gaze swept across the moon-bathed rooftops in contemplation. She laughed mirthlessly. "Just the one?"

"Not easy, is it? See, most people would say they want to be rich, but you already know what that's like. Or someone might say they want to be famous, but you already know what that's like too, don't you?"

"Not anymore," Amanda said, turning to face her.

"There," Bunny pointed her cigarette at Amanda. "That's it. Money is money, it comes and goes, and it never really makes anyone happier. Don't get me wrong, being rich is a lot easier than being broke, nobody is going to argue about that. But being famous? Having people recognize you, adoring you, going out of their mind at the mere sight of you? God, it must be the best feeling in the world." She dragged on her cigarette, and when Amanda didn't say anything, Bunny asked, "Is it?"

"Yeah," Amanda said in a very small voice, and then she fell silent a moment, dizzied by the nostalgia. An image slipped out of her memory: eating sushi at an expensive restaurant and ordering wine that cost more than her outfit, before having the entire bill waived by the manager in exchange for a photo. Then, stepping outside only to see a gang of over twenty people waiting in the freezing December rain for autographs. One girl crying with joy, unable to speak through trembling lips because Amanda had hugged her.

She could feel pressure building behind her eyeballs, the sting of tears threatening to blur her vision. The champagne was making her maudlin, but if she was honest with herself, it was more than that. She hadn't spoken to anyone about the death of her career since the label dropped her. She'd had a window of opportunity to vent – offers streaming in from magazines and trashy tabloids – but the pain had been too raw, and she had been too distracted.

"Why am I here, Bunny?"

"Something has come up that you might find interesting. A company contacted me to enquire about your services. I had to explain that I no longer represented you, but that seemed like a great way for us to get back in touch. Perhaps we can work together again if you find everything agreeable."

"Who was the company?"

"They're called The Midori Media Group. You won't have heard of them; they're new."

"They want me to sing?"

"Ah, now here's where it gets interesting," Bunny said, funnelling smoke from the side of her mouth before crushing her cigarette out on the balcony and flicking the butt over the edge. "No, it's not that kind of gig. They're interested in you, your story."

"Story? What story?"

"Hold on," Bunny began calmly. "There's a little bit to unwrap here, but in essence, they want you to take part in a social experiment of sorts."

"Oh brother," Amanda groaned.

"Don't fly off yet, just hear me out. It's not some tacky reality TV show. In fact, it's not even TV. It's all completely private, and you stand to make two hundred and fifty thousand pounds. Tax free."

"What?" Amanda thought she had misheard.

"That's what they want to pay you. One week's work. Quarter of a million pounds. And it gets better. Midori Media are hugely influential behind the scenes. They can put you back in the spotlight if you decide you want to make more music. I could negotiate a great deal for you."

She spoke with a flat earnestness that completely contradicted her previous, easy tone. Her expression became placid and all those emotional subtleties – the friendly smile, the wide, understanding eyes – dissolved.

A cavalcade of questions clogged Amanda's brain. She stuttered before she could get any of them out, and then shook her head, trying to sift away the sludge. "Wh–what would I be... um, doing?"

"They have designed a social experiment, and they believe that your input would be invaluable. Your experience, combined with your personality, make you an extremely attractive candidate for the role."

"That doesn't tell me anything, Bunny. For god's sake, will you stop with all this mumbo jumbo and just say what you mean?" Amanda said, aware of how hard she was breathing, wisps of vapour trailing from her lips.

"In theory, you and five other candidates would live in a secluded mansion for a week. Every day, you will be required to take a pill."

"Pill? What pill? I thought this was a... what did you say? A *social* experiment. You didn't say anything about a pill."

Bunny's hands came up and patted the air between them in a calm-down gesture. "It *is* a social experiment but there is an element of medical research involved. But don't worry. I have it in writing that the pill is completely harmless and has no adverse side effects."

"This sounds fucking insane, you know that? I can't believe what I'm listening to right now."

Raising a hand to hush her, Bunny continued. "Each of you

will be given a pill, but five of you will be taking a placebo. You won't know who is taking what, or what the pill does."

Amanda shook her head. "Is that all the business you wanted to discuss? Because if it is, you can have my answer now: I'm not interested."

"Even though I have a contract that says the pill is completely harmless with no side effects?"

"I don't care if you have a written note from the Pope. You want to let them drug me? Is that what you brought me here for? You want to use me for medical testing?" The confusion made her head throb. She gulped in air, but couldn't seem to get enough to take a deep breath.

"There's only a one in six chance that you would be taking anything at all."

"I still don't like those odds, Bunny. This has nothing to do with my music, does it? This is about turning me into some kind of guinea pig."

"Amanda, think about what I've just told you," Bunny said patiently. "This is a legitimate business offer; a lot of money for no work at all. It's a gig, nothing more."

"And I suppose you get a cut, do you?"

"Naturally." Bunny nodded. "But not from you. If you sign, I settle with Midori. Your quarter mil has nothing to do with me. You and I wouldn't even need to have a contract between us... that is, unless you want me to manage you again when the experiment is done. What do you think? Amanda Pearson rises from the ashes. A new look, a new sound, a new album. It's got a great publicity spin already."

Amanda gripped the guardrail surrounding the balcony ledge and stared out at the skyline, her brain working overtime to process the information while simultaneously calculating the percentage of truth in Bunny's proposal.

"So, let me get this straight, just so I have it all clear in my head," Amanda said, the cool night air kissing her hot face. "A few years ago, you and the label decide to throw me on the scrap heap because you think I'm a fucking drug-addled mess."

"Nobody called you that, Amanda."

"Nobody *called* me at all. I just get a letter saying, *Thanks very much but you're a stupid little cokehead, so your career's over.* That about right?" When Bunny refused to meet her eyes, Amanda continued. "And now you have the nerve to contact me out of the blue as though you didn't just abandon me, and… the punchline is, you want to pay me to take more drugs." A snort of laughter left her then, and she turned away, seeing the cityscape through tear-blurred eyes.

Bunny placed a palm on Amanda's shoulders and said, "It was business. That's all. And now it's water under the bridge."

"Not to me it isn't." She swallowed down a rising sob, adding, "I was only a kid, Bunny, for fuck's sake." She blotted her eyes with her index finger. "I needed your help. You were like a big sister to me. I *trusted* you."

Passing Amanda a tissue from her purse, Bunny said, "I know that. But believe me, cutting you loose was a blessing in disguise. You might not see that now, but the truth is, you were just too young for that kind of pressure." Bunny picked a loose strand of hair from her mouth and gripped the guardrail. "Mental health wasn't top of the list of priorities back then. Now we have psychologists on hand at the show, and at the label. It would be much different for you if it were today."

"Yeah," Amanda said dryly. "Too bad I don't have a magic wand to turn back time."

"No, but this might be a second chance."

"Really? Because it doesn't sound like much of a second chance to me. It sounds like you want to pump me full of drugs, film it to make me look like a fool, and then push it on the public."

"Not at all." Bunny's voice was eerily calm, as though she were trying to lull her into a meditative trance. "There will be cameras in the house, but that's to monitor the six candidates. The footage will not be made public. That's all in the contract, and before you ask, I've had our solicitors go through it with a fine-tooth comb. It's legit, and it's watertight."

"Yeah?" Amanda made a small spitting sound. "That contract won't be too much use to me when I go blind or my arms drop off, will it?"

"The pill has no–"

"No side effects? Yeah. You must think I'm some kind of fucking idiot. You expect me to believe that they're going to pay me all that money to take a drug that doesn't do anything?"

"Yes, that's what the contract says."

Amanda was momentarily lost for words. This proposition had stirred up a confusing cocktail of emotions, and she felt both giddy with frustration and sick with anger. Biting back the encroaching bitterness, Amanda thought very carefully about what to say next. She settled for: "It was nice seeing you again, Bunny. Take care of yourself."

Amanda opened the fire exit door to step back inside. Bunny touched her arm, delicate as a lover. "They're extremely influential." She pointed through the window at a young woman who was crossing the room, waving and smiling at the other partygoers. "They've helped build and rebuild numerous careers. You want to get back to the top of the mountain, don't you? Fortunately, there's always more than one path."

Amanda watched the woman, who couldn't have been older than twenty but looked as young as sixteen, approach the piano. She wore a billowy gold dress that was almost as bright as her perfect smile, her long hair cascading like a black waterfall over her shoulders. The room hushed to silence as the woman straightened up and began to sing. She didn't need a microphone; a large, captivating voice left her petite body, raising the fine hairs on the nape of Amanda's neck. The woman's voice was honey on toast; a sweet thickness flowing with coarse emotion.

"She's good isn't she," Bunny whispered in Amanda's ear. "Maybe not as good as you were. Still, her debut single drops first week of December. Christmas it'll be number one. Album platinum by February. By summer she's headlining the O2."

Amanda opened her mouth to respond, but for a second, she forgot how to breathe. The jealousy held her lungs hostage, and the throb in her head turned into a steady, rhythmic beating. That uneasy sense of familiarity shivered through her as she watched the performance, picking up all the little vocal nuances. She was incredible.

"Does she remind you of anyone, Amanda?"

CHAPTER 4

The lights of the mansion illuminated the surrounding woods, offering, from a distance at least, a warm, majestic glow. Inside, approximately fifty people were gathered from across various industries. It was a private soiree, and, as such, Moshida had security guards patrolling the acres of surrounding land. Upon entering the mansion, all attendees were searched, X-rayed, and required to temporarily surrender all electrical devices. There were a few good-natured grumbles and the odd joke about Moshida's paranoia, but everybody understood it was a necessity. Things were going to be discussed throughout the course of the evening that nobody would want recorded.

Due to the heightened security, Moshida employed his own colleagues – brilliant men and women that had worked under his authority to help create and refine Honeycomb – as waiting staff. If there had been complaints from any of the twelve scientists under his employ, they went unheard.

Due to the nature of the occasion, Moshida wore a hand-tailored grey suit from Savile Row, complete with a pair of Hermès loafers that had already begun aching his feet. Usually, he spent roughly eighteen hours a day in a pair of comfortable running shoes with cushioned soles, and his daily getup was rarely more extravagant than tracksuit bottoms and a t-shirt. Tonight's outfit felt unnatural and restrictive, but he knew the importance of appearances.

He stood for a moment on the upstairs landing overlooking the reception, unnoticed by the rest of the attendees. The mansion's cavernous interior provided the perfect acoustics to amplify their chatter. Some of them were already drunk, while others had bloodshot, bleary eyes from the odd snort and sniff. That was alright by him, all part of the fun. In fact, it was expected and encouraged. Upon their arrival, each man and woman was discreetly told by one of the overqualified waiting staff that there was cocaine in the restrooms, to be used at their discretion.

"Ladies and gentlemen," Moshida called from the balcony, his arms open wide in welcome. The dialogue died down to murmurs, before silencing completely. "I thank you all for joining me in what promises to be an insightful and revelatory night." He paused for their applause; this was the third time in as many years that he had held such a gathering, and by now there was an almost debauched cheeriness in the atmosphere. The attendees were the rare breed of inexplicably wealthy and powerful human beings to which regular rules and laws didn't apply. He was one of their kind, a pharmaceutical genius, known for his monopoly of businesses, and his fanatical – if not deranged – work ethic. "You are all here because, a few years ago, I made you a promise. I promised you that my team and I had engineered something that would change the modern world as we know it." He had practised this speech many times, but the words felt as awkward coming out of his mouth as the suit felt wrapped around his body. In the lab, Moshida spoke in grunts and staccato bursts of inspiration. "You all wisely chose to become partners and shareholders in Honeycomb, and you have generously provided me with your money – and your patience – to make this endeavour possible.

"You all know my reputation. You know my work. You know I am a man of my word." He paused, taking a couple of seconds to drink in their excitement, their pessimism, their anxiety. "Ladies and gentlemen, the time is finally here. If you would like to follow me, the unveiling is about to begin."

There was polite, restrained applause as Moshida descended the staircase, the heels of his shoes biting into the skin. He took time to shake hands, kiss cheeks, hug awkwardly as was necessary, before he and the other scientists led the way through the mansion.

"No rats this time, James?" Richard Flannigan asked, with a goofy grin stretching across his large, redolent face. His tuxedo shirt was stretched so tightly over his barrel gut that it threatened to discharge the buttons if he coughed. Flannigan was an even rarer breed among the throng: a working-class man who had become a billionaire through a series of clever investments with his late brother. The pair opened a chain of affordable tyre repair garages in the seventies, before branching out to provide hot food vending machines to petrol stations across the UK. By the late nineties, he had expanded to the aviation industry, opening an exclusive online travel agency.

"No rats," Moshida replied, returning the smile, though it was so painfully forced. He took great offence at the jibe, no matter how innocent it may have been.

Moshida ushered the shareholders into the Circle Room, where rows of chairs were set out in front of a large TV screen.

"He's used our money to make the world's most expensive snuff film," Andrew Madison said, earning a musical giggle from the fashion designer, Angelina Kwan. It was just another silly joke, except, Madison, a Hollywood mogul who had produced dozens of blockbuster movies, had been known for his dark proclivities, which included a detestable appetite for children. "I hope it's in 3D at least."

More idle conversation flowed as they settled in their seats. Moshida waited patiently, and then cleared his throat to stamp out the last snippets of chitchat. "You are about to watch a promotional video for our new product, Honeycomb. We are on track to start an aggressive, all-encompassing global publicity and marketing campaign later this year, with orders set to ship by Fall of next year." Someone at the back had their hand raised, but Moshida waved it away. "Could we please hold all questions until the end?"

Moshida dimmed the lights and played the video, which lasted a total of three minutes and fifty-three seconds. When it was finished, he turned the lights back up, and said, "Now, Miss Abadi, your question?"

The Saudi socialite, a member of the famous Abadi oil family, shook her head in confusion. "This thing here," she said, fluttering her bejewelled fingers toward the screen, "is this the same thing we saw in the rat video last time?"

"The same product in principle, yes," Moshida replied.

"But the rats went crazy and killed each other. Disgusting." She reminded him with a wrinkle of her nose.

"The same product in *principle*," Moshida said again. "The chemical balance has been refined, retested, and is now," he paused, preparing for their reaction, "ready for human trials. Here, in this very mansion."

Shifting in seats, sceptical glances, idiotic grinning, a few repugnant chortles.

"Honeycomb will be the most addictive, most sought-after drug to ever exist," Moshida continued, talking over the whispers. "Anybody who tries it, present company included, will never want to stop taking it. It is a designer drug with incredible benefits for the morale."

"You mean moral benefits?" someone said, though Moshida didn't see who.

"No. I mean benefits for the morale. To use a vulgar, but fitting, analogy I suppose: it is steroids for the ego. And here is the most important part of all." Moshida raised a finger. "There are no adverse side effects."

A hand went up at the back. Moshida invited the person to stand. The tall, thin man was by far the spookiest person in attendance, which wasn't an easy thing to accomplish given the company. Matthew Nevers, the grandson of a property mogul who began the Nevers hotel chain, had lived his seventy-plus years in relative obscurity. He owned a significantly large mansion on the edge of Knightsbridge, where, it was rumoured, he conducted his own experiments to stave off the boredom. Moshida had done research on all his business partners, and found that Nevers owned six extremely violent chimpanzees, which he kept on one of the floors in his home. From time to time, Nevers had gatherings, where other animals – vicious dogs, for example – were introduced to the chimps.

"Surely there's no way you'd legally – let alone ethically – be able to retail this," Nevers said in a sardonic tone with his unusually deep voice.

"It has no adverse side effects."

"Maybe not to the person taking it," Nevers countered. "But if this drug can do what your…" He angled his chin to the TV. "…little infomercial there says it can do, then there's no way this gets any kind of health approval." He had black witchy eyes that blinked a lot and an emaciated frame drowning in his brown tweed suit.

"Health approval is a separate issue, sure, but one you needn't worry about. It will get passed for public consumption, that much I can personally guarantee. Right now, though, I mean to show you that it works," Moshida said. "That it is perhaps the single greatest medical achievement of our time, if I can be so bold. There are millions of people that could greatly benefit from Honeycomb, but very few that would be able to afford it. Some of you in this room are connected to the entertainment industry and might have a client whose star has begun to dim. Honeycomb can change that."

"If it works," Nevers said.

"It works. Which brings me onto the next point on tonight's agenda. The trial." He began to detail the parameters of the experiment, explaining that they were in the process of securing a marginal celebrity as the main attraction, adding,

"Though I doubt anyone here has ever heard of her. Amanda Pearson?" He searched the room for any sign of recognition and found none. "She was a popular singer a few years ago. A one-hit wonder, no less. We are making her an extremely attractive offer; one I doubt she will refuse." He then went on to explain about the rest of the participants, and ended by saying, "And you're all invited to stay and watch the drug take effect in real time." A sly giggle flittered on his lips. "A slumber party of sorts."

"You expect us to stay here for a week?" The German accent belonged to Troy Irving, CEO of Ballistik Records. Among his dirty laundry was a case of sexual assault, settled out of court.

"I expect you to see what your money has paid for," Moshida said. "And I expect you to see how much money it will make you."

Moshida allowed a few seconds for the murmurs to spread as the congregation talked it over among themselves. That note of sceptical excitement was still among them, as though they were a group of children sitting before a magician at a birthday party, but there was something else too. Moshida could see that crackle of lust leaping hungrily in their eyes.

"James, you're a mad, mad bastard," Flannigan said, his arms folded across his chest. He was laughing and shaking his head, glancing around, and hoping to share his amusement with the other attendees. "But what if something goes wrong? I mean, if this pill is as potent as you claim – as it was with those fucking rats that ate each other – then what's to stop the people in the experiment from... you know."

Moshida thought about the question for a long time before answering. "Well, I suppose that's all part of the fun, isn't it? We'll just have to wait and see what happens."

CHAPTER 5

"I don't get it," Rochelle said through a mouthful of muffin. "So, it's like... what? A TV show?"

"No, that's what I'm trying to tell you." Amanda picked up another biscuit and dunked it into her coffee. Two days prior she had gone to Bunny's office where she read the contract, and then had each clause explained to her by Bunny's solicitor. Due to the confidential nature of the experiment, Amanda wasn't allowed to leave with a copy, but was assured she could call or drop by at any time with any additional questions. "It's not for TV. It's not for anything. It's just someone that wants to pay me to stay in the house."

"Then what's all this shit about the pill?"

"They won't say."

Rochelle shook her head, and then glanced over to the sofa in the living room, where her eighteen month-old son Andre sat hypnotized by *Peppa Pig*. Satisfied that he was satisfied, she returned her attention to Amanda. "I don't know. I guess it won't make you sick, will it?"

Amanda shrugged, regretting the way the packet of biscuits was now half-deflated. She had promised herself she would stop at two. "That's the thing. How do I know I won't get sick?"

"Because it says it in the contract. It's in writing."

The exhaustion made Amanda feel like she had a fishbowl over her head. She hadn't slept much in the last few days, her mind refusing to switch off. She would snatch a couple of hours sleep and then snap awake, replaying the evening over and over again. Amanda had run Midori Media through Google, found a website filled with generic jargon that didn't really tell her anything at all, and then checked the name at Companies House. The Midori Media Group was less than a year old and had filed no accounts.

"It's a dummy company," Amanda said. "This contract might as well be with the Tooth Fairy for all it's worth."

"I suppose that's a bit weird," Rochelle said, shaking her head ominously. "But on the other hand..." She trailed off, one shoulder shrugging.

"On the other hand, what?"

"If this Bunny woman has stepped in then it's probably a real offer, don't you think? And if she says it's all kosher, then I guess you can take her word for it. You trust her, don't you?"

"I did," Amanda said. "Once, a long time ago."

"What I'm saying is, she doesn't really have a dog in the race does she? So she'll get her fee from them, but Amanda, you stand to make a lot of money here. And then, there was all that talk about new music. That's what you wanted wasn't it?"

"Yeah," Amanda said, almost whispering. She allowed herself a few seconds to indulge in the daydream; her face on a billboard again, her songs soaring up the download charts, sitting on the sofa on breakfast TV shows to discuss her comeback.

"The company could just be to protect the real person that's hiring you," Rochelle said. "I mean, I work at the post office, I don't know about these fancy circles that you move in. What was your feeling on it?" Behind her, Andre gurgled. She swivelled in the stool, and said, "You being a good boy over there?"

Andre babbled a gleeful string of nonsense in response.

"If it's a real offer and I turn it down then, well, we won't be neighbours for much longer. They're killing me with these service charges, and between that and the council tax, I'm just about drowning."

"Yeah, it's murder," Rochelle said into her cup as she took a sip of tea, steam rising into her face. Amanda felt a short stab of resentment at her response. Rochelle was a council tenant and didn't have a mortgage on her flat. When the lifts broke down and the building needed new cladding, Rochelle wasn't liable for a penny of it.

"Let's say the whole thing is just some ropey PR stunt," Rochelle said. "What do you stand to lose?"

"Nothing, except time I guess."

"You could sue the balls off them," she said, reclining. "That Bunny woman would help you do that, wouldn't she?"

"I don't have a contract with Bunny, so if this thing goes tits up then she could just abandon ship on me like she did last time." Bunny blew out a laboured breath and retrieved another biscuit. "So basically, I'd be going in there and taking some random drug on face value. And that might as well be the same as going to a club and..." She waved a hand in the air, scrubbing the rest of the sentence away. She was about to make some morally poignant remark about the dangers of taking drugs from strangers in nightclubs, but that was a little too much like hypocrisy. "And then what? They've filmed me doing this and the next thing I know I'm all over the TV and YouTube."

Rochelle's eyes dropped to her cup and she nibbled at the corner of her lower lip.

"What?" Amanda asked, stuffing the biscuit into her mouth angrily.

"Nothing, nothing."

"Rochelle, come on," she mumbled, spitting specks of biscuit. "Tell me what's on your mind."

Rochelle's eyebrow rose and a smirk danced on her lips. "What's on Your Mind?" was the title of track seven from Amanda's album. The irony wasn't lost on Amanda. She huffed and cocked her head to the side, unamused.

"Look," Rochelle began, placing her cup down on the table. "Don't blow up for what I'm going to say, OK? Promise me."

"I can't promise that," Amanda snipped.

"I'm just saying, the way you described everything, and by the sound of this contract, it just seems like... like maybe you're trying to find an excuse *not* to do it."

"That's ridiculous." Amanda shook her head. Her hand inched toward the biscuits, and she caught herself just as her finger touched the packet. "You don't think I have the right to be cautious? I'm just trying to protect myself."

"I guess." Rochelle shrugged. "But, you don't think maybe there's a chance that you're scared for other reasons?"

"Like what?"

Rochelle seemed to tighten, her face wincing. "Like maybe you don't want to go back to being, you know, famous again."

"Yeah sure. And I don't want to pay my mortgage or get these debtors off my back either."

"Well then, there it is. That's a lot of money they're talking about. You could pay the mortgage off completely."

"HMRC takes half," Amanda grumbled.

"You said it was tax free."

"And that doesn't raise any alarm bells at all, does it? How can the tax man not take their cut?"

Rochelle exhaled, wearily. "I think you want me to talk you out of doing it. You want me to tell you it's a bad idea but–"

"Would you do it?" Amanda stabbed a finger at her. "Would you leave little Andre for a week and take a pill that could fuck you up for the rest of your life?"

"For quarter of a mil? I'd take them up on the experiment outlined in that contract you told me about, sure. Especially where it says that there are no side effects. They could be testing a new hay fever tablet or a cure for the common cold. God only knows, right?"

"Then why would they want *me* for that?"

"Shit, I don't know," Rochelle said.

Amanda palmed her forehead and scrunched her eyes closed. She could feel the veins wriggling across her temples. "I've gotta go."

"Come on, Amanda, don't be like that. You asked my opinion and I gave it to you."

"It's not that," she lied, getting off the stool. "I just want some fresh air. I haven't been sleeping well."

"Oh, OK." Rochelle followed her through the living room, watched as Amanda bent down and kissed Andre on his cheek. "You're still coming over to watch *Bake Off* though, right?"

"Wouldn't miss it," Amanda said, and left.

It was mild outside, nowhere near chilly enough to warrant a hat, scarf and fur-lined hood over her head. If the sky hadn't been so gloomy then Amanda would have had a pair of shades on too. She walked with her hands sunk deep in her jacket pockets, her head bowed toward the paving slabs. For the last ten minutes or so, she had been debating whether to buy a coffee, hating that the decision hung on how guilty she would feel for tunnelling deeper into her overdraft. She wished she had kept the tags on the dress she bought for the party so she could take it back.

She never walked more than a couple of blocks from her building. Beyond that, the streets got busier, and the chance of being recognized increased substantially. Of course, she wouldn't have minded if the people were nice to her and approached in a respectful way. She was more than happy to scribble autographs, and even spend a few minutes talking to people, but nobody wanted to do that. What they really wanted was a photo, and in her experience, there was no easy way to refuse someone this without causing offense. As they saw it, she was obligated to pose for their pictures, and anything contrary to that was an insult. It would be no good telling them that she still bore the scars from all those marvellously witty headlines that poked fun at her weight. Or that before deleting her social media accounts she had read so many spiteful comments, everything from her being a bloated coke whore to a haggard old bitch, that she had seriously contemplated suicide.

She walked past the Caffè Nero, circled back, and then went inside. They had plenty of plug sockets where she could charge her phone, stick her headphones in, and whittle away a few hours watching her programmes. There were a couple of yummy mummies locked in conversation toward the back of the room, and a homeless man passed out with his swollen hand coiled around a cold cup of tea at the front. The barista, a handsome Italian man with neck tattoos, took her order with a smile. While Amanda waited for him to prepare the latte, her phone began to vibrate in her pocket. The screen read *BUNNY*. She tasted sick in the back of her throat and swallowed the bitter taste down, her thumb hovering over the red decline icon.

On impulse, her thumb changed course and swept the answer icon. She placed the phone up to her ear and already the screen felt slimy against her face.

"Hello? Amanda?"

Amanda exhaled through her nostrils. "I'm here," she said.

"Is now a convenient time to talk?"

"Sure. What's up?"

"I was wondering if you'd given any more thought to the proposal we discussed."

"No, not much," she lied. Her mouth felt as though it were lined with cotton wool.

"Not to worry." Bunny's voice sounded bouncy, but was there a hint of urgency in her words? Amanda thought there was. "I just wanted to remind you that we're up against the clock on this one. They're still very keen to have you on board but they need an answer."

"I'll bet," Amanda replied dryly.

"I explained that you were understandably still very apprehensive, so my contact at Midori wanted to extend a gesture of good will to help ease your mind a bit. They want to offer you a ten percent advance, which they will pay directly into your account within the next few minutes, just to show how serious the offer is."

Amanda plugged her free ear with her finger to block out the burr of the milk frothing. "Could you say that again?"

"Sure. They want to deposit ten percent of the proposed fee into your account now. My contact understands that you may have some doubts about the legitimacy of the offer, and would like to put your mind at ease. Of course, if you still don't want to sign you can transfer the money back."

The barista handed Amanda her coffee. She floated to a nearby table and sat down, stunned. "They're going to put twenty-five grand in my bank account?"

"Yes. In fact, I'm with their accountant right now in front of a terminal awaiting your sort code and account number."

"Twenty-five... grand," she murmured. It was the most money she had been offered since she turned down *Celebrity Big Brother*, and almost twice as much as a Spanish businessman wanted to pay her to be the resident singer at the Hotel Casa Bonita, three shows a week, twelve weeks a year.

That would make it real, wouldn't it? If they deposited the money in her account, it would go a long way toward relieving her anxiety about the whole thing. Rochelle was right; in a week's time, she could pay off the mortgage and buy herself a lot of breathing room.

"They've already filled the other five candidates and are awaiting your answer. After today, however, they'll have to look elsewhere if you're not willing to commit."

She thought about the panicky text messages her bank would be sending her, and the charges they would apply for going into her overdraft. She imagined what her coffee table could look like once she took the bills and threw them down the rubbish chute. Then, she thought about the Soho studio where she had recorded most of her album years ago. She pictured herself stepping back into the mic booth and slipping the headphones over her ears.

"Amanda, are you still there?"

If anyone deserves a second chance, it's me, she thought to herself, and not for the first time.

"I'm still here," she said, and began to read out her account number.

CHAPTER 6

"Here's the food," Amanda said, holding up the little box of fish flakes. "Just give them a pinch in the morning and one in the evening. Just a pinch, mind."

Rochelle picked up the box and smelled its contents. "Reeks," she said, pulling her head back.

"Well you don't need to eat it; they do," Amanda said, tapping the aquarium. "You're not going to forget to feed them, are you?"

"I've kept a child alive for the past year and a half. I think I can manage a few goldfish."

Amanda didn't bother to make the distinction between the eight different species of fish swimming around in the tank, all of which she had named personally. She bought them after reading an article about how fish could help a person relax and lower their anxiety levels. She started with a dozen, but her anxiety only spiked when they began to cannibalize each other, and she had to flush the floaters away. Now she seemed to have the mix just right and there hadn't been a fatality in months.

"Well that's about it, I guess," Amanda said, plonking down on the sofa, the air whooshing out of her.

"Are you excited?" Rochelle asked, wandering over to the kitchenette area. She found a grease-spotted carton of old Chinese food, removed the fork, and tipped it in the bin.

"What're you doing?"

"Huh?" She put the fork in the sink and ran the tap. "Nothing."

"Stop tidying up. I hate it when you do that."

44

"I can't help it. Do you know how sick you can get eating leftover Chinese that hasn't been in the fridge? I told you about that time with the prawns. It was coming out of both ends all night."

"I don't want to come back home next week and see that you've hoovered up and washed the windows," Amanda said, threatening her with an index finger. "I want to come back to the same palace you see before you."

"Palace? Ha!" Rochelle wiped her hands on the tea towel and then opened the fridge, removed a bottle of orange juice, and looked for a glass. "Have you packed already?"

"Mostly," Amanda said, stretching out on the sofa. She turned the TV on and flipped through the channels. "Bag's right there by the door."

Rochelle walked past the Adidas gym bag and nudged it with her toe. "Feels light. Packed clean panties I hope."

"Don't call them panties, that's creepy."

Rochelle chuckled as she sipped her orange juice, spilling some down her chin.

"I'm only gonna be there a week. I can't take any electrical devices at all, so I just packed light."

"How're you feeling about it?" she asked, sitting down on the sofa.

"A bit better." Amanda shrugged.

"I'll bet that twenty-five grand went a long way toward convincing you, didn't it?"

"Yeah well. It's not like I got to enjoy any of it. It was out my account that same evening. Had to keep the wolves away from the door. But, I've got to admit, there's a huge weight been lifted off my chest knowing I've cleared some of those debts."

"You'll probably sleep like a baby in that house now you don't have to worry about any of that shit," Rochelle said.

"No, I'm sure I'll find something else to worry about." Amanda inspected her nails; they were chipped, the flame design nothing but white specks. "I always do."

"You spend too much time in this flat. You need a holiday. Maybe you can take a chunk of that cash next week and go on a cruise. See if some Caribbean sun can't shift that dark cloud always hovering over your head."

Amanda thought about it a moment, and then nodded. "I'd need some company."

Rochelle shot her a girl, please look, and rolled her eyes. "Well, if you give me a little while to save, I should have enough money by the time Andre goes to university."

"Don't be stupid. I'll pay for both of you. We could go to Jamaica like you're always banging on about."

Rochelle stared at her for a second, and then said, "I couldn't let you do that."

"Why not? You're the one that talked me into doing this thing in the first place. Least you could do is let me give you a little thank you present."

"Serious?"

"As a heart attack."

Rochelle screamed and clambered over to Amanda, squeezing her in a hug that threatened to crush her ribs. She squealed gleefully, almost piercing Amanda's eardrums. Amanda was laughing and trying to tell her to keep the noise down, but she couldn't get a word out.

Amanda realized that for the first time in a very long while, she felt truly happy. The idea of lying on a beach with her best friend – or rather, her only friend, if you didn't include the fish – filled her with warm and dizzying excitement. She wasn't worried about covering up her cellulite or avoiding other holidaymakers in the hotel, or constantly searching the locals for signs of paparazzi. She had premonitions of piña coladas, buffet breakfasts, and suntan lotion.

What Amanda didn't know was that Rochelle wasn't as hard up as she made herself out to be. Shortly after Amanda met Bunny at the solicitor's office and signed the contract, Rochelle's bank balance increased by ten thousand pounds.

CHAPTER 7

Amanda checked her reflection in her hand mirror as the lift descended. She was wearing too much foundation in an effort to conceal the blemishes, and now her complexion was uneven. She rooted around in her bag for a beauty blender, and swore under her breath when she couldn't find it.

"How could you let me leave the flat without telling me my makeup was all over the place?"

"I didn't notice," Rochelle said, bouncing Andre on her hip. "I thought you looked fine."

"Christ, look at the state of me." She shook her head. The lift stopped with a jolt and the doors slid open silently. "My fucking hair's a mess too."

"Language," Rochelle said, tilting her head toward Andre. "He's picking things up really quickly these days."

"Shit, I'm sorry." Amanda stroked the boy's cheek with her index finger and said, "Don't listen to crazy aunty."

They began through the reception and Amanda abruptly stopped, crouched down on one knee, and unzipped her sports bag.

"Forgot something?"

"Just checking I brought my hand cream," Amanda said, rifling through her neatly folded clothes that she had spent most of the previous day ironing. She checked the side compartment and found the small toiletry bag. "There we go."

"You bring lip balm? 'Cos I tell you there's nothing worse than when you have dry lips and you don't have any lip balm. Drives me out my mind."

"Yeah, I got Vaseline." As she stood up, Amanda noticed Rochelle's handbag. "That new?"

"This?" she looked down at it as though unaware that she was wearing it. "Oh, yeah. Marcus got it for me. God knows what he's up to. But he only gets me gifts when he's done something wrong."

"Must've spent a few pennies on that," Amanda said, touching the clasp. "Chanel. Who'd he rob for it?"

"I know, right? You can hardly tell it's a knock-off."

"It's knocked off? Could've fooled me." Amanda had blown most of her record advance money on fancy handbags, all of which she later sold or exchanged to support her habit. There was hardly a day that went by that she didn't regret getting rid of them.

Rochelle shifted Andre onto her other hip and his legs dangled down over the bag, ending the subject. They pressed the exit button for the reception door and were greeted by a thick blanket of fog upon leaving the building. A black Jeep with tinted windows idled by the kerb. Standing sentry by the back-passenger door was a tall, broad man with a face like a lump of playdough.

"Who's this handsome devil?" Rochelle murmured, just loud enough for Amanda to hear.

Amanda shook her head. "What the hell have I got myself into?"

"Think of Jamaica, think of Jamaica," Rochelle cooed, rubbing Amanda's arm. "In seven days from now that car will be dropping you back here, and I'm going to have a Nandos waiting for you." Andre broke in with an attempt at saying Nandos, and Rochelle said, "That's right Andre, chicken, buck-buck." She turned back to Amanda and added, "And this will all be another exciting chapter for your memoirs."

Amanda exhaled gently and offered Rochelle a brave face. "We'll laugh about this, won't we?"

"We'll piss ourselves."

"Language," Amanda admonished. She looped her arms around Rochelle and Andre, gave them a brief squeeze and said, "Don't forget to feed the fish. And do me a favour, just in case, take a photo of the license plate, OK?" Rochelle laughed. "No, I'm being serious."

"If it'll put your mind at ease," Rochelle said, reaching into her pocket for her phone.

"It will." Amanda turned and walked to the Jeep.

"Hello, Miss Pearson," playdough face said. "Please, allow me to take your bag."

"Be my guest." He relieved her of the bag and placed it in the boot. "Aren't you going to search it? I thought you'd wanna go rooting through my underwear."

Playdough face said, "No. We do that back at the house. I trust you followed the guidelines? No mobile phone or electronic devices of any kind. No cameras or recording equipment. Failure to comply would mean–"

"Yeah, I got the memo."

"Good. As long as you know that we'll have to confiscate anything we find at the house when you go through security."

"I can already see this is going to be a fun ride with you, isn't it?" Before she climbed in the back of the Jeep, Amanda turned and waved at Rochelle. "See you in a week."

"Don't cause any trouble!" she yelled back as Amanda got in and the door closed behind her.

Amanda could see Rochelle talking to Andre and squinting from the steps in an effort to peer through the tinted windows.

"My name is Derrick," a voice said from the front of the car. Startled, Amanda's head whipped toward the front passenger seat, where she saw a well-dressed man grinning at her. He had a shock of shaggy black hair streaked with grey. Baggy purple pouches hung beneath his intense stare. Wrinkles etched deep into the loose flesh of his face. "I'll be your guide as we make our way over to the house." His mouth was crowded with large, square teeth. "Our journey will last approximately five and a half hours, depending on traffic. In the compartment by your legs there you'll find a packed lunch and a couple of bottles of water."

He watched her unblinkingly, the goofy smile frozen on his face. She wasn't sure if he had forgotten the lines to his welcoming monologue or whether he was waiting for her to respond, so she said, "Um... that's great."

"It's no problem," he replied quickly. His voice was soft and feminine, timid almost. His friendly façade flickered, and his large Adam's apple bobbed in his throat. "I will have to fit you with the blindfold and headphones before we begin. You're not claustrophobic I hope?"

"Would it matter if I was?"

"Well..." The question unbalanced him. His eyes broke away from her face and darted around the car. "It's one of the requirements outlined in the contract. Of course, I'll try to do everything I can to make it as painless as possible." He tittered. Amanda didn't like it when men tittered, especially at her expense.

"I'm sure you will. Because, I'll warn you now Dennis—"

"Derrick," he corrected.

"If you try to take advantage of me in any way, or if I think something's up, or if I get car sick, I'm going to kick off. I don't care what I've signed, I'll get out, do you understand?"

"Y—yes."

"Good. Just so long as we understand each other."

"You don't have anything to worry about, Miss Pearson. I'm here to ensure your safety and comfort as we proceed and provide you with anything you need. As such, I'd like to inform you that we have an opportunity for a toilet break approximately every forty-five minutes, so if you feel the need to go, you just have to let me know."

"Fine."

Derrick presented her with a blindfold and a pair of noise-cancelling headphones. "You'll have to wear these. There's nothing scary about them as you can see. May I?"

"I think I can manage." Amanda relieved him of the blindfold and placed it over her head. She adjusted the Velcro strap, plunging herself in darkness. "Feels like I'm volunteering to be kidnapped."

Ignoring her remark, he said, "Now when I put the headphones on, you won't be able to hear me at all. However, if you become distressed, or if you need anything, just call my name and I'll assist you."

"What if I want to eat my packed lunch or take a sip of water?"

"I can help you with that," he said, putting the headphones on her.

She heard seagulls squalling, the swish of lapping waves, the slow creak of a wooden boat docked by the shore. She felt the seat vibrate around her as the Jeep's ignition fired, and then she was moving. Within minutes, the urge to tear the blindfold off was almost overwhelming. She imagined that both men were staring at her, watching her through the rear-view mirror, maybe making lewd gestures. The stop-start motion of the Jeep became disorientating, and she lost all sense of time. She conjured the possibility that they were driving down some back alley to have their way with her, that this whole thing had been some elaborate ruse.

She removed one headphone and said, "Where are we?"

"We're just about to join the motorway," Derrick said. "Are you feeling alright?"

"Open my window."

She heard it slide down and felt the car's forward momentum, the cool breeze blowing on her face. She angled her ear to the window and detected the whoosh of passing traffic.

"I'm going to have to ask you to put your headphones back on," Derrick said.

Amanda complied without a fuss. She listened to the seagulls and the waves and was asleep before the Jeep left London.

CHAPTER 8

Amanda felt a hand on her shoulder, shaking her gently. Her mind was muddy for a few seconds as she stirred awake, unsure as to where she was and why she couldn't see anything. Then she heard seagulls and her senses synced with her memory. She snatched the headphones and blindfold off, and saw Derrick standing next to her outside the Jeep.

"Have a good nap?" Derrick asked, smiling with all his teeth.

"We're here?" She unbuckled her seatbelt and massaged her eyelids with her fingertips. Derrick stepped aside, allowing her a view of the house. It was a two-floor Victorian mansion surrounded by forest. Amanda got out of the car with a stretch, drinking in the atmosphere. She could already taste the difference in the air quality, her lungs filled with the heady scent of pine and earth. It was raining lightly, which only served to stir up the smells, intensifying them. The gunmetal sky winked with lightning. "It's beautiful," she said, and now that the grogginess of sleep had passed, she could truly acknowledge how tranquil it was. Beyond the patter of rain, and the occasional birdcall amidst the trees, the area was silent.

"I'm glad you like it," Derrick said as playdough face retrieved her bag. "If you'd like to come this way, I'll walk you through security and then you can explore the house. How's that sound?"

"Perfect." Amanda followed them up the inclining path, her shoes sinking in the spongy earth. "All these trees," she marvelled, pausing to admire the landscape.

"If you think that's impressive you should see the stars at night," Derrick said. "Billions of them. Don't get that in London."

"No, we don't," she replied absently. She thought she heard a woodchuck drilling a tree trunk somewhere in the distance.

They reached the double doors at the entrance of the mansion. Derrick produced a key from his pocket, unlocked the doors, and pushed them open. The smell of dust and the faint odour of furniture polish jumped out of the gloom as she entered. Immediately in front of them was a contraption linked to a monitor that reminded Amanda of airport security metal detectors.

"Do you have any metallic objects on you at all?" Derrick asked, while the driver placed her sports bag on a table before pushing it through a boxlike device. The monitor flickered to life and revealed an X-ray of the bag's interior.

"Earrings," Amanda said, checking herself. "Oh, and I guess my belt buckle."

"Remove them please, and step through the metal detector."

Amanda did as instructed while Derrick watched the monitor. Happy that the contraption didn't bleep at him, he turned to the driver and said, "Is her bag OK?" The driver made a circle with his thumb and forefinger. "Excellent. Well Amanda, you're free to go."

She retrieved her earrings and belt. "So, what do I do now?"

"Have a look around. Make yourself at home."

"Wait – am I the only one here? Where's everyone else?"

"I really couldn't say." Derrick smiled, and as he and the driver made to leave, added, "Enjoy your stay, Amanda."

The door closed, sealing her in the murky mansion. She stood there a moment awaiting further instruction, and when she heard the Jeep's engine turn over and fade into the distance, she realized she was alone.

"Hello?" she called, her voice bouncing around the downstairs hallway and echoing off the high ceiling. The only response was the faint ticking of a clock, though she couldn't be sure of where exactly it was coming from. "Is anyone else here yet?" she said, cringing at the loudness of her voice. She did not relish the idea of wandering around this huge empty mansion by herself, especially when she could barely see anything.

She turned to the wall, located a series of light switches, and flicked them all on. Overhead, rainbow light danced in an enormous, elaborate crystal chandelier, illuminating the entrance hall. She could see the intricate weave of the carpet runner on the staircase, which lead to the first-floor landing. Directly before her was an arched hallway with a series of doors on either side. From her vantage point, she could see another room at the end of it where a suit of armour decorated the wall. She picked up her bag and started to walk, conscious of the way her footfalls echoed off the tiled floor.

When she reached the end of the hallway, passing a table that housed a large ornamental brass bumblebee, she poked her head cautiously into the room with the suit of armour and saw that it was a study, with carved antique furniture congregating around a fireplace. Taxidermy animal heads with glassy eyes stared at her accusingly from the walls. She continued through the room, eager to be away from it, and entered a kitchen. So far, it was the most modern part of the house, boasting a wide refrigerator, shiny unused pots and pans, and a conjoining pantry stocked full of food.

Following through the doors and warren of hallways, she came to another staircase at the other end of the mansion. She had seen an eye-in-the-sky camera on every ceiling, standing out against the archaic décor like an angry boil on an otherwise unblemished surface of skin.

The whole setup sort of reminded her of *Celebrity Big Brother*, a show that had aggressively pursued her to be a contestant about six months after her little YouTube debacle. After reading the tabloids about her grim financial situation, they had lowballed her and offered seventy-five grand, which was still a huge sum of money that she would have ordinarily leapt at. The only thing that stopped her from accepting the offer was the fact she had just started on her road to sobriety and couldn't jeopardize the six weeks of progress she'd made. That, and the knowledge that they would design the show to humiliate and destroy her all over again.

The house was gigantic, and she had a flash of panic imagining the other guests posted in a room somewhere awaiting her arrival. She ventured up the staircase and followed the landing around. She was just admiring the view of the foyer over the banister when a sound startled her. Up ahead, a man was emerging from a room at the far end of the hallway. When he closed the door behind him, the noise ricocheted through the landing.

"Hello?" Amanda called. The man spun around, taken aback by the sound of her voice. His confusion shifted into a smile.

"Hey there!" he yelled back with a wave and began down the landing to meet her. As he approached, Amanda took stock of him. He had dark hair and tanned skin that popped against his white shirt and a handsome, chiselled face, punctuated by dark hazel eyes that, in the chandelier light, looked almost maroon. He was older than her by a few years, probably in his early thirties.

When he was within a few feet of her, he extended his hand. "Hi, I'm Claude," he said, starting to lean in for a kiss on the cheek, but stopping halfway, unsure as to whether the gesture was appropriate.

She had turned to offer her cheek, but upon seeing his retreat, she straightened up and shook his hand. "Amanda," she said, happy to see a friendly face. Her lonely journey through the mansion's labyrinthine hallways had begun to spook her, outweighing her anxiety of meeting new people.

"So you found the lights," he said. He had an easy smile that touched his eyes and immediately put her at ease.

"Yeah, there was a big switchboard thing down there, so I just flipped them all on."

"Are we the only ones here?" he asked as they began to walk.

"You're the first person I've seen. I haven't really looked around up here though. I've just done a tour of downstairs."

"Really? I've been here for about an hour looking for signs of life. I was starting to get a little worried, like maybe they were pulling a gag on me or something."

"I know the feeling," she said. "Have you found the bedrooms yet? I don't know where we're supposed to be sleeping."

"I suppose we each have our own room but I can't remember reading that in the contract."

Outside, a low grumble of thunder provoked a fierce deluge of rain, which pelted the windows angrily. Moments later, through a large rectangular window, they saw the lightning crackle, leaving ghostly afterimages in the clouds.

"Cripes, what a night," Claude said, shaking his head. "Hope the others are OK. Could you imagine having car trouble on a night like this?"

"Like something straight out of a horror film," she said, and as soon as the words left her mouth, she wasn't exactly sure which scenario she was referring to: having your car break down at night during a storm, or being alone in a creepy mansion with someone that could be a lunatic for all she knew. But then Claude chuckled, and his laugh was somehow childish and disarming, and she immediately dismissed the notion.

"So, what line of business are you in, Claude?" she asked as he tried a doorknob that wouldn't budge.

"Some of them are locked," he said, before adding, "I, uh, I work at a Ford dealership."

"Dodgy car salesman, huh?"

"Not at all." He laughed, and twisted another doorknob and this time it granted him access. The door opened to reveal a musty smelling library with rows of bookshelves extending the whole length of the room. "Wow, that's impressive. I'll bet these are all first editions, what do you think?"

Not really understanding the concept of first editions, or what he meant by the comment, Amanda offered a noncommittal murmur of agreement.

"How about you?" he asked. "What do you do?"

Her stomach cramped. She felt a nerve pinch in her neck. "I'm a singer," she said, though the embarrassment of not being recognized made the statement sound like a lie, like something she'd just plucked from the air. "Yeah, do you know that show, uh, *Searching for a Star*?"

"Yeah." He nodded, though it looked to Amanda as though his cogs were still turning. "My mum and sister watch it."

She smiled. "I won it back in 2017."

"Really?" His eyebrows rose with what she assumed was genuine surprise. "Wow, that's really something." There was a beat of awkward silence before he closed the library door and said, "I'm not really good with music, I'm sorry."

"Don't be sorry," she said, waving the apology away, the nape of her neck burning as though the sun were smiling directly on it. "I don't know anything about cars so that makes us even."

The conversation dipped, before Claude said, "They should've given us a map or something. I don't know about you but I'm gasping for a cup of tea."

Or something stronger, she thought. "I saw the kitchen downstairs. It was just after the room with the animal heads – did you see that place?"

"Animal heads? Can't say I had the pleasure."

They turned the corner on the hallway and arrived at the landing that overlooked the main entrance. There were six doors, each of which bore an engraved plaque with a name on it.

"Here we go. These must be our digs," he said, running his finger across the plaque that read *Claude Passos*. He freed his arms of his backpack and said, "Let's see what we got."

Amanda's room was the third door along. As she turned the doorknob, she heard Claude exclaim, "Wow, talk about five-star luxury!"

This, she quickly realized, was sarcasm. She flicked on the light and saw a couple of moths flittering around the bare bulb, making tiny *ting* sounds when they met the glass. The room was spartan: a single bed with a flat pillow and a scratchy-looking brown blanket that reminded her of something you would wrap a dead dog in before burying it in the yard. Faded floral wallpaper, seemingly applied a century ago, curled and bubbled in certain parts of the wall.

"Charming," she muttered under her breath as she went to test the mattress. She sat down on the bed, realizing there was no give beneath her buttocks, and felt the first stirrings of depression creeping toward her.

"Ah, you must have the penthouse suite," Claude said, appearing in the doorway. "No expense spared, look at that – they even went through the trouble of removing the lampshade for you, you know, just in case it made the room look a little nicer."

"I've stayed in hostels nicer than this," Amanda said, pulling the brown blanket away from the bed. "We're going to need some more covers or a duvet or something, surely. I mean, it's freezing in here."

"Well I don't know about you, but I packed a pair of my sexiest long johns, and I brought a woolly hat so I should be alright." He shook his head. "Hey, if you ask them nicely, they might give you a little oil lamp for you to warm your hands with."

"Ask who?" she said, rising from the bed. She was sure the bedding was clean, but it made her feel itchy nonetheless. "We're the only ones here."

"Not the only ones," he said, pointing to the black eye-in-the-sky camera in the corner of her room. "Someone must be watching."

"I'm glad," she muttered. "If I turn blue in the night maybe they can come in and give me an adrenaline shot." She laughed, although there was no real humour in it, and said, "Have you ever done anything like this before, Claude?"

"No. I don't even know how they got my email address. I usually just delete anything from addresses I don't recognize but this caught my eye." He shrugged. "I think there must have been a breach of data protection somewhere, because I know I didn't give them my email address, but hey, it turned out lucky for me I suppose."

"Yeah, I guess so," she said, thinking of Jamaica. "Shall we get that cup of tea now?"

"I thought you'd never ask."

They were at the top of the stairs when they heard the commotion: a man's voice, loud and abrasive, just outside the main entrance door. Claude offered Amanda a quizzical look, but neither of them attempted to descend the stairs. They remained perched by the landing, watching anxiously from above. The main door swung open and a tall, heavyset man stepped through the threshold, dressed in a rain-darkened white cotton suit that did not compliment his figure. Atop his head sat an unusual hat, the bastard child of a beret and a fez, striped all the colours of the rainbow.

"Oh my god, what is this?" Claude said, quietly.

Flanking the man in the white suit was a driver and another woman who Amanda assumed was his guide. The guide was saying, "But Mr Waldon, we explained back at your house and it is also outlined in the contract–"

But before she could get any further, Mr Waldon and his psychedelic hat said, "I am not an idiot. And I'm not going to let you take my personal possessions, and that is simply the end of it!"

"Then I'm afraid you will not be allowed to proceed any further," the guide told him. "As such, you will forfeit all funds."

"This is unethical," Mr Waldon said, his temper simmering. "What guarantee do I have that my phone will be safe in your hands?"

"You have no guarantees other than my assurance," the guide said. "I will put it in a lockbox for you and hand it back at the end of the week."

Mr Waldon stood there, hands on his padded hips, his shiny blue shoes tapping the tiles in contemplation. "Right, well fuck it, here." He reached into his breast pocket and thrust the phone at her. "But if anything happens to it, or I think you've tampered with it, I'm going to sue the bollocks off the lot of you."

The guide didn't rise to the bait but proceeded to put his suitcase in the X-ray machine, before asking him to step through the metal detector. He beeped, was told to remove his belt, and went through again. He beeped three more times, removing a ring, a set of keys, and a fountain pen, before they were satisfied that he wasn't concealing any electronic devices.

"Happy now?" he asked, giving the burly driver and the guide a sardonic grin. "What on earth do you think I have on me anyway? A fucking bomb?"

"You're now free to explore the house," the woman said, giving him a smile and a nod, before she and the driver left.

"Fucking self-righteous arseholes," Mr Waldon said as the door clicked closed. He picked up his bag and spotted Amanda and Claude at the top of the stairs. Rather than introduce himself, he said, "I mean, honestly, you wouldn't even get that at Heathrow would you? I'm surprised they didn't stick a flashlight up my arse to look for contraband. Did you two have to go through that circus when you came in?"

"They X-rayed our bags, yeah," Claude replied. "I'm Claude and this is–"

Before he could finish his sentence, Mr Waldon said, "Is there anything to drink in this dump?"

"We were actually just about to make a cup of tea," Amanda said.

Mr Waldon rolled his eyes, muttered something to himself, and said, "I mean real drink. Booze, my dear."

"I don't know," she replied. "If there is it'll be in the kitchen I suppose."

He furnished her with a grin-on-demand, and said, "Please do lead the way. I fear I might die of pneumonia before I have the chance to get drunk."

CHAPTER 9

Amanda hadn't seen it at first, but there was a section of the kitchen that opened onto a conservatory. Inside was a table that offered a selection of expensive-looking wines and nibbles. Mr Waldon, who begrudgingly informed them his first name was Arthur, wasted no time in decanting a bottle of red, pouring a generous glass for himself and gulping it down. He didn't bother with any trivial pleasantries, but continued to work on his glass until it was all gone, before pouring another. Then he shovelled his hand into a bowl of peanuts and scooped them into his mouth. He was happy to stare out the conservatory window at the darkness beyond without making any attempt at conversation.

"So, uh, Arthur," Claude began. "What do you do?"

"Do?"

"Yeah. Do you work?"

"Of course I work, love. I'm not the Dalai Lama."

"What I mean is," Claude said, opting for tea over the wine, warming both hands around the mug, "well, I'm a car salesman. And Amanda here is..."

"A pop singer. Yes, I know who she is."

"Right," Claude said. "So that's why I was asking..."

"Could we perhaps wait until everyone is here before I give you my biography? You see, I don't really want to be repeating myself over and over again. Tiresome."

"Sure," Claude shrugged, unoffended. He turned back to Amanda and they made pleasant small talk amongst themselves.

About twenty minutes after Amanda's first red wine, another woman arrived. Sherry Holt was a fifty-eight year-old grandmother who had a proclivity for baggy tie-dye yoga clothes. Dozens of metal bangles covered her wrists and jingled when she walked. Each of her fingers was home to a chunky, elaborately designed silver ring. When Amanda complimented them, Sherry thanked her and said, "I make them myself. I used to have a stall down Petticoat Lane, but packed it in a few years ago to concentrate on my comedy."

"You're a comedian?" Amanda asked.

"A *comedienne*," Sherry corrected.

Arthur groaned into his glass, but Amanda wasn't sure if Sherry had heard him. Sherry was drinking the wine like it was water, and within fifteen minutes had already put away more than half a bottle.

"Yes, I've been on the circuit for a long time now. I started off in pubs and bars but now I'm doing festivals."

"Wow," Claude chimed in. He had switched to coffee and was now nursing a black decaf. "It must take some bottle getting up on stage to do that."

"I'm used to it now. To tell the truth, I'm really part of a double act. My dog Sponge helps with a lot of the gags. I use him a bit like a ventriloquist dummy. It doesn't sound like it should work, but it does." Sherry swigged more wine, her mouth batwinged with purple stains.

Arthur sniggered. This time Sherry caught him.

"Something funny?"

"Your act, by the sounds of it." Arthur smiled, sickly sweet, and palmed more peanuts into his mouth.

Shortly before 9pm, they heard the arrival of another houseguest and lingered beneath the kitchen's arch to greet him. Amanda was surprised at how young the boy seemed, even to her. Justin Crawford shuffled toward the kitchen wheeling his case behind him. He had a red streak running through his mop of black hair, and two nose rings in each nostril. He was short and skinny, with a feminine face that made Sherry remark how much he looked like a young David Bowie. "You know, during his Ziggy Stardust period."

Justin said he didn't know what Ziggy Stardust looked like but thanked her anyway. "Is there any food going? I'm starving."

"There's crisps and nuts and things in the conservatory," Amanda said.

"And wine!" Sherry added, gleefully. "Which reminds me, I need a top up."

When they reconvened in the conservatory, Sherry did the rounds with the bottles. Claude refused, admitting somewhat reluctantly that he didn't drink, which earned him a chorus of boos.

"Is there no beer?" Justin asked when Sherry offered him wine.

"Try the fridge," Sherry said, pointing toward it.

In the fridge, Justin found a bottle of Stella Artois, and returned, satisfied. "That's better. I don't drink wine. It's bad for you."

"I hope that's sarcasm young man," Sherry said, mock scolding.

"This place is huge," Justin said. "I don't think I've stayed in a house as big as this."

"Oh, I just love it," Sherry replied. "It's so classic and... I don't know the word. *Debonair.*"

"You won't be saying that when you see the bedrooms," Amanda said, her head becoming heavy with wine.

"They weren't fabulous?" Sherry asked.

"I've seen prison documentaries that have comfier-looking accommodation," Claude quipped, blowing on his coffee to cool it.

"That's got to be an exaggeration," Arthur said, his forehead creasing with concern. "They can't be that bad."

"See for yourself." Claude pointed to the ceiling. "They're upstairs."

"Ooh, yes, that's an idea. Claude my friend, would you be so kind as to lead the way?" Sherry asked, angling the neck of the wine bottle over Amanda's glass.

Amanda placed a hand over the glass and said, "No, I'd better slow down."

"Speed up, girl! Full speed or nothing at all, come on," Sherry said.

"Alright, I guess it's a special occasion," Amanda relented, although she was beginning to feel sluggish. One and a half glasses of red wine was her limit, and she usually ended up regretting that. It always seemed to trigger a throbbing headache and dehydrate her something chronic. So far, though, she had managed two and a quarter glasses, and thought she had a couple more in her. Maybe it was the adrenaline rush of meeting new people or maybe it was because she wasn't drinking the cheap stuff.

Claude led the way upstairs to the landing. Upon seeing the bedrooms, Arthur brushed past him and hunted for his name plaque. He found it and practically knocked the door off the hinges in his haste. He was in there for less than two seconds before he re-emerged onto the landing, his eyes closed, his face flushed with frustration.

"No, this can't be it." He turned to Claude, his tongue probing the inside of his cheek angrily. "This has to be a mistake."

"I don't think it is," Claude said. "Our names are on the doors and everything, look."

"Yes, I can read. But what is that?" He cocked his thumb toward the door.

"Why are you asking him for?" Sherry said, her eyelids droopy from the drink. "He's not the landlord, is he?"

"Well they can't expect us to sleep in these rooms."

"Why not?" Justin said, stepping out of his room, which happened to be next to Arthur's. "It's got a bed and a pillow."

"And probably mice and spiders and damp if the walls are anything to go by," Arthur returned.

"It's only for a week," Justin said, shrugging. "I think it's fine."

"Right." Arthur held up his palms. "How about we make a pact as a group? Why don't we complain and say we don't want to sleep in these conditions?"

"We can't make a pact as a group," Amanda said, surprised at how even her voice sounded. If not for the wine, she wouldn't have spoken at all. "We're still waiting for one more person."

"Well it's a majority pact then, how about that? We could complain to them." Arthur pointed at the eye-in-the-sky lens in the centre of the ceiling above them. "I mean, this is a great big bloody house and they haven't spared any expense anywhere else, but the bedrooms look like they belong in some fucking Hackney crack den."

Amanda wasn't sure which crack dens Arthur had been in, but in her experience, they made these bedrooms look like Buckingham Palace. She had never smoked crack, but had picked up coke from enough different places to know that they were hellholes: bare floorboards, infested with vermin, black mould festering in the crumbling walls like a sickness.

"If they meant us to have something better, we'd have it," Claude said, diplomatically. "Maybe this is part of the uh... the social experiment."

"How can it be?" Arthur almost spat, his face twisting into a sneer. "I don't see any reason why us sleeping on *cots* with blankets made out of Velcro could be anything to do with any experiment."

"Maybe they're testing a drug that helps you sleep, even when you're uncomfortable?" Justin said. He sucked his Stella down to the suds and placed the bottle on the floor. Just then, his theory sounded perfectly plausible to Amanda.

"That's the most ridiculous thing I've ever heard, I'm sorry," Arthur said.

"Don't be sorry to me, pal." Justin shrugged. "I couldn't give a shit either way."

Arthur removed his hat revealing a deeply receded hairline that somehow made him appear oddly sinister. He reminded Amanda of a villain from a film she'd seen, though she couldn't quite recall which one. He threw the hat into his room and folded his arms across his chest. Judging by the way his tongue looked ready to punch through his cheek, he was gearing up to say something else. Before he could, they heard the front door open. They looked over the banister and saw a tall woman with dreadlocks down to her waist, in a tight white bodysuit that clung to her athletic frame. The woman, accompanied by her guide, happened to look up and see them peering down at her.

"Hi guys!" she said, a perfect white smile standing out against her dark features. "Has the party started without me?"

Even from the landing, Amanda could see that the woman was an Amazon. She was more than just beautiful, she was sexy, and Amanda admitted this to herself with a touch of jealousy that she resented instantly. Just one sentence from the woman in that thick French accent went a long way toward denting Amanda's already fragile self-esteem, and she suddenly had the urge to check her face and see if more spots had formed.

"We're just getting warmed up, love," Sherry called back, as they all made their way downstairs to greet her. "Has anyone ever told you, you look like Grace Jones? My god, you're beautiful, woman!"

CHAPTER 10

Wish walked through the empty halls of the university, trying to find the lecture room. The lady at reception had given her directions, and then, upon seeing Wish struggling to remember all the twists and turns, she had drawn a map on a Post-it note.

After passing through a glass tunnel that connected one end of the building to another, and fighting the encroaching vertigo when she looked down into the courtyard, she eventually came to a set of double doors. The placard outside read "Belling Suite" and Wish tentatively opened the door. The rows of pews were empty but the lights were on and so she went in, inhaling the strong smell of air freshener and pine-scented disinfectant.

She saw Jacqueline at the desk, peering over her glasses as she scribbled in a notepad, a small stack of library-laminated textbooks by her side. Wish waited a moment, but Jacqueline was deep into her groove and hadn't even heard the soft whine of the door hinges.

"Bonjour Jacqueline," Wish said, hesitantly, immediately feeling like a student that had been asked to stay behind after class.

Jacqueline's pen came to an abrupt halt mid-scribble, her head turning quickly. She removed her glasses and seemed on the verge of smiling, but didn't.

"Wish. What a surprise."

They spoke in French, which was both rare and pleasant for Wish. She hadn't made many French friends since moving to the UK and conversing in her mother tongue felt fluid and freeing. Her English was very good, but it was sometimes like stopping to jump over a hurdle as opposed to sprinting around the track.

Wish had been about to take a step forward, but seeing that Jacqueline wasn't prepared to rise from her chair, remained still. "How have you been?"

"Busy. You?"

"Well, sometimes busy, too."

After a spell of silence that seemed to stretch almost to breaking point, Jacqueline said, "What can I do for you?"

Same old Jacqueline. No small talk, catch-ups or trips down memory lane. Straight to the point. Wish shifted on the spot, sensing Jacqueline's eyes rolling over her, observing, judging. Wish felt suddenly too warm beneath the bright lecture room lights, even though she was wearing a skirt and t-shirt. The outfit choice had surely not gone unnoticed by Jacqueline, whose dress sense – and physique – was the complete contrast of Wish's.

"I was evicted yesterday."

There was no emotion on Jacqueline's face, though Wish knew her well enough to understand the cogs were turning. Just because she didn't seem outwardly concerned didn't mean that Jacqueline was the stoic ice queen that most of her students thought her to be.

The last time they had spoken was three months prior, in a very brief conversation over the phone. Wish had explained that her landlord was trying to unlawfully evict her from her little flat in East London, because she wouldn't agree to renew her lease for almost twice the amount she was already paying. Wish fought her case, explaining she had spent her own money sprucing the place up, painting and decorating, all to transform it from a crumbling ghetto to somewhere pleasantly liveable.

Rather than sympathize, Jacqueline had said, *"Why would you do that when you don't own the place? You've decorated and now he can charge more money because of it."*

Well apparently, Wish didn't know the rules. She didn't know that she could get ripped off for trying to do something nice.

"You're too naïve, Wish. You always put your faith in silly things. Like when that woman told you she needed someone to choreograph a Beyoncé video, and you believed her. It's childish thinking."

"Where are you staying now?"

"I'm on my friend's sofa, but... she has three kids and her husband works nights. I can't stay there long. Maybe another day, but I'm already imposing. She let me use her garage for my stuff, but... I don't have a lot, anyway."

Putting her glasses back on, Jacqueline returned her attention to her notes. It was strange to think that there were lecturers who still used pen and paper to plan their lessons. The last time Wish had used a pen to write something, it felt like striking a stone to light a fire.

"How is your back?"

"Much better." Wish brightened, happy that Jacqueline seemed to be taking some personal interest in her. "Sometimes aches a lot if I sleep in certain positions but..."

"So, you're able to work?"

"I do work. I told you, remember. Teaching the kids at the YMCA."

"Giving dance lessons to five year-olds is bringing in enough for you to rent somewhere else?"

"Well..." She drifted, because the embarrassment was almost unbearable, and the tension was causing a tightening in the muscles of her lower back that would soon be excruciating if she didn't sit down. "No, it's not enough. But with my back..."

"Don't use that as a crutch, Wish. You can walk, you can work. A proper job, one that will give you a salary instead of pocket money. It's time to stop being naïve."

"Yes, maybe you're right," Wish said. She had to concede because she was standing there with her hat in her hand, about to ask for a favour that she already knew the outcome of. "I went to the Job Centre already. I just... I just need some breathing space."

"And you want to stay with me, is that where this is going?"

Wish could feel the tears brimming in her eyes and bit down on her lower lip in the hope that it would momentarily divert the sadness and shame. It worked, except for two tears that plinked from her lashes when she next blinked.

"It wouldn't be for very long. Just until I get a grip on things."

"No." The word was so blunt, so divorced from emotion that Wish was momentarily confused.

"No? Jacqueline, I'm your sister. I have nowhere else to go."

"You're nearly forty, Wish. You should already have a grip on things, as you say. Don't use your back as an excuse." She glanced over at Wish, eyebrows arched, and said, "Life is not always the way you want it to be, but I have one piece of advice to give you, as your big sister." She stopped, meeting Wish's eyes to ensure she had captured her complete attention. "If you work hard, things get easier. Things are never *easy*, Wish, but they get easier. Now, I have a lot of work to do before my next lecture."

"That's it?" Wish said, her words amplifying in the empty room. "I come to you in crisis, and you give me some fucking big speech about working hard? What, because I don't read all these books like you do, you think I haven't worked hard? Do you know what it's like, Jacqueline? Do you know what it's like to spend your best years chasing a dream like a dog after a bone only to have it all crushed before your very eyes? No, you don't."

"You're being dramatic, and I want you to stop it. This is my place of work, Wish. You need to respect it."

The muscles in Wish's back were beginning to tighten like a knotted old rope. A dull pain was working its way down the backs of her thighs and riding an elevator up her spine.

"You still blame me, don't you?" Wish said, her vision sparkling with tears. "Why don't you come out and say it. You blame me for your divorce."

"I don't want to talk about this. I want you to go. I have a class in fifteen minutes."

Wish strode over to the desk, each footstep setting off landmines up and down her back. She swept the textbooks off the desk, toppling a small mesh container that held Jacqueline's stationery. Pens, pencils, rubbers, and rulers all toppled to the floor. Jacqueline still didn't rise. Didn't even appear surprised.

"This is what I mean," Jacqueline sighed. "Baby tantrums because you can't get your own way. You need to grow up and take some responsi–"

"It's not my fault your husband was a piece of shit. It's not my fault he cheated on you. And it's not my fault he grabbed me. But somehow, you think it is. And you say I'm the one that is naïve."

A storm began brewing behind Jacqueline's dark eyes. Her jaw worked side to side as though she were grinding her teeth. Wish thought there was a very good chance her big sister would get up now, rising from the chair like a boxer from the stool between rounds, ready to go and slug it out.

But she didn't. She just continued to sit there with the pen gripped tight in her fist, her glare growing murderous. Then, in a heartbeat, her expression softened, and all the tension melted from her features.

"Good luck with your flat hunting, Wish. I'm sure you'll find something soon."

Warm, salty tears ran down the valley of Wish's cheekbones, and slipped away to the carpet. "Fine. At least now, I understand something that should have been clear long ago. I have no sister."

"There you go being dramatic." She resumed her work, squiggling rapidly on the paper. "Be on your way now, Wish. Don't make a scene."

"Don't worry. I won't be bothering you again with my childishness," she replied, palming tears away. "I hope you enjoy being lonely and miserable, Jacqueline. Because that's what you are now." She turned, and even that small movement made more landmines go boom. She gritted her teeth against the pain as twin electric shocks ran down the backs of her thighs and crackled in her calves. The door handle felt slippery in her palm as she grabbed it. Flinging open the door, she was just about ready to leave, to weep as she floundered through the hallways trying to find the exit.

"You know something, you're wrong," Wish said. "Before my accident, I *was* going to choreograph for Beyoncé. I even saw a draft of the contract."

"I'm happy for you." Jacqueline returned without allowing any space for Wish's words to resonate.

She did not look up from her notepad.

"You know something else?" Wish said, an almost maniacal smile breaking on her lips. "Now I wish I did *fuck* your husband."

Jacqueline's head snapped toward Wish, but by the time she got out of the chair, Wish was already making her way down the hallway, her laughter bouncing off the walls.

CHAPTER 11

The woman introduced herself as Wish Baptiste, and her name received a round of compliments. Wish Baptiste was a much more exotic name than Amanda Pearson, Amanda thought. After a quick assessment of Wish's waist, Amanda felt like a jam doughnut standing next to her. She thought she had also seen Claude and Justin exchange a secret look between them, a quick glittering of their eyes and a smile tugging at their lips. Between her sculpted cheekbones, ballerina body, and that goddamn accent, Wish was intoxicating, even Amanda had to admit that.

Wish had just taken her first sip of white wine and was politely listening to Arthur vehemently outline the bedroom situation, when a noise silenced the room. It was a *ding-dong* sort of chime, the kind you hear on an airplane before a flight attendant addressed the passengers.

"Good evening, ladies and gentlemen. If you would like to make your way to the dining hall, we have prepared a very special dinner for you." It sounded like a recording. The *ding-dong* chimed again, ending the announcement.

"Does anyone know where the dining room is?" Justin asked, following the eyes around the room that all seemed to settle on Claude.

"I had a pretty good look around, but I don't think I saw it," Claude said. "A lot of doors were locked though. I'm guessing it's on this floor, right?"

"We can find it," Wish said. "Some teamwork is all we need."

"That's the spirit, lovey." Sherry rubbed Wish's shoulder, and Amanda felt herself bristle, ever so slightly. If Sherry was the den-mother of the group, then Wish had somehow become her favourite child in less than half an hour.

Amanda stayed at the back of the pack and cast aside the rest of her wine, knowing that it was triggering some ugly feelings that she probably wouldn't have felt if sober. She exhaled deeply and ran her fingers through her hair. Her face felt hot and feverish, and she suddenly wanted nothing more than to tiptoe up to her icebox and go to sleep. She knew there was no good way to go about ditching the group without looking like a drama queen, so she plodded on after them as they searched for the dining room.

They were down a hallway decorated with large oil paintings when Arthur said, "It won't be this way."

"Why not?" Claude asked.

"Because look how far we've strayed from the kitchen."

"There might be more than one kitchen," Claude suggested, turning his attention to another door.

"For god's sake," Arthur huffed. "This house is big but it's not that big, is it?"

"I can smell food, can you?" Justin said. "We must be on the right path. We just need to follow our noses."

"Well," Claude began. "That's funny you should say that because…"

"It's not down this way," Arthur said, his voice a bored drone. "Doesn't anyone have a map or some idea of the layout of this place?"

"Are you hungry?" Wish asked, and when Arthur said he wasn't, she continued, "Well then it's fun to look around, no?"

"Oh yes, of course. It's a thrill a minute."

"Is this it?" Claude said, opening a door. He stuck his head in the room and said, "We have lift-off!"

There was a round of applause and whooping as they hustled into the dining room, where a long table was dressed with sterling silver cutlery and fine china plates. At the far end of the room, beneath a set of crossed battle-axes, another table offered a variety of food, kept warm on hotplates. A series of flaming lanterns hung in the centre of the ceiling, completing the gothic ambience.

They rushed to the food, removing lids and inspecting the contents. Three large cuts of meat sat on slabs – pork, chicken, and beef – which were to be complimented with a choice of gravy, varying in shade and thickness.

"What a feast," Amanda said, her eyes scrolling across the vegetables. "It almost makes you feel guilty, doesn't it?"

"No," Justin sniggered, moving past her with his plate. For such a slim man he had piled more food than he could possibly eat, or so she thought.

Amanda took her time choosing. The others had sat down with their food, except for Wish, who was heaping indiscriminate portions of veg onto her plate.

"You're not having meat?" Amanda asked as Wish spooned a dollop of English mustard onto her potatoes.

"I try not to," Wish said, smiling.

"That's how you stay so slim I bet," Amanda said, regretting the comment as soon as the words left her mouth.

Before she could fixate on it, Wish said, "I make up for it with dessert, you know?"

"My kind of girl," Amanda said, before heading for the table.

Sherry was saying something about the wine, which she was pouring into the cups for everyone, but Amanda didn't catch all of it. In truth, she couldn't understand much of what Sherry was saying anymore. She was slurring in an almost indecipherable drawl, although the rest of her body still operated competently as far as Amanda could tell.

"The real question is – who put the food here in the first place?" Claude said through a mouthful of chicken. He chewed, swallowed, and said, "It can't have been sitting there all night. I think they have people moving through the house, but they don't want us to see them because of this um… you know, the experiment."

"How?" Justin asked.

"Dunno. They could have hidden doors. This place could be a giant fun house."

"That's a bit spooky, don't you think?" Amanda asked, picking up her cutlery. The scent drifted off her plate and teased her nostrils, and by the time she brought the first forkful of food to her mouth, she realized just how hungry she was. "It's like one of those murder mystery hotel things, isn't it?"

"Oh, they look so fun, don't they?" Claude said. "Like a game of Cluedo or something. You ever been to one?"

Amanda shook her head. Her cousin Celine had gone to a murder mystery themed party in Blackpool as part of her hen-do. She hadn't invited Amanda to the hen-do or the wedding.

"Well this will not be a murder mystery," Wish said, covering her mouth with her hand as she spoke. "This will be a fun week. No murder."

"Why don't we play a guessing game?" Sherry managed, though she pronounced "guess" as "gesh." Her lips were purple from the wine and her face was almost glowing red. "We don't really know what we…" She stifled a burp against the back of her hand. "Excuse me. We could pretend… I mean, guess what we all do?"

"Spare me," Arthur said. He swirled his wine around in his cup and took a long gulp, his eyes flickering in the light. "Why don't we just go around the table and say what we do?"

"Because it's more fun to guess," Sherry said, her eyelids so low they were almost closed. Her face had taken on a meanness that completely transformed her fun-loving demeanour.

"Yes, and we could be here all bloody night," Arthur replied.

Amanda had passed tipsy a few miles back and the next stop was stumbling drunk, but she still had enough presence of mind to know something wasn't quite right with Arthur. His rudeness was immediate, unprovoked, and quickly becoming predictable. She thought it might be a defence mechanism, and she wondered if he was perhaps even more nervous than she was.

"Why don't you go first," Sherry said, almost tripping over the sentence. She slammed an elbow on the table and extended her cup to him. "Please do enlighten us, Sir Arthur."

Sniggers skittered around the table, but Arthur didn't react. He reached for the nearest bottle of wine and filled his cup, his lips glimmering with saliva. He and Sherry sat opposite each other at the table, and to Amanda it looked as though there was some unspoken competition taking place between them. She wasn't sure how much each of them had put away, but since entering the house neither one had come up for air.

"I'm an actor," he said. He pronounced every syllable with dignity, tilting his chin up and pinning his shoulders back. "Theatre mainly, but I've done TV and film too."

"Anything we'd know?" Justin asked. He had hardly made a dent in the surplus on his plate, but had apparently finished, his knife and fork buried among a mountain of potatoes.

"Depends what you watch," Arthur said defensively, and then went directly to the refuge of his cup. "I make a living treading the boards, my boy, have done for over thirty years," he said it as though it were a challenge, although Amanda had detected no malice in Justin's question. "And what is it you do? Sorry, forgot your name."

"I have quite a popular YouTube channel," Justin said. "I do a lot of reviews, like, mostly video games, but some wrestling reviews as well."

"And that's your occupation, is it? That's how you earn a living?"

"I live with my mum still, but I almost have three hundred thousand subscribers, and I get paid from YouTube if that's what you mean. And Twitch. You know Twitch?"

"I'm not sure that was what I meant." Arthur's eyes rolled away from Justin, dismissing him.

"I think that's amazing," Sherry said, although it felt like her enthusiasm was amplified by the need to contradict Arthur. "Three hundred... thousand, that's, well, that's a lot of people. So good for you. Well done." The compliment was meant for Justin, but Sherry stared directly at Arthur as she said it.

Amanda shrank away from the confrontation, feeling like a child watching her parents gearing up for a barnstormer, and concentrated on her food. She didn't really like where the conversation was headed anyway, because any moment now she would have to divulge the embarrassing truth that no, she wasn't really a singer, she was a failed pop act. Her appetite had vanished, the few mouthfuls she'd managed liquefying in her guts.

"I find this digital age all a bit flimsy," Arthur said.

"I bet you've never had three hundred thousand people watch one of your theatre plays," Sherry replied, her lips pulling back into an unsettling grin.

"What do you do, Wish?" Claude broke in, his voice high and urgent. His effort at diverting the attention away from Arthur and Sherry's snips and jabs wasn't particularly subtle, but Amanda was thankful at the attempt. She was beginning to feel sick, so she concentrated on steadying the tide in her stomach.

"I'm a dancer," Wish said. Claude nodded, as though the pairing of Wish's appearance with her occupation was the most obvious thing in the world. Amanda felt another sting of jealousy, wondering how they would look at her if she had claimed to be a dancer. They would probably mask their disbelief with polite smiles, before rapidly changing the subject. "I do music videos. Mostly in the background, but sometimes I do the TV commercials also."

"I thought you meant you were an erotic dancer," Arthur muttered.

"Erotic?" Wish asked, the smile on her lips twitching ever so slightly. She seemed bemused more than anything else, as though she had misunderstood the setup of a joke.

"That was just what popped in my head when you said you were a dancer." He smiled to show he meant no offence, but it was dripping with condescension. "I don't know – perhaps it was your name that set me off. My apologies."

Silence settled around the table. Wish's eyes widened as her lips began working, trying to find something to say, but the embarrassment at his comment quickly crept into her features.

"What the fuck is your problem?" Amanda said in a low voice, not even really sure she had spoken until she saw Arthur looking at her.

"Sorry, dear?" Arthur asked, his face placid.

"You heard me," Amanda said, her heart bouncing in her chest. "You've been acting ignorant and… childish all evening. So, what's the problem?"

He placed a hand on his chest, dramatically outraged. "I didn't realize I had a problem. I apologize if I've upset you."

The anger dissipated, her fire doused. She felt silly for having spoken out like that, and started to wonder if she had made things unnecessarily awkward for the group. Just as she began blaming herself for the fresh current of tension crackling the room, Arthur said, "And what do you do, Amanda?"

"You know what I do, you said as much to Claude earlier."

"Ah, that's it." Arthur snapped his fingers. "Didn't you have a song out a very long time ago?"

"I did."

"Well, I suppose everybody wants to be somebody, don't they? Was it just the *one* hit you had?"

"No, actually." She stared down the table at him, her vision wavering. "I had three top ten singles and an album that sold over half a million copies." She waited for a reply, her breathing laboured from the wine. He looked on the verge of saying something, but instead, gave her an indifferent shrug and swirled his cup.

"That's an amazing achievement, lovie," Sherry said and began to clap rapidly, her rings tinkling as her heavy palms came together. The sudden loudness of the sound made Amanda wince.

"That's a lot of records," Justin said, saluting her with his cup.

The insufferable sound of Sherry's applause had long outstayed its welcome, and still she continued to clap. She looked at the others, provoking them to do the same until a staggered ovation clattered through the room. It was artificial and made Amanda feel awful; their phony, well-intended applause cut deeper than Arthur's belittling, and now she had to get up and leave the room because if she stayed in there a minute longer she would snap. By the sound of it, she was the most accomplished person in that room and somehow, they had all made her feel like a charity case. She pushed her chair back, the legs screeching loudly on the varnished floor, and used the table for support as she rose.

"Are you OK, Amanda?" Claude asked, his voice silencing the applause. The genuine look of worry on his face made Amanda's embarrassment deepen. She didn't want to appear upset, but her lungs felt stuffed with sand and she couldn't suck in the deep breath she needed.

"I'm fine," she said, with a gasp, her head spinning. "I think I'm going to turn in for the night." She smiled but was conscious of the fact that she was panting like a bull. A collective groan rose around the table, followed by obligatory protests, but she needed her bed.

"Are you going to be alright getting up the stairs?" Claude asked.

She sipped the air and nodded, but it was Arthur who answered for her.

"It's a flight of stairs, for goodness' sake. She's not flying a plane."

"Exactly," Amanda said as the room tipped one way and then tilted the other. She reeled, gripped the back of her chair to steady herself. "I think even a one-hit wonder like me can manage a few stairs."

She said goodnight with a wave and had almost made it to the door before Sherry caught her. "Hold on, lovie, hold on. Come here." She swaddled Amanda with her thick arms and squeezed her, planting a slobbery, overly affectionate kiss on her cheek. Amanda smelled wine and perfume tangled in Sherry's hair. "You have a good sleep, alright hun?"

"I will do. You too."

Sherry clasped Amanda's cheeks between her large hands. "You have a good sleep, that's an order."

Amanda hated people touching her face. She had suffered terrible acne as a teenager that left her with craters that she now filled in with foundation. Her skin was naturally very oily, and it didn't take much to provoke an outbreak. She reared away from Sherry's grasp, practically peeling her hands off her, before leaving the room.

Amanda closed the dining room door behind her, thankful for the silence in the hallway. A drum banged in her forehead, and somewhere deep in her drunkenness, a feeble, sober voice told her she was going to be sick. She placed a hand over her mouth and paused mid-step, waiting for the weight to slide back down her throat. Her stomach lurched, and for one horrendous second, she thought she was going to puke right there on the tiles. She kept it down, and forced her uncoordinated feet to ascend the staircase. It felt like she was walking on a bouncy castle. When she reached the landing, she casually strutted to the bathroom, hoping she could trick herself into feeling normal. It didn't work, but by the time she reached the toilet and had her head aimed over the bowl, the moment had passed. She groaned, the pressure turning her head into a cement mixer.

Bed, that's what she needed. She palmed the wall as she stumbled to her room, and just as she pushed her door open, she heard a loud crash from downstairs. She froze, heard another crash, followed by screaming. A stream of swearwords echoed through the house in an almost incoherent jumble. Amanda heard Arthur say, "Now listen here–" followed by something she couldn't quite make out, as it was dampened by the clamour of other voices.

"This place is nuts," Amanda mumbled, and shouldered through her door. "What have I got myself into?"

She fell onto her mattress and waited for the room to slow down.

Maybe I'll wake up and this whole thing will have been a dream, she thought as she drifted to sleep. Her nap didn't last long, because she was jerked awake by a knock at her door. Her eyes snapped open and she pushed herself up off the mattress.

"Who is it?" she asked, startled.

"It's Claude. I'm sorry, did I wake you?" he asked from the other side of the door.

Had he woken her? Now that she was awake, she wasn't actually sure she had been sleeping. She got off the bed and opened the door. "What's wrong?"

"Nothing's wrong," he said too quickly, trying to assuage her worry. "I just wanted to make sure you were alright. I'm not being weird it's just… you seemed a bit upset and I wasn't really sure if I should come by, you know, because we don't know each other very well."

"Yeah, I'm fine," she replied, croakily. "What was all that racket down there?"

"Oh, that." He shook his head. "Things haven't really got off to a good start with Sherry and Arthur tonight." She nodded, waiting for him to elaborate. "Arthur upset her, and she started throwing plates at him. They missed, thankfully, but there's food everywhere down there. I don't know if that means she's going to get sent home. Then again, we haven't exactly had a code of conduct manual or anything like that."

"What did he say to get her so angry?"

Claude scratched his neck, biting his lip to contain the laughter. "It was a bit out of order, really. Well, you know she does the comedy with her dog? He sort of made a joke about, you know, her and the dog… together."

"Christ," Amanda groaned. She was about to say something else, something about Arthur maybe having a mental illness, when she began to giggle. "He's a fucking arsehole," she said, shaking her head, "but that is a bit funny."

"She didn't seem to think so," Claude whispered. "Anyway, I don't know what tomorrow is going to bring, but I'm going to bed. You sure you're alright?"

"I'm good," she said, her eyelids gaining weight. "Thanks for stopping by."

"No problem. Goodnight." He nodded, waved awkwardly, and walked to his room.

When Amanda fell back asleep, she did not dream.

CHAPTER 12

MONDAY: 10 MILLIGRAMS

Her memory of the night before was a kaleidoscope of still images. Amanda lay there, thinking through the hangover, her breath appearing before her lips in misty apparitions. She brought her knees into her chest and snuggled deeper into the blanket, her skin feverishly hot despite the chill in the room. She rolled her head on the pillow, trying to find a sweet spot that would still the marching band in her skull. She could smell the wine on her bitter breath, her tongue like a Brillo pad. She swallowed, felt her throat click. Water could wait, so could the ache of her bladder. She would just lay there and let the hangover run its course and–

Ding-dong.

"Good morning, ladies and gentlemen," that synthetic voice said affably through the speakers. "Rise and shine. Please proceed to the Circle Room for your morning dosage."

Amanda moaned and wriggled against the firm mattress, which wasn't nearly as bad as she expected it to be. She closed her eyes and clenched her teeth when she felt the pain shift positions in her brain. She was beginning to drift back to sleep when an air raid siren filled the house, loud enough to steal the breath in her throat. She slammed her hands over her ears, not caring that the action aggravated the hangover. The overpowering wail of the air raid siren was vibrating through her; she could feel its urgency in her bones.

"Stop it," she shouted to nobody, wrapping the blanket

around her as she made her way out onto the landing. Squinting, she saw Wish in a long nightgown, a headscarf covering her locks, cringing against the sound.

"Do you know what this is?" Wish yelled over the siren. Amanda shook her head, and then winced.

"Turn it off!" Arthur shouted, his hair sticking up around his ears making him look like a mad professor. He was clad in floral pyjamas that rode up his buttocks. "Turn that bloody horrible noise off!"

"What is it?" Wish asked again.

"Sounds like the bloody Luftwaffe's about to strike. Turn it off!" he said, his face reddening with the effort of his complaint.

"It's Sherry," Claude said. He had slept in a faded pair of baggy Nike jogging bottoms and a thin, long-sleeved cotton shirt.

"What is?" Justin was in a vest and boxer shorts, his hands strategically placed in front of what was obviously a lump of morning glory.

"She's still asleep so that's probably why..." Claude broke off, screwed his face up at the horrendous wailing. "That's why they're still playing the siren."

"Well tell her to get her fat arse out of bed!" Arthur said, pointing to Sherry's room.

"Why don't you tell her?" Justin spat back over the siren. "You had no problem telling her what for yesterday."

"I'll tell her," Wish said and thumped on Sherry's door. "Sherry?"

"She's not going to hear that." Arthur stormed to the door, twisted the knob, and flung it open. Sherry was sitting on the edge of the bed, her large bosom barely contained in a silk slip. "Are you fucking deaf woman? Can't you hear that?"

"Do you mind?" She crossed her arms over her chest. Her hair was a knotty jungle, her face puffy from sleep.

The siren stopped just as Claude grabbed hold of Arthur. Nobody was really sure what was happening in the sudden silence, but Claude marched Arthur away from Sherry's room.

"Get your hands off me!" Arthur protested, trying to flail his arms. Arthur was a large man, six-feet-four and eighteen stones at least, but there was a wiry strength to Claude, the ropes of muscle standing out through the cotton shirt.

"Listen to me carefully," Claude said, his voice low. "Don't ever do that again."

"Do what?" Arthur thrashed out of Claude's grasp, and Claude stepped back to give him space.

"Don't barge into a person's bedroom like that," Claude said. "She could've been naked in there."

"Then she should shift her arse into gear when she hears the house shaking apart, shouldn't she?"

"I don't care about any of that," Claude said, calmly. "But these doors don't have locks on them, so you need to respect other people's space."

"I'll do what I want," Arthur said.

"Then so will I," Claude shot back, "and you won't like it when I do."

Arthur stepped around him and stomped off toward the staircase. Claude inhaled and released a shuddering breath.

"What was that noise?" Sherry asked, emerging from the bedroom, scratching her scalp.

"I think that was our wakeup call," Justin said, blissfully unaware that he was groping himself, trying to shift the bulge into a better position.

Groggily, they drifted through the house in search of the Circle Room. Conversation was scarce, yet the morning's small talk centred on how annoying it was that they hadn't been provided with a map to help them get around. They thudded down the hallways, Arthur staying a yard ahead of the herd, Sherry dragging a yard behind, her effervescence from the previous night fizzled out.

They located the Circle Room about halfway down one of the hallways on the ground floor. Arthur flung the door open and thundered into the room, and Amanda noticed with some amusement just how mincing his walk was, his hips swaying to accommodate the heaviness of his arse. He was ungainly, built like a bowling pin. Funny how an early morning could strip a person away like that, Amanda thought, and realized that for the first time since entering the house, she wasn't nervous. She had survived the night without making a tit of herself, as far as she could remember anyway, and that was a win for her.

The Circle Room was a large open space with a black velvet curtain covering the far wall. It sort of reminded Amanda of her high school drama studio, which her teacher sometimes let her use at lunchtimes to rehearse dance routines with her first girl group, Dream. Now there was something to cringe about! Of the five members of Dream, only Amanda and another girl called Charlene Westway could actually sing, but they had all been good friends and putting together their own dances had been great fun. She briefly wondered what Charlene was up to now as she took a chair and faced the front of the room.

"Where's the teacher?" Justin said. "Maybe class has been cancelled for today."

"Or maybe we have the wrong room," Wish said.

"The door said Circle Room, didn't it?" Arthur grumbled, inspecting his nails.

"I don't know, I didn't read it," Wish replied, hugging her bare arms. "There could be more than one Circle Room, no?"

A minute passed. Then another. All the little noises stood out in the silence; the scratching, the shifting of weight on the chairs, the slap of bare feet on the hardwood floor, the click of jaw hinges as they yawned. Then a rustle from behind them as the black velvet curtain was disturbed. Footsteps echoed through the room, and they turned in their chairs to see a man emerge from behind the curtain, carrying a tray. He wore a white medical uniform with a surgical mask covering his nose and mouth. He reached the front of the room and stopped before them, still as a statue.

Ding-dong.

"Hello, ladies and gentlemen," the voice from the speaker said. "Welcome to your first morning dosage. On the tray before you, you will find six dishes, each labelled with a name. Please find the dish with your name, take your pill, and wash it down with the water provided. Failure to comply will result in your immediate removal from the house, and forfeit of all funds, as outlined in section 7D of the contract."

They sat there a moment longer, awaiting further instruction, and when none came, they got to their feet. Arthur was first to find his dish. He picked up the pill, which was about the size of a chickpea, and placed it on his tongue. Then, he took one of the paper cups of water and downed it. Arthur turned to walk back to his seat, when the man holding the tray caught hold of his wrist.

Ding-dong.

"Please open your mouth for inspection. Then raise and depress your tongue slowly." The automated voice on the speaker instructed.

"You just saw me take it," Arthur said to the man in the surgical mask. The man didn't reply. "You just saw me take it," Arthur said again, before adding, "God, this is really petty, isn't it. Here you go then." He hooked his fingers into his mouth and spread it wide, before wagging his tongue at the man.

"This geezer's got a screw loose," Justin whispered, nodding toward Arthur.

"Happy now?" Arthur asked, his eyes bulging like eggs.

The man nodded, ever so slightly, and Arthur sat back down.

"You alright mate?" Justin asked the man as he stepped forward and took his pill. He opened his mouth, got the nod, and went back to his seat.

When it was Amanda's turn, she tried to see if there was any difference between her pill and the others left in their dishes. As far as she could tell, they were identical. She picked it up, turned it over in her fingers, and just before she put it in her mouth, she looked at the man in the mask. His pupils were dark and his eyebrows were bushy. She picked up a cup of water and swallowed. She didn't feel the pill go down and there was no chalky aftertaste. It was just gone. She opened her mouth to the man in the mask, wiggled her tongue, and sat back down.

Sherry was last. She gagged on the water, gulping the pill down exaggeratedly as though it were the size of a tangerine, and then said to the man, "I hope that's a miracle cure for hangovers we're testing."

The man made no sign that he had heard her. He turned and walked the way he had come, disappearing behind the curtain. There was the sound of buttons being pressed, a beep, and a door opening and then closing heavily.

"You are now free to leave the Circle Room," the voice on the speaker said. "We hope you enjoy the rest of your day."

Justin walked over to the curtain and tugged it aside, revealing a metal door with an electronic keypad to the side of it. He thumbed a few of the buttons at random. The door beeped angrily. "Imagine I guessed the code," he said with a laugh, and slapped the door. "Wankers."

"Anyone feel any different yet?" Wish asked as they made their way out the Circle Room.

"No," Sherry replied. "But I'm bursting for a piss."

CHAPTER 13

"I wonder if there's any way to find out which of us has taken the drug," Claude said, chewing his toast. He looked around the breakfast table at the rest of them. "I think I see some symptoms already. Bloodshot eyes, headaches, crankiness. Could be any of you."

"I feel like fucking death warmed up," Sherry said, elbows planted on the table, her head in her hands. "I bet you feel like the smartest man on earth for not drinking, don't you?"

"Well," he began with a smirk, sipping his tea, "I can't pretend that I don't see the appeal of drinking alcohol, especially given the benefits."

"I'll tell you something for free," Sherry replied. "I'm never drinking again. You give me a stack of Bibles and I'll swear on them."

"That's a good point though," Amanda said. She had made herself a bowl of porridge and added a sliced banana, because a friend of hers had once told her that the potassium was the best thing to battle a hangover. So far, she had managed two mouthfuls and thought she might see them again before long. "What if there's a way to find out who has taken the drug. I mean, it will only be one of us, won't it?"

"But there's no side effect," Wish said, spooning yoghurt into her mouth. "No side effect to the person that takes it, so no way of finding out, no?"

"But the pill must do *something*," Justin said. "Otherwise, what's the point?"

"It might not be something we can notice outwardly," Amanda suggested.

"Or perhaps they'll just analyze our stool when we flush the toilet," Arthur said, dipping a piece of crust into the yolk of his fried egg. "Maybe those little pills will give one of us a brain embolism. Given some of the present company, it'd be a welcome reprieve."

"Arthur, come on," Claude said, exasperated. "Can you just knock it off? We have to spend the whole week together. Why don't we just start again? Clean slate, what do you say?"

"I'm not the one that threw crockery like an infant last night. Nor am I the one that assaulted another guest by placing my hands on them."

"No, but you're a fucking wind-up, aren't you mate, let's face it," Justin said.

"No, he's right," Claude told Justin. Claude turned to Arthur and said, "I'm sorry I grabbed you this morning, and I'm sorry if I've done anything else to offend you. Here," he offered his hand. "Please accept my apology."

Arthur let Claude's hand hang in the air with no intention of shaking it. He pushed away from the table, picked up his plate and took it to the bin, scraping the remains of his breakfast inside. "Have any of you considered that *all* the pills are placebos?" he said as he began rinsing his plate in the sink. "For all we know, there is no drug. This whole thing could just be an experiment to see how paranoid people become when placed with strangers in unfamiliar settings. So far, I'd say that's worked. This big spooky house, the business with that silent nurse and the pills, the instructions through a speaker: it's all theatre."

"I think you're wrong," Amanda said.

"I've been in enough plays to know bad theatre when I see it, but of course, you're entitled to your opinion. Anyway, you can argue amongst yourselves until you foam at the mouth for all I care. Good day."

He sauntered out of the room, whistling merrily.

"What an odd duck," Claude said, shaking his head.

"He's a bloody creep." Sherry's pale face soured. "What on earth did they put such a vile person in the house for? I'm telling you, after what he said to me last night about my little Sponge, I have a good mind to tell these people to stick the money up their arse." She huffed, looked like she was going to say more, and then brought a meaty fist to her mouth. Her shoulders shrugged as she began to cry, her washed-out complexion turning red.

"It's OK, don't cry, don't cry," Wish soothed with an arm around Sherry's shoulders. "No need to get upset."

"Well there is." Sherry punched the air. "It's bad enough that I miss my dog so much, but to have him make those... *insinuations*, it's just... evil."

"I think maybe we all had a bit too much to drink last night," Wish said. "We all acted silly."

Amanda could not bring herself to console Sherry. She was too embarrassed by the woman's plight for attention to say anything useful, so she remained silent.

"He could have a point though," Justin said. Sherry stopped crying mid-sob and glared at him through glistening eyes. "No, not about you and your dog, I didn't mean that. I mean, well, he could be right about this place, about the drug. We might not be taking anything at all."

"Then why bring us here?" Amanda asked. "Why stage this whole thing and pay us all this money? The only company name on the contract was the Midori Media Group. There was nothing about any medical research company."

Sherry grabbed a napkin and dabbed her eyes, then snivelled loudly in a last-ditch attempt to retrain the attention on her. It didn't work, and now even Wish had lost interest and was locked into the discussion.

"I looked them up on Companies House," Amanda said. "It's a brand-new company. They haven't even filed any accounts yet."

"Really?" Claude said.

Amanda nodded. "Didn't any of you have a solicitor look at the contract?"

The corners of Claude's lips curled into a smile that made him look like a mischievous boy. "I didn't have the money for it. And after they took me out to that restaurant – it was this posh French place in King's Cross – well, maybe I'm a sucker, but I was convinced. I mean, twenty-five grand is a lot of money to a guy like me. That's more than I'd make in a year. So, I thought, stuff it, I'll take a week's annual leave and give it a go. I didn't really have anything to lose. I mean, I *did* read the contract."

Amanda searched the other faces at the table and thought she saw a spark jump behind their eyes. They had all thought the same thing, and perhaps felt a trickle of shame or embarrassment, for each of them had been paid a lot more than twenty-five grand. But why? Because Claude was just a car salesman and the rest of them were all… what? If Amanda's estimation of the group was accurate then they were all a bunch of *almosts*.

"So far it's been an interesting experience," Claude said, now smiling optimistically. "I'm not a very creative guy but it's nice to be around so many talented people. I'd be lying if I said it didn't make me sound like a bit of a dunce though."

"Dunce?" Sherry scoffed, all traces of trauma gone. "You're the only one without a splitting headache this morning. I'd say that makes you a bloody genius."

He looked down at his lap, his face colouring.

"So, you all just signed up without getting advice from a solicitor?" Amanda said. The two mouthfuls of porridge felt as though they had hardened to concrete in her stomach.

"Not me," Justin said. "I had my mum look at it. She didn't want me to do it, but when it said there were no side effects, she told me to go for it."

"I have a friend who is studying law in France," Wish said. "She looked at it, but her English is not great. I had to translate some of it, but she said it seemed like a nice contract. Well…"

She giggled, and even her laugh sounded like musical notes. "It's a nice contract as long as we get paid. But it is strange that the company was not like, you know, medical, especially if we are taking pills."

"It's a smokescreen I think," Amanda said. "They're using a dummy company to protect the real people that are putting this thing together."

"Oh." Wish nodded.

"I suppose the only question would be why they would want to remain hidden." Amanda pushed her cold, congealed porridge aside. Sunlight poured through the kitchen window and dazzled her, searing into the back of her brain. She shielded her eyes and said, "I don't think we'll run out of things to talk about this week. There's plenty of conspiracy theories we can cook up if we get bored."

"God, Arthur's right. We've all taken a paranoia pill," Claude said.

"Yeah," Justin snorted, "and by the end of the week we'll all be believing the Earth is flat. What do you guys think about that, by the way? You reckon the Earth is round or flat?"

CHAPTER 14

After breakfast, Amanda snuck back up to her room and crawled under the blanket with her temples pulsing. She fell asleep quickly and dreamed that she was alone on a spaceship that was flying to the sun. She was terrified, her face pressed up against a small round window as she was propelled through space, the interior of the ship growing brighter and hotter until sweat was bursting out of her pores. She jerked awake, expelling a breath that had been locked in her lungs, and was surprised to find that she was actually sweating profusely. She touched her clammy forehead, and then noticed that her pillow was damp. Perspiration dripped off the curls of her hair, and she could smell the odour rising from her body. She rummaged around in her bag, grabbed a towel, and made her way down the hall. The bathroom only had a sink and a toilet, so she continued through the upper floor until she located the shower rooms. When she opened the women's shower door, a bank of steam curled out to meet her. At the far end of the room, Wish was showering, her body hidden by a partition that came to her shoulder.

"Bonjour," Amanda called over the crashing water. She cringed, wondering why she had said that when Wish probably spoke better English than she did. But before she could worry whether the greeting was offensive or not, Wish scooped water out of her eyes and waved.

"Bonjour."

"You don't mind me joining you, do you?" Amanda asked, before quickly adding, "I mean in my own shower, not yours."

"Yes of course." Wish laughed. "It feels so nice to have a shower, oh my god." She tipped her head back, the water spraying her lathered locks. "How are you feeling today?"

"Better now." Amanda stepped out of her slippers and entered the cubicle, leaving an empty one between her and Wish. She began to undress, discarding her clothes in a pile in the corner of the cubicle. "It's a weird experience, isn't it?"

"Yes, but so far I think all the people are very nice. Even that man, what's his name again? Sorry, I'm bad with names."

"Arthur?"

"Yes. He is a bit, um, aggressive, but I don't think he is so bad. Maybe just nervous, you know?"

Amanda twisted the hot tap and sighed when she got the temperature right. The water drummed against her skull, tattooing her back and shoulders. "He seems to have a big chip on his shoulder," Amanda said, raising her voice to accommodate the noise of the shower.

"The most insecure people usually do." There was a faint whine as Wish shut her water off. She wrapped a towel around her hair and another around her body, and then stepped out of the shower. Amanda raked her fingers through her hair, massaging her scalp with her nails. She watched Wish pass, guiltily admiring the muscle tone in her legs, marvelling at how slender her shoulders were. Amanda saw a thick beige scar running parallel to her spine. "Enjoy your shower," Wish said, wiggling her fingers in a wave.

"Will do," Amanda smiled back, but wondered whether that remark about insecure people was an indirect shot at her.

"Oh, Amanda?" Wish called when Amanda was at the door.

"Yeah?" She turned back.

Wish rested her chin on the cubicle wall. "You're a singer."

Unsure as to whether it was a question or a statement, Amanda gave a noncommittal "Mmm-hmm." That about summed up her status as a singer anyway.

"I was thinking, well, you know how I said I'm a dancer? Well, actually, I'm a choreographer. Retired, you know? But… I would love to work with you." Her smile broadened. "On the outside, I mean."

"Thanks," Amanda said, the embarrassment blossoming until she could do nothing but stare down at her feet. She would have bet her life that Wish had no idea who Amanda Pearson was before stepping into this house.

"You are going to make more music, yes? On the outside," she giggled, rolled her eyes. "I make it sound like prison. But will you? Make more music, yes?"

"I hope so," Amanda said, forcing an airy, nervous laugh. She wanted to backpedal out the door and run away from this conversation as fast as possible. But why? It was true, wasn't it? She did want to make more music. Wasn't that the reason she was in the house in the first place?

"I hope so, too. You should let me choreograph your next video. I'm very good. When we get out, I'll send you my work on YouTube. You'll see. I'll do your next video for free. Would be an honour."

The crashing water drowned out the silence that followed. "Alright then," Amanda said quickly, before making her escape.

After a wash and a change of clothes, Amanda felt like a new woman. The hangover had receded to a dull murmur in her skull that she thought she could vanquish completely with a cup of coffee. She wandered through the house, her slippers silent against the carpet, her forearms prickling from the draught. She passed a window, saw the last rind of sunlight swallowed by an ocean of grey, and could almost feel the shadows stretching through the hallway around her. She couldn't hear the others, which only magnified her awareness of how huge the house was. Unconsciously, her pace quickened until she was almost skipping to the kitchen, humming under her breath to chase away the encroaching spookiness.

There was nobody in the kitchen but the lights were on, and by the time she had filled the kettle, her uneasiness had ebbed. She turned the kettle on and leaned against the counter, satisfied by the comforting burr of the boiling water. Her thoughts trailed like vapour from the kettle's spout as she wandered about the house. What had its purpose been before the six of them arrived? The general layout suggested that it might have once housed many people, if the segregated showers and rows of bedrooms were anything to go by. The décor hinted at an old boarding school, or perhaps a children's home. The house brooded with character, the air charged with events and memories that would remain secret to her.

The kettle clicked, distracting her. She opened a cupboard by her head in search of the coffee when a hand dropped on her shoulder. She screamed and jerked away from the touch, her heart a battering ram against her chest.

"I didn't mean to scare you," Justin said, his lips pulled into a wide grin. His eyes darted about her face, and for the first time since meeting him, she noticed a smattering of freckles across his nose and cheeks. "I've been looking for you."

Catching her breath, Amanda said, "Oh my god, you scared the daylights out of me." Her nerves still tingled from the shock, and she was not quite ready to laugh along with him.

"I'm so sorry," he said, his hand reaching out to pat her arm. "Where were you?"

His hand rubbed her bicep gently, before casually settling there. His touch was light, delicate almost. She rolled her shoulders, expecting his hand to drop away, and when it didn't, she moved to the fridge to fetch the milk.

"I had to take a shower. Felt like death."

"We found the games room. You need to see this place, it's awesome."

"Oh yeah?"

"Yeah. It's got a pool table. Do you play pool?"

She fixed her coffee, stirred, said, "I'm not very good, but yeah." She shrugged. Beneath the bright kitchen lights, she thought his face looked distinctly ratty.

"You can be on my team then," he told her. "We're going to set up a doubles game, but so far it's only me, Claude and Frenchie that want to play. So, you should be on my team."

"Sure." She shrugged. "Where is it?"

He led her to the games room, firing questions at her as they walked. It was less of a conversation and more of an interview, or rather, an interrogation. He spoke quickly and cheerfully, barely giving her time to answer one thing before he moved onto another. How was your shower? How was your nap? How are you finding the beds? How is your hangover? What do you think of the house?

She thought that he had been dipping into the liquor cabinet, or that he might have smuggled in something stronger. His fevered tone and jittery mannerisms reminded her of too many nightclub bathrooms, hoovering lines off a toilet lid. He was certainly speaking frantically enough to suggest the latter, and yet he wasn't gurning or bleary eyed. His ramblings were distinctly focussed, and now she thought he seemed more like an excitable child at a party that had gorged on too much sugar. It was like listening to a person on fast-forward.

The pill. Could this be it? Some form of legal high that gave you all the rush of a coke bump without any of those pesky "adverse side effects" like crippling addiction? There were beads of sweat dotting his forehead and his cheeks were flushed red. Yes, she was beginning to think that Justin had taken the little mystery pill, and the more she considered it, the less comfortable she became in his presence.

He pushed open the door to the games room. He was babbling about his YouTube channel, trying to convince her to be a guest on his weekly film review show, when Wish exclaimed, "You found her! Wonderful."

Wish dropped her cue on the table, scattering the balls, and approached Amanda with her arms outspread. "How was your shower?" But before Amanda could answer, Wish was hugging her. She inhaled and said, "Oh yes, you certainly smell clean," before giggling into her hand.

"She's on my team, we've already decided," Justin said, trying to wedge his arm between Wish and Amanda.

"No, how could you decide?" Wish said with a frown. "It should be girls against boys."

Sherry had been lying on the wide suede sofa, using a damp tea towel for a bandana. She sat up so quickly that the tea towel slipped from her head, and said, "I'm playing too then."

"No, you said you were too ill," Justin replied. "Anyway, we can't have three on two."

"Why not?" Sherry asked, wincing from the effort it had taken to speak. She flopped against a mound of cushions, one arm resting on the back of the sofa. Amanda thought she looked a bit like Ursula from the *Little Mermaid* just then, and had to bite her lip to stop herself from laughing.

"Because you can't. Anyway, we have already organized the game," Justin said.

"It's OK," Amanda told him. "I'm really not that bothered. I'll just watch."

"Sure you don't want to play?" Claude asked, re-racking the balls.

"Yes, play," Wish cooed, looping an arm around her shoulder. Then to Justin, she said, "Come on, girls against boys. Unless you are too scared?"

Justin's body seemed to flounder on the spot, as though unsure of how to react. The smile on his lips straightened, curled, and straightened again as he shuffled through his expressions. He was embarrassed to the point of anger, but was doing his best to mask it. His best wasn't good enough, because he sulked away like a wounded dog, joining Claude at the table.

"I want to play too," Sherry said again, her voice on the edge of outrage.

"You can play next game," Wish told her sternly.

Claude picked a speck of lint off the felt on the table then leaned on his cue. "So, do we have a game or are we just going to *talk* about playing?"

"Yes," Wish said quickly. "Yes, boys against girls."

"Fine." Justin shrugged, not looking at any of them. "But we get to break. And we are changing teams in the next game."

"Don't worry, Justin. We can handle a couple of girls." Claude's comment was supposed to lighten the mood, but it only seemed to rankle Justin further.

Justin broke, clacking the balls loudly, potting a yellow in the side pocket. He looked up at Amanda and smiled, proud to have sunk a ball. His eyes lingered on her expectantly until she said, "Lucky shot."

"Oh, you think so?" He lined up another ball, potted it, and looked at Amanda. "Still lucky?" Again, he waited for her to respond, making no effort to get in position for another shot.

"Well done," she offered reluctantly.

It was enough to appease him. He went around the table, mapping out his route, and bent to take another shot. He missed and yelled, "Fuck's sake," and then spun around, turning his back on the table. Wish laughed tauntingly.

"You take first shot," Wish encouraged, but suddenly Amanda had no desire to play. She didn't want to provoke an argument, and she didn't want to look silly in front of the others, especially with how seriously they were taking the game.

Amanda spotted a red ball on the edge of a pocket and decided to go for it. When she bent over the table and set her cue on the felt, she became aware of Sherry rising from the sofa. Now everyone was watching her. She pulled her arm back, remembering how she used to play pool at college and in The Peacock pub, and realized this was the first time she had held a cue since before the record deal. She took the shot, missed her intended target. In fact, the cue ball somehow miraculously missed every other ball on the table.

"Foul. Two shots to us," Claude said, and moved around the table.

"Why don't you chill out, Claude," Justin said.

Claude paused, looked up from the table. "What?"

"Why don't you just calm down. We're only playing for fun."

Claude looked around the room, his eyes narrowing as though he were missing some key bit of information, and said, "Yeah, I know. But she missed the ball so it's two shots."

"She's a *lady*," Justin said irritably. "Just let her have it."

"No, those are the rules," Amanda said. "Two shots to the boys."

Claude waited a moment, unsure of how to proceed. The interaction had unbalanced him, but he shook it off and continued with the game. Sherry gave a running commentary in an attempt to spur the girls on, but it had the opposite effect. Amanda couldn't concentrate with Sherry's cheerleading, and had done everything except tell the woman to shut up to get her to stop.

When the boys were down to two balls, Arthur walked in. Everyone looked over at him.

"Hey Arthur, how's it going?" Claude asked.

Ignoring him, Arthur said, "Amanda? Could I have a moment? Outside?"

"We're in the middle of a game," Wish protested, her hand waving toward the table.

"I'll only be a second."

"What do you want her for?" Sherry asked, straightening up. She pointed across the room at him. "If you're going to carry on with your offensive comments and your potty mouth then you can just fucking get lost. Have you got it?"

"I just want a minute with Amanda," he said.

Sherry spun to Amanda and said, "You don't have to go."

"No, it's OK." Amanda leaned her cue against the wall.

Before she left the room, Justin said, "Don't you fucking upset her, Arthur. I'm warning you."

CHAPTER 15

"Go on, do it again Arthur," Ronald said, the Diamond White wafting bitterly on his breath. He nudged Arthur in the ribs and almost toppled over from the effort.

"Will you stop that?" Arthur reprimanded, begrudgingly steadying Ronald so that he didn't fall face-first onto the cobbles. He spent a moment trying to prop Ronald back on his own legs, like a painter adjusting a wobbly ladder that he hoped to climb. "Always with the elbows. You leave bruises up and down me when you get drinking, Ronald, honestly."

"Oh, shut up, you big poof," Ronald said, grinning through an overgrown beard that was as coarse as Velcro. He sucked on the bottle of cider again, his face glowing almost demonically in the red aura of the drumfire. "Go on, do it again."

Rolling his eyes, Arthur adjusted the collar of his jacket and then held his palms up to the fire to warm his hands. "I'm not in the mood."

"Bah." Ronald slashed the air with his free hand, and the momentum almost sent him pinwheeling into the fire. Arthur, having refrained from the delights of super strength cider for one evening, just barely caught him.

"You're going to light yourself up like a Christmas tree if you're not careful," Arthur said, releasing him. Roland took a step back, flapped his arms for balance, and then reeled on the spot. "You bloody idiot."

"Then do it!" Ronald yelled, and there was a layer of

phlegmy anger in his voice now, the vehemence bouncing off the alleyway walls. "Cold fuckin' night, nothing else to do."

"I'm not your performing monkey," Arthur said, turning away from the fire and heading back to his spot on the rain-sodden sofa. Springs corkscrewed through the rotten fabric of the cushions, nipping him in the thighs. If he angled himself just right, pressing his body up to the crease at the back of the sofa, he could avoid a lancing.

Ronald's face turned mean, his mouth splitting to reveal the rows of small, brown-stained teeth. His oily eyes narrowed, embers leaping in his black pupils, as he extended one accusing finger toward Arthur. "You're going to do it, Arthur, or I'm going to have to give you a hiding."

Grabbing his sleeping bag, Arthur said, "You couldn't hide your face with your own hands, you silly sod."

"Let me see if I got this straight," Ronald began, moving like a marionette around the fire, the three-litre bottle dangling from his grasp. "You can spend eight hours over there in Hyde Park and fucking... Leicester Square doing it for the tourists, but you're not going to do it for me?"

"Shut up and go to sleep." Arthur stretched out on the sofa and used a sheet of clear plastic, which had once been a rain guard for a pushchair, to keep the drizzle off his face.

"Who was it that came and helped you when those lads wanted to kick your head in? Hey? It was me, you big fucking poof. So, you get up and you do it."

"Poof, poof, poof," Arthur grumbled. "You really are a wordsmith, Ronald. A regular Hemingway."

"You–" Ronald made a lazy beeline for the sofa, but his advance was betrayed by his trousers, which fell around his knees and tripped him over. Ronald slammed to the ground like a plank, the bottle bouncing and rolling from his hand. A gargle percolated in his throat, and some approximation of a sentence spilled from his lips. "Do it... you bastard."

"Why don't you just put him out his misery, for Christ's sake,

Arthur," Colin said from his spot in the doorway, curled up in the shadows on a mattress of cardboard, untouched by the firelight. Two months ago, his thick Dublin accent was almost intelligible to Arthur, but now he understood approximately four of every five words he said. "You like torturing old Ronald, you really do."

"Oh, for f…" Arthur tore the sheet off and sat up. He saw Ronald lying sideways on the ground, his hand outstretched for the bottle that was already spilling the precious elixir onto the cobbles. He felt a stab of regret at the sight of the man and immediately tried to bury it. There was a simple old chant his mother used on him as a child when Arthur refused to go to bed at night. She would say: "Lie down, close your eyes, turn over, and go to sleep." Now that's exactly what he did. But after a few seconds he thought about the vapour curling from Ronald's mouth, and then about that night when he chased away those school kids with a traffic cone. Encouraged by sheer boredom, the wayward teens meant to cave Arthur's head in with a Jack Daniel's bottle, and they would have surely done it if Ronald wasn't so downright frightening.

"Alright, alright." Arthur got off the sofa, bent to Ronald and heaved him upright. All the muscles in Arthur's back tightened from the strain, and as he walked over to retrieve the bottle of Diamond White, a flare of pain shot up his spine. Gritting his teeth, he said, "What one do you want tonight then, you spoilt brat?"

Ronald's lips slit into a grin, his eyes glittering with drunken glee. "Do the *Macbeth* one. The 'Tomorrow, tomorrow' one."

"No, not that," Colin called from the darkness. "I'm sick t'death of *Macbeth*. Do *The Merchant from Venice*. That's a better one."

"*Merchant of Venice*," Ronald chanted, raising the bottle to his mouth, sucking deeply. Cider spilled down his chin, and as he went to speak again, he burped. "The quality of mercy is not

strain'd, It droppeth as the gentle rain… that fucking one." He
set the bottle down between his legs and clapped his gloved
hands together. "There you go. I started it off for you. Go on,
now. You do it."

Sighing, Arthur said, "Very well. *Merchant of Venice* it is. And
you better bloody leave me alone when I've finished." He
straightened up, smoothed down his jacket, and cleared his
voice. "Here, pass me that bottle and let me have a swig to
lubricate the pipes."

Ronald eagerly complied, and for that moment, he
resembled a child in the afterglow of the fire. Arthur took a
gulp of the cider, swished it around his mouth, gargled, and
then swallowed. He handed the bottle back to Ronald, and
then laced his fingers together to pop his knuckles.

After a deep breath to compose himself against the bitter
night air, he began: "'The quality of mercy is not strain'd,
it droppeth as the gentle rain from heaven upon the place
beneath: it is twice blest; It blesseth him that gives and him
that takes…'" With each sentence, his voice grew in strength,
bolstered by thespian muscle memory, until it swelled and
filled the alleyway. Ronald mouthed the monologue along
with him, rapt in the performance.

As Arthur continued, the alleyway began to fade and
darken, and he was transported back to the Peacock Theatre,
standing not before two derelicts, but a sold-out audience on
opening night. At the peak of his powers, when his agent was
aggressively rambunctious with the auditions, he had secured
slots on daytime dramas, a summer residency in a West End
theatre, and a walk-on part in a film with Ray Winstone. Then
his father was diagnosed with dementia, and suddenly, all
those years spent chasing stardom, pursuing roles, hounding
casting directors… none of it seemed important. His career had
been his life, his *vocation*, and then when his father could no
longer recognize him, the acting became silly somehow. Yet he
couldn't deny that there were moments, like the nights spent

reciting Shakespeare to the unfortunate souls drifting in the alleyway or the shopping centre car parks, when he thought about what could have been.

What could have been.

Amanda stepped into the hallway and closed the door behind her. "What's up?"

Arthur bowed his head. He wrung his hands together and cleared his throat. "This isn't very easy for me."

"What isn't?"

"I'm…" He stopped, released a shaky breath. He shook his head as though trying to clear it, and said, "I know how I can be. What I mean is, I know I'm not always the easiest person in the world to get along with." His eyes widened and he quickly added, "But that's something I've been working on, personally and… professionally."

"Are you trying to apologize, Arthur?"

"Yes. That's what I'm trying to do."

"Fine. Don't worry about it." Her words loosened the tension in his face, and his expression softened immediately.

"I'm sorry. I said some hurtful things but that's just… it takes me a little while to get… well, I struggle with new people sometimes."

"Look, if you get nervous then that's fair enough," Amanda said. "But that isn't an excuse to act like an idiot and be mean to people for no reason. I don't care if it's a defence mechanism or whatever. It's just not nice. Do you know what I'm saying?"

"Yes. Yes, I do, and believe me, I know what a bloody pig-headed sod I can be. It was just… I don't know, opening night jitters. Can you forgive me?"

"It's already forgotten," she replied. "But maybe you should apologize to some of the others, too. Clear the air."

"Can I give you a hug?" he interrupted, lurching like a dog on a leash, extending his arms awkwardly.

She declined, flustered. "No, I don't think that's necessary."

"Sorry." He let his arms drop to his sides, his face colouring with embarrassment. He scooped his cotton wool hair back over his ears and then wiped his palms on his shirt. "I'm sorry," he said again, his voice little more than a whisper.

"It's fine. Why don't we just forget the whole thing?"

"I'd like that," Arthur muttered. He hadn't shaved and his cheeks bristled with coarse white stubble. "Do you think the others would mind terribly if I joined you in there," he said, pointing to the games room door, "or have I well and truly ostracized myself?"

"I'm sure it's fine. Come on."

When they went inside, Sherry asked, "Everything OK?" She struggled to a sitting position on the sofa. Her chest heaved as she laboured for breath. Her cheeks were blotchy red, and even from across the room Amanda could see the muscles in her jaw pulsing.

"Peachy." Amanda gave her a smile and walked back over to the pool table where Claude was playing by himself; Wish and Justin were now engaged in a game of darts at the opposite end of the room.

Claude racked the balls again. "Fancy a game?"

Amanda shrugged. "Sure." She looked over at Arthur, who remained stationed by the door. He hadn't taken more than two steps inside the room, and was quite content to just stand there with his arms behind his back, observing the others. She thought he looked a bit like a little boy on his first day at a new school with nobody to play with, and couldn't help but feel sorry for him. She conjured the previous evening to mind, remembered how he had belittled her for no reason, and felt her pity evaporate.

"What was all that about?" Claude asked, chalking the tip of his cue.

"Oh, nothing much. He wanted to apologize for acting like an idiot." She spoke quietly so as not to be overheard by the others.

"Yeah?" Claude snorted and shook his head. "I think we've just worked out who's taking the drug." He nodded toward Arthur and out the side of his mouth, said, "I think the pill offers relief if you're a pain in the arse."

She nudged him with her elbow and giggled. She might have imagined it, but Amanda thought she saw the others turn and look at her the instant she laughed. Was everyone paranoid in the house? Did they think she was laughing at them? Before she could dwell on it any longer, the speaker chimed.

Ding-dong.

"Good evening, ladies and gentlemen. We hope you have been enjoying your stay so far. Please proceed to the Circle Room for your first assignment."

"Assignment?" Arthur spat the word as though it tasted disgusting in his mouth. "What's this now?"

Claude shrugged. "Dunno. Maybe they've got plans for us, like a game or something."

"I don't think I like the sound of it, actually," Arthur said indignantly. "I am not a performing monkey. I do not dance to their tune. I am here to take pills and spend a week in this *marvellous* environment. Nobody said anything about assignments."

"Why're you stressing out so hard?" Justin asked. "You don't even know what it is yet. Could be something fun."

"I hate to agree," Sherry started, "but that *man* over there has a point. We're not at school and they…" She pointed at the camera in the centre of the ceiling. "…are not our governors. Nobody said anything about assignments."

"Didn't you read your contract?" Amanda asked, searching each of their faces. "It's in there."

"Must've missed it," Sherry said, turning away. "Still, it stinks of omnipotence to me."

"Omnipotence," Arthur murmured. "God in heaven."

"Why don't we just go and find out, no?" Wish offered. "Amanda says it's in the contract, so no reason to worry."

"I mean," Amanda began, "wasn't it in yours?"

Then a peculiar thing happened, Amanda was quite sure of it. Wish looked her dead in the face and lied to her. There was no way to prove it, but she saw Wish's eyes widen, the flash of uncertainty in her features.

"Yes. In my contract," Wish said. "Of course. Come, let's all go."

When they made it to the Circle Room, they saw that a small whiteboard and a black marker pen sat on each of the six chairs. They sat down, and immediately Justin uncapped his pen and began drawing on his board. He turned his masterpiece to the group, revealing a crude doodle of a veiny, ejaculating penis. Sherry was the first to laugh, but changed her mind halfway through, deciding that she was offended instead.

"That's disgusting and crass," she chided, shaking her head. "There are ladies in the room you know."

Justin cackled, taking delight in his creation.

"Is it a self-portrait?" Arthur asked.

Justin held up his middle finger and wiped the board clean with the sleeve of his other arm.

"Hello, ladies and gentlemen. Thank you for making it to the Circle Room," the voice in the speaker began. "Each of you has a pen and a whiteboard. Your first assignment will be to write the name of the person you like most in the group. You will have thirty seconds to complete this task. Do not reveal the name on your board until instructed to do so. Failure to comply will result in your immediate removal from the premises and forfeit of funds."

The speaker went silent. Amanda uncapped her marker and let the tip hover over the whiteboard's surface. She didn't need to think for very long about who she liked the most, but still she hesitated. She wrote a C, and then quickly wiped it away with her palm. What would the others read into it if she admitted that she liked Claude the best out of them? What would *he* read into it?

"You know something? This *is* dumb," she whispered.

"What is, dear?" Sherry asked, craning her head for a better look at Amanda's board.

"This assignment," Amanda replied. "What does it have to do with anything? What is this, a popularity contest now? Who cares? It's pointless."

"Could just be a cognitive test," Claude suggested. "Maybe the pill affects memory, I don't know. Or like you say, could just be completely pointless."

"Mind games," Arthur said with a sigh, capping his pen. "Misdirection. Bad theatre."

Amanda became fidgety and anxious, and just the slightest bit annoyed. This *was* a little too much like school, not wanting to admit she fancied a boy for fear of embarrassment, not having the right answers during an exam. She looked up from the board, scanned the room, and quickly wrote WISH, and added a smiley face for authenticity.

There was a hiss of static before the voice on the speaker said, "Justin, please reveal the name of the person you like most in the house and give a brief explanation why."

Justin turned his board over. The name AMANDA was emblazoned in bubble writing with lightning bolts jumping from it. He scratched the back of his head and said, "I picked Amanda because... I'm not really sure. Me and her have a lot in common I'd say. Also, we're almost about the same age, so there's that too. So, Amanda." He straightened in his chair and looked away, pretending that something had caught his attention on the opposite wall.

"Thank you, Justin," Amanda said, but received no response. She wasn't exactly sure what they had in common, considering that she still didn't know an awful lot about Justin beyond the fact that he was a blogger who lived at home with his mum.

"Wish, please reveal the name of the person you like most in the house and give a brief explanation why."

Wish sat up straight in her chair and smiled. Her teeth could have been on a Colgate advert they were so perfect. "I chose Amanda also because I think we could be good friends if we met outside of the house. I think she is a very nice, warm person."

"Aah, thank you hun," Amanda said. Her face became hot with embarrassment at having been picked twice in a row, but she could live with it. After all, it was a lot less embarrassing than if nobody had written her name on the board. "I think you're nice and warm too."

"Like a pain au chocolat?" Wish asked and broke up laughing. Amanda joined her, genuinely amused by the comment. Wish derailed the laughter by adding, "I can make them, you know. Maybe I make them for you tomorrow? Would you like that?"

"Um... sure." Amanda smiled, but the gesture seemed to take much more effort now. "But don't put yourself out or anything. I mean there's plenty to eat already."

"Sherry, please reveal the name of the person you like most in the house and give a brief explanation why," the voice on the speaker commanded.

"I'm going to give you my explanation first," Sherry said, cocking her head back and addressing the eye-in-the-sky directly. She scooped her frizzy hair away from her face and tied it in a ponytail, and then leaned forward in the chair. "Seven years ago, my sister died of cancer," she began, her eyes now fixed on the floor. "It was the darkest time of my life, and coincidentally, it's when I started doing comedy as a way of dealing with the loss. Joy was a wonderful person, so full of life, so graceful, so giving... and when she went it broke me into little pieces." Her ringed hand rose to her face, and she ran a thumb off the corner of her eye to catch a tear. "Since then, I've been a bit of a lost soul really. I don't have many friends, just my little Sponge. But then I came here. And I met..." She turned the board over. "Amanda."

Amanda's cheeks pebbled with gooseflesh. She tightened in the chair, her toes curling so tightly in her trainers that she heard them pop at the joints.

"Amanda," Sherry said, "you remind me so much of Joy that it makes me wonder if we're related." She smiled suddenly, eyes bulging, and said, "That was a joke. And not a very good one apparently." She swallowed, knuckled another rogue tear from her other eye, and said no more.

"That's very sweet," Amanda said cautiously. "I'm really flattered, thank you. And I'm sorry about your sister."

The cord of tense silence was broken by the voice on the speaker.

"Claude, please reveal the name of the person you like most in the house and give a brief explanation why."

Claude's lips curled up bashfully. He clucked his tongue, opened his mouth to say something, and then closed it again. His brow furrowed and he said, "This might be a bit awkward." An airy giggle sailed from his mouth. "I put Amanda down too, but I promise I wasn't copying anyone's board. I um..." He made eye contact with Amanda and said, "I met you first, remember? And I think I've probably talked to you the most so that's why I put your name down. I'm not trying to be weird or anything. Have I made it weird?"

Amanda shook her head. She wanted to tell him that she understood completely, that no, he hadn't made things any weirder than they already were. The weirdness that permeated this whole experiment was now teetering on the edge of bizarre, and soon, she thought things might even get frightening. But the real truth was she felt a pinch of disappointment that he didn't offer more, that the real reason her name was on his board was because he genuinely liked her, that maybe he could see himself taking her to dinner when this whole thing was finished.

"Arthur, please reveal the name of the person you like most in the house and give a brief explanation why."

Amanda felt the flesh tighten on the nape of her neck. It was cold in the room, but she could taste sweat on her upper lip. She held her breath as Arthur turned his board around. She couldn't see what he had written because the flowery writing was too small, but it looked about the right length.

"I was horrible to Amanda yesterday," Arthur began, his chin resting on his fist contemplatively. "I can't tell you how ashamed I am to admit that. But thankfully, she's forgiven me. Even an old fool like me makes mistakes from time to time, but that's all in the past."

"You said some pretty horrible things to the rest of us too," Sherry said, "or don't you remember? What is it? Selective memory?"

"If I said anything to upset you," Arthur said over his shoulder to Sherry, "then you probably deserved it. If you chose to be offended, then that's also your problem."

Amanda's mouth was dry, her throat constricting to a pinprick. She had learned how to receive attention from thousands of fans while performing but was now having trouble accepting praise from a handful of people. During her short, blazing moment of fame, it hadn't been unusual for the media to shower her with compliments whenever she entered a room or left a building. Paparazzi would tell her how great she looked, asked if they could get a smile for the camera, told her they loved her music. She had enjoyed that, had come to crave it. So why did this now feel so... *wrong*? Was it because this wasn't a roomful of publicists and agents, but just a gaggle of civilians? *No, come on Amanda, tell it like it is: we're a group of has-beens here*, or perhaps never-have-beens would be more apt for most of them.

Avoiding the unblinking eyes that settled on her around the room, she suddenly realized that everything felt so wrong because it was fake. Arthur was right; this whole thing was nothing more than a bit of theatre, and they were all in on it. She hadn't done anything spectacular since arriving at the house, had barely gone out of her way to make conversation with any of them, and yet they all voted her the nicest. It was all a game and they were playing her. She just couldn't figure out why.

The speaker asked Amanda for the name on her whiteboard.

"You don't have your own name on that, do you?" Claude asked. "You could make it a clean sweep."

"Uh, no," she turned it over and said, "Wish," but before she could say any more, Wish clapped her hands together sporadically and yelped with delight.

"Oh my god, thank you so much Amanda." She clutched her hands over her chest, her expression one of such sincere gratitude that Amanda thought Wish was going to drop to her knees and start bawling. She looked like she had just won an Academy Award and was getting ready to give a speech. "I knew it. I *knew* it. Dieu merci."

Amanda laughed, but it was nothing more than a release of tension. Now that the time had come to explain her choice, she realized that she couldn't think of a good enough reason to have written the name.

Before she could elaborate on it, Sherry said, "I see. Well that's typical, isn't it?"

Nobody seemed quite sure what Sherry meant, and half of them hadn't heard her over Wish's celebratory singing.

"Why her?" Sherry asked, folding her arms across her chest. "Hmm? Why Wish? Go on, tell us. This should be interesting."

"Is there something wrong?" Amanda asked.

"Wrong?" Sherry shrugged petulantly. "What could be wrong?"

"I don't know. But I picked Wish because I had to pick someone, and I think we hit it off." It sounded lame and forced, especially considering that it wasn't true. Wish was still grinning, almost bouncing in the chair. "It's nothing personal."

"Why her and not me then?" Sherry said, scratching the black polish off her fingernails and letting the tiny curls flitter to the floor. "I know it's your choice, and you say it's nothing personal, but I can't help but feel like maybe it *is* personal. I'm the only other woman here, and you chose her." She cocked a thumb at Wish. "Is it because she's pretty? Because I'm old?"

Amanda shook her head. "It's none of those things. It's just a stupid assignment. It doesn't mean anything."

Sherry kept her focus on her swollen, pink hands, still peeling away nail polish. Her mascara was clotted around her eyes from where she'd been crying, and sludgy black lines trailed down her cheeks. "I'm sorry. I'm sorry, I think I just got emotional about my sister. I... I miss her a lot." She looked across at Amanda, tried for a smile. In the low light of the Circle Room, her face puffy with sadness and booze, Sherry appeared much older than a woman pushing sixty, and if Amanda was being honest, she looked a little crazy too.

"It's this house," Sherry said. "It plays tricks on you. Being away from home, you know – no TV or anything, it forces you to think about stuff that you don't want to think about. I'm sorry Amanda."

"Don't apologize, I completely understand," Amanda said, but she was fed up with compliments and apologies. She could quite happily ride out the rest of the week in her chilly room, only popping down for the morning pill and the evening's assignment. Now that she thought about it, that might not be such a bad idea.

The speaker crackled. "You are now free to go. Please return to the Circle Room tomorrow at 8am for your morning dosage."

Amanda got up and hurried out of the room, feeling a lot heavier than she had when she walked in. The assignment had taken no more than twenty minutes, but it had been an emotional workout. The one and only time she had gone to a Narcotics Anonymous meeting, Amanda had left feeling so pummelled and drained that she never went back, even though she knew it would help her sobriety. She felt a little like that now, like a piece of her was still in the Circle Room, and she didn't like it.

CHAPTER 16

Every Wednesday, The Horse and Cart held an open mic night. It was a tried-and-tested ploy to pull punters in during the lull, but with a twist: anyone who wanted their five minutes on the microphone – to sing, do magic tricks, tell jokes, whatever – would have to pay ten pounds. At the end of the night, the audience would hold an anonymous vote, writing the name of the person they thought was most entertaining and placing it in a pint glass. The winner took all the money home. After four weeks of consecutively crushing the competition, Sherry had won a grand total of two hundred and ten pounds; a fortune for a woman living in a nearby hostel.

It was fate that drove her to the microphone. She had been in The Cart, enjoying a pint of wallop ale, sipping and savouring it, not knowing when she might next be able to afford such a luxury. Despite the neon cardboard signs decorating the walls of the pub advertising the open mic, she'd had no clue that such an event was taking place until a young man with a bowler hat began playing an acoustic guitar and singing "Hey Joe." He was not half bad, and his act was followed by a singer who looked as though she hadn't finished high school, yet had the vocal maturity of a much older woman. After a few more acts, Sherry went back to the bar and enquired about how she might be able to enter. The barmaid told her.

"Don't suppose you can spot me a ten, can you?" Sherry had asked, only half joking. "I'll win tonight, I can promise you that. If these lot have any sense in their heads, I'll win that's for sure."

"Afraid not," the young lady said, smiling through a lip piercing.

"Well that's alright," Sherry said, and it was then that she spotted the little black dog lounging in a fluffy bed behind the bar. It was a West Highland Terrier, and she knew that because it was the same dog that her elderly neighbour owned when Sherry was little. Except, her neighbour's dog, Daisy, had been a light brown, yappy little thing. "Hey there, rascal," she said to the dog, stepping to the opening of the bar. She crouched and held out her hand, wishing that her palm was full of doggy treats. "Hey there. What's your name, huh?"

The barmaid took no notice of Sherry and nor did the dog, who was quite content to lay its head on its forepaws and go back to sleep.

The following Wednesday, Sherry returned with a crinkled ten-pound note in her pocket. She deposited the money into the pint glass and wrote her name down on the performance sheet. She was the third act up and having already spent her beer money to enter the contest, she was sober and in desperate need of a drop of Dutch courage.

When her name was called, Sherry approached the microphone with absolutely no routine rehearsed at all. She knew she was going to *do jokes*, and that's exactly how she thought of it in her mind – doing jokes – and she hoped that a few would spring to mind, good ones like her dad used to tell her. She vaguely remembered one about a man that runs over a gang of motorcyclists' bikes, but forgot how it started. She knew the punchline of another joke, which ended with *follow the yellow-prick toad*, but the setup evaded her.

She stood behind the mic for perhaps twenty seconds, braced against a shriek of feedback, her mind a blank, humourless void. About twenty or so people stared expectantly at her over their drinks, a few already laughing at her apparent stage fright.

"Don't start my five minutes yet. Just one moment please ladies and gents," Sherry said, and shuffled over to the bar. In a low voice, Sherry said to the barmaid, "Would you mind if I borrowed the dog?"

"The dog?" the barmaid looked over her shoulder at the terrier, which was glancing back at them with questioning eyes. "What for?"

"Just to hold. I promise I won't hurt him. Or is it her?"

The barmaid, still bemused by the request, hesitated a moment, and then hoisted the terrier up in her arms. The dog came without a fuss. "A *he*. Don't drop him."

"Not a chance," Sherry said, noticing the name engraved on the dog's collar. It read *SPONGE*. She carried the dog back over to the microphone, her fingers buried in its curly fur. Every time she stroked Sponge, she felt a lap of calmness wash over her. When the dog licked her hand, a pervading sense of fearlessness overtook her, and the jokes just began to roll out of her mouth like those prizes in the toy vending machines.

A homeless man, an alcoholic, and a gay guy enter a bar... What's the difference between a clown and a woman's vagina... A man takes his wife to the zoo, she's wearing a fur coat with nothing on underneath...

She didn't stop to accept their applause, but instead steamrolled straight over their laughter with the beginning of the next joke. If she paused to take even a small sip of that warm feeling of accomplishment, she risked losing the momentum and the bucket in the well of her memory from which she drew the jokes. It was almost as if she were speaking in tongues, the punchlines popping like fireworks, provoking uproarious laughter in the audience.

When she felt herself slowing down, she changed course, went off-script even though she didn't have one to begin with. "You people like this dog? I'm a dog person. I don't care for cats. I'll kick a pussy through a cat flap, no problem." The segues weren't even particularly funny, but the manic, off-kilter delivery was, and so the laughter continued.

Before she knew it, the barmaid with the dyed pink hair raised her wrist and tapped an imaginary watch, then mouthed: "One more minute."

Sherry fired off a couple of rude knock-knock jokes, her palm smoothing the fur on Sponge's head. Then, she said, "OK folks, they tell me I've gotta get off now." This admission earned her collective groans of protest. "Last one from me, alright? Some of you have friends here that might be going on the mic, whatever. But at the end of the night, you have to write my name on the paper so that I win, OK? I mean it. I'm living in a fucking hostel and sharing a bathroom with a bunch of drug-addicted foreigners." The audience were too invested to stage any objections to her politically incorrect wording. In fact, that hostel line got the biggest laugh of the night. "So, if you vote for me and I win, that's a bit of beer money for your old Aunt Sherry. And if you don't vote for me... someone you love will die within one week, so the choice is yours."

As she stepped away from the microphone, the people dotted around the pub clapped and cheered and whooped rambunctiously. Even Sponge barked his approval. "You're a good boy, Sponge, aren't you?"

Sherry remained The Horse and Cart open mic champion for four weeks, until she was narrowly defeated by a ventriloquist. A fucking *ventriloquist* of all things. And she knew that the vote had been rigged somehow. That pouty, pale, pink-haired barmaid had some sort of vendetta and had fucked around with the pint glass containing the slips of paper.

So, she stole Sponge.

She wanted the dog, even though she'd never be able to sneak him into the hostel. They had a strict no animal policy, but from what Sherry had seen, heroin was perfectly acceptable apparently. Well, it was about time she left that dungeon anyway. She could go back to the Citizens Advice Bureau for all the bastard good that did, and she could say that she felt unsafe at the hostel, that some Albanian had held a knife to her throat. They could recommend that she be placed somewhere else, somewhere that accepted animals because – and she'd heard this was true – the dog was part of her therapy, it calmed her down because she had PTSD from childhood or something. Nobody was going to tell her otherwise. If you could take a dog on an airplane because you were scared to fly, then she could have a dog while she lived in some little shithole of a hostel and shared a bathroom with fifty other people. Or maybe they could put her in a house somewhere with a garden – why not? Then little Sponge could prance around, and Sherry could grow some vegetables.

In the end, however, she hadn't needed the CAB, the council, or some homeless shelter, because two days after dognapping Sponge and sneaking him into the Queen Victoria Hostel, fate intervened again. She wasn't even remotely religious, in fact she thought anyone that was had to be a gullible arsehole, but the word *miracle* was starting to sound extremely profound to her. First, she wins the open mic and gets enough money to buy some desperately needed new clothes. Then, she meets Sponge, which was just the thing she needed to prevent her slitting her wrists in the shower. And while the universe was arranging all this good fortune for her, the stars continued to align because during her second week at The Horse and Cart, some Good Samaritan had the sense to record Sherry's five minutes on the mic. The Samaritan uploaded the footage to YouTube under the headline "CRAZY HOMELESS WOMAN DOES STANDUP." Though Sherry disagreed with the particulars of the title, she conceded that it was enough of a hook to get people clicking. A week after being uploaded, Sherry's clip went viral, racking up almost four million views.

When the man knocked on her door at the hostel, she assumed by his attire that he was with the management, and that she'd been rumbled about Sponge. She picked the dog up, placed him in the dented metal wardrobe, which was really nothing more than a filing cabinet. Sponge barked and it echoed loudly in the confines, but there was nowhere else for her to hide him in the tiny box room.

Huffing as though the man's presence were a massive inconvenience to her, she said, "Yes? Is there a problem?"

The man, who looked like some executive on his way to a board meeting, furnished her with a friendly grin. "No problem, Miss Holt. Actually, quite the opposite. I'm a huge fan of your comedy. Is there somewhere we can talk?"

"Talk? What do you want to talk to me about?" she said, unable to shake the suspicion.

"I'd like to talk to you about an opportunity that will change your life."

Inside the wardrobe, Sponge began barking erratically.

CHAPTER 17

"No, honestly, let me make dinner," Sherry said, her voice echoing around the kitchen. "I was a dinner lady for almost twenty years. I think I can handle a bunch of scoundrels like you lot."

"Are you sure you don't want help?" Wish asked.

"No, that's sweet of you, but honestly, I can get it done a lot quicker if I just crack on." She slapped her hands together and rubbed them vigorously. "How does chicken casserole sound?"

There was a general murmur of appreciation, although having watched the woman pick at her nail polish, Amanda wasn't over the moon at the prospect of eating her cooking. Still, she didn't think she could refuse it without causing another emotional breakdown, even though a ham and cheese sandwich would have suited her just fine.

"I'll make my own if it's all the same," Arthur said, rooting through the pantry.

"You suit yourself, sunshine," Sherry said, turning her back on him. They were like an old married couple that were only staying together for the kids, and the whole routine was beyond tiresome.

Amanda grabbed a glass, retrieved a bottle of wine from the cooler, and took it to a table in the conservatory. She admired the misty glow of the full moon and the star-speckled sky through the double-glazing. She took a few deep breaths in an attempt to open up her lungs that had shrivelled to the size of walnuts amidst the day's drama. She was still feeling delicate from the previous evening's debauchery, but it didn't stop her pouring a large glass of wine. She brought it to her nose, inhaled the fruity fragrance, and took a long, deep gulp.

"Hey. Mind if I join you or did you want to be by yourself?"

Startled, Amanda looked up and saw Claude standing in the entrance of the conservatory, sipping a Coke through a straw.

"Course not. Come on in."

He sat down in a round wicker armchair and gazed up at the moon. She wondered why he hadn't joined her on the sofa but quickly pushed the thought away. He could have a girlfriend, or even a wife and children, for god's sakes. She sipped her wine and chanced a look at the fingers of his left hand. No ring.

"What a crazy day, huh?" Claude said, easing back into the chair. He stretched his legs out and rested them on the large footstool. "What did you make of that assignment then? You just won Miss Popularity."

"It's creepy. This whole thing is creepy."

"Yeah, you can say that again. It was weird how everyone wrote your name though, wasn't it? Like what are the odds?"

"I don't know." She brought her legs up onto the cushion beside her and leaned against the arm of the sofa. "You tell me."

His eyebrows rose as he sipped through the straw. "What do you mean?"

"It is weird. It's so weird it makes me think there's something going on. Some little game you're all playing."

"Game? Not me."

"Then how come you all wrote my name? I'm not exactly Princess Diana and I've barely said two words to anyone except for you since we've been here. And statistically is it even possible to win a vote like that?"

"I don't know. I've never really been good at maths, so…"

"Are you an actor, Claude?"

"Actor?"

"Yes."

"No. I told you already that I'm a car salesman. I work at Ford."

She eyed him closely, looking for signs of deceit in his face. His expression shuffled from bemusement to discomfort and he quickly turned his attention back to the moon. "Maybe it's the pill," he said, rattling ice in his glass. "Maybe it's got you thinking things."

"Making me paranoid? Why is everyone talking about paranoia today? If people didn't act so fucking strange, then none of us would be paranoid."

He shrugged and placed his glass down on the windowsill. "If it helps, I think something has changed in the house, but I can't put my finger on it. The problem is, we didn't know any of these people before yesterday so we can't really compare how they're acting to anything. Does that make sense?"

"So, you think they're acting odd too?"

"Oh sure." He nodded. "Couldn't say really what it is, but... they're all a bit aggressive today. Did you pick up on that?"

"Aggressive? No."

"They weren't aggressive toward *you*, that's the thing. They wouldn't be, would they? You're the queen bee." He smiled, warmly. "But they're all at each other's throats. And mine for that matter."

"You were at Arthur's throat this morning when you grabbed him."

Claude bowed and chewed on his lower lip. "I shouldn't have done that. I shouldn't have touched him. Not an older man. That's why I apologized."

Amanda felt a twinge of regret for poking him about it. She sensed that she was creeping into one of her spiteful moods and the wine wasn't going to alleviate that any time soon. She set the glass down. "He's a bully. You were right to stand up to him."

"The only reason I did anything at all was because he opened Sherry's door, and I don't think it's nice. The doors don't have locks on them so he shouldn't do that." He lowered his voice and said, "She might be a bit eccentric, but she's still a woman of a certain age, know what I mean?"

"I do. And you don't have anything to feel bad about. I'm sorry I brought it up."

Pleasant silence settled over them. She didn't want to shatter the moment by rushing in with small talk, but a question was burning on her lips. "Was there any other reason why you wrote my name, Claude?" As soon as she had spoken, she became aware of how needy the question sounded, and bit the inside of her cheek to stop from cringing.

"I have a bit of a confession to make. This is slightly embarrassing, but, I'm afraid I haven't been entirely truthful with you," he began, wringing his hands together.

Concern creased her brow. "What is it?"

He scratched his neck, a nervous grin appearing on his lips. "I made out like I didn't know who you were when we first met. But I recognized you as soon as I saw you." He spoke gently, offering the confession reluctantly. "I've got your first album downloaded on my phone."

She could almost see his face flushing red in the dim light of the conservatory. "Really?"

"Yeah," he laughed. "That song 'Prowl' is on my workout playlist, not that I would admit it to another man for all the money in the world."

Suddenly, she erupted with laughter. Knowing that she was living in his phone, encouraging him to run faster on a treadmill, made her immensely happy. She thought the buzz of having people tell her they listened to her music had worn off. She had worried she would never get that feeling back again.

"You like 'Prowl'?" she asked, grinning. "How gay are you?"

"Hey." He pointed a finger at her, a smile twitching on his lips. "It has a fast tempo and a booming bassline."

"And it's about girls going out looking for boys at bars."

"Yeah well, I told you I wouldn't admit it, and you can't prove I told you that anyway."

The conservatory door opened. They turned and saw Wish and Justin entering, each of them holding a glass of something clear – probably vodka. Wish bent down and hugged Amanda, their cheeks pressing together, and whispered, "Thanks again for picking me." Her breath tickled Amanda's ear, sending a shiver through her. Then, she sat down and clasped Amanda's hand, linking fingers.

"What are you two up to?" Justin said, opting not to take a seat, but rather, to stand sentry between the armchair and the sofa.

"Just admiring the view," Claude said, pointing to the moon. "Beautiful, isn't it?"

"Yeah, very romantic," Justin snipped.

"So, what should we do tonight, guys?" Wish asked.

"How about strip poker?" Justin replied, trying to make eye contact with Amanda. When nobody answered him, he added, "There's a poker set here, you know. Could be a laugh."

"Or we could play truth or dare." Wish offered the suggestion so sultrily that for that one moment she resembled a teenager at her first sleepover. Amanda feigned a yawn to free her hand from Wish's grasp.

"Spin the bottle's a better game," Justin said, punching his palm. "That would be so jokes, wouldn't it? I mean, we could get wasted and play spin the bottle and just, you know, have a laugh with it. We don't even need to do tongues unless you want to. Could be jokes."

"You think so?" Claude asked. "And what if you spin the bottle on Sherry, or Arthur, or me. You still going to think it's a good idea?"

"No." He screwed his face up as though he'd just drunk a mouthful of sour milk. "Don't be fucking gross, Claude. We won't play with them, just us four. And obviously we'll have a no man-to-man kissing policy."

"Oh, but girl-to-girl is fine?" Amanda asked, her tone tinged with agitation. In truth, she was bored of the whole stupid discussion, but she felt like being confrontational to shut the stupid twerp up.

"I'll try it if you will," Wish said, chuckling.

CHAPTER 18

Sherry assembled her ingredients, momentarily marvelling at the range of food before her. Without even washing the vegetables or slicing a single piece of chicken, she could tell that she was handling the best quality produce, probably all locally sourced. For a few minutes, she simply stared at it all, content to let a wave of nostalgia wash over her. It had been many years since she'd had the luxury of preparing a home-cooked meal, and standing there now, excited and intimidated by the task, it almost brought tears to her eyes. She had forgotten the simple joy and freedom of cooking, and god only knew how she missed eating regular hot dinners. Most nights she either went without or spent what little money she could scrape from her benefits on booze, because it was much easier to forget the hunger when you were drunk.

She shouldn't have thrown her plate at Arthur. If it had hit him, it might have been worth it. But wasting that food, plentiful though it may have been, was an unforgivable sin. She knew there would come a time, perhaps not too long after they left the house, when she would not be able to afford to eat, and the memory of that wasted food would torture her.

What's done is done, she thought. *You can be a good girl tonight. No throwing food. No drinking.*

"Well, hang on," she muttered at the thought, uncorking a bottle of red and pouring herself an oversized glass. "Can't cook without a drink. It's against the law."

The wine washed away the guilt, and, smacking her lips after another large gulp, she went straight to work. It was all muscle memory, the cutting, the frying, the seasoning, and before too long she had created a wonderful ambience of sizzle and smells.

She began to daydream as her body moved on autopilot. Sometimes, when the alcohol lured her into a trance, she was able to conjure up the saplings of a new joke. Though she had mostly relied on the good old knee-slappers she already knew, there was a certain satisfaction to creating *new funnies*, as she liked to put it. The process was a welcome distraction to reality. Now, however, her mind wandered elsewhere. Propping herself up with a hand on the kitchen counter, the other hand swirling the wine, she thought about cooking, living in a house, somewhere away from the city; Sponge barking contentedly in the background, a CD player with Kate Bush's greatest hits on repeat. If life would stop kicking her in the arse so hard, she would be more than happy to live the rest of her life throwing a ball for the dog, falling asleep in front of the TV, and–

Wish. The whiteboard with the name scrawled across it. Amanda had written Wish's name. *Why?*

Sherry set her glass down, shook the frying onions and garlic, and frowned as she thought. The assignment was meaningless. And still there was a pinch of something... anger? Jealousy? Was that it? No, not quite. Or maybe both those things and more, a thorny hybrid of emotion that Sherry couldn't quite account for. Why had Amanda written *Wish*? No, that was the wrong question. Why *hadn't* Amanda written *Sherry's* name. Had she not gone out of her way to make Amanda feel welcome? Perhaps Sherry hadn't tried hard enough to bond or maybe she'd accidentally said something offensive while deep in her cups. Sometimes these younger people were especially sensitive – she knew that from her nights doing stand-up; a gay or Jew joke wasn't always embraced no matter how soft it may have been. A young white woman had complained to the pub landlord about Sherry's black robot joke, even though that one was a classic.

Was that it? Was there just too much of a gulf in years between Sherry and Amanda?

Of course, she thought. *I'm old enough to be her mother, for fuck's sake.*

Then why couldn't they have a mother-daughter bond? Sherry only had the vaguest idea of Amanda's status as a celebrity, but judging by the girl's haunted eyes, she needed someone to look after her... to love her.

"What?" Sherry said aloud, shaking her head.

Where had *that* come from?

Noticing she was burning the garlic, Sherry swore, tipped the vegetables and diced chicken in, and added a glug of wine (one for the pan, one for herself). Then she began stirring it all around, dimly disturbed by the sudden intrusion of that random thought. Switching focus, she meditated on a much simpler fantasy: a cottage out in the country. Sponge yipping excitedly. Kate Bush on the radio. And...

Amanda. Sitting on a sofa reading a magazine, or if it was a nice day, lying out on the grass with a pair of shades on, the sunshine bronzing her skin.

Why not?

"Because you don't know her," Sherry said as though someone had actually been standing there and asked the question. She spun around to make sure she was still alone, and then gulped more wine.

Harmless. These thoughts were completely harmless. And it wasn't such a bad idea, was it? When this whole thing was over, Sherry would have a big chunk of change, enough to at least rent somewhere nice. And it'd get cheaper the further away from London she moved, and she liked that idea very much. Fuck London; the Muslims and foreigners could keep it. She could get a job then – nothing fancy, just something part-time and local, and frugal as she had grown to become, she'd be alright. All three of them would – her, Sponge, and Amanda.

But she wrote Wish's *name.*

Sherry tightened, her fist clenching around the wooden spoon. Her heart did a little skip in her chest that, for a couple of seconds, made her feel unpleasantly giddy. She was suddenly very hot in front of the frying pan. Grabbing the tea towel, Sherry dabbed her head and neck, then slung it over her shoulder.

A name on a whiteboard didn't mean anything. What did Wish have that Sherry didn't? A firm arse and long legs, whoopdie-fucking-do. Father Time would soon change that. *But what if... what if Amanda and Wish get close, have too much in common...*

"Then I'll think of something," Sherry snapped, her voice large and animated in the empty kitchen. Quieter, she added, "I always do."

The chicken casserole was delicious, exceeding all of Amanda's expectations. She hadn't been looking forward to dinner, but once Sherry brought it into the dining room and began serving it up, Amanda realized just how hungry she was. Gathered in the dining room, they ate heartily and drank steadily, but Amanda made a promise to herself to only have the one glass. She considered the idea that her surliness was a direct result of her bad night's sleep, and planned to hurry off to bed as soon as she got an opening. She noticed that there was a streaky brown stain on the wall, and fragments of a broken plate on the floor below it, presumably from Sherry's tantrum the previous evening. Amanda wanted no part of that tonight.

Throughout the course of the meal, Amanda would catch Arthur watching her from the opposite end of the table. He was eating bangers and mash that he had prepared himself. The mound of mashed potato was garnished with spring onions and cracked black pepper and doused with gravy. On the table next to his plate was a bottle of vodka, which he poured into a large drinking glass like water.

"I think the chef deserves a big cheer for that fantastic meal," Claude said, instigating a round of applause and whooping that didn't seem to embarrass Sherry at all. "That was absolutely delightful, Sherry."

Sherry rested her elbows on the table, her hands clasped together as if in prayer. "I'm glad you liked it, and I'm glad some good came out of all those years at St John's Primary." She looked past him to Amanda's plate. "How was it dear?"

"It was amazing," Amanda said patting her stomach. "I'm stuffed. Thank you so much for cooking tonight."

"You're quite welcome," she said, and then her face changed, became mischievous. Her eyes gleamed slyly. "I suppose it's just a shame I didn't cook yesterday, otherwise it could have been my name on your board tonight."

Amanda sighed and shook her head.

"Why don't you give it a rest?" Arthur said, the words oozing contempt. "You've already made quite a show of yourself this evening. Just leave the poor girl alone."

Over her shoulder, Sherry said, "Why don't you shut up and drink your vodka like a good little boy?"

"You really are tiresome," he replied.

"And you're a fucking joke," Sherry snapped, a cord standing out in her neck.

"Then perhaps you should use me in your act. Might get a few more laughs than your dog does."

"Jesus Christ," Claude muttered, rubbing his eyes. "Not this again."

"What's *your* problem?" Sherry, full of venom, turned to Claude.

"No problem," he said softly, holding up his hands. "I just don't want to dodge any more crockery tonight, that's all."

"Honestly, I don't believe this," Sherry started to say, lips trembling, her eyes welling up. "I've just slaved away in that kitchen to cook for you, and all you've done tonight is gang up on me."

"Nobody is ganging up on you," Wish said, her accent making even a weary sentence sound melodic. "The meal was fine. Why can't you just leave it at that?"

"I'm going to go home," Sherry muttered, turning her back to the table. "Honestly, I don't think I've ever been as insulted as I am right now."

"Really?" Arthur slugged back more vodka. "Give me a minute, I think I can top it."

Justin tipped his head back and began howling with laughter, almost toppling from his chair.

Sherry started to cry again. She snatched a napkin from the table and covered her eyes.

The atmosphere in the dining room took on a hysterical, surreal quality that was quickly bewildering Amanda. She was struggling to cope with the schizophrenic changes in mood, and her inability to predict the sudden shifts in tension shot her body full of anxiety.

"Guys, guys?" Amanda began, her words lost amidst the sobbing, rambunctious laughter and mutterings from around the table. Her head began to throb again, and she raised her fingers to her temples, massaging them. "Can we just act like adults for five minutes?" They appeared not to hear her. She slapped a palm against the table, causing the cutlery to jump. Now she had the attention of the room. "I don't know what's the matter with you all, but this is a fucking mess. We've been here for one day and we've turned this place into a circus. I don't understand it. What's the matter?"

Through hitched breaths, Sherry said, "I cooked you all dinner and–"

"And we thanked you for it," Amanda interrupted. "It was a lovely dinner, we're all very full. That's the end of it. OK?"

Sherry's neck inflated as she struggled to keep the sobs at bay. Miserably, she nodded.

"And Arthur?" Amanda turned her head to him. "Quite frankly, you've been antagonizing everyone here since you arrived."

"I... I apologized to you earlier," he said, his face slack with worry.

"Yes, you did. But I think you should apologize to everyone."

"Wh–what?"

"Look, I have a fucking stress headache that's climbing into my neck and I think we should just clear the air, wipe the slate clean, and start this whole thing again."

"Do you need a massage?" Wish said quietly.

Ignoring her, Amanda continued to watch Arthur expectantly. "Well?"

"I..." His lips snapped shut, his jaw sliding from side to side as though he were grinding his teeth. "I don't see why I..."

"Because it would be a nice gesture," Amanda said, exasperated. "Come on. A man your age should know better than to behave like this."

There was a long, pregnant pause. Arthur took another drink of vodka and said, "Alright then. Everyone, I'm sorry if I've mistreated you, said something to upset you. If you'll let me, I'd like to start again."

"Thank you. Now can we all make a pact right here and now? Can we get through these next six days without any more arguing?"

There was a general murmur of agreement. Amanda pushed her chair back and stood up with her plate. "Sherry, can I take your plate?"

"I can take my own. I'm not a complete invalid."

"Whatever." Amanda turned and left the dining room. She had exhausted her quota of fucks that she could give for one day, and could no longer muster the strength to feel anything for any of them. She pushed it all away and thought about

Jamaica, the sun on her skin, the sand between her toes. She padded off to the kitchen and began scraping the remains of her meal into the bin. When she started to wash her plate, she heard footsteps behind her.

"I can do that for you," Justin offered.

"All done," she said, towelling off the suds and placing the plate onto the drying rack. She stepped to the side to move around him when he adjusted his stance.

"Hey, um, I thought that was a really good thing you did in there. Keeping the peace and all that."

His red-rimmed eyes were glossy from the drink. She couldn't smell the alcohol on him, but he was swaying ever so gently on the spot.

"I just want to get through the week with my sanity." She forced a smile, and said, "Anyway, I'm off to bed. I'll see you in the mor–"

His hand seized her wrist. "Wait. What about poker?"

Amanda glanced down at his hand and felt his fingers slowly uncoil. "I'm tired, Justin. I'm going to get some sleep."

"You sure you don't want to do something? Play pool? Anything?" His tone became whiny, his expression almost pained with disappointment.

"No thanks. I'm going to bed."

Before she could take another step, he leaned in, eyes closed, lips pursed. Had he not been so drunk he may have pulled it off, but as he neared for contact, Amanda managed to get her hands up. "Whoa, whoa, whoa."

His eyes opened and his lips moved wordlessly. There was a second of painful realization before he chuckled and shrugged his shoulders. "Was only going to give you a peck goodnight."

"That's alright," she said, patting him on the arm, before blurting, "OK then, see ya."

She hurried down the hallway, wheeled on the staircase, and raced up to her room. Upon entering, it felt so chilly that she expected there to be dew on the bedsheets. She shivered, rooted through her bag for her quilted onesie, and began to undress. She was down to her knickers when she heard a slow creak and thud of footsteps on the stairs. Covering her chest, she turned to the door, located the bolt, and slid it home, locking it.

The footsteps continued on the carpet, becoming louder and more prominent. It sounded like whoever was on the landing had stopped right outside her room. Her first instinct was to ask who was there, but instead she just stood shivering, her ear cocked toward the door. Was it Justin? Had he come up to try to kiss her goodnight again? What if he meant to do something more forceful? She held her breath, could almost hear her heart beating in her ears. Then, the footsteps began again, except this time it sounded as though the person were heading back down the staircase.

Amanda released the breath she had been holding and saw a cloud of vapour appear before her face. She slipped into a t-shirt, stepped into the onesie, zipped it up and jumped into bed.

It was the first time she had felt something like fear since being in the house, although she wasn't exactly sure why. The attempted kiss had been awkward and embarrassing, but there had been something in Justin's expression she didn't like; a subtle sneer, a look of contempt? Or maybe she was overthinking it. He was almost drunk and she was drained; it was a concoction for confusion if ever there was one.

She curled up beneath her blanket, thankful for the bolt on her door, and tried to push Justin's beady eyes out of her mind.

All the coffee Claude had been drinking was finally starting to pay off. He was able to stay awake without the risk of dozing, until each of them had returned to their room. When he heard the last door click closed, he waited a while longer before getting out of bed. He guessed it was somewhere near 2am.

After the stress and pressure of the last couple of evenings, he desperately wanted to tiptoe downstairs and fix himself a stiff drink just to help ease his nerves if nothing else, but of course, the stipulations in his contract forbade it.

He opened his door and stepped out onto the landing, the chill nipping at his bare feet. A symphony of snoring rose and fell from the neighbouring rooms. That was all the confirmation he needed. He retreated and gently closed the door behind him, before padding across to the corner of his room. He knelt down in front of the wall, and if someone had burst in on him in that very instant, it might have appeared as though he were preparing for prayer.

Instead of praying, however, he began whispering.

Amanda's room was the only one with a lock. His was the only one with an air vent.

CHAPTER 19

TUESDAY: 15 MILLIGRAMS

The air raid siren woke Amanda from a wonderfully vivid dream about Jamaica. She had been lying on the beach, shielding her eyes from the sun as she watched the surf lap against the shore. The weather had been pleasurably hot, and the sound of the ocean drove the tension out her body, exorcizing the stress from her muscles. Then the siren cut across everything and she was gasping, waking up with the cold air numbing her cheeks and nose.

They congregated on the landing before heading to the Circle Room. The routine was very much the same: the man in the white uniform and mask held out the tray, and one by one, they took their pill. When they were dismissed, the man in the white uniform disappeared behind the curtain. There was the beep of buttons and then the click of a lock. Justin ran to the curtain, pulled it back, tapped a few of the buttons at random, and earned a loud electronic squeal from the door.

"I bet I guess it by the end of the week," he said, his hair sticking up in corkscrews. He looked around the room for a laugh, found none, and grinned wider at Amanda.

They flocked to the kitchen and Amanda noticed there was a definite shift in the atmosphere. The tension that had coiled like a spring the previous day was now unwound, and conversation was flowing freely as they went about fixing their breakfasts. Arthur was more talkative than she had ever seen him, offering an exposé from his theatre days.

"Believe me, these actors you see on TV, especially the British ones, they're all up their own arse. Oh sure, when they're on the chat shows they're all lovey-dovey, but when you have to work with them they're a bloody nightmare." He dipped a triangle of toast into his boiled egg, yolk spilling down the side. "You should hear some of the things they come out with, honestly."

"Who have you worked with?" Claude asked.

"Who haven't I worked with?" He rolled his eyes. "Let's put it like this, Sir Ian McKellen and Patrick Stewart are as good as gold – you won't hear me say a bad word about either of them. And wild horses wouldn't make me slag any of my fellow actors off by name, but some of them..." He put a hand up by his cheek and spoke out the side of his mouth, "Some of these new actor types can be difficult. Honestly, they wouldn't know Shakespeare from their own arseholes."

There was a low note of tension as Arthur's face grew grim, his eyes narrowing to slits. Then, that bitterness that threatened to overboil and become something worse melted away. "Oh they're alright if you're having a drink with them, but when you're treading the boards and stuck in a rehearsal all day, things quickly become tiresome."

Light-hearted laughter fluttered around the breakfast table. Amanda reached for the teapot to refill her cup. The pill had left a chalky taste in the back of her throat and so far a glass of orange juice hadn't been able to wash it away. She angled the teapot over her cup but only a squirt left the spout.

"Is it empty?" Sherry asked, wiping marmite away from the corner of her mouth.

"Yeah." Amanda stood up. "I'll refill it."

"I can do that for you," Sherry said, rising from the table, an avalanche of crumbs falling from her pyjama top. "Pass it here."

"No it's OK, I can do it," Amanda said.

"Actually I was going to make the tea," Wish chirped, also standing.

Now there was a Mexican standoff around the table.

"I'll make the tea," Amanda said, trying to sound firm, but lacking the conviction she needed to make it stick. It was still early, and she was hesitant to rock the boat now that it was sailing on gentle waters.

"It's no bother," Sherry said, wagging her hand for the teapot.

"It's no bother for me either," Wish added.

"Yes, but I offered first, didn't I?" Sherry said. "It doesn't take three of us to make a bloody pot of tea." Her easy laughter juxtaposed the vaguely menacing tone.

"You made that pot and it tasted awful," Wish quipped. "You're English and you can't even make tea."

A storm began brewing behind Sherry's eyes, and Amanda could almost see the lightning crackling in her pupils. Sherry glanced at Amanda, smiling wistfully, and slowly sat back down.

"I think I'll have coffee anyway," Sherry said.

"So shall I make?" Wish asked Amanda, hopefully.

"No, sit down, sit down, please." Before Wish could protest or mount another case, Amanda went to the sink and started the ceremony, painfully aware of how quiet everyone at the table was now. She turned and saw the others looking at her, as though awaiting permission to begin eating again. All except Claude, who was now studying their faces, his eyes flicking between their expressions. Then he looked over at Amanda, one eyebrow arched.

"David Jason, now he's a gentleman," Arthur said reluctantly. "I did an episode of Frost with him back in '92 and he was just the epitome of what an actor should be…"

A bead of perspiration dropped down the back of Amanda's neck. She touched a hand to her forehead and her fingers came away slick. She suddenly realized that her armpits were moist and the fabric of her t-shirt was sticking to her back. She tore off a piece of kitchen towel and dabbed her face, sopping up the sweat, and finished the tea.

When she returned to the table, Wish was talking about her early years as a dancer. She had been front and centre in music videos for numerous French house musicians, and had choreographed a dance routine for a French musical, Le Grand Mariage, which earned her a meeting with Beyoncé.

"You met Beyoncé?" Justin asked, dipping a croissant into his tea. His breakfast had consisted of nothing but pastries. "That's crazy."

Arthur stiffened in his chair, his jaw shifting from side to side. He fiddled with the teaspoon he used to crack his egg. Wish had trumped his celebrity story, and no amount of acting could conceal his bitterness.

"Yes. She wanted me to do the dances for one of her videos, but... I had a bad accident." She prodded her muesli. "I was in a car crash. Doctor said if the impact had been an inch to the right, I would have broken my spine. But I had to have lots of operations on my back to repair it." Her eyes dropped to her cereal and she shrugged slightly. "So now I can't dance so well. But it's not such a big deal. I was twenty-eight when that happened, and when you get to about thirty you don't get so many jobs anyway. I always said I would retire gracefully at thirty, but fate had other plans." She dropped her eyes to her cereal, momentarily lamenting her career. Then she raised her chin defiantly. "Not such a big loss. Because I plan to work again, as soon as we get out, in fact. Big plans."

Wish's eyes pinballed to Amanda. When Wish winked at her, Amanda quickly looked away.

The sound of scraping cutlery and chewing filled the silence until Claude said, "The most famous person I've met, apart from you guys of course, was a guy called Ian Dalton. He went to my school."

"What was he famous for?" Amanda asked. She felt sticky and was almost sure she could smell the odour of sweat rising from her body.

"He killed his girlfriend with a hammer about ten years ago," Claude said. "They did a documentary about him and everything."

"Sounds like a catch," Amanda said.

"That the kind of guy you're into, is it?" Justin asked before stuffing a sticky bun into his mouth.

"It's called sarcasm," Amanda said, without returning his smile.

"Do you have a boyfriend though?" Justin asked, his words barely audible through the bun.

"That falls into the category of none-of-your-business." And with that, she decided that breakfast was over. She stood up with her cup of tea, felt another bead of sweat slip down her back. "Is it hot in here?"

"You're having a laugh, aren't you?" Claude said. "I don't think they've put the heating on once since we've been here. Probably take hours to heat this place up."

"Freezing," Arthur said. "We should have complained about it ages ago. We're bound to catch colds if we're not careful. We'd all better bundle up if we don't want to get frostbite."

"That's what I thought," Amanda said and went upstairs to take a shower.

CHAPTER 20

When she removed her onesie, t-shirt and underwear, Amanda could feel how damp they were. She raised the clothes to her face and inhaled. She wasn't sure if it was the sweat mingling with the fabric, or whether it was her imagination, but she thought she smelled something faintly acidic, like vinegar almost. She raised her arm and sniffed.

No adverse side effects. Sweating profusely wasn't an adverse side effect though, was it? It was uncomfortable, and if others could smell her then it was offensive too, but she wasn't sure if that counted as an adverse side effect. She ran the taps and as she washed, her attention wandered to the eye-in-the-sky camera in the centre of the shower room. From its vantage point, she was sure it couldn't record her naked body behind the stall door and partition.

She wondered how many people might be watching her right now.

That chalky residue still coated her tongue. She opened her mouth and let the showerhead fill it with water, before spitting toward the drain. Maybe one of the others would have mouthwash.

"You have company," Sherry's voice echoed through the steam. "Only me, love."

"Hey," Amanda called back.

Sherry had a towel wrapped around her body, her flip-flops slapping the floor as she walked. As she passed Amanda's stall, Sherry removed her towel. Amanda saw her thick body, the

146

meaty slabs of her buttocks, and then Sherry turned, giving her a full-frontal view.

"How is it?" Sherry asked, still standing outside the neighbouring stall.

Amanda looked away, hoping that Sherry was asking about the water and not her body. "It's great. Nothing like a hot shower."

"You've got that right. How was your breakfast?" Sherry was still standing there, stark naked, trying to strike up a conversation.

"Yeah, good."

"Most important meal of the day."

Amanda didn't say anything, and Sherry didn't move. Was she waiting for Amanda to look at her, to acknowledge her nakedness before going in the shower? Amanda hadn't washed her hair yet, and didn't think she was going to be able to unless Sherry went into the stall.

"You're so right. Nothing like a hot shower."

Finally, Sherry stepped into the stall next to Amanda and turned the water on.

"Amanda?"

"Yeah?" Amanda hesitated, squeezing shampoo out of the bottle.

"Do you like me?"

Amanda poured the shampoo over her head and began to massage her scalp. "Of course I do."

"Good. Because I like you. And I don't think I could stand going through the week knowing that you didn't like me. It would... it would hurt too much, I think."

"Well you don't need to worry." Amanda quickly rinsed the foam out of her hair and shut the taps off. "Let's just try to enjoy the rest of the week."

"I'd like that." Sherry's voice was toneless beneath the crashing water. "I'd like that very much."

Amanda grabbed her towel off the rail. She was wrapping

it around herself when Sherry's eyes appeared over the top of the partition. Amanda yelped, tucking the towel into the fold to secure it in place.

"Can I tell you something? Just between us?" Sherry whispered.

Amanda groaned internally. "Um… OK."

"I know everybody is looking at Wish like she's a goddess. I've certainly seen the boys ogling her, checking her out. And god, she loves the attention, even if she tries not to show it. But, in my opinion, your body is a hundred times nicer than hers."

Sherry's stall door flung open and she charged out, dripping wet. Amanda shrank back, and her first thought was to turn and run out of there, because just then, with her hair stuck to her face and her body exposed, Sherry looked completely out of her mind. And what would happen if Sherry decided she wanted to attack Amanda? Would they pick it up on the camera and rush in to rescue her? Would they even get there in time?

"What's wrong?" Amanda asked, backing up.

"You're perfect exactly as you are. And I don't just mean that physically. Inside." Sherry tapped her chest. "You're just as beautiful. You're an angel."

"Sherry!" Amanda shouted. Sherry stopped in her tracks, rivulets of water running down the contours of her face. "I get it." She laughed nervously because it was all she could do to keep from screaming at her, and said, "Now stop being mushy and enjoy your shower."

"I just want you to know your worth."

"I appreciate it. Look, I'll see you downstairs, alright?"

"Sure." The word was flat and dead as it left her mouth. Her face was a blank void, her eyes filmy and lifeless.

I am looking at a mad woman, Amanda thought. *They have put me in the house with a mad woman and she could be dangerous.*

With a mixture of trepidation and awe, Amanda watched Sherry turn and stomp back into the shower without another word.

Amanda rushed out of the shower room. Claustrophobia closed in on her as she hurried down the hallway. She barely dried herself before changing into a velour tracksuit and heading downstairs. The dry, dusty atmosphere of the house felt like it was clogging her throat and filling her lungs, and now she was hot because she was teetering on the edge of panic. She made it to the conservatory undetected and made a beeline for the door. It was locked. She twisted the handle up and down rapidly, and then slammed her palm on the glass.

"Why won't you fucking open?" She slapped it again, harder and harder. Realizing it was useless, she turned and stormed to the entrance of the house. It was the only other door she could remember seeing that led outside to the real world where she wasn't smothered with forced compliments. But hadn't that been her life not too long ago? And hadn't she spent every waking moment trying to reclaim that feeling since the world decided that Amanda Pearson wasn't relevant anymore?

She reached the front door, tried to open it. Wouldn't budge. She looked for locks, bolts, something that she could work with. Nothing. She pressed her forehead to the heavy oak and could feel her heartbeat in her neck, the blood rushing in her ears. She inhaled slowly through her nostrils and exhaled. "Easy, Amanda, easy. There's nothing wrong. There's nothing wrong." She stepped back, saw a shiny, round smear on the door from her clammy forehead, and started toward the Circle Room. She had to speak to someone in charge, to vent, to ask the questions she should have asked before she signed that piece of paper. Now, that twenty-five grand advance she had spent didn't seem like that much money. It was a carrot dangling in front of her nose, and she was the donkey that followed it without question. She tried to think back to what she had read in the contract, the questions she had asked Bunny's solicitor. Sure, maybe the pill they were all taking was fine, but what about the people they put her in here with? What was the vetting process? She was at their mercy, and if there was no way to get outside then she was as good as a prisoner, wasn't she?

She tried to change her train of thought, to settle her temper. Think of Jamaica. Rum and jerk chicken, reggae and hot sand, Bob Marley and palm trees, whatever. Because if she thought too much about this experiment, this trap she had willingly bumbled into, then she would unravel. Christ, she was unravelling already, wasn't she? What about a bump of the white stuff up the hooter? Wouldn't that help, right about now? Wouldn't that just be the ticket she needed?

The door of the Circle Room wouldn't open. She twisted the knob, bumped the door with her shoulder, a scream of frustration revving in her throat. Sweat rolled off her brow and stung her eyes. She wiped it away, whirled in the hallway, located the eye-in-the-sky camera, and waved her arms.

"I need to speak to someone," she shouted at the camera. She felt like an idiot for yelling at an inanimate object, and maybe that's exactly what they wanted: some juicy footage of her going out of her mind, acting a fool. She waited for a response, her embarrassment boiling down to anger in the silence. "I know you can hear me. I want to speak to someone, right fucking now!" She kicked the door, the impact vibrating up from the sole of her foot and exploding in her knee.

That's it, Amanda, you keep acting like a lunatic and see how far that gets you.

"It's locked," Claude said, walking down the hallway, hands in his jeans pockets. "They only open it when we have to take our pill and in the evening for the assignment." He eyed the camera, and in a low voice said, "This house is only old on the surface. Everything in here is electronically controlled."

"How do you know?"

"Follow me. And don't say anything until we get there."

Without another word, he began to stroll, finally leading her to the staircase on the opposite side of the house. A grandfather clock ticked loudly beneath the arch leading to another reception area. "Were you any good at word searches when you were a kid?"

"Word searches? No, not really."

"Neither was I. That's why I completely missed this." He ran his hand over the wooden panels beneath the staircase. Then, he pulled the panel and it gave way, creaking open, revealing a passage. "Sneaky bastards, eh?"

"What is that?"

"Come on, I'll show you." He bent down and sidled through the small rectangular opening, disappearing into the musty darkness.

"Are you crazy? I'm not going in there. Claude, what is this?"

"It's fine. I was in here earlier."

"Where does it lead?"

"Down," he whispered. "I've got to admit, it was a leap of faith for me too, but you'll have to trust me."

She shook her head, took a step back. A waft of stale, gritty air blew out of the opening, tickling her nostrils.

"It's dark in there," she said feebly.

"Only for a while. But believe me, there's light at the end of the tunnel."

Hearing his voice without being able to see his face unnerved her. She hugged herself, craning her neck for a better view into the passageway. "How narrow is it?"

"Tight. About four feet across," he said. "Come on. Trust me, there's nothing to be scared of."

The clock ticked behind her. She didn't move.

"Amanda, I don't want the others to know about this," he said, half-emerging out of the passageway.

"Why not? Why's it such a secret?"

"Because right now I think you and me are the only two normal people in this house." He held out his hand. "Come on. Trust me."

CHAPTER 21

The door closed behind her, silencing the grandfather clock, and sealing them in darkness.

"Put your hand on my shoulder," Claude said, standing in front of her. "There's no banister, so just take the steps slow. There's twenty-three of them."

The draught blew through her, tossing her hair in front of her face, the fusty odour of damp wood and wet earth filling her nose. "I can't see a thing. I'm going to break my neck."

"No, you won't. If you fall, I'll soften the impact."

He placed a hand over hers on his shoulder, and they descended deeper into the darkness, which gradually began to soften as they neared the bottom of the stairs. She started to feel itchy, imagining insects crawling over her skin, spiders nesting in her hair. Once she summoned the image to mind, she became sure that she was covered in creepy crawlies and swept her free hand across her face to rid it of imaginary cobwebs.

When they reached the bottom of the stairs, Amanda felt something drip on her, and this time she was sure she hadn't imagined it. Another drop tapped her on the crown of her head.

"What is that?" she asked, shrilly, her voice echoing through the passage.

"What is *what*?"

"Something wet just touched me."

"It's just rainwater, condensation, something like that. Look."

Before them was a narrow passage about two bus-lengths

152

long. A puddle of light splashed onto the floor at the end of the passage, and as Claude guided her toward it, Amanda saw that it was coming from an opening in the ceiling about fifteen feet above.

"Is that daylight?"

Claude chuckled gently. "Yeah, it is. It feels like we're escaping from prison, doesn't it?"

"We can't get up there though, can we?" She saw that the column of light bled in through a barred grille that covered the opening.

"There's a ladder. And that thing up there is on a hinge. If we push it, it opens."

"And then what?"

"Then we're outside."

"You're joking."

"Come and see for yourself."

When he got to the end of the passage, Claude grabbed hold of the ladder and started to climb.

"Wait, don't leave me down here."

"I'm not. You're coming up with me."

She reached out, her pale hands finding purchase on the cold, wet metal ladder. Above her, Claude was already at the top rung. He reached out and pushed the grille, which opened with a tired whine of the hinges, and then he was lifting himself out.

She hurried to keep up with him, suddenly fearful that something would reach out and grab her from the darkness below. In her haste, her foot slipped on the rung, a scream shot out of her mouth and her heart lurched in her chest.

"What happened?" Claude's concerned face filled the square opening.

"I'm fine, I'm fine," she said, her feet still tingling from the fright of almost tumbling. When she was a couple of rungs from the top of the ladder, he reached in, grabbed her wrists, and heaved her the rest of the way out. She could feel the strength in his grip and was mildly surprised.

While still on her knees, she dusted off her palms and looked around. They were in a small, square courtyard, surrounded by brick walls too tall to climb. All they could see of the outside world was the dishwater-grey sky.

"How did you find this place?" she asked.

"I didn't. They told me about it."

Her head whipped toward him. "*Who* told you?"

"Whoever's in charge, I guess. Last night when I went to bed, there was a typed note just next to my pillow. It said, 'Push the panel opposite the clock.' It's actually a noticeable door when you know it's there, but you'd completely miss it if someone didn't bring it to your attention."

Had he broken eye contact abruptly there? She thought that the rhythm of his speech had become a little singsong, the words not quite flowing naturally as they had in their previous conversations.

Rehearsed. The word pushed through her paranoia and refused to budge.

"Why do you think they told *you* that?"

Oh, and haven't you just been the voice of reason this this whole time, Mr Claude? her mind whispered slyly. *The cool head, the only one that isn't acting skittish and weird?*

"It's probably part of their little social experiment. Maybe they want to see how I would react, who I would tell. But what I'm more interested in is that thing behind you." He nodded with his chin.

Amanda turned around and saw a smooth metallic booth the size of a phone box, with a clear glass window in its centre. Engraved on a plate beneath the window were the words QUEEN CAGE.

"What the fuck is this?" she said under her breath, hesitantly starting toward it.

"Any ideas what a Queen Cage is?" Claude asked, joining her side.

"Not a clue," she said, running her fingertips over the

engraving. "What is that, a door?" She felt along a ridge in the booth and pulled gently. There was a hiss and then the door opened slowly and smoothly on its own accord, releasing the dull scent of new leather. Amanda flinched back, wiping her hands on her thighs.

"It's creepy, right?" Claude said. "Looks like something from a sci-fi film." He stepped around her to inspect the booth's interior; it was padded, as though ready to accommodate a person. "Dare you to go inside."

"No way. You do it."

"Double dare me?" he said with a grin and prepared to step inside the booth.

She stopped him at the last instant. "No, better not."

"Why?"

"I don't know. Could be dangerous."

He scratched his head. "They wanted me to see this, otherwise they wouldn't have left me the note. Could be a test."

"If they wanted us to go messing with it, they would have said so in the Circle Room," she said, taking another step back. "I don't like this thing sitting here. And I don't like all this Indiana Jones stuff with the secret passageways and god only knows what else."

Claude pushed the door on the booth closed. It glided slowly back with an audible click as it locked in place. "Notice anything else?" he said.

She gave the surroundings another cursory glance, glad of the cool wind against her skin. "What am I looking for?"

"A camera. I can't see one and I had a good look around here. That doesn't mean that we're not being watched and listened to. In fact, I'm certain we're still being listened to. But not being able to physically see a camera makes me feel a bit better. How about you?"

"I'd take a camera over that space shuttle thing over there," she said, pointing to the Queen Cage.

"That's rattled you, hasn't it?"

"Hasn't it rattled *you*?"

"I think we have bigger concerns, such as the others. Something's wrong with them. Don't tell me you haven't noticed."

"Oh… I've noticed. I've also noticed that you seem perfectly fine."

"What's that supposed to mean?" He gave a short, breathy laugh. "You seem a little annoyed."

"Shouldn't I be? This secret passageway like something out of Batman, the sci-fi phone booth over there. I don't know." She gave a half shrug. "You just seem a little clued up on everything."

"I told you, they left me a note." His brow furrowed. "And I immediately told you because I thought you'd want to know. Would it make you feel better if I started following you around and getting all creepy?"

"Of course not," she said, her face flaming with embarrassment. "It's this place, it messes with your head."

"I know it does. That's by design." Claude shook his head. "They lied to us."

"Who?"

"Midori Media or whatever it is. Do you remember they told us that only one person would be affected by the pill, and the rest of us would be taking placebos? That was in the contract."

"Yeah, I read it."

"I don't remember exactly how it was worded, but they said something like only one person would be taking the drug, and that one person wouldn't experience any adverse side effects. But as far as I can tell, the four of them are taking the drug, and me and you have placebos."

"What makes you think that?" Amanda felt sweaty again, and her heart skipped with worry.

"They're drawn to you, Amanda. All four of them are

climbing over each other to get close to you. It isn't just that silly shit with the whiteboards yesterday, although that was what got me thinking originally. You must be able to see that surely?"

A strong wind swept through the courtyard. Amanda tucked her hands into her armpits, her teeth chattering. She thought about Sherry standing in front of her, naked, the dull, vacant expression on her face. She thought about the hungry way Justin had leaned in for that kiss, and how Wish had almost burst into tears when her name was on Amanda's whiteboard.

"You don't think they're just eccentric?" Amanda asked.

"Yeah, I do, but something's changed. I know we only really had a few hours to talk to each other before we had to take that pill, but even still, I felt like something shifted with them. It's like all their focus went on you."

"Are you sure you're not just..."

"Just what?" His eyebrows rose expectantly. "Paranoid?"

"I was going to say jealous."

Rather than take offense, Claude asked, "Jealous of what?"

"The attention," she sighed, and shook her head. "There's no way for me to say this without sounding like a complete tool, but I'm the most famous person in this house, even if I'm not famous anymore. With normal people – people that haven't experienced that kind of fame before – it can be... I don't know. Intriguing? They could just be trying to impress me because I'm..." She faltered, was about to use the F word in present tense again, but caught herself at the last instant. "...I was *really* famous. And I think that even when you're washed up like I am, you still carry a bit of mystique. Does that make sense, or do I just sound like a self-centred bitch?"

He was looking at her strangely. She couldn't decide whether he seemed sorry for her or was repulsed by her overinflated ego. He seemed in no hurry to speak, and in the lingering silence, she began to wonder if he was going to lean in for a kiss. If he was – and she suddenly found herself hoping he would – she would embrace it. What harm could there be in a secret fling? Even if their romance only lasted the duration of the week, it would certainly help the time go by quicker. And wasn't she due a bit of fun? God only knew her body needed it.

His lips parted and his head tilted to the side. She stepped toward him. Hesitantly, his lips neared hers. She closed her eyes and waited.

"We should get back," he said, so close to her that she could feel his breath on her face. "The others might get suspicious if they can't find us."

Her mind stuttered. The anticipation, that campfire in her lower stomach, fizzled out, leaving only wisps of smoke in its wake. "Uh, yeah. I think you're probably right."

He nodded, walked to the square opening, and bent down to the ladder. "I can prove it, you know."

"Prove what?"

"That the others have taken something."

"How?"

"Follow my lead, and I'll show you."

CHAPTER 22

They decided to split up when they re-entered the house, taking different routes to the games room. Claude arrived first, to a frosty reception. Wish, Sherry, Arthur and Justin had been sitting on the sofas, a Monopoly board set up in the middle of the coffee table. Their heads snapped toward him, their expressions morphing from hopefully expectant to angrily disappointed. He saw that the Monopoly money and game pieces hadn't been moved at all. It was as though they were trying to give the impression that they had been playing, when really they were waiting for Amanda.

"Where is she?" Arthur asked, his mouth locked in a sneer.

"Amanda?" He shrugged. "I don't know. I thought she was here with you."

"No, you didn't," Wish chimed in. "You're lying."

"Whoa," he chuckled nervously, "why don't you tell me how you really feel?"

Justin stood up slowly, his wiry arms dangling by his sides. He had the body of a scarecrow, but Claude recognized something unpredictable and maybe even cruel in his pointy features. "Do you expect us to believe that both of you just went missing for an hour?" A smile split across his lips. "Don't fucking bullshit me, Claude. Where did you go?"

"Don't worry about where I went," Claude said, casually moving over to the pool table. He began to rack the balls. Justin stood at the foot of the table, his shadow stretching over the felt. "It's none of your business what I do."

"Are you trying to make a move on her?" Justin hissed. "You trying to fuck her?"

Claude bent down with the cue and went to break. Justin caught the cue ball before it could make contact with the rest. Claude stood up, glanced over at the sofas where the others sat, eyeing him closely.

"Is there a problem?"

"We looked for her," Sherry said. "We looked all over the house and we couldn't find her. And don't you think it's convenient that you were nowhere to be seen either?"

"Not really. It's a big house. How come you all wanted her so badly anyway?"

A mist of confusion settled over them. Claude could almost hear the record skipping in the room as they tried to untangle his question.

"We just wanted her," Arthur finally choked out, breaking the spell. "And we don't have to explain anything to you, either."

"Fine by me," Claude said with a laugh. He put the pool cue down on the table and approached the dartboard. He pulled the darts out of the cork, took a few steps back. Something jabbed him in the back of the shoulder. He turned and saw Justin extending the cue like a sword.

"You're lying," Justin said, darkly.

"Don't touch me with that again," Claude replied, his playful demeanour calcifying. "Say what you want, but you don't touch me."

"Ooh," Justin quivered. "And what if I do? What if I wrap this cue around your head?"

"Then you better make sure you knock me out and put me in a coma," Claude said, squaring up to Justin. "Because if I get up, I'll paste you all over this room. Do you understand me?"

"You think you could do that to all of us?" Wish asked, and now she was standing up too, shoulders pinned back, the long ropes of muscle taught in her arms. "Because if you want to talk violence, you better be willing to do it to all of us."

Claude's fist tightened around the darts he was holding. He knew not to push them anymore. They were a pack of hyenas regarding him like a limping antelope, waiting for their opportunity to pounce. Now he could feel the aggression rolling off them, polluting the air around him.

"Guys," he began, slowly raising one hand to simmer them. "What's going on here? Why are you all so upset?"

"Are you lying? Were you with her or not?" Wish asked, her eyes widening until they threatened to pop right out of their sockets. "Just tell us the truth!" Her accent thickened with frustration, losing its lilt.

The pool cue that Justin was holding rose until it was just under the point of Claude's chin. "Tell the truth, Claude. The truth will set you free."

Slowly, with as much care and confidence as he could muster, Claude delicately moved the cue away from his face. "I don't know what's got into you," he said. "But I went exploring the house. I was bored, and I thought there might be a way out to a garden or something, or that one of the other rooms might be open. I saw a library the other day but couldn't remember where it was, and I wanted something to read. There's nothing in the contract that says I have to stay cooped up with you all twenty-four hours a day. And as for Amanda, I don't know where she is. I haven't seen her since breakfast. She's probably in the swimming pool. Did any of you check there?"

Justin squinted, the light catching his nose ring. "All the doors are locked in this house. There's no getting out. You know that, don't you?"

"So?"

"So, you'd be wise to remember that. There's still five more days to go."

The door opened. Amanda walked in five minutes later than Claude, as planned. The flow of her movement came to an abrupt halt when she saw their faces. Startled, she shot a glance at Claude, but before she could ask one of the dozen questions that were running through her mind, Wish exploded.

"Where have you been?" She clambered over the sofa, losing her footing, and fell to the floor with a hard thud. Her sudden gracelessness completely contradicted the lithe, almost feline movement she had exhibited since entering the house.

"I... I was looking for somewhere to smoke..." Amanda tried to say, but Sherry and Arthur were rushing toward her, cornering her by the ping-pong table.

"We've been out of our minds with worry," Sherry said, her large hand shooting out to stroke Amanda's upper arm. "We couldn't find you anywhere. We didn't know whether you'd fallen down and hurt yourself, or whether you'd got lost or..."

Arthur waved his hand irritably at Sherry. "We were just concerned," he said, and now there was a richness in his voice she hadn't heard before, one reserved for projecting at audiences in auditoriums. "You see, we were talking today and we think... well, we..." His attention was snagged by Wish, who was still on her knees, a pose that was half suggestive and half worship. "Will you get up and stop being so bloody childish, woman!" He reached down and yanked her arm.

Wish allowed herself to be dragged to her feet without quarrel. Arthur's face soured with contempt, and with a small shove, he dismissed her. "As I was saying, as I was... what *was* I saying? Oh, you stupid, stupid woman!" He spun on Wish, his face purple with anger.

"We think that it's best to stick together," Justin told Amanda, eerily calm amidst the clamour. "We've decided that we shouldn't be straying from each other. The house is too big. If one of us went off and took a fall, or god forbid," he glanced over at Claude, "something worse, then it could be catastrophic. I'm sure you understand."

"There's about twelve million cameras in this house," Amanda said, flinching away from Sherry's caress. "I think we'll be fine."

"Still," Arthur said, a smile struggling on his lips. "If we all just spread out and do our own thing, it goes against the whole ethos of the house, doesn't it?"

"I don't have a clue what you're trying to say, Arthur."

"What I'm saying is, this is a once-in-a-lifetime sort of deal, isn't it? I mean, when are you ever going to be locked in a house, taking pills with five strangers? It's an experience. We should try to get the most out of it."

"Good idea," Claude said dryly. "And how do you suppose we should do that?"

"Monopoly," Wish said, pointing excitedly at the board. "We could play Monopoly."

"Yeah, because that's never caused any arguments before, has it?" Claude muttered.

"I don't think I'm in the mood." Amanda stretched, yawned and massaged her neck.

"One game isn't going to hurt you," Sherry said, her face faltering between a smile and an expression of such sincere worry that, for a second, Amanda felt the smallest twinge of pity for her. "Go on. Be a sport. *Please.*"

"Please," Wish echoed.

"Please?" Arthur cocked his head to the side. "I'll be the banker and I promise not to let any of these heathens cheat."

"Come on Amanda. One game won't hurt you," Justin added, although Amanda was sure there was a thinly veiled threat implied in his words.

CHAPTER 23

The black felt-tip writing on the corrugated cardboard sign read: Homeless and Was In Army. Please Spair Change. God Bless. Next to it was an old Pret A Manger cup with a few strategically placed coins; not enough to buy a filter coffee from the place it was promoting, but just enough to give an impression that this poor young man had been ignored in the cold all day.

Justin lay on his bed, which amounted to little more than a bundle of blankets, just beneath the light in the underpass. He liked to be in full view of any late-night commuters that were taking a shortcut to and from the tube station, so they could see his face, see how dreadfully young he was, how vulnerable. Pleading for change was usually a waste of breath no matter how pitiful the performance. People either ignored him, or fixed him with a short, sharp look of disdain, as though he were a puddle of vomit that had just learned to talk, before striding away. Occasionally, about once every four days, some Christian do-gooder would want to take him somewhere to buy him food, or just crouch by his side and talk, see if they could understand and sympathize with his plight. They were full of concerned looks and soft tones; friendly vibes, sure, but not much use to him. Conversation was not a currency he cared for. All he wanted was cash.

That night, he hadn't been able to sleep much. A Romanian busker had been playing the accordion down the other end of the tunnel, and the music had funnelled through to Justin. It was *The Godfather* theme, over and over again, and Justin was just about ready to smash his head against the tiled wall.

What made the whole thing even more irritating to him was the fact that people were throwing money at the Romanian, the coins clattering audibly into the accordion case. There Justin was, filthy and malnourished like a mangy fox, and people were practically stepping over him to give money to a busker. Although it was a lie, the cardboard sign declared that he was an ex-soldier, but that didn't seem to matter much to the commuters. Well, he couldn't sing, dance, or play any instruments, so until he thought of some hustle to better his position, he would have to make do with the sign.

It'd been almost a week since he'd last seen Haley, and he supposed she was as good as gone. She didn't like hanging around in Baker Street or Marylebone, even though Justin assured her it was far more profitable than lurking around Victoria train station. Baker Street still profited from the city crowd, but there was a lot less competition on the streets. If you hung around with too many other unfortunates, then you ended up like a pack of mad dogs all fighting over the same bowl of food. Haley didn't seem to agree. She was always talking about taking a train out of London, heading down to the coast, and starting a new life, maybe getting a job as a waitress or a barmaid, something like that. Said she had spent a week in Blackpool when she was a kid and could see herself working the amusements on Pleasure Beach. Problem was she couldn't keep the spoon out of her hand or the needle out of her arm. And with a habit like that, she had to do a lot of work to keep up with her fix, otherwise she got sick. Justin had never much got the appeal of heroin, especially having seen so many people hooked on the fucking stuff. Alright, so it apparently sent you nodding off to heaven for a while, but the compromise was that you spent the rest of your time in living hell. It had only taken him seeing her go through withdrawal once to know that he was never going to get involved. Witnessing her puking and shitting herself, while writhing in pain and shivering, wasn't exactly his idea of Disneyland.

Haley was only a few years older than him and still had the echoes of prettiness in her face, which was why she was usually successful in soliciting men for quick back-alley business. Having not seen her for a week, Justin assumed that one of three things had happened to her. The first was that she made enough money to get that train ticket she was always promising herself, although, having borne witness to the ferociousness of her addiction, he doubted it. The second thing he thought might have happened was that she had taken up with a pimp, someone who would take her off the street and put her to work privately. Though, given the state she was in the last time he saw her, Justin thought this might also be off the cards. The last scenario he had imagined for Haley was something he had actively been trying not to think about: her curled up in the corner of some abandoned building, stiff and cold, bruised, blotchy and bloated from decay.

No, no heroin for him. Even when things had been really rough after his stepdad tried to lay down the law and his mother just looked the other way, as though preoccupied by a sheen of dust on the TV that she had forgotten to clean.

"You're not going to sit up in your room all day, playing computer games and smoking that god-awful stuff. Not under my roof."

How had his mother replaced his dad with that horrible ogre of a man? He was ugly for a start. His head the size of a sofa cushion, his eyes like poached eggs behind the thick lenses of his glasses. Justin looked over at his mother, appealing for backup, but she was wandering away, deliberately disinviting herself from the altercation.

"Well it ain't your roof, is it, *Howard*. It's my mum's."

"Yeah? Then you might want to think about who's paying the electric so you can play those stupid video games, and who's putting food in the fridge, and who's getting up at six every morning to go to work so we can have hot water. Because I'll tell you something, *sunshine*, it certainly isn't you."

He had prodded Justin in the chest, and it hurt. Impulsively, Justin slapped his stepfather's hand away. "Don't you fucking touch me."

A slap came back across Justin's jaw, strong enough to make his teeth click together and a swarm of ants crowd his vision. The shock was like a jolt from an exposed plug socket. Justin hadn't gone crazy or begun windmilling at Howard. He had just been sort of stunned, unable to comprehend that this man had actually hit him.

Howard was shouting something at him, about how he had always had this coming. But Justin tuned it all out as though turning down a dial on the radio. Instead, he once again glanced at his mother, the unofficial umpire in their game of slap tennis. When she still refused to meet Justin's eyes, he said, "Mum? Mum, you gonna let him do that to me?"

What she said next severed their ties forever. Even days and weeks later when he replayed the argument back, he could not quite believe the words had left her lips.

"This is really your thing, Justin. I'm going to leave it for you to sort out."

And so, he had. With nothing more than a few handfuls of clothes in his backpack, he left the house and had spent the entire night on a park bench unable to get comfortable enough to sleep. He had been reminded of something he had heard in Scouts as a child, back when his real dad was still alive to take him. On the occasional camping jaunts that they used to go on, the scoutmaster – Scott? Had that been his name? – had said, "If it's been raining, you don't want to make your camp under a tree. You sleep under a tree, and you get rained on twice." Justin hadn't thought of that advice in years. Hadn't thought of a… what was it called? Those funny fucking sleeping bags that were like tents. Bivouac. Christ, a bivouac. He wished he had one now.

Eventually *The Godfather* ceased, and the Romanian took his winnings and disappeared. It must have been close to three in the morning, if Justin's internal clock was correct. He lay on his side, the blankets pulled up to his chin, his woolly hat pulled down to his eyes, his fleece zipped up to his mouth. The underpass was empty, as it usually was at this time, and that feeling of isolation filled Justin with a conflicting sense of tranquillity and unease. He'd heard stories of nutcases going around beating up beggars or dousing them in petrol before flicking a lit match. Then there were the sadistic bastards going around offering tramps food that they'd poisoned, and he'd heard about a couple of instances where the poor saps who gave in to the temptation ended up in A&E, or dead. Nothing so heinous had ever happened to him, but his youthful appearance had attracted a different sort of unwanted attention.

The tiredness teased him, and he closed his eyes, listening to the steady burr of the traffic on the road overhead. There was continuous dripping sound from the moisture on the underpass ceiling pooling in a small puddle. He was almost asleep when he heard footsteps echoing toward him. Through the cages of his lashes, he made out a tall figure striding through the underpass, the silhouette becoming clearer as the volume of the footfalls increased. Justin braced, knowing that he would relax once the person passed, but then the footsteps stopped.

"Excuse me," the gentle voice said, and Justin's eyes snapped open at once. Justin didn't trust the soft cadence of the man's speech, and he sat up, the tiredness vanishing from his body like an exorcized demon.

The man was well dressed, a sheepskin coat over a tailored suit, and shiny black shoes that didn't have creases near the toes, as though they were on their maiden voyage out of the box. The man might have been Japanese or Chinese, something like that, Justin wasn't sure – his geography had never been great.

"What do you want?" Justin asked, putting as much bass into his voice as he could, his back to the slick, graffiti-defaced wall.

The stranger smiled, and Justin distrusted it instantly. The man looked down one end of the underpass, and then the other, before returning his attention to Justin.

"I was wondering if I might have a moment of your time," the man said. "To discuss some business."

"No, absolutely not," Justin returned without taking a breath. A lot of older, rich men thought that because Justin was homeless, they could pay to use his body for a couple of hours, and that he would even be grateful for the opportunity.

The man's gloved hands came up in a defensive gesture. "It's nothing sordid if that's what you're thinking."

"I don't care. Keep it moving, before I lose my temper with you."

"Very well." The man furnished Justin with a placating smile, and said, "But before I do, I just want to reassure you that I'm not after anything... sexual. I have a legitimate business opportunity for you."

So, he was a Christian, was that it? A Jesus freak that wanted him to come and stay at the church or something like that? He'd had similar offers in the past, all of which ended up sounding as though he were being inducted into a cult that would cost him a lot more than it paid.

"I don't want to know," Justin said, and found himself glancing down the underpass, hoping that someone else would come walking by and spook this creep off. Beneath the blankets, Justin's hand spider-walked to the neck of a broken Heineken bottle he kept there for emergencies such as this.

"You don't want to know about earning twenty-five grand for one week's work? You don't want to know about a hot bath, a haircut, a bellyful of food, a warm bed?" He pulled a face and shrugged, as if to say, well, I tried my best, and added, "Alright. In that case, I bid you farewell."

The man walked off, trailing the delicate yet powerful scent of expensive cologne that was apparent even over the damp stink in the underpass. He left whistling, and Justin only recognized the tune when the stranger had neared the mouth of the underpass. It was *The Godfather*.

Justin was fairly sure that the sheepskin coat had been real. The gloves seemed expensive too, as did the shoes. And did the man seem like a queer? Justin didn't think so. He'd been wrong before, but right then and there, he didn't think so.

"Hey," Justin shouted, his voice ricocheting toward the man. The man stopped mid-step, turned, and pointed at his own chest. *Me?* "Wait a minute. Are you talking about a job-job? Like a real job?"

"As real as you and I," the man said, and for some reason, that didn't seem like an odd answer to Justin at the time. It did later on, but by then, it was too late.

"What kind of work is it?" Justin asked, and even from a distance, he saw the man's grin stretch across his face.

CHAPTER 24

They were called to the Circle Room just over an hour after their second excruciating game of Monopoly. The dull drone of the speaker's voice was a welcome reprieve from the icy silence of the game. The only time anyone spoke was to wish Amanda good luck before she rolled her dice, and then to congratulate her when she finished her go, even if she went straight to jail, which they immediately dismissed.

When they shuffled into the Circle Room, Arthur said, "Thank god Monopoly's over. It made me realize how much I absolutely loathe that bloody game."

"Only because you were losing," Sherry huffed, as they played musical chairs, bidding for the spot next to Amanda.

"You know, the last time I played Monopoly was with my sister when we were about nine or ten," Arthur continued. "I got so worked up, I could have killed her. I mean, I think I really could have killed her in that instant."

Ding-dong.

"Good evening, ladies and gentlemen. We hope you are enjoying your stay. Please listen carefully for the instructions of your second assignment." A brief pause. "Please assemble yourselves into two groups of three. You will have an hour to complete the assignment. All parties must agree on the groups. Failure to comply will result in a forfeit."

They waited for more. The hiss dampened in the speaker, and then the room was silent.

"Then what?" Arthur asked. "Assemble ourselves into two groups and then what?"

"We might have to do the first half of the assignment before they tell us anything else," Claude suggested.

"Me, Amanda, and Wish," Justin fired. "There you go, done." Then to the camera, he yelled, "We're done."

"It most certainly is not done," Sherry bellowed, turning on Justin. She looked as though she was getting ready to pick him up and snap him like kindling. "Excuse me young man, but you don't get to call the shots here. This is a *group* assignment. And we all have to agree."

"Fine. Me, Amanda, and you then," he replied, shrugging dismissively.

What happened next unfurled like a scene from a wacky cartoon: Wish and Arthur began to vomit a tirade of abuse at Justin, their arms flailing, their faces clouding with rage. Amanda and Claude remained seated, watching the scene descend further into madness.

"Don't you dare think for one second that you're in charge here, little boy," Arthur said, enunciating each syllable, his voice trembling. "Because from where I'm standing, you're not in charge of a bloody thing!"

"I don't care what any of you say. I'm going on Amanda's team," Wish said, raising her hand like a child in a classroom.

"We all want to go on Amanda's team for Christ's sake." Arthur's hands balled into fists so tight that his knobbly knuckles whitened. With a great deal of difficulty, he inhaled, and there was an audible rattle in his throat. "But you don't just get to announce it. That's not how it works!"

"Then how does it work?" Sherry said, spittle flying from her lips. "And don't you go raising your voice like you're talking to a bunch of children either. Because I'll tell you for free, I've had it up to here with you." She stuck her hand out level with her forehead.

They continued to argue, creating a cacophony of curses and

undecipherable babble. The argument evolved into a peculiar four-way dance that saw them push and pull at each other, bordering dangerously close to physical violence.

"Believe me now?" Claude asked Amanda. She almost didn't hear him over the clamour.

"They're like a..." She wanted to say *pack of wild dogs*, but couldn't quite get the words out. She was mesmerized by the display, entranced at the intensity of their entitlement. The only thing she could clearly distinguish from the rabid din was the name "Amanda", barked from their snapping jaws.

Arthur broke away from the melee, picked up his chair and slammed it down on the ground. The boom of the impact erupted in the Circle Room, and instinctively, Amanda reached out and grabbed hold of Claude's hand. He quickly pulled it free of her grasp.

"Don't," he said without looking at her. "Not in front of them."

"I think you're forgetting something." Arthur, who was able to project his voice the loudest, won their attention. "They said all parties need to agree, and we only have an hour to do it or we forfeit funds."

"You're the one that heard wrong, you silly old bastard." Justin stabbed a finger in the air at him. "It didn't say we would forfeit funds, just forfeit. What are they going to do? Take away our alcohol? Turn the hot water off? Who gives a fuck?"

"I don't want to forfeit *anything*," Arthur returned, "especially as I don't know what it is I'm going to be bloody forfeiting."

Sherry ran her fingers through her frizzy hair and shook her head. "Alright, alright, come on now, let's get sensible." She stuck out her arms, appointing herself as the referee. "Now let's just hold on and think about this. We're not going to get anywhere like this, so we need to just take a little chill pill and gather ourselves." She inhaled deeply like a yoga instructor before a class, and then rubbed her hands together. "Problem and solution. The problem is that we can't decide who gets to go with Amanda. So, what's the solution?"

Nobody offered anything, until eventually Wish said, "I'm going on Amanda's team. Nobody is going to talk me out of it. She picked me the other day, so that means I should be with her. That is common sense."

"Oh, that doesn't mean a fucking thing," Sherry said, "and I'm sick of you using that as your little trump card. The real issue is that you feel special, and that's because–"

"Because what?" Wish's head cocked to the side. "Because what? You might as well say what is on your mind, no?"

"Yeah," Sherry laughed humourlessly, "I'll say it. Because you're the only black one here and you think you deserve special treatment. And with that silly fucking accent you think that makes you somehow better – yes, better than us."

"You're a stupid ugly cow," Wish spat back before cackling contemptuously. "Look at you. Fat lonely idiot, never done nothing with her life. Why don't you do what you do best – go in the corner and cry like a baby."

"There's that sassy black attitude," Sherry said, her neck winding as she spoke. "I was wondering how long it'd take to show up. Bravo! You'd better watch your mouth before I break it like your back, you fucking stripper."

"Whoa, Jesus, Sherry. That's way out of line," Claude intervened, standing between them with his arms outstretched as Wish began cursing vehemently in French. She slashed an arm through the air trying to get at Sherry, who taunted her in return.

"I'm out of line?" Sherry began sidestepping Claude, hoping to find an opening and charge at Wish. "Tell this stupid stripper, or do you prefer the term *exotic dancer*? You're a whore in anybody's book!"

Wish lunged like a cat, clambering up on Claude as he struggled to referee, her vitriol manifesting in a boiling broth of English and French.

Amanda could feel screws tightening in her skull, the tension centring in her forehead and burrowing deep into her brain like an engorged maggot chomping through an apple core. The acoustics of the room made it feel like their voices were assailing her from every direction. Each time someone yelled, she cringed, and the screws did a full turn in her temples.

"Will you stop it!" Amanda screamed, and as her voice ricocheted around the room, Wish and Sherry immediately fell silent and stood to attention, panting raggedly. "Both of you, just..." The enthusiasm to regain control fled as suddenly as it arrived, leaving her tired and slightly giddy. "Will you both just stop?"

The unbearably awkward silence that followed stretched until Claude eventually said, "I have a solution. If any of you wants to listen and behave like adults, I have a solution that will make this thing fair for everyone and then we can pass the assignment, hopefully, without killing each other."

"Oh, I just bet you do, lover boy," Justin said, his face a landscape of furrows and creases that aged his otherwise boyish features. "You might think you're some kind of Romeo, but I can see straight through you. You've been trying to sniff her knickers since the minute you got in here and don't you try to deny it."

"Does he speak for all of you?" Claude asked the others, regarding them one by one. "If he does, I'll shut my mouth and let you lot keep arguing until the time runs down and we fail." He shrugged, looked at his wristwatch. "But you've already spent almost half an hour down that road so let me know, and I'll just save my breath."

"Half an hour?" Arthur's jowls shook as he spoke. He looked up at the camera before casting a worried glance at Amanda. "We're already halfway through."

Claude zipped his lips, locked them, and threw away the key.

"That twerp doesn't speak for the group," Arthur insisted. "He isn't the leader."

"More of a leader than you," Justin said, petulantly.

"Yes, sitting up in your room wanking over *Tomb Raider* while your mum prepares dinner. I can already see the leadership qualities clear as day," Arthur returned.

"Will you shut up and listen to Claude?" Amanda said. She had not wanted to get involved in their squabble; if truth be told, her anxiety had escalated along with their vehemence, but she could not stand another half an hour of this utter madness. She wanted to get out of the room and away from them.

Her words struck them like a gavel, and they were immediately silent. They *obeyed* her. She realized then that they would do anything she asked, and the prospect intimidated her. She did not want to be their cult leader. She did not want a flock of devoted followers. She already had John Meadows in Birmingham with tattoos of her face on his body, and that was plenty.

Claude got up from the chair, keeping his distance from them. "We have to split ourselves into two groups, three in each group. The problem is, only two of you can be on Amanda's team."

"Me," Wish muttered. "I already said that from the start."

Claude ignored her. "So, unless anyone else can think of an easier, fairer way to go about it, why don't we do egg and bacon?"

"Egg and... what are you on about?" Sherry asked.

"Amanda and I will be the group captains," he explained. But before he got any further, Justin shunted in.

"No way. You don't think I know what you're up to?"

"Put a sock in it," Arthur hissed. "He's saying he won't be on her team. Why don't you try using these." Arthur pulled on his own earlobes.

"We'll go on the other side of the room," Claude continued. "One of us will be egg, the other bacon, but we won't tell you until the end. Then, between the four of you, all you have to decide is which two will be egg and which two will be bacon. When you've agreed, Amanda and I will reveal which we are, and, you know, egg goes with egg, bacon with bacon." He frowned. "You're all looking at me like I'm speaking Arabic. What's so difficult about what I'm saying?"

"But how do we know which one Amanda will be?" Justin asked.

"You don't, that's the whole point," Amanda said. "That's what makes it fair."

"No." Justin shook his head. "No, sorry, I'm not doing it."

Claude looked at his watch. It was coming up to 20:40. He sighed and said, "Fine, then you think of something. But we have just over twenty minutes to get this done."

"You're going to try to cheat me," Justin snarled. "You're going to try to make it so that I don't end up with her, no matter what."

Claude exhaled. "Personally, I don't give a shit about this task, but I don't want to forfeit anything, especially when the task is so easy a group of five year-olds could do it."

Just as they seemed about to comply, Wish said something that Amanda didn't quite catch. Judging by the way they broke apart and started arguing afresh, she assumed Wish had reiterated her right to be on Amanda's team.

"Fifteen minutes." Claude tapped his watch.

"Come on guys," Amanda said, "this is getting boring now. Let's just get this done and have some dinner. I'm starving."

Gradually, they shambled to the opposite end of the Circle Room like a herd of scorned sheep. When they were out of earshot, Claude said, "You see it now? There's no denying it. They're obsessed with you and they don't even know why. It's like they're under a spell."

"You think that the pill's making them crazy?"

"Crazy about you, yeah."

"But what kind of drug is it? Have you ever heard of anything like this before?"

"No. Not ever."

"We've got to tell them then." She became aware of how thirsty she was and could almost feel fresh sweat pushing up through her pores.

"Do you think they'll listen?"

"I don't know. But they're acting like a bunch of fucking psychos. One of them is going to do something stupid soon, I can feel it. And what if they do get into a fight or hurt each other? What happens then? You think these Midori people are going to jump in and separate them?"

As if on cue, Sherry released a shrill shriek of defiance, and Arthur thumped the wall. There was a lot of head shaking and hissing, punctuated with sudden outbursts and exclamations.

"They don't even know why they want to be close to you, they just do. Look at them. They seem like the same people we met on Sunday night but it's like their whole personality has altered to centre on you." Claude shook his head, amazed. "Was it like this when you were famous?"

"No," Amanda said quietly. "Not even when I sold out the O2 and had people waiting outside the arena for autographs. They wanted to see me, or even touch me, but it wasn't like this. This is… this is something else."

Claude nodded. "So, it's some kind of love potion. You think that's it?"

"Whatever they have for me isn't love. How can it be? They've known me for five minutes. They're not being nice to me because they like me, they're doing it to satisfy themselves. It's just some sort of…"

"Selfish impulse," Claude finished. He checked his watch and called to the other side of the room. "Ten minutes. Speed it up, guys."

"Will you shut up?" Sherry volleyed back, grabbing two fistfuls of hair. "Do you think we need this pressure from you?"

Claude sighed and said to Amanda, "You try."

Amanda got to her feet and clapped her hands. "Time's up. Come on."

At the sound of her voice, they broke out of the huddle and straightened. Their expressions were placid, the muscles in their faces slack. *Zombies*, she thought. *The pill is turning them into a horde of zombies.*

Claude stood by her side, leaned close to her ear, and said, "I'll be egg, you be bacon." Then, to the others he said. "Which two are bacon?"

Nobody spoke. They just stood there, bristling with anticipation, and Claude imagined that the adrenaline would be pumping hotly through their muscles, setting their heartrates galloping.

"I said, which two are bacon?"

With the care and concentration of tightrope walkers, Justin and Wish slowly stepped forward, their eyes locked on Amanda. Justin looked to be chewing something angrily, and Claude thought it was probably his tongue. Wish wiped her palms on her sheer blouse, leaving dark grey smears.

"Wish, Justin," Claude began and saw them gulp in unison. Wish opened her mouth and gasped like a fish out of water. "You're in Amanda's group."

A riot of sound rushed through the Circle Room. The cries of protest clashed against the screams of delight, creating an ugly, hysterical whirlwind. As Wish and Justin celebrated, racing over to Amanda hand in hand, a chair sailed through the air and bounced off the wall.

"No," Arthur bellowed, his shoulders heaving. "This isn't fair. We need rules, real rules to dictate how we do this, not some ignorant children's game."

"You lost," Justin countered, one arm around Wish, another looped around Amanda. "You lost fair and square so get fucked. These are the groups."

"Oh really?" Arthur, teeth bared, stomped to the centre of the room. "I disagree."

"I don't like this at all," Sherry said, pacing in the corner like a caged panther, coiling her hair tightly around her finger. "I want a do-over."

"No do-over, you lost, and we are with Amanda," Wish proclaimed, and shimmied on the spot, winding her waist rhythmically in a victory dance. "Boo-hoo, you don't like it, go and cry, ugly cow."

Jostled between her new group members, Amanda could see Arthur's and Sherry's complexions drastically darkening, as though the blood vessels were bursting in their faces. She tried to say something about how it was a fair deal, but her words were drowned amidst Justin singing the chorus of "We Are the Champions."

"You rigged this," Sherry accused Claude, clawing at her billowy shirt as though about to rip it straight off her body. Her breath chugged out of her like fumes from a broken exhaust, and coupled with her frighteningly dark complexion, Amanda feared she was about to have a heart attack.

Amanda wriggled out of Justin's grasp. "Sherry, calm down," she said, crossing the room with the caution of a person approaching a wounded animal. "There's no need to get worked up. Come on, why don't you sit down?"

"Worked up? Worked up?" White globules collected in the corners of her mouth. "We've been cheated. We've–" She drew saliva from the back of her throat and spat it on the floor. Amanda flinched away, disgusted. "That's what I think of this assignment. It's less than shit to me."

Amanda became giddy, the stress gnawing at her, pulling her down.

"Rules! We need real, tangible rules, not some Micky Mouse–" Arthur's declaration was cut short by the voice on the speaker, who Amanda had begun to think of as the Overlord.

"You have now exceeded the time limit. Have you all come to an agreement on the groups?"

A clash of disagreeing yells filled the room.

"No, we don't agree on the groups," Arthur said, unmovable in his stance.

"Yes, we do," Justin countered. "We do. The group is me, Wish, and Amanda."

"No, it *isn't*," Sherry yelled, her voice thick with injustice. "NO IT IS NOT! We don't agree on the groups at all."

"You're going to fuck this all up," Justin threatened, but before he could say any more, the Overlord spoke again.

"As you have been unable to reach a final decision regarding the groups, within the specified time limit, you will now face a forfeit. You are free to go."

There was a low hiss, and then silence. For almost a full minute, nobody spoke.

"Well done." Wish gave Arthur and Sherry a mock round of applause. "Now you have got us all in trouble because you are so selfish. I hope you are proud of yourselves."

"Fuck them and fuck you," Sherry said, slashing a hand through the air.

"Arthur," Justin called as Arthur was heading toward the door. "If this forfeit is something bad, I'm going to beat the shit out of you, you got it? No ifs, no buts, I'm just going to thrash the fucking life out of you."

"I'm quivering in my bloomers," Arthur muttered.

A tide of unreality swept Amanda out of the room. She flashed back to that night at The Butterfly Lounge, coked out of her mind, the music too loud, the lights flashing frenetically. In that moment, she hadn't felt real, but more like an avatar in someone else's dream. Now, that uneasy sense of helplessness swirled within her again.

She was in a madhouse and she had no control.

And there were still five days to go.

CHAPTER 25

It was time to rehearse.

Arthur sat on the edge of his cot, his eyeballs aching in their sockets, heavy as snooker balls from the tiredness. He hadn't been sleeping well, only managing to nod off for snatches at a time, before jerking awake with his mind racing a million miles a second. That inability to think coherently had to be due to his new environment; the frigid air, the tough mattress, the infuriating itchiness of the blanket's weave. Of course, one also couldn't discount the eerie silence that seemed to be constantly swelling through the house, which was somehow more intrusive than it was soothing. He was used to falling asleep to the city ambience, lulled by the symphonic dissonance of traffic and chatter. Now the lack of noise was conspiring against him, keeping him awake deep into the night. Except...

Except none of that was true. Lying on that mattress was like floating on a cloud compared to the sodden sofa in the Shaftsbury Avenue alleyway. And it wasn't like sleeping in a house full of strangers was any worse than having pedestrians step over him as they made their commute to work.

He stood up with his knees popping loudly and began to pace up and down his room with his bare feet slapping the cold floor.

"There are fields of daffodils beneath a blazing hot sun, where the taste of cider dances in the mouth, and at night – that great purveyor of death, an endless ocean of stars dim in the presence of your smile..." Whispering the monologue went against his training, and his body urged him to project, to parade his voice so that it stirred the fine hairs of the audience members in the back row, but of course, that was not an option now. Anyway, he had the first couple of lines pinned down, but it had taken all his mental dexterity to compose them. Out of necessity, he had long since stopped using a pen and paper to concoct his monologues, choosing to draft, rewrite and memorize his work instead. It had developed a keen mental muscle, one that had never failed him before. Yet, now, the stress of coming up with a new burst of words that might somehow convey the complexity of his feelings was provoking a rather tremendous migraine.

He massaged his temples, hoping to find gaps in the roaring chaos of his thoughts. *"Amanda,"* he said, pronouncing the syllables with extra care, intoxicated by the way they rolled from the back of his throat, vibrating in his mouth, before sliding from his tongue. Speaking her name was like a magical incantation that brought a gentle stillness inside him. He conjured her image; a beautiful, smiling apparition, extending her hand, so that they might both take a bow together before the audience, before the world. It didn't matter that she was less than half his age. She was his muse, his motivation, his ambition, and his redemption; these things were much more important than fickle concepts like lust. He just had to be near her, to appease her, so that she might shower him with her glow. If he could really hold her hand then, as they say, fortune would smile upon him again.

Arthur had only ever been in love once before. As an undergraduate theatre student, he had fallen deeply for Tracey Wells, a stunning blonde beauty who went on to do a bit of TV and some film walk-ons, before trading the cutthroat world of acting for the humdrum life of a housewife. Her last role had been in 1992, as a barmaid in a long-forgotten police drama series. He'd been besotted with Tracey, enamoured with her charisma, enthralled by her talent, but had never had the courage to put himself on the line and tell her as much. He made a promise to himself that he would do it on the last day of term, and when that failed, he swore he would announce his feelings at their graduation ceremony. But he never did. Eight years later, balding, and unable to rein in his ballooning belly, he married Linda Humes, whom he had never really loved and barely even liked. A year later, she was pregnant with Frazer; five years after that, she was filing for divorce, emigrating to Canada, and engaged to a new man who had started off as a pen pal of all things. Arthur had not tried to stop her. As a selfish, barely working actor, he felt a sense of mild relief at their departure, that the loss of their weight might offer him the necessary freedom to finally fly.

The big break never came.

Arthur had only seen his son once since then, and that was a photograph of the boy's seventh birthday. He was tall and handsome, but it was difficult to know from the slightly blurry picture whether he resembled Arthur or not.

It wasn't productive thinking of that now. Arthur shook it away and recalibrated his focus.

"Amanda. Am-an-da."

Throughout the day, it was easy to steal glimpses of her, providing the necessary sustenance for his imagination. At breakfast, he had sat across from her and caught the timing of her chewing – *the machinations of her masticating*, he thought, committing that witty line to memory and hoping to relay it to her later, when they were alone. She would get a *real* laugh out of that, not like the polite titters she gave that bloated dumb oaf Sherry whenever she tried cracking one of her useless jokes.

He did another lap of the room, lightly punching himself in the side of the skull, hoping that it might kickstart the machinery. "There are fields of daffodils beneath a blazing sun," he began again, and groaned as he encountered a blank. He rested his forehead against the door, could almost feel the *thump-thump* of his migraine vibrating against the metal.

It was useless. Better to go with what he knew. *The Merchant of Venice*. He could knock her socks off with that. If it was good enough to calm a lunatic like Mad Ronald down from one of his tempers, then it would work wonders with Amanda. Arthur was certain of it.

"'The quality of mercy is not strain'd. It droppeth as the gentle rain from heaven upon the place beneath. It is twice blest: It blesseth him that gives and him that takes.'" He recited it like a prayer, his strength growing, his confidence mushrooming. He didn't think there was a working actor alive today that could recite *The Merchant of Venice* better than he.

All he needed was the courage this time. Arthur couldn't afford to play the cowardly lion again. He'd been a coward his whole life and the only thing it had brought him was a demolished sofa in an alleyway. Fear had stripped him of any happiness he might've attained, but if there was ever a time to change it all, by god, it was now. Here in this house.

I just want to hold her hand, he thought, though this scene morphed into an embrace, and at once, he imagined the scent of coconut shampoo that he'd smelled on her hair as he passed her in the kitchen.

Quietly, he turned the doorknob and poked his head out into the darkness of the hallway, half expecting one of the others to be standing there already. Seeing that he was alone, Arthur stepped out of his room, and padded down to Amanda's. With one quivering hand, he reached out and touched the plaque on her door, his fingers tracing the grooves of her name.

AMANDA.

His heart bumped in his chest. Something like a shiver ran from his scalp down to the soles of his feet, causing him to cringe violently, pulling a small sigh from his mouth. His hand deviated from the plaque, found the doorknob, and rested there. She had touched this doorknob, left traces of her energy on it. Impulsively, without really considering what he was doing, Arthur bent over and licked the doorknob. The taste of metal brought him back to his senses, and confusion flowed through him. He wasn't sure why he had done that, but he wasn't exactly sure he regretted it either.

All it would take is a twist and then he could go inside… go inside…

Go inside and do what?

Not sure, he thought. But soon, he would play his hand, *The Merchant of Venice*, and he had a good idea that it would seal the deal. She would see the magnificence of his talent and lend him her friendship, her support, her positivity, and with that, he could conquer the world. It was never too late to start again.

"Everybody wants to be somebody," he whispered, unable to keep the words locked behind his lips. Swallowing, he released the doorknob.

Not now, he thought. *But soon.*

CHAPTER 26

Amanda had been in bed for hours when she finally gave up. She couldn't seem to switch off, to block out the carousel of worrying thoughts that spun through her tired mind. She had climbed out of bed three separate times to check that her bedroom door was locked. When she returned to the mattress, struggling to settle into a comfortable position, she found herself undressing her current predicament. When she waded through the sludge, it really came down to this: they had her over a barrel. They had done their due diligence on her, acquired knowledge of her dire financial situation, and then they had taken advantage of her. And when she broke it down, analyzing it from the outside, it made her feel cheap. So now what could she do? She couldn't leave, because that would be breach of contract. Perhaps she would be in better position to bargain if she hadn't snatched up that twenty-five grand advance and paid off her credit card bill and her backdated council taxes. As it stood, all she had really done is transfer her debts to Midori, and for the rest of the week, she was at the mercy of the Overlord.

In the darkness of her room, Amanda began to feel smothered with worry. She had often sat on the edge of her mattress as she did now, head in her hands, wondering how things had gone bad so quickly. The fame had disintegrated gradually, and she had been able to feel it slipping away like sand passing through her fingers. It had been that awful feeling of transition – going from being somebody that people cared about, to somebody that people laughed at – that hurt her the most, because it wasn't fair. Being recognized and adored was a harder habit to kick than coke, and the withdrawal symptoms far more severe. Yet here she was, theoretically rich again, with a cluster of people that apparently loved her, and it felt terrible.

Then it occurred to her, realization popping in her head like a firework. This wasn't just a group of random strangers. They were a group of failures, to one degree or another. She was a one-hit wonder, scrambling for her handful of sand, trying to reclaim her glory. Arthur was an actor who had been grafting for years and probably still worked other jobs to make ends meet. Sherry was a comedian who hadn't given them the slightest inclination that she had a funny bone in her body. Wish was a damaged dancer who was now unable to make a living off her talent. Justin was a YouTube nerd who had a sizeable online following, but hadn't there been a ring of truth to Arthur's jibes? He was still just a boy living in his mum's house, making videos in his bedroom.

And then there was Claude. A used car salesman. The civilian among them. He was the only one that didn't really seem to fit in with the showbiz group dynamic. He was also apparently the only one who wasn't completely enamoured with her. Why was that? Why would they choose to give the drug to the others and a placebo to him and her?

Something wasn't right and it bothered her like an itch in the back of her mind. She drifted about the room with the blanket wrapped around her shoulders, trying to make sense of it. Had Claude given her any reason not to trust him? Well, there was the secret passageway that only he seemed to know about. Why would they be communicating with him, offering up all the house's secrets? Now that she mulled it over in the silence of her room, she realized that something just didn't ring true.

He had lied, she was almost sure of it, although she had no real evidence to strengthen the notion. It was just delayed intuition, and now that she had settled on the idea, she had to find out why. She didn't know what time it was and didn't particularly care if he was sleeping. She slid the bolt back and opened the door. Cold air whistled into the room as she stepped out onto the landing, her feet encased in blocks of ice.

The house was pitch black, and she waited a moment for her eyes to adjust to the darkness. Claude's door was the last one on the left. She placed her fingertips on the wall and felt her way down the landing, listening to the ghostly whisper of the wind as it haunted the hallways. She felt along the ridges of Wish's door, could hear her snoring softly beyond it, and carried on.

Two steps later, and her fingers made contact with something solid. She stopped, tentatively touched the shape in the darkness. It was an arm.

Rather than scream, the terror seized hold of her breath and pulled it violently back down her throat, squeezing it in her chest. She choked on her fear, hiccupping on her breath, backing away from the person she had touched.

"Calm down," a cold voice said.

It was Justin.

"Wh–what are you..." she panted, whispering fiercely. "What are you doing out here?"

"I had to use the toilet," he said. He hadn't been moving when she touched him. He had been pressed against the wall between the bedrooms. It was almost as if he meant to go undetected as she walked by.

"What are you doing up?" he asked.

"Toilet," she lied, walking past him.

"Do you want me to come with you?"

"What for?"

He didn't answer, his silhouette as still as a cardboard cutout.

"Go back to bed," she said, her heart still pounding. "I'll be fine."

"As long as you're sure," he said, slowly. "Alright then. Goodnight."

"Goodnight," she said, and carried on to the bathroom.

Justin returned to bed, although he knew sleeping would be an impossibility. His brain was a kaleidoscope of unfinished thoughts. Every time he closed his eyes, he imagined him and Amanda in one scenario or another. The most prevalent fantasy he had painted in his imagination was a simple one: he and Amanda were walking down a nice, clean suburban street on an autumn day, the sun lowering on the horizon, casting the neighbourhood in an orange-pink hue. They were holding hands and talking casually. He was saying something to make her giggle, and through the laughter, she would reach out and swat him playfully. Then, for no reason at all, she would stop them dead in the middle of the street, the sunset giving her a golden aura. "I'm so glad that I found you," she would say, so sincerely that to him it looked like her dark eyes were about to well up with tears of joy. Then, she would lean in so that he could smell the faint coconut fragrance of her shampoo, and their lips would meet. Her full, wonderfully soft lips would slowly part, and then her tongue would enter his mouth.

So far, he hadn't been able to build anything beyond a kiss, before imagining something else: him and Amanda sitting in Pizza Hut, him and Amanda planted on the couch at his house watching Netflix, him and Amanda playing video games. No matter what he thought about, it always featured Amanda.

He thought it might have been love at first sight, but when he tried to trace it back, he realized that the constant fixation really only started yesterday. He had seen her in the games room beneath the glow of the pool table light, and it was as though a switch flipped on inside his brain. He couldn't look at her without staring. His stomach became fluttery, his face breaking out in gooseflesh, the hairs stirring on the nape of his neck. She had infected his thoughts like a virus, and now he was feverish for her.

Something was wrong with him; he knew that much. He had held secret crushes for girls at school, been smitten over women he met online, had even thought he was in love with the waitress at Sergio's Italian Bakery. But he had never experienced an emotion so forcefully. The excitement bubbled in his blood, his skin prickling as though covered in static, and he frequently shuddered from the sensation until he thought he would scream or burst into hysterical and uncontrollable laughter. At one point, he thought he was going to come involuntarily.

And yet, beneath it all, he was frightened. He wasn't sure why exactly, not when he had so much to look forward to with Amanda, but beyond the butterflies in his stomach, there was a low thrum of apprehension. He could feel himself changing, his thoughts bending and reforming against his will.

He realized that he was in love with Amanda Pearson. He knew this with unwavering certainty, and once he had acknowledged it, it presented him with some rather difficult questions. If he failed to win her over in the next few days, then how would he see her again once they left the house? If she rejected him outright, then was it worth going on at all?

"Shh, don't think that," he said aloud with only the darkness to hear him.

There was always the chance that he could *make* her love him. He didn't really have any idea of how to go about it, but he supposed that some grand gesture was needed, a declaration of his love to show just how serious he was about her. He had to do something, and he had to do it quickly, because if he was honest with himself, he knew that the others were already plotting against him. Arthur was a big, bumbling idiot, far too old to be any kind of real rival, but Claude was a different story entirely. Claude was closer to Amanda's age than he was. Claude was taller, and, for fuck's sake let's just get it out in the open, he was *handsome*. In the sanctuary of his own mind, Justin could readily accept that Claude was a good-looking bastard, and he had been spending an awful lot of time with her. Claude had become close to her in a way that Justin hadn't been able to, and it physically sickened him.

Then another thought boomed out of the darkness and hit him like a lightning bolt. He snapped up into a sitting position, his fists full of bedsheet, his teeth clenched so tightly together that the lining of his jaw throbbed.

What if she's falling for Claude?

"No," he panted, shaking his head. He ripped the blanket off himself, picked up the pillow and placed it over his face. Somehow, he held back a scream, but the effort made his neck inflate painfully. The anger pulsed inside him like a living organ. He threw the pillow and then brought his hand up to his mouth and bit down on it. He sank his teeth deep into the flesh until he could taste blood and feel the grinding of his metatarsals. He leapt up, every muscle in his body taut, his heart like a cannonball in his chest. His first thought was to go straight to the kitchen and get a knife. Then he would creep back up to Claude's room and make him look ugly. He would pin him down and draw on Claude's face with the blade, and then poke his eyes out with the tip of the knife and then–

What was he thinking?

He stood there, panting in the darkness, quivering all over. He felt nauseous, the bile slowly working its way up his oesophagus. He swallowed it back down, burning his throat, and gasped for air. In that one moment of madness, he had seriously contemplated disfiguring Claude, could even envision himself holding the knife, the blood dribbling over his hands, Claude's petrified screams filling his ears. Now that it had passed, Justin became very afraid.

As quietly as he could, he left his room and made his way down the landing.

He had been comfortable standing outside her room earlier, wondering if she was asleep, hoping that she was dreaming about him. He had found it peaceful. Now, he stood directly outside her room again, his hand tentatively reaching out to touch her door. His fingertips made contact, and he immediately felt a gentle balm of relief passing over him, slowing his heartbeat, stilling his thoughts.

He mouthed her name, and slowly slid to the floor. Touching the door was good enough.

For now.

CHAPTER 27

WEDNESDAY: 20 MILLIGRAMS
They lined up in the Circle Room, the nurse in the white uniform and mask holding the tray of pills. Amanda watched as the others took their pill without question. Each time one of them had gone to take a sip of water, she had wanted to scream at them to spit it out. When they had their mouths inspected, Amanda's nervousness increased. She began to feel like that nineteen year-old from Croydon about to step on stage, ready to sing her heart out live on TV.

When it was her turn, she picked the pill out of the dish and held it on the tip of her finger, inspecting it. Strangely, she felt no trepidation at placing it on her tongue. It was a placebo, and so was the pill in Claude's dish, she was sure of it. That was the only thing that made sense. The rest of them were taking some kind of acute endorphin enhancer. She didn't know how it worked or what signals it was sending through their brains, but she knew it was making them sick. They were beginning to look drained and faded somehow, as though the pill were leeching their vitality day by day.

She picked up the water, took a sip. The others stood in a pack, studying her with bloodshot stares. When they had all taken their pill, the nurse took the tray and disappeared behind the curtain.

They stood a few paces behind Amanda, shuffling along after her as she made her way out of the Circle Room. Rather than head for the kitchen, Amanda went in the opposite direction, heading back to the ground floor staircase.

"Where are you going?" Justin asked. "You're not going to have breakfast?"

"I am," Amanda said. "But I'm having a shower first."

"Good idea," Wish said eagerly. "I'll come with you."

"And me," Sherry said, "us girls have to keep clean."

Amanda halted, turned on her heels to face them. "I'd like to shower by myself if that's alright?"

"Why?" Wish recoiled as if Amanda had struck her.

"Because I do," Amanda told her irritably. "So, you guys go on and have breakfast and I'll be back down in a bit."

"I think I'm going to shower with you," Sherry said. "I mean, there's enough room, and it's not like we'll be invading each other's privacy, is it?"

"I don't think that's the point," Claude said. "She wants some time to herself."

Wish's head snapped toward Claude, and for a second, an ugly grimace flickered on her face. It completely changed the landscape of her otherwise flawless features. "The shower room is for all of us, you know. What do you think we are doing? Breaking the law?"

"Can't I just have ten minutes alone?" Amanda said, palming her forehead. She was sweating as though she had just run a half-marathon. She didn't *feel* sick, but her body seemed to be displaying all the symptoms of a fever. She did feel warmer than usual, and she assumed that her headache was more the result of another bad night's sleep.

"I'm sorry Amanda," Sherry began sweetly, "but you don't own the showers."

"Yeah I know, it's just–"

"What do you think we are going to do? Try to have sex with you?" Wish said before breaking up with laughter.

"Yes, I like you Amanda," Sherry said, her tone amiable, "but not enough to turn into a full-blown lesbian over it, am I right?"

They giggled together, and then Sherry held up her hand for

a high-five. When Wish slapped it, Amanda thought it was just about the weirdest gesture she had ever seen. She didn't stick around to watch any more of it.

"Do you need us for anything?" Arthur called, struggling to sound pleasant. "Perhaps *we* can wash your backs?"

"Not fucking likely," Sherry shouted from the staircase.

"I think we need to establish some ground rules," Justin said, leaning against the kitchen counter while Claude buttered his toast.

"Ground rules?" Claude looked at him contemptuously, before returning to the shelves to hunt for the marmite.

"Yes. Something me and Arthur were discussing. Weren't we Arthur?"

Arthur uncapped a bottle of whiskey and poured a large measure into his black coffee. "Quite."

Claude scraped marmite over his toast. "You have a problem with me I guess?"

"You're not as dumb as you look." Justin's hand slapped Claude in the centre of the back, pushing him forward.

Claude set the knife down and turned to Justin. He wanted to keep the boy in full view, just in case he had any ideas of throwing some kind of cheap shot at him. "If you have a problem, I'll hear it."

"We don't like that you sit next to Amanda all the time," Justin said. "And don't try to deny it either, because we've been watching you. We've seen how you worm your way in at the breakfast table, or in the Circle Room. You're like her fucking shadow. So, no more of it, you hear? It ends now."

Claude could scarcely believe what he was hearing. He smiled, sure that at any second Justin would return the gesture and they would break up laughing, because surely he was pulling Claude's leg. But Justin didn't smile. He didn't quite look capable of it even if he had wanted to. Purple grooves carved the flesh beneath his eyes, standing out against his ashen grey complexion. He was breathing heavily through his nose, grunting like a bull.

"With all due respect, I don't think that's a law you can enforce, Justin. You see, you can't tell me what to do, or who to sit next to." Claude looked across at Arthur and saw the older man chomping down on his thumbnail, frantically clipping at it with his front teeth. "We're all adults here."

"I need you to understand something," Justin said, gripping the counter, a blue vein visible on his temple through his almost translucent skin. "We know what you're trying to do. And we don't like it. Now, you can either take this friendly warning. Or..."

"Or what?" Claude straightened. He turned his attention to Arthur. "Come on, Arthur, don't be shy now. What's going to happen?"

Arthur removed his thumb from his mouth and spat a chip of nail to the floor. "We'll have to hurt you," he said, without menace.

"Hurt me?" Claude barked laughter. "Well let's have it now, then." He stretched out his arms. "Come on. You want to be tough guys? Let's have it now."

"Why don't you just take the warning," Justin said. "Amanda is out of bounds from now on. No more secret rendezvous, no more sitting together like a pair of schoolgirls."

"No more private jokes," Arthur added. "In fact, it would be best if you just didn't speak to her at all anymore."

"Or you'll hurt me, is that it?"

"Yes," Justin said. "And you'd better believe it."

Claude stood there a moment longer, trying to process what he'd been told. "Is there anything else? Any more rules you want to run by me?"

"You can do whatever you want in here," Justin replied. "But as of right now, Amanda is out of bounds. I don't even want to see you looking at her."

"No looking," Arthur agreed.

They stared at him with eyes as dull and lifeless as old buttons. Perhaps it was a trick of the misty morning light, but Claude thought Arthur's brow looked more prominent today, Neanderthal almost. The crows' feet scraped out from the corners of his eyes, and a network of wrinkles congregated across his forehead that Claude was sure hadn't been there before. The two looked like they hadn't slept in a month.

"We need to look out for her," Justin said. "We need to protect her."

"From herself if need be," Arthur added.

"And you're not going to be a bother to her anymore." Justin paused, his lips pulling back to reveal a row of jagged, overlapping teeth. "Say it."

"Fine, you win." Claude held his hands up. "If you feel that strongly about her, I'll back off."

"Good," Justin grunted and sat down at the breakfast table. "That'd be best for you."

"By the way, I didn't mention it the other day, but you have lovely tits," Sherry's voice clattered around the shower room.

Amanda immediately covered her chest. With Sherry and Wish flanking her in the cubicles, Amanda did not want to make a song and dance about washing herself. She quickly soaped her palms before hurriedly running her hands over her body.

"I've never had nice tits," Sherry said even louder than before, ensuring that Amanda could hear her over the crashing water. "But I bet men love yours, do they Amanda?"

Amanda pretended not to hear. She quickly rinsed the suds off her, eager to be away from them. She thought she might be able to catch them unawares and hurry out while they were still showering. Then she saw Sherry's face over the cubicle.

"Do they?"

Amanda turned the water off and snatched her towel from the rail. "Do you mind?"

"Do I mind what?" Sherry's face screwed with confusion.

"Can we not talk about my... body while we're trying to get washed?"

"Why not?" Amanda's cubicle door opened, and Wish stood before her naked, her athletic physique glistening. "You have got a sexy body. Men must love to fuck you." A meanness had crept into Wish's face. Even her smile, which had seemed dazzling only a couple of days ago, did little to offset the intimidating gleam in her eyes.

Amanda wrapped the towel around herself. "Excuse me," she said, trying to step past Wish.

Wish didn't move. Amanda heard the creak of Sherry's cubicle door, and then they were both blocking Amanda's path, staring straight at her.

"I bet you fuck good," Wish said, barely moving her lips.

"She definitely looks the sort, doesn't she," Sherry added.

"This isn't appropriate," Amanda said, the words trembling out of her mouth. It seemed like such a stupid thing to say, but she could think of nothing else. "Can you please excuse me, I'd like to go and get dressed."

Amanda clapped her hands in front of Wish's face as though trying to catch a fly. Wish blinked rapidly. "You're getting dressed now?"

"Yes, please move out of the way. Now."

Wish and Sherry parted, leaving a gap between them just big enough for Amanda to sidle through. She still brushed against their naked bodies as she left the cubicle and heard a breathy moan escape Sherry's lips.

The soles of Amanda's feet thumped the tiles as she hurried out. She jogged down the hallway, gripping tightly hold of the towel to stop it from falling. Breathless, she reached her room, and once behind the safety of her bolted door, she began shaking. The tears sprang out of nowhere, and her stomach muscles clenched as she fought the sobs. Crying only made her angry, and she whirled in the room, looking for something to use as a weapon. Now the towel fell away, and she stomped around the room, strength rippling through her body. The only thing she could see was the table and chair, which were no good to her. But downstairs there were utensils, knives, forks, frying pans. Yes, a frying pan might do it. Once she cracked it around one of their heads and told them to fucking back off, they would get the idea.

Oh, is that what you're going to do? A voice whispered inside her. *You're a tough girl now, is that it? Sure you are. Go on then, go downstairs and get your frying pan. What are you waiting for?*

Amanda gulped, suddenly feeling weak and shivery. The anger reduced to a gelatinous film of shame that swam on her simmering blood.

She quickly got dressed and headed downstairs. That was it; she wasn't going to be taken advantage of again, not in this house, and not anywhere outside of it. She had repeated some variation of this mantra during times of stress, but now, more than any time before, she had to mean it.

When she'd weathered the storm and calmed down, she realized that perhaps a frying pan wasn't the answer. It would probably fracture one of their skulls and then she'd be arrested for attempted murder. But she didn't care what drug they were testing; she was done being the object of their affections.

She entered the kitchen, saw Claude fixing bacon and eggs in a pan, and for a second, she imagined that he was her boyfriend, making her breakfast. God, how she could have spent this whole week entertaining that daydream, flirting with him, maybe even taking it further. She was about to say something, to ask if she could share his breakfast – he'd give her the whole thing and not because he was under some chemical spell, but because he was nice. He was the first nice man she had been around in such a long time that she had forgotten they existed.

"We saved you a seat," Justin said proudly, dabbing his mouth with a napkin.

Ignoring him, she went straight to Claude, the smell of bacon grease and fresh coffee perfuming the air. In a private voice, she said, "Hey. Mind if I hang out with you today?"

Claude, fussing over the food with a spatula, turned and gave her a wry smile. He looked back at Justin and Arthur, and said, "Sure. I'd love to."

"Amanda?" Justin called. "Amanda, we've set a place for you at the table."

"I don't want it."

"B–but..." he spluttered. "I... I've set you a place here. So, you can sit down and have some breakfast. What would you like?"

To Claude, Amanda said, "How about breakfast to go?"

"What was that?" Justin asked, the volume of his voice rising. He walked around the table, arms folded over his thin chest, and strode across the kitchen toward her. "What's the joke?" He smiled venomously. "You guys have some little gag going?"

"Justin," Claude began softly, turning away from the pan. "She doesn't want to eat with you."

"But she wants to eat with *you*? Huh? You two are going to go off and have a little picnic somewhere?"

"Yes," Amanda spat. "Yes, if that's what I want, then that's what we'll do. So why don't you just fucking leave me alone. Go on, fuck off."

"Wait, Amanda." His smile didn't reach his beady eyes. There was no confidence in his tone, but he snorted with fake laughter and said, "Hold the phone a minute, will you? No need to fly off the handle."

"No need to fly off the handle," she repeated with a humourless laugh. "Please get away from me," she said coolly. "Please just go back to the table, eat your food, do whatever you're doing, and leave me alone. I'm asking nicely."

"But…" His eyes darted back and forth as he attempted to make sense of what was happening. "Will you just listen to me a minute? I don't–"

"I don't want to listen to you. I don't want to talk to you. I don't want anything to do with you."

"I just want us to have breakfast together," Justin finished, his words trailing out in a fragile whisper. "*Please.*" He bowed his head and began to cry, a runner of snot trailing from his nose.

Amanda grabbed a plate from the cupboard, slapped a few slices of bread on it, and snatched a banana from the fruit bowl. "Those eggs ready?" she asked Claude.

"Now hold on a second." Arthur, straight-backed, his finger wagging in the air, approached her. "You can't just walk out of here."

"I can't?" Amanda's eyes narrowed. "Did you just say that I *can't* walk out of here?"

Startled, Arthur reset himself. He frowned and said, "Yes. That's exactly what I'm saying. That's not polite. Don't you have any etiquette? We have prepared a space at the table and… and…"

"Listen to me very carefully, Arthur. Fuck you and your space at the table. Got it?"

"No, I'm sorry I really must insist," he began to flap, babbling with his eyes closed, his mouth moving ahead of the words.

She reached out and grabbed hold of Claude's hand, linking fingers.

The sound of Justin's sobs ceased abruptly. Arthur gasped as though she had slapped him across his face.

"Come on, Claude, let's get out of here."

When she turned to leave, she once again saw Wish and Sherry blocking the kitchen door, wearing matching blank expressions. There was nothing in their eyes.

"Boyfriend and girlfriend, are we?" Sherry asked, pointing to their hands disgustedly.

"So, what is this?" Wish asked. "You take him upstairs to fuck now? You are his whore now?"

Years of online abuse had gone a long way toward thickening Amanda's skin, but she almost bit at the jibe. If anyone had called her a whore to her face in any other setting, she would have exploded. But as it stood, Amanda was just about able to keep her temper in check. She could feel Claude's hand wriggling in hers, trying to free itself. She clutched it tighter, their palms meeting slickly.

"Amanda, maybe we should..." Claude started to say, his arm tensed and rigid pressing against her.

"I'm glad you're all here," Amanda announced, the outrage stoking her fire, strengthening her. "Because I want to tell you all, right now, that I don't want to see or speak to any of you again if I can help it, and I certainly don't want to be in the same room as any of you outside of my contractual obligations. This is not up for discussion."

"Amanda, don't," Claude whispered, almost whining. He was about to add that this was dangerous, that perhaps her anger was blinding her from the very real threat circling them there in the kitchen. They were snarling, their faces twisting with hatred. A clear line of drool hung from Wish's lower lip as she clenched her teeth. Sherry was brushing her fingers through her damp hair, coming away with twisted strands and matted clumps each time her hand ploughed over her scalp. Arthur's nostrils flared, his lips moving wordlessly as though he were repeating a silent prayer. Perhaps most worrying of all was Justin. He was gnawing his lower lip until his teeth were stained with blood.

"I'm sorry if you feel a certain way towards me," she said, more evenly now. "But you don't even know me. And you can't control me. You don't own me."

"You can't just shut us out," Arthur said. "We won't stand for it."

"Then you need a big reality check," she replied. "Because I'm here to make money, not friends, and that is it."

There was a blur of movement. Amanda saw Justin reach for something, cat-quick, and then he was in front of them, so close that she could smell the tea on his breath. The odour of fresh and stale sweat rose from his body like steam.

"Let her go, cunt," he said through bared teeth, his nose wrinkled, tears shimmering in his black eyes. His hand was tightly curled around the handle of a kitchen knife, its tip in line with Claude's navel. "Let her go or I'm gonna pull your fucking guts out."

"Justin what are you doing?" Amanda almost reached out to make a grab for the knife but thought better of it. She couldn't afford to make any sudden movements, especially not the way his fist was shaking, aching to plunge into Claude's body. "Don't do this, Justin. Put the knife down."

His head snapped toward her, his face a portrait of pain. "You're giving me no *choice*. Why *him*? Why him and not me?" he elongated the words, the sentence coming out in an agonized moan.

Amanda chanced a look at Arthur, then back to Sherry and Wish. They weren't alarmed. In fact, in their stillness they were condoning Justin's actions, perhaps even eager for him to take it a step further.

"I love you," Justin told Amanda, straining so hard that his face had become beetroot, his temples pulsing on either side of his narrow head. He released a strangled cry and brought the knife up to Claude's throat.

"Please Justin," Claude said, inching away. When he tried to take a step back, he bumped into Wish, who had crept up behind him so quietly he hadn't even heard her move from the doorway. "We're just friends."

"Friends don't hold hands, you fucking..." He shook his head. He dragged the heel of his free hand across his eyes, wiping the tears away. He inhaled sharply, drawing the snot to the back of his throat. "Have you kissed her? I'll know if you're lying so you'd better just tell me the truth."

"If you're going to do something then do it," Sherry said. "Either cut him or put it away."

"Shut your mouth!" he boomed, the knife wavering in his grasp.

A wild thought sprouted in Amanda's mind. She saw a premonition of her hand flying out and slapping the knife away from Justin. Then rationality returned, except her hand was actually reaching for the knife. No, not the knife, his hand. She touched him lightly and saw his lips quiver. His face was an amalgam of emotion, the muscles working overtime in an effort to express his feelings. Eventually, he sighed deeply, and he took on that same vacant glare she had seen on Wish and Sherry in the showers.

"It's the pill," Amanda said. "That's what's making you act like this."

"No, it isn't."

"Can't you see? Can't any of you see?" She tried to turn but felt herself blocked in by Arthur's girth. "Think about it. Why are you all so interested in me all of a sudden? They lied to us. They said that only *one* of us would be taking the drug but it's not true. You're all taking the drug. I'm the only one that's taking the placebo. You have to see that, surely?"

"She's right," Claude said, his Adam's apple bobbing in his throat.

The sound of his voice lit a new fuse in Justin, reanimating his features. His eyes widened and glared, he pulled his arm back, raising the knife.

Then there was a scream from outside.

INTERLUDE

In contrast with the chaos around him, Moshida continued to watch the monitors in silence. The breach in House 2 was fascinating, offering a new layer of exploration to the experiment. A whole new scenario had presented itself: what would happen if the Queen in House 2 was able to communicate with the Queen in House 1? Fear, yes. Heightened paranoia, undoubtedly. But what of the others? Would this force them closer to their Queen? Would the threat of outside intervention accelerate the Honeycomb effect psychologically? So many delicious possibilities.

Someone was speaking at him. He had successfully managed to ignore the voice, his concentration sinking deeper into the monitors, his eyes darting from screen to screen, but then the speaker blocked his view. Moshida felt a pinch of pain in the meat between his neck and shoulder, and then an almost unbearable surge of anger coursing up through his body like lava from an active volcano. Before it could erupt, he calmly said, "Please step out of the way. I'm trying to watch this."

"Yes, I know, sir." It was Hitchson, his main assistant; his round, pale face was flushed with worry and reminded Moshida of a child's drawing of a full moon. "But I really think we should activate the shutters. Queen 2 is–"

"Her name is Rebecca."

"Sorry." Hitchson's face twitched, his cheeks blooming with colour. "But Rebecca is at the window of House 1."

"I know," Moshida said, pointing lazily toward the bank of monitors not five feet from his face. He had eaten little in the last few days and slept even less. "I was the one that opened the door for her. Now if you don't mind, I'm trying to watch."

"But..." Hitchson turned, appealing to the other technicians in the main viewing room, who were shambling around and muttering amongst themselves, keeping their attention locked onto their tablet screens, monitoring the progress of each housemate more closely. "She's going to tell."

Moshida might have laughed, were he not so irritated by the man's helplessness. And wasn't that ironic? He found Amanda's and Rebecca's helplessness intriguing, their resilience endearing.

"Tell them what, exactly?"

Hitchson's face stuttered with confusion, morphing through a series of frowns. "Tell them about the pill... She might..." Again he looked back at the others. "She might try to get in."

"And you think she will? Three-inch reinforced glass?"

"I don't..."

"You don't *what*?"

Hitchson's mouth opened, closed again with an audible click. "But the other shareholders will be watching."

"Exactly. They're about to see just how powerful Honeycomb is."

"I understand that Mr Moshida, but we're already in dangerous territory at twenty milligrams. And with this added to the mix – I mean, the Queen in House 1... if she gets in..."

"She won't," Moshida said firmly. "She's nothing but *incentive*."

He continued watching the monitors, and gradually the rest of the world fell away. He was back with Amanda, drinking in every exquisite movement, cherishing the subtle nuances of her body language. He wanted to reach out and touch the screen, his finger itching to stroke the image of her face, but, of course, he resisted.

For now, he would have to make do with the screens and keep his hands to himself, counting down the hours until morning dosage when he could see her up close and in the flesh.

"Mr Moshida, the guests in House 1 are going to become even more unstable. They're going to turn *primal*. I know it's not my place to say, but I would strongly advise that we terminate the experiment. The shareholders have seen more than enough proof that Honeycomb works."

"No," Moshida said absently. "For all they know, this whole thing could be a trick, a piece of tightly choreographed theatre. They have to know for sure."

Hitchson swallowed so hard that Moshida heard his throat click. "What are you going to do?"

Moshida's hand hovered over the instrument panel, his finger primed by the button that lowered the shutters.

CHAPTER 28

The scream cut through the kitchen. There was a pregnant pause in which nothing stirred, and then the sound of hammering.

"Help me please you have to help me oh my god please!"

The animalistic panic in the woman's voice perforated the house. It seemed to be coming from the direction of the conservatory.

"They're going to kill me please help me someone help me, oh god, please!"

The hammering on the conservatory glass sounded like hoofbeats. That moment the bubble of tension popped in the kitchen, and Justin's knife clattered to the floor. They dispersed, hurried through to the conservatory, and saw a woman standing at the window in a ragged dress, her face lumpy and swollen, her hair blowing in the breeze. Bloody handprints splattered the glass from where she had slapped it to get their attention. Amanda thought she had read relief in the woman's damaged expression upon seeing them, but now there was only terror.

"Please…" she started to say again, the impact of her palms weakening as they beat the conservatory. "Oh god, are you safe?" she said, and tears rolled down from the one eye that wasn't puffed closed. "Let me in."

"We can't." Wish was the first to speak. "We are locked in."

"Break the glass," she said, her teeth painted pink with blood. "Break it and let me in. Hurry, hurry, hurry, please."

"What is this?" Sherry asked, placing her hand on the inside of the conservatory window. "What's going on?"

"Amanda, get back," Justin commanded, his voice full of purpose. He had stopped crying, but his unusually long lashes were still wet. He turned to her with his hands out, ready to grab her by the shoulders, when he thought against it. "You'd better stand back. She looks crazy."

She looks a whole lot saner than you did two minutes ago, Amanda thought. She didn't want to give him the satisfaction of complying with his instructions, but the sight of the woman was filling her veins with ice water. The woman looked as though she'd been thrown in front of a bus, and yet there was a frightening urgency about her. They were looking at a person driven mad by terror, and Amanda thought she was beginning to know what that felt like.

"Break the glass and help me," she said again. "They'll be here soon!"

"What do we do?" Wish asked, turning to the others for advice. Wish looked at Amanda almost pleadingly, awaiting an answer. There was no malice in Wish's face; no sign that she was the same woman that had been back in the showers or blocking Claude from exiting the kitchen just a moment ago.

"We need to break the glass," Amanda said, and separated from them to find something practical to do the job. The chairs at the breakfast table wouldn't make a dent, and the stools at the breakfast bar were secured to the floor. "Come on, help me look," she ordered the others, and they immediately sprang into action, rifling through the kitchen.

While Amanda rooted through a cutlery drawer in search of a rolling pin or a meat tenderizer, Justin slithered up next to her.

"Amanda, I'm sorry about what happened just now. I wasn't going to cut him, I promise. I just... I wanted us to have breakfast, that's all."

She showed no sign that she had heard him. She was not

going to forget that he had pulled a knife on Claude, that he had in fact looked capable of stabbing him. But she had to tackle one crisis at a time and right now there was a terrified woman outside who needed her help.

Once she located the rolling pin, she realized that it was completely inadequate. She abandoned the drawer and glanced back at the conservatory. Claude was talking to the woman from the other side of the glass, telling her everything was OK, that it would be alright. He spoke so calmly and confidently that Amanda believed every word he was saying.

"What about this?" Arthur asked, holding a stainless-steel pot.

"Don't ask me, just try it on the glass," Amanda snapped. She heard Arthur grunt as he lugged it, then the dull thud as it hit the glass and banged to the floor.

"Hurry! I'm bleeding!" the woman screamed.

Amanda cringed at the words and bit down on her lower lip. She couldn't stand to hear the woman so afraid, the panic straining her vocal cords. Justin was whacking a chair against the conservatory window, but it bounced back without so much as a chink. Then she remembered something she had spotted in the hallway leading to the kitchen.

"Where are you going?" Wish asked, almost hysterical.

"Getting something to smash the window," Amanda called back over her shoulder, and jogged down the hallway until she came to the small table. On top of it was a brass bumblebee ornament about the size of a small watermelon. She picked it up, satisfied by the weight of it, and brought it back to the conservatory. "Everyone move, out the way," she demanded, before hurling the bumblebee as hard as she could at the glass. It made a small fracture amidst the collage of scuffmarks.

"Again, again," Sherry said as Amanda picked the bumblebee back up. Amanda hurled it, aiming at the crack in the glass as best she could, and heard a small crunch as the glass chipped.

"What's this window made out of? Adamantium?" Justin said, and used the metal leg from one of the breakfast chairs to chip away at the fracture.

"Yes," the woman shrieked, her good bloodshot eye widening with exhilaration at the sight of progress. "Keep going."

Amanda had the bumblebee poised like a shotput ready for another throw when she spotted something in the field beyond. A cluster of shapes cresting the hill on the horizon, sprinting down toward the house.

"What's that?" Amanda said, pointing to the distance.

"I have no idea," Claude replied. "But we'd better get this glass broken before–"

A sound rumbled through the kitchen, taking them all by surprise. Before anyone could ask what had caused the noise, their answer was provided. Metal shutters were slowly sliding down the windows.

"Oh, mon dieu," Wish uttered as shadow stretched across the kitchen.

"No!" The woman slapped the window. "No..."

Amanda turned to Claude. "We have to help her."

"*How*?"

"I don't know but..."

There was a loud clunk of finality as the shutters completed their journey, pitching them into darkness.

Nobody moved. For a few seconds, there was only the collective sound of their laboured breathing. This time, Claude's hand sought Amanda's, clenching it tightly.

Then, the woman on the other side of the shutters began to whimper miserably. "Don't take the pills," she said. "It's a trick. Don't..."

"What just happened?" Sherry asked, sounding small and afraid in the darkness.

Then they heard a drone of jagged voices, yelling manically from outside. The woman made one last protest, smacking the shutter with the remainder of her strength, before the commotion descended on her. Screams pierced the house followed by violent rattling of the shutters.

Inside, there was a collective gasp, followed by a prolonged moment of stupefied silence. Amanda's heart punched in her chest so hard that it felt as though it were trying to leap into her throat. Outside, the hideous sound of the woman's suffering was like nothing Amanda had ever heard; animalistic and primal, with a pitch she had never heard accomplished by human vocal cords.

Amanda's lips began moving numbly but no words formed. Then she said, "We have to do–"

The rest of the sentence was stolen by the music blaring through the house speakers, drowning out the woman's suffering.

It took Amanda a minute or so to realize that they were playing one of her songs on the speakers.

It was "Prowl."

CHAPTER 29

They were summoned to the Circle Room, but Amanda changed course and went to the mansion's entrance. She knew the front door would be locked even before she tried the handle. When it didn't open, she felt her guts slowly twisting. She hadn't thought of herself as a prisoner until that very moment, and now a hot, suffocating dread rose inside her. The mounting tension culminated in her forehead, a screwdriver slowly turning in her temple. The gritty, dense air of the house became thicker until she felt like she was wading through treacle, unable to take more than a sip of breath at a time.

Of course, the rest of her fan club had followed her to the front door, shuffling dumbly behind her like a herd of cows. Arthur asked her what was wrong. She didn't answer, couldn't afford the breath.

"Is it locked?" Wish asked. The group banded together behind her, now moving in tandem like a herd of sheep – all except Claude, who stood as far away from them as possible. "The door won't open?"

Amanda gave a slight shake of the head.

"We should go to the Circle Room," Claude said. "They'll have to tell us what's going on. The shutters… they're probably a security measure."

"I don't want to agree with him," Sherry began, "but he's right. All of a sudden, I'm feeling rather disturbed about this whole thing."

Yeah? I drove past disturbed about a hundred miles back, Amanda thought. Her tongue stuck to the roof of her mouth, and every time she swallowed it hurt her throat.

"I don't know what's going on," Arthur said, talking to the carpet, unable to make eye contact with anyone. Even in the gloom, she could see his forehead glistening with sweat. "But I think we'd better go and speak to them about that woman. They will have a phone. Yes, maybe they can call the police or an ambulance."

"Who…" Justin started to speak, but lost his confidence. His voice quavered, threatening to break. It may have been some trick of the shadows, but standing there with his shoulders hunched and his thin neck craned forward, he looked like a frail old man. "Who was she?"

"How can we know?" Sherry replied, although she was staring straight at Amanda, as if expecting her to answer.

"And who were those people chasing her?" Justin asked thinly.

"We're not to know," Sherry said, sharper this time.

"They were going to kill her," he whispered.

A hush fell over them as they contemplated his words. Amanda cleared her throat, saw their faces brighten with expectation, and said, "And you were going to kill Claude."

"I wasn't," Justin replied.

"You wanted to. And the rest of you." She inhaled sharply, her lungs filling with thorns. "The rest of you wanted him to do it."

"Not me," Wish blurted. "I don't want anyone to die."

"Shut up," Amanda hissed. "Shut up and listen to me. All of you." She looked at Claude, saw that she had his full attention despite the haunted expression on his face. "You saw that woman, you heard what she said. We need to make a pact, right here and now. I know you're all scrambled from these pills they've been giving us, but this is where it ends. We can't take any more pills. None of us."

"We have to, or we'll be breaking the rules," Justin said.

"So what?" Amanda said.

"That's breach of contract," Arthur added almost shyly, hands in his pockets. "We won't get paid."

"We won't be able to spend the money if we kill each other before the end of the week," Amanda said, massaging her chest to alleviate the tightness. She lacked the fire needed to deliver the sermon in a way that would get through to them. The weighty atmosphere of the house was pressing down on her, squeezing the strength out of her muscles. She tasted sweat on her upper lip and licked it away. "Look, we can't take those pills anymore. Didn't you hear that woman?"

"I think I might have a very simple explanation," Arthur said, raising his hand. They all gave him their full attention, which he seemed to enjoy. Now that he had an audience, his posture changed. "I think that it was more theatre. Think about it: her turning up out of nowhere, shouting her head off about the pills. It's supposed to sow discord, to see if we would refuse to take our daily dosage. It's a test."

"What about her face?" Amanda asked. "She looked like she'd had the shit beaten out of her. Was that theatre too?"

"Makeup," he said with a slight shrug.

"Then I tell you what," Amanda began. "She's the best actor I've ever seen in my life, because to me she looked absolutely terrified."

"He could be right," Wish said, shifting from foot to foot, one fist in the small of her back. "How else would she know about the pills?"

"You keep asking me these questions like I have the answers," Amanda fired back at her. "I don't know a fucking thing more than the rest of you, except that those pills are doing something to you. And you all know it too." She thrust a finger out accusingly. "You all know you're changing. All you've done for the last three days is try to cling to me, and it… it isn't normal."

"Have you thought that maybe we just think you're a fun person?" Arthur said.

"No, because I'm not," Amanda returned. "The pill is making you all sick. I can see it in your faces. Now we need to make a pact, right here, right now. None of us are going to take any more pills, especially not until we get some kind of explanation." She wheezed and wiped her forehead on the crook of her arm. She had thought they looked like sheep huddled together earlier but now she knew that was wrong. They looked like cows in a field, their dumb, gormless expressions reflecting no sign that they had taken on board anything she had said.

"I need the money," Claude said, weakly. He looked at her, his face pained, his brow crinkling with concern. "I'm buried in debt. They're going to take my house. I'm..." He slapped a hand over his eyes. "I have a problem. I..." He turned away, unable to face her. He made a sound that might have been a trapped sob, and then said, "I gamble, Amanda. I've pissed it all away and this was my one and only shot." He made a motion with his hand as though wiping his eyes, and then he turned back to her. "I don't care if they don't like me." He cocked his thumb at the others. "Or if they pull knives on me. It's not a big deal to me. I've had people pull knives on me before. I've had a gun shoved in my mouth. I've been to prison. This house is nothing. We only have three and a bit days left. Can't we just play along until then?"

"Who's to say that we're going to get paid, Claude? Who's to say they're even going to let us out of this fucking place?" Amanda shrieked.

He shrugged dismissively. "Of course they're going to let us out."

She shook her head, felt the perspiration fly off her hair. "What about that woman? She said, 'Don't take the pills.'"

"I don't know what that was," he admitted. "But I know it doesn't have anything to do with us. She could be an escapee from a nuthouse for all we know. Maybe those people were nurses and–"

"Just stop it. Listen to what you're saying for Christ's sake." She looked at Claude, the disbelief etched across her face. "Not you, too," she whispered, before barging through them and charging down the hallway toward the Circle Room.

Sherry jogged to keep stride with her. "Hey Amanda. Why did the golfer change his trousers? Because he got a hole in one."

"Why don't you take your jokes and fuck off, Sherry."

"There's no need to speak to me like that. I'm just trying to cheer you up. I'm worried about you."

"It's not me you should be worried about," Amanda yelled, the frustration filling her head until she thought it would pop. "I'm taking a placebo. It's you idiots that are being drugged."

"I know," she whispered.

Amanda stopped. "You know? What do you mean, you know?"

"I suppose it makes sense, doesn't it?" She wiped her nose with the heel of her hand. "I have noticed that we all seem drawn to you, sure, why not? But is that so bad?"

"Yeah," Amanda laughed humourlessly. "It is for *me*."

"Why? All we do is talk about how great you are. I mean, we'd bend over backwards for you, Amanda. We'd do anything for you. Why is that bad?"

Because you're crazy and you're dangerous, Amanda thought. If they were taking this pill in the outside world, what extremes would they be going through to show their love for her? Were they so different to John Meadows? If his rambling emails were anything to go by, then he was a hundred percent dedicated to her. But did he have the potential to be violent? If he was unstable enough to get those tattoos, then he was surely unstable enough to defend them if someone tried to mock him, or god forbid, mock her.

Sherry opened the Circle Room door for Amanda. A TV was set up on a stand in front of the chairs.

"What's this?" Arthur asked.

"A microwave," Justin replied irritably. "What does it fucking look like?"

"Yes, I see that," Arthur snipped. "I mean why is there a TV here?"

"Why don't you turn it on and find out?" Justin thrust a finger toward the TV.

"You turn it on. I'm not turning it on."

"Jesus Christ," Claude muttered. He got up, found a remote on the stand, and switched the TV on. The screen came to life, revealing footage from the eye-in-the-sky cameras. The screen was split into four segments, showing them in different parts of the house.

They stood around the TV and watched in silence. The footage was grainy but not to the point of obscuring the actions on screen. The different camera views changed to reveal someone playing pool, someone sat in the library reading, someone waiting for the kettle to boil. And then it dawned on Amanda. "That's not us," she said.

Arthur stood up, leaned closer to the screen, and squinted.

"It looks exactly like this house," Wish said.

"It might be this house," Amanda began, "but the people aren't us. Look closely. Who is that woman?" Amanda pointed to the top right angle, where the shape of a tall pale woman was drinking alone in the dining room. "It isn't me or Sherry," Amanda said. "And it certainly isn't you, Wish."

"I'll be buggered," Arthur said. "Then who the bloody hell are they, then?"

Ding-dong.

Their heads snapped toward the speaker.

"Good evening, ladies and gentlemen. We hope you are enjoying your stay in the house. We would like to inform you that for health and safety reasons the emergency shutters have been activated. You are completely sealed in the house, but please do not be alarmed. We have medical staff on hand, and there are first aid kits in the bathrooms on the ground and upper floor.

"On the TV, you will see six guests in another house – a house that looks very similar to the one you are in now." The Overlord paused to let that information sink in.

"And there I was thinking we were special," Sherry said, with a short snort of laughter.

"Yesterday, you failed the group assignment, and as warned, there is a forfeit. As section 8C on the contract states, failure to comply with any rules or regulations of the house, including group assignments, will result in a financial penalty. As such, you will all be docked two percent of your earnings."

There were grumblings of annoyance, but to Amanda it sounded forced, as though they were actually relieved the penalty wasn't more severe.

"Nobody cares about that," Amanda said. "What's going on outside with that woman?"

"However," the Overlord started to say, ignoring her question. "This pay deduction is a preliminary warning. If there is one more act of disobedience, then Amanda Pearson will be removed from the house and replaced with a new guest from the house you see on the screen before you."

"Excuse me?" Amanda said, but the indignation she felt was second to the overpowering sense of helplessness that loomed over her. An invisible entity was playing chess with her life. She was nothing more than an ant beneath a magnifying glass.

"Amanda will be placed in the new house for the duration of the experiment, and her replacement will continue here in her absence until the week is over," the Overlord said flatly. "Due to the security breach earlier, there will be no group assignment this evening. Morning dosage will resume as normal at 8am"

"Hey!" Amanda shouted at the camera. "Hey, I'm talking to you! Who was that woman outside? We want some answers." She froze, waiting for an explanation, but there was only silence. She picked up a chair and carried it to the back of the Circle Room.

"What're you doing?" Arthur asked.

Amanda pulled back the curtain covering the door that the nurse used in the mornings. She knew that beyond it there was probably a corridor leading to a lab, or some kind of monitoring room. In her mind's eye, she saw a pale, skinny man hunched over a microphone, reading from a script, inflated by the sense of power it gave him. Then she thought about *The Wizard of Oz*, and the anger rocketed through her. She picked up her chair and began battering the keypad with it.

"No, don't do that Amanda," Wish said.

The sound of her voice only made Amanda swing harder. She retrained her attention on the door's keypad, using the chair legs as a battering ram, trying to damage the buttons. The keypad gave off a manic electric squeal, and Amanda thrust the chair harder.

Someone touched her shoulder. In one deft movement, Amanda wheeled around and swung the chair through the air, not caring who was standing there, just hoping to connect with their head. Claude leapt back, narrowly escaping the chair's arc.

"Hey, take it easy. Calm down," he said.

"Don't touch me!"

He flinched, hurt by her reaction, but he did not press the issue. She went back to work on the door, the impact vibrating through her arms. She held the chair by its legs and continued her assault until the moulded plastic splintered and shards were flying past her face.

When she had finished demolishing the chair and her muscles throbbed and burned, she stood there, puffing hoarsely, her face dripping with sweat.

"I want to leave," Amanda whimpered. "I want to get out of this house."

Ding-dong.

"Further vandalism of company property will result in pay deductions. This is your first and final warning," the Overlord said.

Amanda tossed the remains of the chair into the semi-circle where the others stood. "Suck my dick," she said to the camera and made her way to leave. When she was at the door, she sensed that the herd were trying to shuffle along with her. She felt a new surge of fury and turned on them with her eyes blazing blackly. "Don't any of you dare come near me!"

"Amanda, maybe... maybe you're not well," Arthur suggested, but it was him who looked sickly. His skin had taken on a waxy quality, his lips lined with white foam like a rabid dog. His blue eyes became oceanic stones in the centre of his ghoulish face.

"Do you want to talk about it?" Justin asked.

Amanda threw her head back and cackled. Sweat trickled from her hair and spattered on the floor. She began laughing so hard she had to bend over, her lungs aching from the hilarity. *I'm the mad one*, she thought, and this only made her break into new gales of laughter until she could no longer see clearly through her tears.

Then, she began to run.

CHAPTER 30

Amanda raced to the kitchen, took a small steak knife, and stuck it in the pocket of her tracksuit top, the tip jutting through the fabric, and then traversed back through the hallways. Her first thought was to go back to the passageway, get into the courtyard and try to scale the wall. There had to be some way over, even if it meant forcing her fingers into the grooves between the bricks and clambering up with her bare hands.

As she neared the archway with the ticking grandfather clock, the words Queen Cage stirred in her mind. What was that thing and why was it just sitting there, so out of place in the courtyard? Was it some kind of puzzle or just another mind game? She didn't care about any of it. They could keep the money and they could send bailiffs to her flat for the twenty-five grand she had already spent. Good luck to them, because the first thing she planned to do when she got over that wall and found her way back to safety was phone the newspapers. She was going to spill everything to anyone that listened, even if she came across as a conspiracy crackpot. Why not? Add another layer to her ruined reputation; it might land her a couple of magazine deals.

"Going somewhere?" The voice sliced through the silence behind her.

She pulled the knife out of her pocket and spun.

"Easy," Claude said. "I'm your friend. You don't want to end up stabbing me accidentally, do you?"

"Stop sneaking up on me then."

"What's that for?" he asked, gesturing to the knife.

"I was going over the wall. Wanted something to use as protection."

He shook his head. "You won't get over the wall. Too high."

"Then I would have stayed out there until the end of the week if it meant being away from *them*."

"What about me?" He shrugged. "I thought we were friends?"

"I don't think we can be," she said, and kicked the panel once for good measure, then she started to walk. "I think I'm the only one in this house who still has any sense left in their head."

"Well I'll be the first to admit I'm not the sharpest tool in the box but…"

"This is *wrong*," she whispered. "Can't you see it Claude? Justin had a knife on you earlier. He was going to…"

"He wasn't going to do anything," Claude said. "I saw it in his eyes. He pulled the knife to impress you, and once he had, he didn't have a get-out clause."

"Yeah? You seemed pretty convinced earlier."

"I didn't want to antagonize him any further. He was riled up, but he's just a spoilt little kid."

"How can you be so casual about this?"

"What do you want me to do? Start smashing things up so that they deduct even more of my money? No, not a chance."

"Is that all you care about?"

"It was," he told her, and let the implication – if there was one – linger a while. "Frankly, yes it was. Look, cards on the table time, alright?" He inhaled, held it, and then said, "I didn't think I'd meet someone like you here, but I need this money, Amanda. I don't have the luxury of being a celebrity, OK? I'm in a giant hole, and unless I dig myself out of it soon, it's going to bury me completely."

She turned away from him with her arms folded and said nothing.

"I'm going upstairs to the library. It's peaceful in there, and they have some decent books. I started reading *Dracula* yesterday. It's a bit hard going at first but it's like the movie. If you get restless and want company, that's where I'll be." He walked on ahead of her toward the staircase.

"So, it's just business as usual for you, is it?"

"What do you want me to do?" he asked wearily.

"And it doesn't matter to you at all that we saw that woman? She was terrified, Claude. And someone had used her for a punchbag."

He leaned over the banister. "Do you want my honest opinion?"

"No, I want you to lie to me."

He didn't rise to her bait. "I think she looked dangerous, and she looked like she was out of her mind. Let's not blow this out of proportion, Amanda. We're here for a harmless experiment. Those shutters came down to protect us, probably from her."

"I actually can't believe what I'm hearing right now."

"When I was a kid, we had crazies like her walking around our estate all the time. There was one woman that lived a few buildings over from me and she tried to gouge her own eyes out. You'd always see her walking around talking to herself with claw marks up and down her face. But she did it to herself. That woman out there earlier, she could be a paranoid schizo." He shrugged. "I don't know, I'm not a doctor."

"Out here in the middle of nowhere? She's just going to randomly try to get into this house, screaming for help, telling us not to take those pills?"

"She probably hasn't been taking her pills and that's why she's having an episode."

She shook her head. "Do you really believe that?"

"I do."

"Then we don't have anything further to say to one another."

He nodded. "I'm sorry you feel that way." Slowly, he began to lumber up the stairs. "If you change your mind, you know where to find me."

She listened as his footsteps began to fade, and deep down through the warrens of the house, she heard the library door shut.

And then, she was truly alone. He had been right. There was no way she would get over those walls in the courtyard, and his clear rationale made her plan seem like the protest of an angry child.

She walked on the balls of her feet, hoping to make it back to her room unnoticed. The house had a way of amplifying even the tiniest sounds, but that worked both ways. She would hear footsteps or voices from afar, travelling through the otherwise silent hallways, and this would give her enough of a warning to change direction, or, if need be, hide completely.

So far, she had traversed the ground floor, taking the long route back to the to the bedrooms, and hadn't heard a thing. All the lights were on but that didn't make the silence any less intimidating. What exactly did the others do when they weren't trying to crawl all over her? Did they sit in a room and talk about her for hours on end? Did they try to dissect her personality, swapping titbits of trivia, competing with one another to see who knew her best? Or, more worryingly, did they try to drum up tactics to get even closer, to find some common ground in an effort to share her?

As she crept along, she scanned for soft spots in the house, trying to find some feasible way out. The shutters were still down over the windows, so that option was out. She tried the other doors as she went along, most of them locked. She began to wonder whether the house would slip up and reveal any more of its secrets, but that didn't seem likely. It was obvious now that the whole experiment was centred around her, and that the Overlord wasn't going to free her until the game was over.

Amanda lost her nerve and gave up. Mindful of not wanting to bump into the others, she strategically navigated her way back to the staircase, putting her weight on the banister to reduce the creaking underfoot. She came to the bedrooms. Now, she did hear something. It was coming from behind Arthur's bedroom door. She didn't stop to listen, but caught a snippet as she hurried past. It sounded as though he were reciting Shakespeare in a slow, morose voice, the monologue only broken by his sobbing. This disturbed her for reasons she couldn't quite understand, but she didn't let it linger. She entered her room, closing the door carefully to reduce the noise, before sliding the bolt home.

She undressed, keeping hold of the knife the whole while, and got into bed. The stress of the day had sucked the energy out of her marrow, and she lay there, her body a tapestry of aches and pains, her mind too overworked to settle on a coherent thought. Sleep took her quickly.

She had no way of knowing that Justin was lying beneath the bed, listening to her breathe.

CHAPTER 31

THURSDAY: 25 MILLIGRAMS

The siren shrilled through the house, snatching Amanda out of an almost unbroken night's sleep. She had woken once briefly, her internal clock estimating that it was somewhere between three and four in the morning, because she thought she had heard something. With the residue of a dream lingering in her mind, she had slipped easily back to sleep and thought nothing more of it. Now, however, the siren was penetrating her brain, and for an instant she thought she was the cause of it. Perhaps everyone else was waiting on the landing, too timid to rouse her for fear of rebuke. But when she stumbled out of her room and saw the others, she realized Justin was also missing.

"If that boy can sleep through this poxy bloody noise then he must be an even bigger idiot than I had him pegged for," Arthur moaned.

With his fingers in his ears, Claude said, "If you want to go in there and wake him, you won't find any complaint from me."

"Thank you for your permission, Father," Arthur said.

"This noise makes my skin crawl," Wish said, cringing over to Justin's door. It was the first time Amanda noticed that she walked with a very slight limp, one that was probably more severe in the morning just after waking up. Wish banged a fist against Justin's door. "Justin? I'm coming in, OK?"

She opened the door and shuffled in. From her vantage point, Amanda could see something on the walls of Justin's room.

"He's not here," Wish said, stepping back out. When she tried to close the door behind her, Amanda walked over and pushed it back open.

"What's wrong?" Wish said, angling her body to prevent Amanda from entering. It didn't matter. Amanda could see the black scribbles that covered almost every inch of wall in Justin's room. At first, she took it to be juvenile graffiti, a way of entertaining himself during the long, boring hours in the house. Then she saw her name, ballooned in foot-high letters on the wall next to his bed.

"Wish, would you excuse me please," Amanda said.

"He's not in there," Wish replied, unmoving.

"Yes, I know." She looked at Wish and gave her a smile, and, for good measure, reached down and squeezed her hand. Wish responded to Amanda's touch with a gasp, her mouth forming an O of surprise before stretching into a grin of almost orgasmic bliss.

"We should probably respect his privacy," Arthur called. "Isn't that what you said, Claude? I don't see you going over to manhandle Amanda."

Their dialogue and the siren drowned out as Amanda's eyes drifted over the extent of the writing. He had obviously taken the Magic Marker pen from their first group assignment to create this mural to her. She could almost see where his obsession increased as the scrawling became bolder, more prominent. At a glance, she could see some variation of her name at least thirty, maybe even fifty times. There were love hearts dotted around and inscribed with their initials like something a schoolgirl would doodle in her diary. Turning slowly, Amanda noticed that he had defaced the space behind the door with what she thought was a poem. Upon closer inspection, she saw that it wasn't a poem at all, but rather a list of statements:

AMANDA PEARSON IS MY GIRLFRIEND

WE WILL LIVE IN A NICE HOUSE TOGETHER AND HAVE 1 OR 2 OR 3 DOGS

AMANDA IS MY WIFE AND WE LOVE EACH OTHER
I LOVE AMANDA
AMANDA PEARSON IS MY WIFE
JUSTIN AND AMANDA WILL GET MARRIED AND HAVE 3
CHILDREN AND 2 DOGS

The tribute, which he had attempted to illustrate with a cartoon drawing of the two of them holding hands in front of a sunset, made the fine hairs on her arms stand to attention. A sliver of ice slipped down her spine and she shuddered, shaking the tension out of her hands.

"What the bloody hell has he been doing in here?" Arthur said, poking his head in. "Are we living with Banksy and don't even know it?"

Amanda shot a look at him. "Do you find this funny? Do you think this…" She waved a hand at the mess of writing. "Do you think this makes me feel nice? Do you think it's normal?"

"Well he's obviously got a soft spot for you," Arthur said casually. "I wouldn't let it bother you though. He obviously has a soft spot in his head, too. I mean the boy is as thick as two planks."

"It's just vandalism if you ask me," Sherry said, scratching her stomach. "I would be very surprised if they don't dock his pay or, better yet, kick him out completely."

Amanda couldn't hear most of what was being said, but she had to get out of that room. It felt dirty somehow, as though she were being contaminated by his sick mind from just standing there.

"Where is he?" Amanda went back onto the landing. "Where the hell is he?"

"I don't know," Sherry called back. "Perhaps he's already in the Circle Room? Is there any chance we could get a move on?" she asked, one hand slapped across her forehead. "This wailing is going to drive me mad."

Amanda strode ahead of them. What right did he have to obsess over her, to proclaim his love so shamelessly? For an instant, she imagined him lying on the bed repeating her name in a fast, breathy mantra as he brought himself to climax. The revulsion sat in her stomach, curdling like bad milk.

They got to the Circle Room door. The door wouldn't open.

"This fucking noise," Wish said. "Why won't they turn it off?"

"Because he isn't here," Claude said.

"Then where is he?" Sherry asked. Her tongue was purple from last night's wine and her bangles rattled as she ran her hands through her hair.

"There," Amanda said as Justin rounded the corner of the hallway. The siren abruptly stopped, and there was an audible click as the Circle Room door unlocked. With her ears ringing, Amanda approached Justin. His face went through a process of surprise and then delight. He patted his hair and adjusted his t-shirt, before appraising his pyjama bottoms.

"Morning sunshine," he rasped, fingering a spec of crud from the corner of his bloodshot eye. "How did you sleep?"

"I'd like to have a private word with you," she said.

"Me?" He straightened, his expression caught between joy and suspicion. "We have to do morning dosage."

"Morning dosage can wait," she said.

"Yeah, but we might have a forfeit if we don't..."

"Either you speak to me in private or I say what I have to say here in front of everyone."

He looked around her, saw the group watching him with what he assumed was jealousy, and said, "In private is fine." He swept his arm through the air in the direction of the bend in the hallway and said, "Shall we?"

They walked around the corner and stopped when they were about halfway down the hallway, standing just outside a parlour room that she had explored on the first day. He licked his lips, which were dry and peeling. She could almost see his heart beating through his t-shirt, his eyelids lowered showing only a chip of his pale blue pupils.

"What's on your mind," he breathed, his shoulders rising and falling dramatically. "Like your song, remember? 'What's On Your Mind?'"

"I saw what you wrote on the walls in your room."

"And?" His pierced eyebrow rose expectantly. His lips began curling into a smile.

She wondered how many times he had played over this encounter in his puny little mind, and how it had ended.

"I don't like it," she said. "And I want it to stop."

He blinked rapidly as though the information was not processing correctly. The smile quivered on his lips. "Well, what does that mean?"

"It means that I don't like you. I will never like you, especially not in that way. Not in a million years, do you understand? You can write over every inch of this house that you're in love with me or that we're going to get married, but that's only going to happen in your imagination. Is this getting through to you?"

He started breathing heavily. He bit down on his lower lip, caught a piece of dry skin between his teeth, and worked on tearing it free.

"I just didn't know how to tell you," he began.

"Well now you don't need to waste your breath, because I've explained exactly how I feel. It stops here, do you understand?"

"I... I..."

"Do you understand, Justin? Just because you want something it doesn't mean you will get it, and no amount of wishing or daydreaming is going to change it." She heard a small, pained whine escape his throat and added, "We have a couple more days here and then we will both leave and never see each other again."

"No," he barked, so feral that she reared back. "Don't say that. I mean, don't make it so final. You're angry, alright, I get that. I shouldn't have written all that stupid shit all over the walls, I'm sorry. If it makes any difference, I didn't mean for you to *see* it. It was just for me, you know, like a diary. But don't say that when we leave here that's the end of us."

"There is no *us*, Justin. Don't you get that?" She was shouting now. "Isn't anything I'm saying registering with you? We're here to make money and that is it. This is a gig and nothing more. Now will you at least do me the courtesy of not being so…" she almost said creepy but pulled herself back at the last instant, "…*overwhelming*. It's bad enough that you pulled that knife on Claude–"

"Oh Christ, is that what this is?" His face soured, his bloody lower lip pulled down into a snarl. "You love him, don't you? You love him and you think I'm ugly."

"I don't love either of you!" she roared back, so ferociously that she became dizzy. "But you can't go threatening people with knives like some fucking psycho."

"I wasn't going to–"

"I don't care anymore, Justin. I've said everything I'm going to say to you." Her fingernails bit into the palms of her hands as she clenched her fists. The stress made her heart work harder, the veins in her neck straining until she was sure something was going to pop inside her.

"Please Amanda," he wailed. "Can't we start again? Can't we… can't we pretend that it's the first day and… and…"

She turned and thundered down the hallway and into the Circle Room. The others were sitting down waiting for her. The nurse held the tray like a mannequin, unmoving, unblinking. Only two pills remained in their dishes – hers and Justin's. Amanda picked up her pill. The nurse watched her expectantly.

"I want to speak with someone in charge."

The nurse didn't reply.

"If I don't speak to someone in charge of this experiment in the next two minutes, I'm not taking this pill. So, you can look at me like a gormless fucking idiot all you want but I assume you can hear me, yes? Go and run off and tell whoever is back there that I don't give a shit about my money, you can deduct it all if you want. But I'm not taking another pill until I get my answers."

The nurse blinked, and in a birdlike motion his head angled toward the eye-in-the-sky camera, but he didn't move.

"I'll wait," Amanda said and took a seat.

Justin swung the door open, his face red and puffy from crying. He looked like a toddler after a tantrum, his hand pressed to his mouth, chewing on it like a leg of lamb. He snatched his dish from the tray, put the pill in his mouth, and swallowed it dry. Then he opened his mouth to the nurse and screamed in his face. The nurse flinched, ever so slightly, but his eyes barely changed. Without another word, Justin turned and left. He slammed the door so hard that the impact vibrated through the walls like a tuning fork.

"Did you give him a telling off, Amanda? Well, too blooming right, he needs to grow up," Sherry said.

"We're going to get a forfeit," Arthur said, scratching his neck. "Amanda, it might be wise to just take the pill. After all, if yours is a placebo like you say it is, then you have nothing to worry about."

"I'm not taking anything until they talk to me." She looked up at the camera and waved her arms. "You get that? Come and answer my questions and I'll take the pill. That sounds like a fair trade to me, I'd say."

"Yes, but they said they were going to take you out of the house," Arthur said. His attention fixed on the camera, the colour slowly tipping out of his face. "You don't want that, do you? You don't want to be put in another house with a bunch of strangers."

"They're not taking me anywhere I don't want to go. What are they going to do? Force me out of here at gunpoint?"

"They could do something spiteful, you know?" Wish told her, fiddling with the bottom of her vest. "Might be best for everyone if–"

"I don't care what's best for everyone."

Wish's head flicked to the nurse, then to the camera, before settling on Claude. "Tell her, Claude."

"Tell her what?" He shrugged.

"Tell her she has to take the pill."

"She can hear you," Claude said. "She's a big girl. She can make her own decision."

"But her decisions affect all of us," Sherry said. She turned to Amanda and got down on one knee. "Honey, what's the matter? Do you want to talk about it?"

"I've done all the talking I'm going to do."

"Alright, sweetie, but…"

"Don't call me sweetie. I'm not a five year-old."

"I'm sorry, I'm sorry, but… well, they said they would take you out of the house if…"

"That's what I want," Amanda shouted. Her sudden outburst unbalanced Sherry and she fell down on her behind with a short yelp.

"Claude, for god's sake." Arthur stomped toward him. "Speak to her. Make her see sense." He grabbed Claude's arm.

Claude snapped out of his grasp. "Get off me. You want to say something to her, be my guest. It's none of my business."

"You fucking selfish… cunt," he finished, spitting the words at Claude. "You've just doomed us. Any minute now they're going to exile her and it's all your bloody fault."

"I can't force her to take it," Claude roared, wiping Arthur's spittle from his face.

"Maybe we can," Wish offered. "It might be for the best if we just… I'm sorry Amanda, but maybe we have to force you. For your own good."

Amanda could not speak. Her jaw hung agape. She took a few seconds to analyze Wish, trying to get a read on whether she was serious or not. Apparently, she was.

"Are you out of your fucking mind?" Amanda was on her feet before the sentence even left her mouth. "You try to touch me, Wish, and see what happens to you."

At the scolding, Wish went through her entire repertoire of emotions in a few short breaths, eventually settling on an unreadable blankness. The light seemed to dim in her eyes, and her arms became limp as her muscles relaxed.

"Nobody is forcing anyone to do anything," Claude said, taking a strategic step closer to Amanda. "The ball's in their court." He pointed at the camera, and in response there was a hiss on the speaker.

Ding-dong.

"Amanda, you are required to take your morning dosage. Failure to comply–"

"Fuck your forfeit of funds," she blurted.

"–will result in a forfeit of funds. We would like to give you the opportunity to change your mind."

"I'm not changing shit unless I speak to someone in charge. Not this fucking dummy you send in here with the tray, either. I want to know why that woman was banging at the window and why the shutters are still down."

Ignoring her protest, the Overlord said, "For every minute that you refuse to take your morning dosage, we will dock Claude one thousand pounds from his total earnings."

"Wait, what?" Claude walked toward the camera. "Hold on a minute." He was waving a hand as though trying to get their attention. "That's not fair. I haven't broken any rules since the minute I got here."

"They can't do that," Amanda said, trying to reassure him, but even as she spoke, she knew instinctively that it wasn't a bluff.

Claude turned, seemed about to say something more, but only a gust of breath left his mouth. He shook his head, screwed his face up, and appealed once again to the camera. "Why are you docking my wages? I've taken my pill already. He saw me." Claude pointed at the nurse, before walking in front of him. "Tell them. Tell them you saw me take the pill."

"One thousand pounds have been deducted from Claude's earnings," the Overlord said.

"It's a bluff Claude," Amanda said.

His brow knitted together. "How the hell would you know?"

"Because they can't just take money out of your earnings."

"Why can't they?" he shouted. "I'm not a millionaire like you, Amanda. I need that fucking money."

She was about to put him straight about her financial situation, but could not bring herself to do so. The hurt had twisted the features in his face until it looked like a tragedy mask. A pang of guilt stabbed at her, but she couldn't give up. She couldn't let them manipulate her into doing something she knew was wrong.

"They have to pay you what you agreed in the contract," she said, unsurely. "It's against the law…"

"Against the law? Haven't you figured this out yet?" his pitch rising an octave. "This is the government we're dealing with. They can do whatever they want to us."

"No." She shook her head, wanting to say more, but could not summon the words.

"What kind of media company is going to have us taking these pills? This is the British government testing these pills on us like lab rats."

"Two thousand pounds have been deducted from Claude's earnings," the Overlord said ominously.

"Fine." He threw his hands up and slumped down in a chair. "Don't worry Amanda. In less than half an hour I'll be down to zero. Why don't you go and have your breakfast?"

She shook her head. "That's not…"

"That's not fair? Is that what you were about to say?" His eyes widened.

"This could get out of hand," Arthur said, levelling his arms out as though separating them from a physical confrontation. "Amanda, once they're through punishing him they'll start on the rest of us."

"I don't care about the rest of you," she said, accidentally letting the implication slip. Her mouth clicked shut, and she bit her tongue.

"Just yourself," Claude said.

"There really isn't any reason for you not to take the pill," Sherry said, her tone light and cajoling. She smiled but it didn't reach her crinkled eyes. "After all, if you say you're taking the placebo then there's nothing in that dish to worry about."

No, everything I have to worry about is right here with me in this house.

"If this really is some secret government experiment then what guarantee do we have to get out at all?" Amanda said. "That's what I've been trying to say all this time. They're just going to watch us through their cameras while we tear each other apart."

"Three thousand pounds have been deducted from Claude's earnings."

"Jesus, Amanda, you're killing me," Claude said, before leaning forward, resting his head in his hands. "You don't make the rules here. *They* do. You think they're going to spend all this money on an experiment like this just to have one of the participants back out halfway through?"

"I'm sorry, Claude." She shook her head. "But this isn't right. None of it is right."

"You picked a great time to take the moral high ground. And what do you think they're going to do once they fleece me of my earnings? You think they're just going to go around the houses? No, they're going to hit you with something else. The only reason they're doing this to *me* is because I'm your only friend in here." He paused. "Or at least I was."

"We could force her," Wish said again.

"You're speaking like I'm not even here, Wish, and I'm really getting sick of it."

"I'm sorry, believe me, I'm very sorry," she said, sucking up her bottom lip. "But I'm saying this for your own good. We could make you take the pill just to… to keep you."

"Keep me?"

"She means to *keep you* from being swapped into another house," Arthur amended clumsily, smoothing back the wispy tufts of white hair. He flexed his fingers, the knuckles popping rhythmically. "And I happen to agree with her."

"You would do that to me, Arthur? And you, Sherry? You would gang up on me and force the pill down my mouth against my will?"

"If it meant protecting you," Sherry began. "Then yes. And..." She looked down at her bare feet. "I think they would let us."

Slowly, Arthur crossed the room and stood in front of the door, guarding it. He may have had almost thirty years on her, but she wasn't naïve to think she could overpower him. Wish was slim but lean with muscle, and even with her bad back she probably had enough fire in her to outgun Amanda in every department. And then there was Sherry, a slab of a woman, probably with the strength of an ox. Amanda could tell by her thick legs and broad shoulders that Sherry could tear apart the whole room if the mood took her. If that did happen, would Claude help her? Would he be able to? No, Amanda realized. He couldn't hold off three of her most rabid fans, not even if he had some kind of weapon to do it with.

"Four thousand pounds have been deducted from Claude's earnings."

"Just take it all," Claude muttered. "Take it all. I don't care anymore."

Amanda felt the electric charge in the room, could almost hear it crackling like static. They had manoeuvred her into a corner and were moving in for checkmate. She was at their mercy, and she knew that she could not depend on help from the people behind the scenes. She doubted even the Overlord's voice would do anything to dissuade them if they decided to set upon her.

They could love her to death if she wasn't careful. She realized that they had banded together to form a fan club of sorts, finding solace in their despair. She hadn't given them anything to hope for, no sparkle of promise to keep their appetites at bay. All this time she had practically beaten their affections away with a stick, and now they were going to rebel.

Then, a cold, slimy thought slithered into the forefront of her mind: they could kill her on a whim. Hadn't there been cases of obsessive stalkers murdering the object of their affection for fear of losing them to someone else?

You don't hold the cards anymore, girl, she thought. *They're past that now. The honeymoon is over.*

"I think you better take your dosage," Sherry said, the lopsided grin slipping away.

"Yes," Amanda said reluctantly. "Yes, I think you could be right. I'm sorry I created a fuss."

She placed the pill on her tongue and swallowed it with a mouthful of water.

Oh Amanda you better think of something quickly.

"Good girl," Wish said.

CHAPTER 32

Amanda touched the window in the upstairs hallway that used to overlook the grounds at the back of the mansion. Now, the shutters blocked out the sunshine and the house had never felt so foreboding. There was something desperately depressing about not being able to see any natural light in the morning. It made the house seem smaller somehow. She tapped a finger against the glass, heard no echo, felt no give, and fresh torrents of sweat leaked from her pores. Even if she could break this glass – which would take a sledgehammer and a person a lot stronger than her on the other end of it – there would be no getting through the shutters. They were sardines, trapped in their tin.

A drop of sweat dripped from her nose. Her palm almost slipped off her head when she touched it. Perspiration pooled in the hollow of her neck. She looked down and saw that her blue t-shirt was soaked through, sticking to her skin, clinging to her.

"What's happening to me," she whispered, pulling the t-shirt away from her skin. She was sweating as though trapped in a sauna, and yet she could still feel the chill in the air, the cool draught sighing through the hallway. "Oh god, what on earth is going on?"

She rushed to the women's bathroom. The reflection in the mirror caused her mouth to drop open. Her skin shone slickly, the tendrils of her curly hair sticking to her cheeks and forehead. She ran the tap, splashed herself with cold water.

Leaning over the sink, she drew saliva from the back of her throat and spat the chalky taste out, and then rinsed her mouth. She slid to the floor, her clammy back resting against the frosty tiles.

It was the stress, had to be. She remembered when, during her darkest days trapped in the flat, she blacked out the windows with shoe polish after a cocaine binge left her insanely paranoid. She would huddle in a corner with the quilt over her like a tent, watching TV on her phone, expecting to see herself flash up in a news story. Her body temperature would alternate between hot and cold, and the sweat would leak out of her until she was practically soaked through. Now it was happening again, except she hadn't been near a white line in over a year, but...

But.

No adverse side effects. Sweating didn't count, did it?

After everything she'd gone through these last few days, her mental health had taken a battering, and she was unable to concentrate long enough to follow this train of thought. Not that it mattered. She was positive that four people in the house were taking a drug that tore up the contract's small print and pissed all over the "No adverse side effects" clause. The swirl of emotion that came with this realization funnelled down to outrage, yet she was powerless to fight against it. Maybe after, if she got through this week with her sanity intact, she'd think about a legal case. Right now, though, her biggest concern was that there were no locks on the bathroom doors. Now that she thought about it, the only lock she had seen in the whole house was the one on the inside of her bedroom door. Why was that? Some anomaly in the house's design? Perhaps they had wanted to remove all the locks and overlooked one. But no, she knew there were no accidents in this house.

Sleep began tugging at her gently. The energy was oozing out of her like blood from an open wound. Her body had to be working overtime to make her sweat like this, even though she had taken less than a thousand steps since waking up. How was she producing so much sweat and doing so little physically? What was going on inside her? Using the toilet for support, she pulled herself up to her feet, her soles slippery against the tiles. It occurred to her then that she might have been taking some radical new dieting pill that made her sweat all the weight off her body. This thought was followed by something far more sinister. If she *was* taking a diet pill then that would mean the others were just naturally insane, and this was scarier to her than the idea that their behaviour was being chemically altered. Either way, it amounted to the same thing: they were out to get her, by any means necessary. She began to replay Wish's words in her mind – *We can force her* – and only then did the real threat of that sentence hit home. They could have held her down and done anything they wanted to her. Anything.

The knife. She would have to keep it on her at all times, when she prepared her meals, when she went to the bathroom, when she slept. She left the bathroom and paced down the landing, wiping moisture away from her eyes, an almost compulsive need to hold the knife overriding all the other signals in her brain. She was just outside her room when she heard someone yelling maniacally. Her heart bounced in her chest, her shoulders tightening at the intensity of the sound.

She wandered to the balcony and peered down at the reception. More jumbled, frantic yelling funnelled out to meet her. Through it all, she heard her name rolling through the hallways, bouncing off the walls, shuddering in a jagged wave toward her. Someone was shouting for help while the others engaged in a fiery argument. It was a mishmash of confusion, and the only thing she could really make out was her name again, but she had never heard it sound so ugly, so strange.

"Amanda, quickly, where are you?" It was Wish. Now Amanda could hear the staccato of her rapid footsteps as she ran through the ground floor. "Amanda, please, we need your help."

No, you don't, Amanda thought and took a step back from the balcony. She quickly went into her room, retrieved the steak knife, and stuffed it into the zipped pocket of her hooded jumper.

When she emerged from her room, she heard Arthur call, "Try her room or the showers. Hurry for god's sake, *hurry*."

A distress flare shot up inside her, urging her to go back in her room and lock the door. Whatever madness was happening downstairs, she knew that she wanted no part of it. But then she heard, or thought she heard, Sherry say, "He's bleeding everywhere." Her voice seemed to come from both the ground floor and through the upstairs hallway at once, the house's acoustics bewildering her.

Claude, she thought. *What have they done to Claude?*

Wish was chugging up the stairs just as Amanda turned the handle.

"Amanda, you need to come quickly. Come now." She reached out and clasped her wrist.

Amanda pulled away. "Get off me. Don't touch me."

"He's bleeding, you need to come."

"Who's bleeding? What's happening?"

"Justin," she gasped, swallowing hard. "He's cutting himself."

CHAPTER 33

Approximately fifteen minutes before Wish reached Amanda on the landing, Justin had gone to the bathroom with his disposable razor. He had been crying on and off like a sprinkler system, bawling until all his organs seemed to retract. And then there came a point when his eyes were all out of moisture, and he was only moaning from a pain he couldn't pinpoint or understand.

That fucking fat old bag Sherry was right: he had made a spectacle of himself by not plunging the knife into Claude's stomach, and now he mourned the opportunity. Stabbing Claude would have shown Amanda just how serious he was about her; it would have been the single most romantic gesture he could offer her. Sure, she might not have understood his actions right away, but with time, she would have worked it out. She would have understood the depth of his devotion and realized what he had known all along: they were soulmates, two hearts beating as one, whatever cliché you wanted to apply.

Now a new gesture was needed.

He snapped the blades out of the disposable razor, slicing his thumb in the process. Then he pulled his top up and tucked it under his chin so that his chest was exposed. He placed the corner of the razor against his ribs on the right side of his body, and carefully concentrated on the first cut. He hissed as the razor broke skin, but whenever the pain became too intense, he refocussed his energy, her name flashing up in his mind like an SOS signal. Blood seeped down his body, soaking the top of his jogging bottoms. Writing her name from that angle was a damn sight harder than he had first imagined, and the difficulty of the task helped distract him from the pain of the wound.

By the time the others wandered back in from their morning's dosage, Justin was sitting at the breakfast table with his t-shirt pulled down and the razors resting on his lap. He could feel the blood wetting his stomach and the sharp, seething pain as the fabric of his t-shirt made contact with the cuts. Calmly, he proceeded to eat a large bowl of Rice Crispies, the milk turning pink as blood dripped from his fingers each time he dipped his spoon in the bowl.

Claude noticed first. Of course he did, the fucking bastard. He had sat down with a buttered crumpet and had casually looked over at Justin. His eyes were drawn to the bloody finger smears on Justin's cup, and upon closer inspection, Claude saw that Justin's t-shirt was dark with blood.

"Justin…you're bleeding," he said, scraping the chair away from the table. "Don't move. I'll get something." As Claude charged for the kitchen towel, he said, "What have you done, Justin? Tell me. You need to trust me for a second, OK? Tell me what you've done, and I can get help."

Laughing, Justin ignored his offer and wandered through to the drawing room with the animal heads glaring down from above the fireplace, the blood dripping from his chest and leaving a red trail behind him. When Amanda finally caught up to him, he was sitting in one of the leather armchairs staring into the pile of unlit logs.

Arthur, Sherry, and Claude remained a safe distance away. Amanda wondered why they weren't trying to help Justin until she noticed that he was still holding a razor blade between his fingers.

"Ah, here you are," Justin said, in a voice that sounded very far away. He looked over at her, his skin curdled pale, his eyes bulging inside their dark hollows. "I've got your attention now, I see."

Amanda surveyed him quickly. She saw that he was bleeding profusely but only had the vaguest idea of what had actually happened. She looked over at Claude for an explanation.

"He cut his chest up," Claude started to say, but was drowned out by Justin.

"Don't spoil it," he mewled. "It's not your news to tell. This isn't yours, Claude. This is mine."

"Alright, I'm sorry," Claude said, "but you don't look so good."

"You're right about that," he replied flatly. "Might've nicked something important."

"Someone get a wet towel or something," Amanda said, and then looked up at the cruel, black eye of the camera. "For god's sake he's bleeding all over the place! Send some help."

"Who are you talking to?" Justin asked, his thin lips seeming to darken against his sickly complexion. "Nobody's there. I finally figured it out. We're in hell. Don't you get it?"

She looked at the others, appealing for help. That awful feeling of helplessness closed in on her when she saw their blank stares, like a row of window display mannequins.

"Claude," she began, noticing that his was the only face with some semblance of rationality remaining in it, "we need a doctor."

"What are you telling *him* for?" Justin demanded, drunkenly. "He can't help you."

"It's you that needs the help," she replied, noticing that the blood was still flowering through his t-shirt. "How deep did you cut?"

"I'll show you." He started to stand, sweat speckling his bone-white brow.

"Perhaps you'd better stay seated, old boy," Arthur said. "You don't want to keel over, now do you?"

"He's right," Sherry added. "Let's take a proper look at you. I'm first aid trained, so I can get you a nice clean bandage and–"

"I don't need a bandage," he groaned, slumping back down. "It doesn't hurt." Gingerly, he began to peel the t-shirt up, hissing as the fabric unstuck from the clotting blood. The cuts made some jagged approximation of Amanda's name like an angry billboard. His stomach was awash with crimson that had seeped down over his crotch.

"Oh Holy Jesus," Claude whispered, the words trembling from his lips.

"I'm going to get help," Amanda said. "The rest of you just stay with him and–"

"If you go I'll kill myself," Justin said hoarsely, bringing the razor tip to the soft, stubbly flesh beneath his chin. "No rehearsal this time."

"Justin, stop that," Amanda snapped. "Just stop it. What's the matter with you?"

"I don't want you disappearing," he said.

"Don't be silly," Wish said. "You don't have to do this."

"Maybe I do. I have to show Amanda what she means to me."

"OK just hold on a second." Amanda, thinking on her feet, took a step closer. She saw his whole demeanour change, the muscles loosening ever so slightly in his arms, his nostrils flaring. "Justin, those cuts need to be treated. Sherry can do first aid and we can get you bandaged up. Will you let her do that? For me?"

"Do you like it?" he asked.

"Like it?"

"The tattoo!" he screamed with his eyes closed. "I did it for you. Your name on my skin forever."

"I don't like that you hurt yourself." She tried for a smile but wasn't sure what appeared on her face. She turned to Sherry and saw that she and the others had their attention glued on Amanda. They were entranced, breathing deeply, their eyes clouded with something that Amanda couldn't readily identify. Lust? Hatred? Amanda turned her attention to Claude. "Can you get the first aid kit, and try the Circle Room for a medic?"

"If a medic was going to help, they would be here by now," Claude said.

"Try anyway," Amanda barked back at him. "I'm not going to get any help out of anyone else."

"Yes, that's it," Justin said. "Get him out of here. I can't stand looking at his ugly fucking face any longer."

"Amanda, I don't think it's a good idea," Claude said. "I don't think I should leave."

Justin dragged the razor across the inside of his own forearm. Blood spilled out from the wound in a neat, alarming line. The muscles in Amanda's legs softened, her knees buckling slightly. She felt like a buoy at sea. Numbness crept across her skin like a rash. She had never been squeamish at the sight of blood, but the savagery of his mutilation unglued her from reality. She was going to faint, she was sure of it.

"I'll end it here and it will be your fault Amanda," he screamed.

"He's going to pass out unless one of you get help," Claude said.

"You go," Sherry replied. "We're not leaving Amanda with him. Not in this state."

"I'm not leaving her either," Claude said, defensively. "He's dangerous."

"Only to himself," Arthur said. "We can protect her better than you can. You're only setting him off, making him more volatile."

Justin wiped his bloody arm across his forehead, smearing it with crimson war paint. "Look at that. I think I nicked an artery. I'll probably bleed out in a little while. But that'll be good, won't it, Amanda? You'll understand then, won't you?"

"What do you want?" she said through frozen lips.

"You," he said. "I want you."

He sprung up and stepped toward her, clutching his arm, blood drooling between his fingers. Arthur, Wish and Sherry huddled in front of Amanda, forming a protective barrier against him.

"Keep back," Sherry said to Justin. "We're going to patch you up but don't do anything stupid, young man."

Over her shoulder, Wish said to Claude, "Go. We won't let anything happen to her. Get help."

Claude looked at Wish, tried to see past her drug-induced mania. A few days ago, he had thought she was pretty – no, more than that, stunning. When she entered the house, she had looked like a model with a smile that gave off an almost radiant glow. Now, that burning beacon of light had fizzled to cinders. Wish's face was drawn, her eyes rolling around like marbles, never fixing on anything except Amanda. Her teeth bared as though about to viciously snap at anything that got too close. He didn't want to leave Amanda but knew how feverishly loyal they were to her. Not one of them would harm a hair on her head, and in many ways, Amanda was safer with these maniacs than anyone else on earth.

Amanda was their queen.

And still, Claude could not help but feel that it was all a performance, as though their forced concern for Justin was part of some bigger conspiracy.

"Alright, for god's sake," Claude shouted, his voice booming through the vast room. "Amanda, I'll be right back, OK?"

"Yes," she said. "But hurry up."

Reluctantly, Claude turned and ran out of the room. He was in good shape, and at the pace he was moving, it would not take him long to retrieve the first aid kit and fly by the Circle Room.

When Claude was gone, Justin's thin lips tugged into a ghastly grin. "Now we have her," he said.

Before the words had fully registered, Amanda saw Arthur whirl on her. His shovel hand clasped around her bicep. Her lips parted to protest, but before anything could leave her mouth, Arthur punched her, once, twice, and when his arm raised for the third blow, the darkness claimed her.

CHAPTER 34

Movement. Pressure in her head and eyeballs. She was upside down. Swaying.

"We'll build a fortress." Sherry's voice emerged from the fog. "The landing. That's the only place to do it."

"Don't be stupid. We have to put her in a room," Wish said.

Amanda looked through her lashes, keeping her eyes as closed as possible. She saw the floor moving away from her. Judging by the feel of the body beneath hers, it was Arthur carrying her.

"Why don't both of you... shut up and... keep your eyes peeled for god's sake." Arthur was breathless, constantly adjusting her weight on his shoulder, his hands pressed lovingly against the backs of her thighs. The motion stopped.

"What are you doing?" Justin hissed.

"She's heavier than she looks." Arthur was gulping in air. "And I'm not as fit as I used to be."

"Then let me carry her."

"I'm surprised you're still standing at all with the amount of blood you've lost. No, you've done enough," Arthur told him. "Sherry, Wish, you might need me to help me get her up the stairs."

"Wait, what was that?" Wish whispered.

Amanda's hair was splashed across her face. She took a chance and opened her eyes a little wider. She couldn't tell where in the house she was. The lining of her jaw ached, felt off kilter. Was it broken?

Somewhere in the distance, Claude was calling her name.

"Don't worry about him," Justin said icily. "There's four of us and one of him."

"There's three and a half of us," Sherry said. "You look like you've just walked out of a fucking slaughterhouse."

"You don't need to worry about me. I can take care of him."

"You should have taken care of him yesterday when you had the chance," Sherry replied. "And why are we still standing around talking about this? We need to get her upstairs on the landing so that we can have all bases covered. We can see the ground floor and the–"

Amanda's name echoed through the hallway.

"That's him again," Sherry said.

"So what?" Justin said. "He won't have anything on him."

Maybe not, Amanda thought hazily. But I do.

Wish said to Justin: "I will go to him and end it."

"You'd fuck it up," Justin replied.

Arthur groaned, and then Amanda felt her body being lowered. He placed her down softly on the carpet and she let her hand drop strategically near her zipped pocket.

"She makes a point," Arthur said, wheezing. "We could just go to him and get the fly out of the ointment now. I don't know why we scurried off like thieves in the night in the first place."

"Because he could still be dangerous," Sherry said. "He's young and strong."

"So am I," Justin interjected.

Slowly, Amanda's thumb and forefinger began pulling the zip.

"You're young and stupid," Sherry corrected. "And you happen to be pissing blood all over the place." She lowered her voice and said, "Even with four of us, Claude is still a threat. So let's just get her up to the landing where we have upper ground."

"Why even take her upstairs?" Wish burst in. "What is the point? Let's just take her into one of these rooms."

"We can't back ourselves into a room. We need a way to see everything that's going on," Sherry informed her. "If it's not Claude coming for her then it will be one of those nurses or a guard or something. Because god knows we're not making it to tonight's assignment, and when we don't, they'll come for her. And we can't let anyone take her, I think we're all in agreement, yes?"

Amanda's hand slithered into her pocket. She heard Claude shouting for her, his voice growing louder.

"If we do this right, there's a chance we can share her. But if we don't work together now, we'll lose her forever. So get your fucking heads screwed on," Sherry continued. "We stick together and let him come for us. Then we can deal with him and not a moment before. Now, have you had a sufficient tea break, old man? Or do you want to wait until they send in a bunch of guards to come looking for her?"

Arthur bent down by Amanda's side and shoved one hand under her legs and another hand under her back, his fingers pressing against the side of her breast as he began to lift her. She waited until he had raised her a couple of feet off the ground, and then her hand withdrew from her pocket. She drove the knife into Arthur's neck and twisted the handle as hard as she could, and felt his arms loosen. Before she hit the floor again, a warm jet of blood shot out of his wound and sprayed into her face. The wetness registered dully in her mind, as did Arthur's cough-scream, but she was already on the move, scrambling to her feet and bolting like an animal down the long hallway toward the sound of Claude's voice.

CHAPTER 35

In the first three years of high school, Amanda had been a part of the athletic program and on two occasions had almost come first in the hundred-metre dash at the county championships. She had not needed to run for anything other than the school bus since she was fifteen, but thankfully, her muscles had retained the memory. The extra weight she was carrying didn't slow her down. The adrenaline was burning through her system, numbing all feeling, sharpening her senses, and she became acutely aware of the space around her. Her arms and legs worked to propel her forward at a speed that almost bewildered her. She saw Claude passing down the adjacent corridor carrying the green first aid kit like a suitcase. He stopped, turned, saw her sprinting at him, and his eyes widened.

"They're coming," she blurted, but needn't have wasted the breath. She realized that Claude was in fact looking past her at Wish, who was less than fifty yards behind her.

Claude braced himself, a deer in the headlights, and called out, "What's happening?"'

Claude dropped the first aid kit, and when Amanda reached him at the end of the hallway, he grabbed her hand and ran with her. He took the lead, almost dragging her. Behind them, Wish was screaming, an angry cocktail of French and English.

They were on the opposite side of the house from the passageway. She knew as they approached the staircase that he meant to take her up and around to the other side. When they were trampling up the stairs, Amanda saw Wish emerge into the reception, her head whipping around until she locked eyes with Amanda. Wish released a horrendous sound that almost stopped them dead. It was more than a scream of rage; it was a primal war cry, something that belonged in the Jurassic era.

"Quicker," was all Claude said, and Amanda found the energy from somewhere. She broke free of his grasp and began to run side by side with him. Soon, she overtook him and led the way, bringing them to the T–section where the end of their hallway joined the middle of a new one.

When she turned right, he said, "No, this way – we need to get to the other staircase."

"They'll be waiting for us there. Come this way, trust me."

They had created enough of distance between them and Wish, but the sound of her feet thudding on the hardwood floors was still audible. Amanda stopped at the library door, twisted the handle, and went in. Claude followed, closing the door as quietly as he could. Amanda hurried down the middle of the aisle between the rows of bookcases to the very end of the room. There, they posted up in the corner, which gave them a vantage point of the door yet offered enough cover to remain concealed.

Her heart felt like trampling hoofbeats in her chest. In the dusty silence of the library, their panting was as loud as a chugging train engine. Amanda closed her mouth to regulate her breathing, but her lungs caught fire.

"You're bleeding," he whispered.

"It isn't mine."

CHAPTER 36

"Is he dead?" Justin asked, holding the cut on his forearm. His sodden t-shirt had grafted to the cuts on his chest and created something of a bandage, although every time he moved he could feel each individual slice.

Kneeling down by Arthur's body, Sherry said, "There or thereabouts." Her knees creaked and popped as she stood up. "Fuck him anyway. We need to find her."

Arthur lay in a pool of his own blood, the knife handle sticking out the side of his neck.

He looks like a Christmas turkey, Justin thought. Justin knelt to retrieve the knife, releasing a jet of arterial blood from the wound.

"And then what?" Justin asked. Worry had crept into his words and he now sounded like a scared little boy, turning to his mother for reassurance. "What do we do when we find her? She's not going to want to come with us."

"Come with us where? Where is it you think we're going to go, Justin? Hmm? Do you think that they're just going to open the doors and we're going to walk out of here hand in hand into the sunset? You think we're all going to move in and live together happily ever after?"

"We could apologize. We could say we're sorry and… maybe if we put all our money together she'll want to…"

Sherry slapped him hard across the face. The impact almost knocked him off his feet.

"Pull yourself together and stop feeling so fucking sorry for yourself. I need you thinking clearly and coherently."

He shied away from her, fearing he would be struck again, and said, "Please don't hit me. I'm dizzy."

"Of course you're dizzy, you stupid idiot. Look at what you've done to yourself."

"It was for her," he said, almost slurring.

"Fat lot of good it's done."

From the ground, Arthur gurgled and hiccupped. A blood bubble burst in his mouth. Sherry regarded him and groaned with contempt. "Useless men. You have so much bravado don't you." She kicked Arthur's legs. "But you're all soft as runny shit when it comes down to it. Aren't you?" She stomped down on Arthur's kneecap, but he gave no response. She spun to face Justin, her cheeks redolent with rage, the blood vessels bursting in her eyes. She was snarling. "Go upstairs and sweep the whole floor. Check every door, every nook and cranny. If you find her, yell for me."

"I will," he said. He had paled so much that his skin had taken on an ashy, almost green hue.

"Then get a move on with it." She watched him struggle down the hallway, palming the wall as he walked, leaving a red trail along the wallpaper. Her eyes fixed on the knife in his loose grasp, and she knew that in his weakened state it would be about as effective as a croissant if he came up across Claude.

"Ple…"

Distracted, Sherry looked down at Arthur. She had momentarily forgotten about him and was vaguely surprised that he had enough strength to almost form a word. She thought he had been dead these few minutes. He was white as a milk bottle, which made the splatter about his lips look almost neon red.

"Please?" she said softly. "Please what?"

"Pl…" The word was stolen by a guttural groan.

"Please?" She laughed darkly. "What do you want me to do, Mr. Arthur? She stuck you good. No coming back from that. You know something, I think I admire her even more for doing such a service to the house." She towered over Arthur's prone body, delighting in the way his white hands weakly groped at the air. "Does it hurt? Well, you have been nothing but a pain in the neck, am I right?" She giggled, and then guffawed at her own wit. "I like that one. Perhaps I'll run it past Amanda. That'll tickle her, I'm sure." She lifted her foot and stepped in the centre of Arthur's chest, pressing her weight down. Black blood pumped out of his neck. Arthur's mouth opened to allow one final rattling breath to escape. "That's for Sponge."

Drifting now. Vision fading, all sound silencing. Tumbling down a darkened tunnel, Arthur recalled that blurred photograph of his son, who might even have children of his own by now. The photo bubbled and melted away, and was replaced with Amanda, standing on a West End stage, glittering, glowing, calling for him to take one final bow.

Thoughts slipping away like grains of sand through cupped hands. All except the last…

The quality of mercy is not strain'd, it droppeth as the gentle rain from heaven upon the place beneath: it is twice blest; It blesseth him that gives and him that takes… that takes…

Wish flung the door open to a room she had not previously come across. She reached up and clicked the light switch on. A sodium glow washed over a study with leather-backed chairs, desks, lamps, and a large rectangular window that would have allowed light to pour in had the shutters not been down. She did a quick tour of the room, prowling around to check all the potential hiding spaces, and decided it was empty. She was on her way out when something caught her eye: a pair of battle-axes crossed in front of a wooden shield, about ten feet up the wall.

*

"What are we going to do?" Amanda whispered. She had spent the last couple of minutes containing a cough from the dust that tickled her throat.

"I don't know," Claude said, peering around the bookcase, scoping the door. The nightmare image of Wish sprinting down the hallway holding a knife bled into his mind. He briefly considered whether stuffing one of these books down his shirt would make a good stab-proof vest, and shook the idiotic thought out of his mind. "We can't stay here for long. We need to get to the passageway."

"What if it's locked?"

"It won't be."

"It was the other day when I checked."

"Then I'll kick it down. I don't care if I break every bone in my foot, I'll get us in there. If I remember rightly, the door wasn't that thick. It shouldn't take too much persuasion."

"They might dock our wages," Amanda said dryly. She could feel nervous laughter bubbling up in her stomach and bit down on her lower lip to keep it at bay.

"I hope you're joking."

"Sorry. I'm just really scared. They're going to kill us."

"Not us," Claude corrected. "Me. They're going to kill me so that they can get you all to themselves."

"And then what? Why aren't the company doing anything about this? Why are they just letting this happen?"

"Amanda, I..." He stopped, swallowed. His throat clicked.

"What? What is it? What were you going to say?"

"I'm not who you think I am. I'm not a car salesman."

Amanda's head turned to him. A dozen cliché horror moments flashed through her mind, variations of the scene where the killer is finally unveiled to be the person you least expected. She felt her muscles tighten and edged away from him. Her back made contact with a row of books.

"Then who are you, Claude?"

"Don't look at me like that. Please Amanda."

"Don't please me, Claude. You know what's going on, don't you?"

Slowly, he nodded.

"You've known all along. And you're choosing now to let me in on this?" She lurched, both fists tightly clenched.

"Now's not the time for this. We need to work together."

"Tell me what's going on!" She spoke too loudly and cringed at the imagined amplification of her voice.

His face was stricken. He wouldn't look her in the eyes. He leaned forward on a bookshelf, using it for support, and rested his forehead against a stack of encyclopedias. "I work for them."

A gust of air rocketed out of Amanda's mouth. "You... what?"

He shook his head. "It's too long for me to explain now. But I will do. I'll get us out of here and then I'll tell you everything. Amanda, please... they lied to me. I didn't know... I didn't..." Without knowing he was doing it, Claude reached for her hand. She drew away from him.

"Don't touch me. I..." She could feel her eyes aching with tears. She took a deep breath, refusing to break the promise she had made with herself, that she would never let another man make her cry ever again. "I trusted you, Claude."

"And I trusted them. This was supposed to just be a harmless experiment. I got the same brief as all of you, you have to believe me. I was just told to... play along, help things go smoothly. There was a little machine in the air vent in my room. I got messages like the one that told me about the Queen Cage. They said if things get out of hand that's where you must go. It's completely safe, bulletproof glass, locks from the inside. They wanted you to know that."

He began toward her. She slapped his hand away again.

"I stabbed Arthur and it's because of you," Amanda said, still walking backwards.

"No, not because of me, Amanda. I didn't want this to happen. You think I wanted people dead? It isn't my fault. It was just a job."

"And it isn't theirs either. They're taking a drug."

"No, they're not," he said, slowly shaking his head. "They're taking placebos."

She stopped, the confusion swirling around her mind like dense fog. She tasted salt on her upper lip. She opened her mouth to speak but the library door clanged open. Amanda almost yelped in fright. She ducked down behind a bookcase, peering between a gap in the dusty tomes, and saw Wish walking down the aisle, dragging the axe behind her.

"Come to do some reading, have we?" Wish said, her words echoing through the books. "Amanda, I know you can hear me. Please just listen for a second. The rest of us just want to keep you safe. There is evil in this house and we need to protect you from it. So please, come out from wherever you are hiding, and I will take you back to the others. That sounds nice, doesn't it?"

Amanda stared at the floor, saw a smattering of sweat spots from where the perspiration had dripped from her forehead and chin. She tried to judge the distance between Wish and the library door, wondering if she could outrun her.

Before she could make her move, Claude grabbed her from behind.

CHAPTER 37

"Don't make a sound," he breathed in her ear, one hand covering her mouth. He was so close she could smell the faint aroma of his shaving cream. "I'm going to distract her, and when I do, make your move."

He removed the hand from her mouth and reached out for a book, carefully sliding it free from its place on the shelf. He stepped in front of Amanda, gave her one last hopeful smile, and then started to creep down the far aisle. A floorboard creaked underfoot, and Wish locked in on the sound, cocking her ear in Claude's direction.

"No need to be sneaky, Amanda. I haven't given you a reason to be upset with me, have I? Remember, we wrote each other's name on the board that first day. Best friends, remember?" As Wish spoke, she heaved the axe up.

And that's when Claude threw the book high in the air. Wish didn't see its ascent, but the flapping of pages overhead snagged her attention and she turned just in time to see it thump on the floor at the other side of the library. With her back turned, Claude broke into a run and dashed for the door. Wish saw him, and this time there was no dramatic scream, but instead, she took after him with the axe raised high in the air. He reached the door, and Amanda's body clenched for the second and a half that it took him to turn the handle and get it open, Wish swiping the air after him.

Amanda heard Wish shout something in the hallway, and a moment later there was only silence. Amanda's wet hair stuck to the back of her neck. She was thirsty and the library felt like it was swaying, but she continued to pad down the far aisle, remaining hidden behind the bookshelves. The door was twenty feet away. All she had to do was open it and brave the hallway and pray to god that she didn't bump into the rest of them.

She opened it a crack and peered out. In the distance, so far away that it was difficult to discern whether it was her imagination or not, she heard shouting. There was nothing else. She pulled the door back, gritting her teeth against the screech of the hinges, and stepped back out into the hallway.

She has an axe, Claude thought, his mind unable to process the image. It was almost like one of those wacky cartoons. He could hear her rhythmic exhalations behind him, and through the panic he tried to assess how much ground he had on her. *Not enough*. He had seen her limping around the house, placing a fist in her lower back to alleviate the nag, but right now it seemed she could run a marathon without much of a problem. He, on the other hand, wasn't so sure of his own abilities. He was scared, and the fear was emptying him. Where could he run to? Amanda's room had a lock and it would take an awful lot to batter the door down, but between them he was sure they would manage it given time. He came to the T-section in the hallway, feinted as though he was going to continue going straight, and at the last instant changed direction, cutting to the left. He had hoped that Wish would copy his movement, maybe lose her footing, and go sprawling to buy him some preciously needed seconds of ground.

It didn't work. If he continued going down this hallway, he would emerge into the landing that led to the western staircase. Once there, all he had to do was scurry down it and make his way over to the passageway. But what if the others were waiting for him? Well then, he would deal with them when he crossed that bridge and not a moment before, because right now he had a rabid dog on his back. He could hear her swiping the axe through the air, making a violent whooshing sound that made his stomach clench with fear.

How sharp could that axe be, anyway? It was an ornament, probably couldn't cut its way through a cardboard box. No, but with a strong enough swipe it could break a bone. If she caught him about the neck, she could crack his spine, paralyse him. Hit him in the head and he was dead.

Wish was close enough to see the fine hairs on Claude's nape as he ran. Each time her left foot made contact with the floor, a jolt of pain surged up that side of her body, culminating in her lower back. The pain, while enormous, also seemed to be very far away, like a rumble of thunder in a receding storm. The muscles in her neck ached tremendously from the stress of the chase, but she was gaining on him.

A single reel of footage jumped and skipped on the projection screen of her brain: Amanda, holding the whiteboard with her name written on it: *Wish*. And had she ever seen such beautiful handwriting before? No, never. People often complimented Wish on having such a unique and pretty name, but somehow, Amanda's delicate cursive script breathed poetry into it almost as if… as if that single syllable attached to her at birth had never really had any meaning until it slipped from Amanda's lips. As if the name was invented for Amanda. As if…

This is wrong. You know this is wrong, Wish.

The intrusion caused her to slow a step, the footage flickering as though the reel needed replacing. Somewhere in the theatre of her exhausted mind, Wish knew that she wanted to watch something else, but she was powerless to do so. Her thoughts were a constant montage of Amanda's face – with her guarded smile, and the sometimes fierce intensity behind her eyes – and Wish knew that it was killing her somehow, draining her.

She could almost feel the circuit breakers in her brain frying from the constant focus, from the desperation of meditating so hard, mentally blocking out anything else that dared invade her conscience.

Do you want to lose her?

No, obviously not. Amanda needed protecting. She needed Wish's friendship. She needed her love.

Wish picked up the pace again, renewed by the memory of Amanda's husky yet lilting voice, cooing in conversation. God, when Amanda spoke, said something even as mundane as, "Could you pass the salt?" it was like listening to a choir, full of soul, oozing emotion. She was nearly crying now, thinking about how Amanda had wished her a good night before bed, and how beautiful those few seconds were as she watched Amanda leave.

Not for the first time, Wish considered the notion that Amanda was her real sister. Perhaps that explained the strength of their bond, the fusion of their souls, the marrying of their personalities. Yes, it was possible – not in any physical way – but in the spiritual sense, that God put two people together at a specific point in time, like pieces of puzzle slotting into place, completing a perfect picture.

That was why she'd had the crash; not because the brake pads on her ancient Peugeot were shot to bits, but because it was divine intervention. Wish needed that crash to happen, to break her body so that her soul was free to find Amanda. All the pain she went through, the surgeries, the excruciating physio, the mental anguish, the trauma of reliving the accident every time she fell asleep, the depression of losing her career, the PTSD when she heard a Beyoncé song, it was all for a reason. She went through that nightmare to find her true calling in life, and nothing was going to stand in the way of it. There wasn't a force on earth strong enough to take Amanda away from her now.

She pushed her body harder and viciously swung the axe.

Its edge was a couple of inches away from shaving the back of his head. He tried to zigzag but she didn't falter. There was six feet between them. Wish sprung through the air with the axe clutched in both hands.

The hallway darkened with each step Justin took. He leaned against a door, the floor spongy as a mattress beneath his feet. He thought he could feel the cuts opening as he walked, and a terrible image floated through his mind. He saw Amanda's name opening up in his flesh, allowing enough room for his innards to poke their way out. He saw his intestines pushing through the slits like sausage meat through a butcher's grinder. His mouth was very dry, and the stink of blood hung about him in a coppery cloud. The cut on his arm was deep enough so that he could see the yellow sliver of fat beneath his skin, but not deep enough so that he could see bone. It would not close on its own, would likely need several stitches to do the job, but it had stopped bleeding. Now, only a clear yellow puss seeped from the crimson chasm in his arm, and he was sure that it had a faint odour, something that reminded him of disinfectant and the medical bay at his primary school.

He thought he might pass out on numerous occasions, and yet he was still lucid. He felt completely weak, as though a strong draught could topple him like a bowling pin.

"Amanda," he muttered, the name sitting bitterly on his tongue. "Oh, my sweet Amanda."

He could not understand any of this. Why had she run away from them? Didn't she see that they were trying to keep her safe from the evils of the house, and beyond? And now here he was, torturously plodding through the barren house in search of a woman who would only reject him. He knew there would be no sharing her. It was impossible. Each of them had made some claim to her, but only he was truly worthy. There was no going around it. A bigger sacrifice was needed, and what could be more romantic than ending her life before ending his own? He could send their souls to paradise, entwined for eternity.

He shook his head, trying to clear his rapidly darkening vision. He imagined waiting nervously at the altar as she slowly made her way down the aisle, trailing a long train, holding a beautiful bouquet to her bosom. When he looked into the imaginary congregation that packed the church pews, he saw his mother and father – divorced, but reunited for this special moment – and they were watching Amanda too, smiling proudly because he had made such an excellent choice. He could hear his father's voice telling him that he had nailed it, that she was a stunner. Then his mother was telling him how pretty their children would be, and what a wonderful mother Amanda would make.

In his mind's eye, he saw Amanda reach him, with a smile on her lips that melted his heart. She pulled back the veil, her dark eyes meeting his, her full lips waiting to be kissed. Sunshine flooded in through the stained-glass windows, and at that very moment it was like a personal present from God, pointing the spotlight right on them.

He would take her hand, and while the preacher – or priest or deacon or whatever they were called – addressed the congregation, he would lean in close to her and say, "You will never know how happy you have made me today." She would bat her eyelashes and say, "No, you don't know how happy you've made me, my love." Then they would exchange a look that would begin as a loving gaze and evolve into an unspoken, lustful agreement. That evening, after they ate and danced and he made a speech where he would tell their friends and family how lucky he was to have her, he would take her to bed. They would make tender love, and she would find out she was pregnant while they were on their honeymoon, somewhere exotic with a beach and sunsets.

She would look at the sunset, her face glowing, and then she would turn back to him with a flower in her hair. Softly, she would say, "And just think, Justin. This almost didn't happen."

He tried to think of more, but the sand had slipped from his grasp, and the vision fell apart.

The scream built up in his throat. He opened his mouth and her name tore free from his body, loud and thunderous.

Amanda had crept through the upper floor, her head on a swivel as she checked her surroundings. She heard her name ricocheting through the house and ice flooded her veins. It was Justin screaming, his voice sounding as though it came from a bigger, older man. He sounded as though he were possessed by the devil. She stalled for the couple of seconds it took for her heartbeat to get back on track, and then continued creeping. The landing was up ahead, and all she had to do then was get downstairs. It occurred to her that if she was correct, Justin was on the upper floor with her. If Claude had managed to lose Wish on the other side of the house, then that could mean that only Sherry was downstairs patrolling. *Only Sherry*, she thought humourlessly. Sure, she would be able to outrun the older woman, but what if Sherry caught up to her and made it a physical exchange? Sherry, who had slipped deeper and deeper down the dark well of obsession, would easily ragdoll Amanda. *I just can't let it get to that point then*, Amanda thought. *I can't let her back me into a corner and have her way with me.*

The side of her face ached constantly from where Arthur had attacked her, and the hinges of her jaw felt as though they were rusting closed. She had been hit in the face before by a complete stranger, when she was doing a CD signing at HMV to promote her album. A deranged fan slapped her after posing for a photo with her. In court, his defence had been that he was doing it as part of a YouTube prank show and he had never meant to cause Amanda any physical harm, and in a way he hadn't. The slap had been unexpected and, when the adrenaline died away, her cheek tingled. But the psychological impact had lasted deep into her career.

She inched closer to the end of the hallway, sidling along with her back to the wall. The acoustics in the house played tricks on her. Several times she thought she had heard Claude shouting but couldn't be sure where it was coming from. She couldn't think of him now. He was on his own and so was she. She had to survive.

When she neared the landing, her footsteps were muted by the carpet. She stopped, cocking her ear to try to pinpoint any movement. Nothing. The house throbbed with eerie silence, which was disturbed every so often by a creak from the foundations, the wind rattling through the window shutters.

All she had to do was turn the corner of the hallway and follow the landing around to the staircase. If she was quick, she could make it to the passageway beneath the stairs on the other side of the house in a minute or so. She mapped it all out in her mind, took a deep breath, and then emerged onto the landing.

"Hello," Sherry said.

CHAPTER 38

Over the course of the day, the remaining shareholders drifted into the main viewing room, their curiosity piqued by the pandemonium. Hitchson had mentioned that boredom had got the better of just over a dozen shareholders, who had decided to leave and withdraw their support for project Honeycomb. Moshida knew they had probably all branded him a madman. That was OK though. Part of this process was to weed out the wheat from the chaff, to get rid of anyone who didn't have the imagination to extrapolate on what they were seeing.

Richard Flannigan had been the first one in, which didn't surprise Moshida. He supposed that Flannigan, being one of the few self-made millionaires among them, was the most inquisitive, most eager to expand. Moshida could smell his shaving cream from ten paces, and the Listerine on the man's breath, probably to help mask the cognac that he drank like a fish, even in the morning.

The leather sofa squeaked as Flannigan hefted his bulk and sat down. Moshida heard a spark, a puff, and then smelled the pungent smoke. "Did she stab him for real?" he asked around the cigar.

"I assume you zoomed in and saw the blood for yourself?" Moshida asked without diverting his eyes or attention from the screens.

"I did, yeah. But it's just... she stabbed him? It wasn't a gimmick blade?"

A gimmick blade? Moshida had absolutely no answer for

such nonsense, and so remained silent. That didn't seem to bother Flannigan, who continued watching the screens intently. Moshida heard a rattle and knew that Flannigan was shaking a glass with ice cubes in it, waiting for Hitchson to refill him.

"Nice rooms you put us in, by the way," Flannigan said. "I've been meaning to ask you – those fish you got in the walls, the uh... the purple ones with the yellow eyes. What are they called?"

"Kole Tang," Moshida said, barely moving his lips or raising his voice above a whisper.

"Kole Tang," Flannigan repeated. "Sounds like something you'd order from a Chinese takeaway." He laughed, puffed on the cigar, and said, "You're not Chinese are you, James?"

"No."

All the rooms that the shareholders stayed in were fitted with a bank of screens, depicting different areas in the two houses. Complete with sound options that could be toggled between screens, the experiment was a voyeur's wet dream. The fact that most of the shareholders had remained in their rooms was evidence enough of the experiment's entertainment value. It was a beguiling alloy of morbid fascination and compulsive curiosity that held them prisoner, keeping them glued to the screens.

More voices filled the main viewing room, but Moshida did not turn to see who was there. Their conversation was little more than elevator music to him. Tuning in and out, he picked up little snippets that he found particularly revealing. They were discussing the stabbing in hushed tones, and the breach in House 2.

"...I mean did you see the blood? It was like a fountain." The voice, which was tinged with amusement, belonged to a crypto trader who also ran a plethora of illegal services on the Deep Web. "Guess he won't be doing any musicals from now on. She got him right in the Adam's apple."

"...I know he said that the footage would be kept confidential and everything, but I think we're well within our rights to get a copy of all this. The best bits, I mean. Not all the sitting around and playing Monopoly. I mean, some of it is fucking gold."

"Like the stabbing?"

"*Especially* the stabbing."

A chorus of hilarity ensued. Andrew Madison, the American movie producer, said, "I once saw a homeless guy smash another bum in the head with a hammer on 44th Street. I mean he just bludgeoned him right there in the open for everyone to see. And that was in *Manhattan*. This kind of thing happens all the time. They're animals. You can take them off the street and scrub them up a bit, but they're really one step removed from hyenas."

The conversation drifted back and forth, recapping and reviewing the past few days' activity. Someone said, "You know, I was really hoping that Amanda and that Robert guy would fuck. It's like watching a sitcom, isn't it?"

"Claude, you mean," someone corrected.

"Yeah whatever."

They were all there in the main viewing room, which was the size of a small cinema, drinking, smoking, and jabbering away. The subject of the chitchat moved from Amanda's stabbing and refocused onto which of the other housemates might kill her. Bets were being made, with shareholders offering up larger wagers for predicting the particular manner of the murder.

But not one of them was discussing the pill and the effect it was having on them. They seemed more interested in the savagery of the beating administered to Rebecca in House 2, rather than what had driven the other housemates to behave in such a way. The daily dosage had been slightly higher in House 2, and the outcome had been remarkable, even if none of the shareholders had appreciated the significance. With just a few extra milligrams per pill, the housemates in House

2 had turned on their Queen, their obsession morphing into entitled rage.

"So, what will they do to Amanda? Kill her?"

It was Nevers, the eerie cadence of his speech finally distracting Moshida. He turned, saw the straggly older man standing there like a mantis in a V-neck, with his hands stuffed deep into his corduroy trousers. Nevers pointed absently at the screens and said, "They're going to kill her now, right?"

"I don't know," Moshida admitted, though he was fairly sure that Amanda's admirers weren't quite there yet. They would cycle through a gamut of emotions before reaching their nihilistic conclusion: Amanda was theirs, and nothing was going to convince them otherwise. If they couldn't have her, then nobody could. "If she's as clever as I think she is, she'll go to the Queen Cage. If she doesn't…" Moshida shrugged. "Then it's anyone's guess."

Nevers nodded in understanding and then stroked his cheek. Staring at the screens, his eyes had become filmy and distant, the light flickering against his face. "I don't suppose you would sell her, would you?"

At this, the talk around the viewing room began to subside, and the shareholders' attention diverted to Moshida. Apparently, Nevers' bizarre proposal was more interesting than the action on screen.

"Sell her?" Moshida was momentarily confused.

"Yes. You could stop this…" He gestured to the screens. "And give her to me. I'd be willing to offer you a fair rate for her."

"What're you gonna do, Matt?" Madison called over. He was sandwiched between a former Formula One driver and the South American heir to a coffee dynasty. "You gonna feed her to your baboons?"

A Mexican wave of laughter rippled through the viewing room. Matthew Nevers' mouth twisted to the side, and he muttered something about chimpanzees that went largely unheard.

"Or are you going to get her to spank your arse?" It was Henry Victor, an obese online trading entrepreneur. He was referring to the other rumour that often circulated about Nevers, and how he liked to be viciously spanked with a metal-studded paddle. Apparently Nevers' buttocks were like raw mincemeat when you got his trousers down.

Ignoring the jibes, Nevers' attention locked solely on Moshida now. He said, "Name your price."

"She's not for sale," Moshida said, though the admission came with a sense of propriety. He found that he was slowly growing outraged. "Just what kind of business venture do you think this is?" He pushed away from the console and shot to his feet. "This is your money you're watching here," he said, thrusting a finger toward the screens. "The greatest... the greatest, most revolutionary medical breakthrough the world has ever known, and you want to... buy her, like she's a ham at the market?"

A few sniggers. A bored sigh.

Nevers shrugged. "What difference does it make? Even if she gets out alive, you're going to kill her anyway, aren't you?" His gaunt face had all the emotion of a catatonic patient in a mental asylum. "I mean, you're going to kill all of them, surely. That would seem to be the only logical conclusion to all of this. Why not let me buy her?"

Because she's mine, Moshida thought. *All mine.*

CHAPTER 39

The flat edge of the axe caught Claude on the buttocks, whacking him like a punishment. There was a quick flash of pain, but it wasn't enough to drop him. Two things occurred to him almost simultaneously. The first was the idea that the axe had slashed his cheeks, and if it had, then so what? If he could escape this ordeal with just a bloody arse to show for it then he could consider himself very lucky. The other thing that he realized, perhaps a second slower than he should have, was that Wish was on the floor. She had jumped to try to split him with the axe, and now he had a choice: he could use this time to try to lose her in the hallways, or he could turn and really slow her down.

He had taken two steps when he chanced a look over his shoulder. She was on all fours, reaching for the axe that had clattered away from her grasp. There was a moment that lasted perhaps for half a heartbeat when Wish looked up at him, unsure what he would do.

Ever since he was a little boy, Claude had played football. He had been on the school team, and had played for Arsenal Youth's under-16s. Until recently, he had met up with a group of friends every Wednesday night to play five-a-side in the Power League, but then he had taken a job at the Midori subsidiary and had to put his extracurricular activities on hold. Now, Wish's head was a football, and he was about to take a penalty to score the winning goal in the World Cup. He took a run up, pulled his right leg back, and let it swing. Just before his trainer made impact with her cheekbone, he saw Wish's face soften, all signs of menace melting away. For an instant, she was just Wish again, that bubbly, happy-go-lucky woman he had met only a couple of days ago. There was a loud smack, and the impact of the kick resonated through the bones in his foot, pain shooting up his shin. Wish rolled over limply, groping for her face, and Claude felt another beat of uncertainty. She should be sailing into unconsciousness now, but when she regained her senses, she'd get right back on after him. A kick wouldn't be enough to dissuade her. She would keep getting up no matter how badly injured she was, because her mind would make her. Right now, her brain would be feverish with signals flashing, forcing her to find Amanda, touch Amanda, be with Amanda, *become* Amanda. Amanda had rewritten her mental hardware and taken control of her body.

Claude picked up the axe. It was heavy and blunt, but he could drive this damn thing through her chest and count her out of the game. He stood over her, saw her eyes rolling around unable to focus, the side of her face already swelling to the size of an orange. She tried to sit up, her hands set into claws reaching for him.

"Stop it," he said, and planted a foot on her chest, the axe raised high above. "I don't want to hurt you, Wish, but I'll have to if you don't stop."

Her lips peeled back revealing teeth and gums, her nostrils flaring. She was growling at him, her chest rising and falling rapidly with each shallow breath she took. She grabbed hold of his trousers and tried to pull herself up.

Slowly, Claude could see realization dawning on her. The dizziness and discoordination had subsided, and she was rising to the count, getting ready to fight again.

"Wish, stop," he pleaded, the weighty axe wavering in his grasp. If she got up, then she would not think twice about trying to kill him. He had heard horror stories about tests they had run on lab rats using the Honeycomb pill, and he had assumed they were largely exaggerated; conspiracy theories that had spiralled wildly out of control. But what he was seeing now, what he had seen all week, was all the proof he needed.

None of the rats ever made it out alive.

Zombielike, Wish opened her mouth and tried to set her teeth around Claude's ankle. He pulled away, the axe vibrating in his grip as fresh torrents of emotion washed through him.

"Kill you... *putain de batard*... Amanda... Amanda..."

He couldn't do it. No matter how crazy Wish was or how afraid he felt, there was no way he could murder her in cold blood. He stepped back, ripping his leg free of Wish's hungry hands, and lifted his foot again. This time the sole of his shoe crunched down on Wish's face and he felt her nose break. Her head slammed back to the ground and her arms became wet spaghetti. Blood poured out of both nostrils as she groaned, her hands making small circles in the air in an attempt to find her face.

"I'm sorry," he said, knowing that she would not extend him the same courtesy, and ran for the staircase.

"Here we are, just you and me," Sherry said, the words dancing dreamily. She had her forearm pressed against Amanda's chest, pinning her to the wall. Amanda could smell the sour, thick stink of her morning breath, and up close, could see just how badly Sherry had degraded over the days. Her hair was lank and greasy, her skin oily and ripe with blemishes.

Amanda tried to squirm away but had little room to manoeuvre. The weight of the woman, the power surging through her arms, was incredible. It was like being pinned to the wall by a car. Amanda reached up to Sherry's face, her fingers coiled to gouge at her eyes. In response, Sherry turned her head away and moved her thick, muscular forearm across Amanda's neck.

"Don't be a fucking moron, Amanda. You touch my eyes and I'll crush your windpipe. That's the top and the bottom of it."

Amanda was caught between gasping for breath and gagging to be sick at the pressure on her throat. She had to tiptoe to keep the pressure from building, and now her hands scratched weakly at Sherry's wrist.

"Oh, sweet Amanda. Look at you. You're sweating." Sherry leaned in to inhale Amanda's scent. She breathed her in, and in Amanda's ear she made a small, almost orgasmic sound of pleasure. "You're so cute I could eat you with a spoon, do you know that?"

Amanda couldn't concentrate on what was being said. Her efforts were dedicated to staying conscious and alleviating the pressure on her neck. Sherry's large, wide tongue lapped Amanda's cheek, her taste buds tingling from the flavour of her perspiration.

"What is it about you? I wish I could understand. You drive me so crazy and I have no idea why. At first, I thought I was jealous of your youth, your beauty, but it isn't that. Do you know – the girls at school thought I was a lesbian for the longest time. I have never fancied a woman, not even remotely, and when you're called a dyke on a daily basis it tends to have the opposite effect. In fact, I used to do anything I could to prove I wasn't a dirty dyke. I would give it away to anyone that was remotely interested. How old were you when you lost your virginity, Amanda?"

The forearm loosened against her neck. Straining, Amanda said, "Please Sherry, you're hurting–"

"I was twelve. But I was big for my age you see. The first person to have their way with me was my friend's dad. I seduced *him* if you can believe that." Sherry snorted, and a low, throaty chuckle built up inside her. "I've never told anyone that before. Do you suppose a reputation as a slut was better than being a lesbian? Now that I think about it, I'm not entirely sure."

"I... don't... know..."

"Have you ever kissed a girl, Amanda? Ever had a little fumble with one of your friends on a drunken night out?"

"Nnn... no."

"Will you kiss me?"

"No," she spat defiantly.

"I think you should. It would be an experience for both of us. It might be weird but it could also be sweet, couldn't it? Why don't we give it a try?"

"No," Amanda choked again, trying to twist her head as Sherry brought her lips closer.

Sherry's forearm shunted harder against Amanda's neck. "If you keep being a fucking baby about it, then I'm going to spank you like a baby, got it? Now stop making this into something sordid and just go along with it. Believe me I'm as nervous as you are."

I won't, Amanda's mind screamed. *You have no right. You have no right to do this to me.*

Sherry pressed her lips firmly against Amanda's. Amanda squirmed, could feel Sherry's teeth behind her lips as she kissed harder. Sherry sighed internally, and her free hand found Amanda's waist, settling there. When she eventually pulled away, Sherry was gasping, her cheeks flaming, her dry tongue making a slow, sultry circuit around her lips.

"Bitch," Amanda said, not even really meaning to, but the word found its way out of her mouth all the same.

"That," Sherry began, sucking in air, "was beautiful. Don't look like that, my sweet." She stroked Amanda's clammy face. "You don't have to wear a mask now. We can be open with each other. We can say how we really feel. It was beautiful. Tell me you thought so too. Just say it."

Against Sherry's forearm, Amanda shook her head.

"Why do you look so sad? It was lovely."

"It wasn't."

"It *was*. It was special. Come on, I know I'm a good kisser, and

I bet you've never met a woman that has a sense of humour like me, have you? We'd make good roommates I think. And you'd love Sponge, honestly, he's so clever he's just like a little human. Oh, come on, what are the tears for?"

"Let... me... go."

"I don't think I can do that," she said hesitantly, though the grip around Amanda's neck loosened ever so slightly.

Suppressing a cough, Amanda said, "You can. You can, Sherry. If you feel anything for me then please, just let me go."

"Feel anything for you? Oh, my sweet Amanda, you don't know the half of it, do you? No, I don't suppose you do. I feel *everything* for you. Every drop of blood in my body sings for you. I can..." She paused, mouth closed, expelling air through flared nostrils. "I can feel you alive *in* me. It's like you've turned on a light and brightened up my world and now there is only... there is only..." She trailed off.

"I'm not a toy, Sherry, or a dog, or an object. I'm a person, and I want you to let me go."

Sherry's face frowned in thought. For a couple of heartbeats, it appeared as though Amanda's words had made it through the fog and struck a chord somewhere deep in Sherry's cluttered mind. But then her face softened again, each muscle relaxing until her placid, nothing expression returned.

"No, I don't think so. You might get a knife and try to stab me like you did with Arthur. He's brown bread by the way. Good job." Sherry's heavy hand fell on Amanda's breast and squeezed it. Pain rushed through Amanda's chest, and when she opened her mouth to scream, Sherry was there with her other hand to silence her. In Amanda's ear, Sherry said, "I dream about us Amanda. Me in the kitchen cracking jokes, cooking you dinner, Kate Bush on the CD player. Living together, going on holidays. I... I see us growing old together, walking in the park, shopping, reading magazines in a garden, drinking champagne. Do you know, I've never been to Paris?

We could do all of it. I could... I could take care of you. Look after you. Like a mother. I could be your mum, but your bestie as well."

Amanda reached up and scraped her nails down Sherry's face. Amanda felt the friction in her fingertips as her nails peeled away skin and Sherry inhaled with shock.

But Sherry did not scream. Instead, she grabbed Amanda's head with both hands and thumped it against the wall behind her. Amanda felt a boom of hollow pain occupy her skull. She saw Sherry's face lined with vibrant vertical scratches start to disappear as the darkness ate her vision.

Then she was sliding to the floor and Sherry was on top of her.

CHAPTER 40

"What are you doing to her? You disgusting, dirty old bitch, just what are you doing?"

Sherry's head flipped up toward the sound of Justin's voice. She had no way of knowing, but the shock of getting caught in the act gave her an almost adolescent quality that shaved a decade or so from her face. But then her features turned mean, and she morphed into the wicked witch again. She had been bent over Amanda, lapping at her face like a thirsty dog over a water bowl, sucking the sweat from her pores.

"I'm keeping her sedated," she said, dragging the back of her hand across her mouth to clear any excess moisture.

Somewhere on his travels through the house, Justin had received his second wind. He had dragged himself through the hallways that seemed to stretch endlessly like an optical illusion, his vision warping like mirrors in a funhouse. He had tried to do too much too soon and was going to shut down completely if he didn't wise up. On his search for Amanda, he had stumbled into a small room that had a sink, and he had gulped down water until his belly was bloated with it and the fog dissipated. He washed his arm, hissing as the water trickled over the cut, and then threw handfuls of water on his chest. The blood had clotted and closed the cuts that spelled Amanda's name, but if he stretched too much or raised his arm beyond a certain point, they would open again. He had succeeded in keeping the pain at bay by moving gingerly, but now, seeing Sherry preying over his wife, he thought he might have to reopen his cuts.

Sherry got to one knee, and then stood all the way up. "Where's Wish?"

"I don't give a shit about Wish," Justin replied. In his hand was an iron poker, which he had found by a bricked-over fireplace in another room. He pointed the poker at Sherry. "What were you doing just now?"

"Doing? I wasn't doing anything. I've had to restrain her otherwise she would have run away again. That's all."

Justin's eyes flicked to Amanda and then back to Sherry. "What's wrong with her?"

"I just told you."

Justin whacked the poker against the wall, the sound ringing through the house. "Why is she unconscious?"

"Because I knocked her out," Sherry said, through gritted teeth. "She was struggling. But calm yourself down. She isn't hurt."

"She better not be." His hand tightened around the poker. He took a step closer to Sherry, desperately needing to kneel by Amanda's side, to check her pulse, to stroke her hair and give her the kiss of life, but he would not allow his focus to waver.

"I don't know what you're thinking about doing with that," Sherry said, pointing to the poker. "But you need to get it out of your head. We have work to do. We have to secure this area, make it so that nobody can come up those stairs and interfere with–" She faltered, had almost said "my love" but caught herself at the last instant. "We can't let anyone come in here and take her, and that means we are going to have a siege. Do you know what a siege is? They'll have to negotiate terms with us."

"Like terrorists?" he said, disgusted. "Do I look like a fucking Arab to you? I'm not negotiating with anyone. That," he pointed with the poker, and then amended, "*she*, is my wife."

Now he held the poker like a baseball bat, cocked and ready for a home run.

"You won't be able pull this off without me, Justin." Sherry tried to sound firm but found herself taking a step back from Amanda. "Look, with all due respect, you're not smart enough to get us out of this, but I am."

"You're a fucking dinner lady not a detective."

"Yes, alright, but I have almost thirty years of... of life experience on you," she said, pointing a ringed finger at him. "If we start fighting now, then all they'll do is wait for us to finish and sweep her up. Is that what you want?"

"I'm not sharing her with you or anyone."

"That's something we can work out once we've escaped this bloody house, isn't it? You won't do it alone, do you hear me? You won't get out of this house without my help!"

Careful not to tread on any part of his bride, Justin stepped around Amanda. "Who says I intend to get out?"

The confusion disrupted Sherry's stride and she froze mid-step. Her eyes narrowed in understanding. "You're going to kill her?"

"I'm going to release her," he corrected, and swung the poker before Sherry could say any more.

CHAPTER 41

For one terrifying second, Amanda thought she was dying. Darkness swarmed her vision, and someone was slowly turning the volume down in her head, killing all sound. A flaming tide of panic rose inside her then, because although she was having no trouble breathing, the darkness was suffocating her. She tried to call for help but didn't know whether her mouth had been able to perform the task. The world was pulling away from her, her vision closing to a pinprick. Disembodied, she was painlessly drifting deeper into the abyss.

Oh Rochelle, please help me. I think I'm going to die and I don't want to die before we get to Jamaica. Please can I just wake up now from this nightmare and be back in my flat with my bills and my damp walls? Please Jesus God help me I'm dying.

Then, there was light. The raft she lay on became solid beneath her, and the wind rushed out of her mouth. In that instant, her mind was empty, perfectly serene. She was looking up at the slanted roof but did not know anything about the house or the people in it. She did not know about the last few days and the pills she had taken. All she knew was that she was awake again, that her jaw and her head ached with a pain that sent bright red warning signals through her body. Black fireworks occasionally popped in her vision, but she could mostly see and make sense of everything. Then she heard voices, male and female, arguing ferociously, and that kick-started her brain again. She rolled onto her side and saw

Justin locked in a tussle with Sherry by the top of the stairs. They were both wrestling over something, but Amanda could not quite make out what it was, nor did she care. She crawled along the carpet like a toddler, the house shuddering around her. She saw her bedroom door and sluggishly groped for the handle. Every move she made felt off-balance and wobbly. She turned the handle, and the dizziness provoked her stomach into action.

"Wait, wait, look–"

On all fours, Amanda scuttled into the room. She did not like to move this fast because it made the house shake around her like a snow globe and the vomit roil in her stomach. Clumsily she closed the door, palmed the wall, and reached up to the bolt.

She slid it home just as something heavy banged into the door from the other side.

CHAPTER 42

If he hadn't mutilated himself earlier and lost so much blood, Justin might have had the strength to swing harder. All things considered, he still managed to get a lot of his body into the motion, but Sherry had seen it coming and adjusted her stance accordingly. She closed the distance on him, getting her hands around the poker before it could make contact with its intended target – her head. She saw his eyes widen with surprise, and then with fear as she screamed and yanked at the poker. His whole body jerked forward, but he did not let go. The move gave her a good estimate of his weight and strength. He was skinny but not completely powerless. There was a ropy kind of strength in that flimsy body, but Sherry had grown up with three older brothers and was well versed in fighting men stronger than herself. She never did have a sister, as she had claimed during their first group assignment, but it hadn't been a lie she told just for Amanda's benefit. It was simply what she told people when they asked about her family, because a dead sister usually quelled any further conversation on the matter. The truth of it was she hated her brothers, who had beaten and humiliated their fat little sister any chance they got. Frank, Eddy and Howard were as good as dead to her, and could actually be six feet under for all she knew, having not spoken to any of them in over twenty years.

While Sherry had been evaluating his strength, Justin had been doing the same thing. He wondered whether he had the energy to drive her back a few more feet to the top of the staircase, and give her another nudge to send her sprawling. If he wasn't able to do that then he was bang in trouble, because now she looked beyond mad. An H-shaped vein pulsed in the centre of her dark forehead, and her red-threaded eyes looked like they might explode from the pressure. She was wiggling the poker and he could feel her winning the battle. He ground his feet into the carpet and leaned all his weight toward her, hoping to steal some of her momentum. She turned, spun him around, and drove him toward the wall. She had opened her mouth and meant to sink her teeth into his face or neck – whichever she found first – when he said, "Wait, wait, look…"

Knowing that it was a ploy, Sherry did not look. But then, she heard a door close and, in no danger of losing the poker, glanced over her shoulder. Amanda wasn't there.

"She's got a lock on her door!" Justin yelled, his voice shrill with panic.

With one final yank, Sherry snatched the poker out of his grasp. She did not even think about hitting him with it. All thought was devoted to Amanda, who was now behind the safety of her bedroom door. Sherry ran down the landing and charged the door with her shoulder. If this had been a film and she a police officer, the door would have collapsed in its frame and she would have access. But it wasn't a film, and the door was thick, heavy wood. She slammed her shoulder into it again and felt no give in the integrity of the door, but her arm screamed with pain. She grabbed the poker like an ice pick and started to chip at the door. The poker was blunt as a butter knife, and she was only succeeding in scratching the wood. Sherry took a step back, and then stomped at the door. A bolt of pain shot up through her heel and exploded in her knee, and Sherry tumbled backwards.

"Won't it open?" Justin asked, staring down at Sherry who, in that instant, resembled an upturned turtle. Without waiting for an answer, he picked up the poker and thrashed at the door.

"Amanda, it's Justin," he said, breathlessly. He rapped the poker against the door and said, "Do you want to open up so we can talk about it?" He pressed his ear up to the door. He might've heard movement on the other side, but he wasn't sure. "Amanda, I didn't have anything to do with what's been happening. I don't want to hurt you. Please believe me babes, I wouldn't hurt a hair on your head."

Had there been laughter? He didn't know. He pressed his palms against the door, a bonfire of frustration and confusion kindling inside him.

"Amanda, you can't... you can't stay in there forever. And I know we've been acting a bit... goofy, but we're your friends, your only friends. Can you hear me in there?" He looked down at Sherry. "Get up and do something, will you?"

"My knee," Sherry groaned.

"I thought we were going to build a fortress to protect her. I thought we were going to negotiate terms with the house to let us have her and you're there complaining about your fucking knee? Get up. Get up or I'll smash your brain in." Turning back to the door, he said, "I'm not going to let anything happen to you Amanda. Just open the door and we can talk about it?"

"She's not going to open." Sherry, using the landing balcony to pull herself up to her feet, limped to the door. "There's no way she's going to open up, and that door is solid as a rock. We'll have to smoke her out."

"Smoke her?"

"You heard me." She nudged him out the way and banged a fist against the door. "Amanda? I know you can hear me, so listen to this: you either open this door up and surrender to us peacefully or..." She paused for effect. "We burn this place down, starting here." She scraped her nails lightly against the wood. "It can be as simple or as difficult as that, my love."

There were small sounds on the other side of the door; footsteps, a clank, a soft thud.

"What's she doing?" Justin whispered.

"She's looking for a way out," Sherry told him. "She isn't going to find one." She turned to Justin, placed a reassuring hand on his shoulder and said, "Go downstairs to the pantry. Get as many of the vodka and whiskey bottles as you can carry and bring them up here."

"We're really going to do it?" he asked, their scuffle forgotten.

"If she doesn't want to be saved then perhaps you're right. Perhaps it would be better to release her. In fact, I think that might be just right. It could be…"

"Romantic," Justin finished, and turned to head downstairs before Sherry could see him crying.

CHAPTER 43

"Do you know why I've called you in here today, Claude?"

Claude had spent a couple of minutes in front of the mirror in the men's room, adjusting his tie, straightening his hair, ensuring that his shirt was tucked in.

Now, the knot of his tie was pressing against his Adam's apple and he wanted to rip the damn thing off. He ran his palms over his thighs to dry them, and said, "I'm not really sure, no. I hope I haven't done anything wrong."

"Not at all." Mr Moshida smiled, and in that instant he looked like a kind uncle, someone who would get drunk at a Christmas party and get up to sing karaoke. "In fact, quite the opposite. You've done everything right. It may come as a surprise to you, but it's no secret to some of the directors, that I am a big fan of yours. Do you remember the hot dog meeting?"

Claude must have involuntarily made a face because Mr Moshida's smile widened, touching his eyes. Yes, of course he remembered the hot dog meeting. He had gone home that night and bought a bottle of Jack Daniel's and drunk half of it in his room, sure that he was going to lose his job.

"I should maybe let you in on a little secret," Moshida began, and now the smile was gone, and he was all business. "The hot dog assignment was a test, although you might have worked that out already for yourself. Did you?"

"I thought..." He bit back the sentence, realizing that he was allowing his stream of consciousness to dictate his speech.

"You were wary?"

"Yes. If I can speak openly?"

"Of course. Always."

"I thought it was designed to bring me down a peg or two. I'm not accusing you," Claude quickly added, but could feel his face burning. "But there are a lot of office politics on the ground floor. I may have spoken my mind one too many times and ruffled a few feathers. I can't help it. I just..." He lowered his eyes. He smoothed his tie, fidgeted with the noose around his neck, and continued, "I believe I could be a real asset to the company and for a long time I felt stuck in the mud. I felt..."

"Like you could run the ship better than your manager? That your ideas were worth exploring? That you could think outside of the box while the rest of the team were happy within the confines of it? You were right on all accounts. You see, working for Lavender Sky is not about sitting at your computer day in, day out, feeding data into a spreadsheet and regurgitating statistics at board meetings. Well, maybe at some level it is, but there is another level to it." He picked up a piece of paper from the desk, and briefly glanced over it. "You've worked here for almost two years, and in that time, you have stood out among the throng. I've seen you in some of the creative sessions. I've seen your passion, your ability to think laterally. And more than that, I've seen your ambition. You want to climb, and you'll do whatever it takes. The hot dog assignment was designed for one reason only. I wanted to see you under stress, to hear you talk your way out of an obstacle. You exceeded all my expectations."

Again, Claude looked away. The hot dog meeting had been a source of almost constant regret and humiliation, one that he had spent a long time trying to bury in his mind.

Four months prior to this meeting with Moshida, Claude had received an email from a higher-up, informing him that his presence was requested for a board meeting at 3 o'clock that afternoon. There had been no further instruction, no agenda attached to the email as there usually was in all the dozens of pointless meetings he had every month. He thought nothing more of it, and at ten to three, he made his way up to the eighth floor with a notepad and pen in hand. Before he entered the room, he saw numerous people sitting around the long boardroom table through the window, and assumed that a meeting was already in progress, perhaps running over as they sometimes had a way of doing. He waited, checking his phone, and after a minute realized that he was the only one standing outside the boardroom. The cogs had just begun turning when a woman he had never seen before opened the door, smiling at him. She was in her forties, wearing an open-collar shirt beneath a black pinstripe suit, the confident body language of an executive exuding from her.

"Hello, Claude. Please come in."

With a mixture of bewilderment and that unsavoury flavour of panic that always assaulted him when he neared a deadline, Claude did as he was bid. The faces around the table didn't return his smile. The woman that had invited him in, who still hadn't offered her name, told him not to take a seat. She handed him a picture of a hotdog logo, at the bottom of which were a series of bullet points detailing the nutritional information.

"Claude, we would like you to give a presentation on Porkies Thick Dogs. We are preparing the budget for marketing and publicity now, but would like to hear your spin on them. Would that be OK?"

"Sure," he replied rapidly. "When do you need it by?"

"Right now." And then her smile died.

"Oh," he began, the panic turning feral, clawing at the walls of his chest. His scrotum tightened as the embarrassment bloomed. "I don't believe I've received any info on this. I can check my emails again. It might have gone through to my spam folder."

"No information was sent. This is something of a pop quiz."

"A pop quiz," he repeated under his breath, desperately scanning the bullet points. *More like a stitch-up*, he thought.

"Whenever you're ready to begin."

I can be ready tomorrow afternoon after I've researched the damn product and had longer than two seconds to draft some ideas. He walked to the water dispenser, got himself a plastic cup, filled it and gulped. He hadn't even stopped for lunch that day and the shock of this presentation had stolen the last of his saliva.

"Well, depending on budget, I think social media advertising would be a great place to begin. Tube adverts, of course. And if we're just talking about the UK, then..."

"Claude?" the woman interrupted. "That's not what we want to hear. We don't want your *ideas*. We want you to sell us on Porkies Thick Dogs. Sixty seconds. Go."

His stomach tightened like a clenched fist. He wasted the first ten seconds looking around at the blank faces staring back at him. Then, his mind went into autopilot and the words began tumbling out his mouth, his voice loud and important.

"Alright ladies and gentlemen, you've all had a hot dog before, maybe at a fun fair or a football game, that's all very well and good. But forget your gristly, greasy sausages with less pork content than the buns you're eating them with, OK? You can throw that out the window. There's a new kid on the block, and his name is Porky's. That's right, Porky's Thick Dogs are delicious, they're nutritious, and they're blinding with chips, or 'French fries' if we have any of our friends from across the pond with us today. So, you've come home from work and the kids are playing up, moaning about their dinner, and you've already done an eight-hour shift and you don't want to hear it. No worries – Porky's Thick Dogs can be prepared in less than ten minutes, and yeah, you don't want that guilty feeling of thinking the kids are going to turn into a pack of porkers – no pun intended. Porky's Thick Dogs are less than ten percent fat per sausage. Not only that..."

"Thank you, Claude," the woman said with a dismissive smile. "That'll be all."

He had heard no more about his hot dog presentation, and when he ran the name through Google nothing seemed to match up. They had brought him up there for the sole purpose of humiliating him, reducing him to a fruit-and-veg trader at the market stall trying to rally enthusiasm for a box of strawberries.

Through the window behind Moshida, a series of cranes were working on a new structure. Claude had not seen the progress of the new building being erected from this height, and was dimly surprised.

"I'll cut to the chase, Claude. I want you for a very special task that we're putting together. However, I really can't overemphasize how confidential this is. In fact, if you were to take part, you would be required to sign an affidavit in the presence of our solicitors, legally binding you to secrecy. I can see in your face that you're already interested."

"A hundred percent," Claude said, without missing a beat. "Am I allowed to ask what it is I'll be doing at this point?"

"No," Moshida said. "That comes later. There are some people who would like to meet with you, ask you some questions. Think of it as an informal job interview, except you already have the job."

Claude nodded, trying to wrap his mind around the contradiction.

"I think you have what it takes, Claude. You want to get to the top of the mountain, but you have to remember there is always more than one path. Fortunately, you've just been offered a shortcut."

The excitement made him giddy in his chair. He started to smile, not really knowing why he was smiling, but unable to stop himself. He had always envisioned a flat overlooking the Thames, driving a new BMW, a Rolex on his wrist. Lavender Sky was the right place to work if you wanted those things, but it was more cutthroat than a pirate ship. He could do without the headache.

"I want to thank you for picking me," Claude said, trying to taper his enthusiasm in an effort to maintain an air of nonchalance. "And I just want to let you know that whatever it is, I can do it. You won't regret it, Mr Moshida."

"No, I don't think I will." He smiled and extended his hand, bringing the meeting to a close.

Now, snippets of that meeting stuck out in Claude's brain like shrapnel. As he tiptoed down the western staircase, he wondered – and not for the first time – if he would still have taken the job knowing what he did now. He would like to have thought not, but then he would only be lying to himself. Claude knew that he would have accepted the role as the house spy no matter what he knew, because he would always believe he could do a better job. If they had prepared him thoroughly, offered him more than just a vague outline of the character he had to play and the rundown of the week, then he could have really protected Amanda. But how was he to know?

He stopped halfway down the staircase when he saw Arthur, splayed out on the floor like a starfish, a puddle of almost reflective blood pooling around him. Large, crimson footprints walked away from his body. Arthur's dull eyes were staring up at the ceiling, his porcelain-pale skin clashing with the vibrant red blood. Claude fell against the wall, one hand covering his mouth to keep the threat of sickness at bay. Amanda had done that to Arthur; she had told Claude as much back in the library, but he had not been able to fully process the horror of what Arthur's corpse might look like. He had seen countless cadavers on TV and in movies, but even the most gruesome horror scenes could not prepare him for the real thing. Claude was overcome with a queer sense of sadness that he couldn't control, but equal to this feeling was the disgust that cringed through him and made his flesh crawl. When he was a teenager, he had been made to help bury the family cat when it finally kicked the bucket, after fifteen years of faithful service. His father had made a deal with him: Claude would dig the hole, and his dad would deposit Snowy and fill it in. Claude had liked the bargain because he knew he wouldn't have the stomach to pick Snowy up and feel the dead weight of her, not when he was so used to having her purr on his lap or slink across him on her way to the radiator. So, he had dug the hole and stood by as his father carried Snowy, wrapped in her favourite, moth-eaten blanket. And just before his dad lowered Snowy in, the blanket slipped from her head, and Claude saw her awful, lifeless eyes, her mouth hanging open stupidly.

He did not think he had the nerve to just step over Arthur as though he were a misplaced draught excluder. Claude wasn't sure he would be able to avoid treading in any of his blood, as so much of it was splashed around, covering the floor.

How had things become so crazy so quickly? On Sunday he had come to the house full of hope and optimism, already looking forward to that call to the mortgage advisor that he would make. Now, four days later, he was looking at his first dead body, and there were people rabidly eager to leave him the same way. Then he thought of Amanda, helpless and alone in the house.

He brought a fist to his mouth and began the game of avoiding Arthur. He decided not to look down as he walked, but he could smell the man's blood and the unmistakeable stink of his evacuated bowels. He held his breath and just walked, one foot at a time, even though his legs felt about as sturdy as breadsticks. Claude's foot made contact with Arthur's shoe, and a shiver went racing up his spine. *I've just been kicked by a dead man*, he thought crazily, and inched over to the panel beneath the stairs that would lead to the passageway.

He traced his fingers along the ridge and pulled. The panel came away with a small creak, and a gust of musty air blew into his face. All he had to do was get in, fumble his way through the dark, find the ladder and climb up to the courtyard. Whatever else happened in the house wasn't his business. He had done what they had paid him to do: he had played the game and had been a participant in the experiment. He had risked his life for this madness, and enough was enough. He opened the panel wider, turned sideways and began to edge into the darkness, when he stopped.

She was still here, somewhere in the house.

He allowed himself a moment to think. Whatever happened to Amanda wasn't his fault. If they ended up killing her then that was down to Lavender Sky, and anyway, what was to stop them from offing him as soon as he reached the courtyard? It would be a whole lot easier and less expensive than paying for his silence. He stepped into the passageway and began to pull the door closed behind him.

If you go, they'll kill her and you know it.

He struggled for a counter-thought, something that would force him further into the passage. *She could already be dead. They could be up there playing with her corpse, rolling around in her blood, and I'd be stumbling into a fucking alligator pit.*

He started to close the door again.

But how would you know?

CHAPTER 44

There were no weapons in the room, and now that she had backed herself into a corner, Amanda realized just how stupid she really was. She should have stocked up, stolen every knife in the kitchen from the moment they began sniffing around her. But she hadn't, and now she was in an empty cell, with two rabid animals banging at her door.

She pulled the drawers out of the small bedside table and fished through the wardrobe for anything that could be of use. She found wire hangers and cobwebs. A scream of frustration was building up in her throat and she kept it locked behind tightly clenched teeth. Sooner or later, they would find a way through that door. It may be thick, but they were crazy and determined.

"Come on, come on," she whispered to herself, getting down on all fours to check under the bed. She knew even before she looked that there would be nothing but lint, but she had to make sure. In her fear-flustered mind, she considered sliding beneath the bed on her belly in the hope that they wouldn't find her, but then she heard Sherry cooing from the other side of the door and reality returned.

"Amanda, honey? Are you still with us?"

Amanda got to one knee, her elbows rested against the thin mattress. If they broke the door down now it would look like she was praying, and the way things were going that wouldn't be too much of a bad idea.

Merciful Jesus, I don't know what I've done to deserve this, but

*I am your child and I need your help and if you can do anything –
anything at all – then I would be eternally grateful.*

If there was a God, He apparently hadn't heard her.

But then again...

She quickly stood up, grabbed the mattress, and ripped it
off the bed. The bed's slats were wooden, just like the ones
on her Ikea bed at home. Amanda lifted her leg and brought
it down in the middle of the slats, which were spongy and
discoloured with age, but still solid enough to hold weight.
She heard the wood crack, but it did not break. She stomped
again and her leg went straight through, shattering the slats
in the middle. The broken shards of wood scraped through
her tracksuit bottoms and drew blood, but she barely felt it.
She was too preoccupied with her work – trying to free the
slats from the bed's frame. With some persuasion, wiggling
the wood like a loose tooth from a rotten gum, she pulled
a piece of slat away that was about a foot long, pointy and
jagged at the end from where it had broken. It was like a
stake to kill a vampire, which was appropriate considering
she had at least two at her door.

But you fuckers can't come in her without my permission, she
thought, and just holding the wood brought her panic to a
more manageable temperature. She had already staked one of
them today and she had more than enough energy to do the
rest of them.

"Amanda, sweetheart? I need you to listen to me for a sec,
OK hun?"

Amanda stood in the centre of the room, holding the slat so
tightly that the wood raised welts on her palm.

"Amanda, this is Sherry. I need your attention because this
is very important. We don't want to fight you anymore."

"Do you think I'm an idiot?" she screamed back. The scream
became a laugh of incredulity. She was having a difficult time
processing the madness and could not believe she had just
indulged it.

"No, we don't think you're stupid. Far from it, my love. But, you see, the thing is, we need you out of that room."

"You need me out? Why? What for?"

"We need to keep you safe."

"I am safe! I'm away from you fucking lunatics."

"Yes, well." Sherry's voice sounded weary. "I think we will have to just disagree on that point. But here is the reality of your situation. You are locked in a room, alone and vulnerable without our help."

Amanda heard a shuffle on the other side of the door. Then, from the centimetre gap beneath the door, a clear puddle began to spread. Her first thought was that Sherry was urinating, marking her territory. Then, she realized.

"This is vodka seeping into your room. It'll catch fire, but it might not completely burn up. However..." Sherry paused. "On the other side of this door we have a vodka-soaked bedsheet that most definitely will catch. It'll burn up this door, and when it's cinders we'll come in and get you, if you haven't choked to death from smoke inhalation, that is."

The puddle spread, inching closer to Amanda. It wet the bedside table, the bedposts, the bottom of the wardrobe. It took her a couple of seconds for the information to sink in, and then Amanda backed away to the furthest wall of the room.

"I want to be reasonable Amanda, but it has to be reciprocated. You have to understand – I don't want to set this door on fire, but I will. I'll burn this whole fucking house to the ground if it means that I get to you."

"Why?" Amanda shrieked. The vodka had pooled across the floor. If the flame caught, she might be able to stomp it out, perhaps suffocate it with the mattress. Or the mattress would catch fire and she would be chargrilled even quicker; she wasn't sure. "You don't even know why you want me. You're going to burn me up because the pill has made you crazy."

"It's made me crazy?" It sounded like she was smiling. "You're the killer, not me."

"Fuck you," Amanda spat. "It was self-defence."

"Yeah, tell it to the magistrate. Did you forget they've got you on camera, lovie? Anyway, we're getting side-tracked here. This is how it's going to work. I'm going to count to five, and if you don't come out, then I'm lighting the match. That's simple enough, isn't it?"

"I'm not opening this door."

"We'll see."

CHAPTER 45

The rumpled bedsheet and the two pillows they had thrown in for good measure were bundled against Amanda's door. Justin had doused the bedding with one bottle of vodka and one bottle of whiskey, and he had three more bottles just in case they needed to feed the flames. If the smell was anything to go by, then the sheet would catch once the match touched it. The thought made him nervous and excited. Then, of course, there was the carpet, the wallpaper, and the ceiling not twelve feet above them. They could take those stupid oil paintings off the walls and toss them on the heap too. Turn it into bonfire night, why not? He supposed the mansion predated asbestos, which meant this whole place would be completely engulfed before long. That is, if they were really going to do it. He thought Sherry had been serious at first, but the reality of the situation had settled in as he poured the first bottle of vodka under the door. If they dropped a match then they were going to burn her alive like a witch at a stake, and now that the time came, he wasn't so sure that's what he wanted.

"She's not falling for it," he whispered to Sherry.

"There's nothing to fall for. We'll see if the heat doesn't persuade her, shall we?" Sherry turned her attention back to the door and tapped her knuckles on it lightly. "Amanda my sweetness. Here is your last chance. I'm going to begin counting. One."

Justin held his breath.

"Two."

Justin began to reel. He should have had a gulp of that whiskey to calm his nerves.

"Three."

"Amanda, just do it, will you?" he said, kicking the door. "Just open up. We only want what's best for you."

Sherry put a hand on his shoulder and pulled him back. Then, she opened the matchbox, removed a match, and struck it.

"Four."

"Amanda, will you stop being so fucking difficult," Justin yelled, his voice hoarse. "She's going to do it. She's really going to do it, you know. She's…"

"Last chance saloon," Sherry said. "Alright. Have it your way. Five."

She dropped the match.

There was a whomp, followed by a funnel of bright blue light. The orange-red flames appeared suddenly like a magic trick, and then raced up the door, already eating their way through the bedding. A backdraft of heat repelled Justin and Sherry, the sudden brightness causing them to squint.

"Look at it go!" Sherry said with a smile, the firelight dancing in the darkness of her eyes.

"Jesus Christ, Sherry," Justin shouted over the crackling. "She's really going to burn up. What have you done?"

"I've done what was necessary," Sherry replied without diverting her attention. She tittered like a little girl. "Fantastic, isn't it?"

"Sherry, you need to put it out." Every modicum of strength Justin had had gone into the sentence, and now he was holding onto the edge of the balcony for support. He needed something to eat, something to drink, some decent sleep. His engine was chugging on empty and about to break down by the side of the road.

"With what?" Sherry asked with a slight shrug of her shoulder. "I don't see any fire extinguishers here. Do you?"

"She'll fucking cook," he gasped.

"No, she won't. She has more sense than that."

The acrid stink of the fire climbed into the back of Justin's throat. His eyes were beginning to weep. He was standing six feet away from the flames but could still feel their heat against his skin. The crackle had grown into a roar as the fire blackened the walls around the door.

"Come out, Amanda," Justin said, but wasn't sure that his voice would be heard above the fire. A column of oily black smoke plumed toward the ceiling and spread out like a waterfall in reverse. He coughed and brought his good arm up to his face, covering his nose and mouth. The fire was beyond stomping out now, but if he went and got a blanket from one of the other rooms, he might be able to suffocate the flames. No, that was stupid. They would need a few buckets of water to put it out now. But of course, there was no chance of that. They would just have to watch the fire and hope she came out.

He peered through the smoke, saw that the metal door handle was blistering. A shard of wood broke off the doorframe and Sherry hooted, threw her arms in the air, and began to dance.

CHAPTER 46

A blue trail raced across the clear liquid and then it caught; fire danced on the surface of the vodka, the flames licking up, hungry for something to consume. Amanda moved on instinct. She grabbed the upturned mattress and slammed it on the vodka. She heard the splash and sizzle as the flames were extinguished, and she knelt down on the mattress with her heart racing. She hadn't noticed that the cuff of her left leg was aflame until she felt the fire burning her skin. She spun over and slapped at it until it was out, and then she saw the smoke billowing into the room from beneath the door.

For an instant, she just stood there watching as the smoke curled into the room like nefarious black fog. She had no idea of the size of the fire beyond the door but began to wonder how safe she was in the room. Would the walls protect her from the fire? Yes, they likely would. But they wouldn't protect her from the smoke, which would suffocate her before the fire had a chance to burn her again.

She pushed the mattress up against the door, hoping to block out the fumes. The smoke thinned, devolving to wisps, and she waved a hand in front of her face, coughing. Already her throat was starting to feel raw, her eyes starting to stream. She could hear the burning beyond the door and it was beginning to frighten her very badly. Her fear grew along with the flames when she heard Justin shouting at Sherry, telling her that things were getting out of hand. And now,

Amanda understood that this was not a bluff; they really meant to burn her alive if they couldn't own her, and she had no idea what to do. Was it better to just go outside and try her luck? How long could this go on for? How long could they torment her, torture her, before someone stepped in to save her? Did this Midori company mean to let the house burn down? No, of course not; they had allowed a lot of things to transpire over the last few days – a lot of things they might be able to cover up. But a mansion burnt to the ground wouldn't go amiss.

She had been so preoccupied with these thoughts that she hadn't noticed that the end of the mattress was now on fire; the fabric mottled black and smouldering, revealing the tufts of cushion and coils of spring. She pulled the mattress away and a gout of black smoke belched up from the gap beneath the door. She turned and coughed, drawing phlegm from the back of her throat.

Again, she thought about opening the door. If she did that, they would swarm her. She might be able to hurt one of them with the broken slat, but the odds weren't great. Then again, she would be blind from the smoke when she came through the door, so she would be swinging into the wind.

The heat thickened in the room. Now, smoke was streaming in from the crevices around the door. The burr of the fire began to build until Amanda could no longer hear their voices – if they were still talking at all. They might just be standing there, admiring the fire, savouring her terror.

She retreated to the corner of the room and held her pointy piece of wood. She might as well throw it on the fire and speed the process up, for all the damn good the thing was doing. She blinked, and tears ran out of her bloodshot eyes. She thought about Claude, wondering if he was waiting for her by the passage. Couldn't he hear what was going on? Could he hear at all? Had Wish caught him in the hallway or was she still chasing him like an episode of Tom and Jerry.

No, Claude was dead. She believed that the way she believed that at any second now she would begin to feel lightheaded and pass out. Did the house have sprinklers? She couldn't recall seeing any. In fact, the only thing that took her notice when she looked to the ceiling were the cameras. They could see what was happening, that the house was going up in flames, and yet there was still no action. Then she understood: if Claude had managed to shake Wish in the hallways, then he was already gone, back to safety. He had probably been feeding information back to them every day, providing reports, recounting all those private conversations they'd been having that the cameras couldn't pick up.

When she coughed again, it felt like something tore in her chest. She buried her eyes into the crook of her arm and covered her mouth with her t-shirt. She curled into a ball on the floor, the smoke enveloping her. She was sliding away, and thankful of it.

CHAPTER 47

Claude had smelled the smoke long before he saw it, but he still had no idea of how bad the blaze was. He stood on the edge of the reception where, directly above him on the first floor, Amanda's door was on fire. Justin and Sherry were shouting at each other, but he couldn't quite make out the specifics. All he could say for sure was that Justin was losing the argument as Sherry's voice bellowed like a rumble of thunder overhead. Whatever she was saying, it was somewhere between anger and hysteria, a maniacal preacher terrorizing their congregation.

With his back to the wall, Claude edged out, angling his face to the landing above him for a better view. A sea of smoke drifted across the ceiling. He wasn't sure what they were burning up there, but he couldn't smell anything that resembled meat, and this made his adrenaline more manageable. When he first got a whiff of the smoke, he had envisioned Amanda burning on some nightmarish pyre they had created. He was almost ready to disregard the smoke completely, putting it down to a crazy quirk that he didn't have time to understand, and then it dawned on him: Amanda had locked herself in her room and they were trying to smoke her out. If the smoke he could see was anything to go by, then she would be sucking those fumes down into her lungs. He knew he had to do something quickly, because the longer he stood there contemplating the situation, the more smoke Amanda would inhale. He coughed, the axe now feeling as heavy as an anchor in his hands.

He stood there, trying to psyche himself into venturing out into the open and up the staircase, when he heard Justin say, *"Please.* We have to stop this. You're killing her! You're–"

"–killing her," Justin poked his foot toward the charred blanket and tried to scoop it away from the door, not that it would have made a slight bit of difference. The door itself was on fire, and around it, the wallpaper melted away to reveal the brickwork. He tried to kick at the blankets again when Sherry shoved him back. Justin lost his footing and stumbled backwards, flapping his arms to stay upright.

"You wanted her dead too, remember?" Snot drooled from Sherry's flared nostrils. She squared up to Justin, blood colouring the whites of her eyes. The blaze gave her a hellish aura, and with her hair snarled in corkscrews, she resembled a demon. "You wanted this, Justin. Anyway, it's out of our hands now. It's for her to choose. She can come out and live, or stay in there and die."

"And if she does die?" he asked meekly.

"Then I suppose we won't be too far behind her."

An image popped in Justin's mind like a flashbulb. He thought of it as more of a projection, a psychic vision planted there by Amanda. He saw her, terrified and alone, her eyes wide, her face a tear-streaked black mask. *"I thought you loved me, Justin. I thought we were going to get married. Why would you let her do this to me? Why Justin? We would have made beautiful children. We…"*

"I didn't mean to," Justin said.

"What?" Sherry's brow pinched. She raised the poker and prodded him in the shoulder. "You didn't mean to what?"

"What about our babies? We were going to have beautiful children, remember? Sunday dinner at your mum's."

"We still can," Justin said, his face scrunching in pain. The thought of her suffering, that he had a hand in destroying their future together, was torture. Something came over him then; he felt a pop in his head, as though some part of his brain had detached, freeing him of any inhibitions. A wild surge of ferocity made his blood fizz, and before he had a chance to reconsider, he was charging Sherry. He came in low, catching her by surprise. He rammed his shoulder into her stomach and heard the scream-gasp as the air rocketed out of her. The momentum propelled them both toward the fire, but youth lent Justin a magical reserve of strength in his weedy legs. He pulled away as Sherry fell into the burning heap, rolling and shrieking. The screams that followed came from some locker deep inside the pit of her stomach; it was a place she had never known existed before, and never knew she had access to. She rolled away, the fire eating through the polyester of her top, her head a torch of dancing flames.

There was no fear in him now. Without a second thought, Justin reached for the door handle. The mottled metal seared the flesh on his palm. He withdrew sharply, the pain so sudden and intense that he almost fainted there on the spot.

"Amanda, it's me," he tried to say, but the smoke tunnelled into his mouth. He hacked and coughed, brought his leg up and snap-kicked the door. His trousers caught on fire, but he did not reach down to slap at them. "Pl–please Ama–" He coughed again and turned away from the heat.

With his eyes tightly closed, he didn't see Sherry swinging the poker. He felt a burst of pain explode through the back of his skull, and the sudden taste of copper flooding his mouth. Instinctively, he reached up to his head, stumbling back toward the balcony, when the poker struck him again, this time catching him on the side of the face and shattering his eye socket. His back hit the balcony ledge and–

Claude had taken two steps toward the staircase when Justin's body sailed past him. It slammed down onto the reception floor with a sickening thud, his skull smashing like a watermelon against the black and white tiles. Claude made a sound, something between a gag and a gasp, his hand flying to his mouth. His breath accelerated, leaving him in short, shallow sips.

"Oh god, oh my god…"

He looked up at the landing balcony and saw Sherry glaring at him. He could see that her face was red raw in places, and the fire had singed her hair down to the scalp. And still, she was smiling.

"Your move, Claude," she said, and raised the poker in the air. There was something distinctly primitive about the gesture, as though she were a Neanderthal waving a thighbone at a rival tribe. "Better decide what you want to do quickly. I haven't heard her cough in a long time."

She began to dance madly, twirling around in front of the fire, oblivious to the pain of her wounds.

Claude started up the staircase.

CHAPTER 48

Sherry did not try to rush him. She just continued to dance. In another setting, under different circumstances, she might have looked like a raver high off her head on ecstasy. But against the amber glow of the fire, she looked like something hell had coughed up.

Slowly, Claude walked toward her, adjusting his grip around the axe handle. He tried to size up the poker to get an idea of its weight and strength, but she would not stop for long enough to allow him to do so. Then, when he was ten feet away, she stopped dead, breathing hard.

"I don't want to hurt you," he said, but even as he spoke, he saw her bring the poker up, ready to duel. "Let me go to the door. Let me call to her."

"Won't do any good, lovie. She's dead."

"Let me try, Sherry."

"I said she's dead!"

"Then what are you so happy about?"

"Happy?" She laughed, and the furrows on her blistered brow wiggled as her expression changed. She exhaled and two black streams exited her nostrils. "Claude, I have never been so sad in my entire life."

"It's not your fault, Sherry. I know what the pill is. I work for them."

"Oh yeah?" she said, disinterestedly. "Are they hiring? What are the perks like?"

"Not great. I have to work weekends."

A smile appeared on Sherry's mouth. Clumps of her singed hair remained on the mottled, oozing flesh of her scalp. Her eyebrows had completely burned away, and that, to Claude, was somehow the most disturbing thing about her appearance. He watched as the smile spread to her peeling cheeks. She began to laugh. The laughter grew and grew until she was howling. The poker slipped from her grasp and hit the carpet with a dull thud, and she bent over breathlessly, gasping from the hilarity.

"I... never knew... you could be funny," she said and then her legs gave out from beneath her. She lay on the floor, quivering with laughter, her eyeballs standing out like bloodshot marbles in her soot-stained face. "Oh Claude, that has tickled me. Claude... it hurts..."

Gradually, the laughter chugged to a stop, and the hacking began, her blistered neck inflating and deflating. She was in no condition to put up a fight.

Claude tossed the axe away, stepped around her, and started toward Amanda's door.

Thick smoke buffeted the room, blinding Amanda. She thought that she might be able to brave the fumes, to allow herself permission to sign off without any more fuss, but the pain was too great. It was the pain that brought her back to her feet. She couldn't swallow, and every time she coughed, she felt the aftershocks tremble through her skull. Her hand fumbled around for the broken bed slat. She found it and crawled to the door. She remembered seeing or hearing something about house fires when she was little, maybe on *Blue Peter* or some other show like that. In the event of a fire, you were supposed to put a wet cloth over your mouth and breathe through that. Well, that was out of the question, but the other thing you were supposed to do was stay low to the floor while heading for the nearest exit. That was it, wasn't it? It didn't make much of a difference now anyway. She was wading through smoke, her skull a field of landmines, her throat a scorched chimney. With her hand outstretched, she came into contact with the wall, and then feeling across, found the door. She reached up to the deadbolt and touched the boiling hot metal for just a second – long enough to make two large blisters appear almost immediately on the tips of her index and middle fingers. Blindly, she groped for something to cover her hand, felt into her open suitcase, and brought out one of her bras. She put one cup over her hand and used it like an oven glove, but the flames would not permit her another chance at the lock.

She backed away and expelled a thick wad of mucus, her head full of slowly dimming fairy lights threatening to pull her into unconsciousness. *I want to live*, she thought. *I want to live*. She hadn't known that before entering the house, her existence a constant blur of shame and disappointment, but these last few days had opened her eyes. There was more to life than being famous. One day, she might meet a nice man and start a real relationship. Then, somewhere down the line, they would get married, possibly have children if that was in the cards for her. Wasn't that a sweet thought? Wasn't that better than the idea of performing a song that someone else had written and produced for her to a sea of strangers? Yes, she thought it was. She didn't give a fuck about social media or getting thousands of likes for every banal comment or picture she posted. She wanted to live. She wanted to love and be loved. She wanted–

Someone was kicking the door in. Through streaming eyes, she peered into the flames, could see the door wobble in the frame. Another loud crash and the door gave. A tornado of smoke billowed into the room, almost pushing her back. The heat caught her by surprise, and the temptation to turn away and retreat from it was almost overpowering. Yet, through the flaming rectangle that made up the doorframe, was freedom, and so she charged it with the wood clasped in both hands. Coughing, her eyes half-closed, she saw one of them reaching for her.

Amanda pulled her arms back and, with the last of her strength, drove the wood toward the figure with everything she had.

CHAPTER 49

The fire had become unruly, and there was no way for Claude to access Amanda's door without getting burned. Still, he did not consider giving up. Even if she was a barbequed corpse in there, he wanted to be the one to carry her out of the room. He owed her that much, didn't he? He had been in on the gag, the only one to go into this fucked-up experiment with any sort of knowledge of what was actually happening, which made him about as awful as Lavender Sky, or Midori, or whatever they called themselves. If it was the last thing he did, Claude would carry Amanda out of that mausoleum of a room and into the fresh air. If she was dead, he would kiss her forehead and admit something that he had known since the second day: he loved her. He hadn't been completely sure, but once he was, he had to work hard at concealing it.

That was the one part of this nightmare that he couldn't quite wrap his head around. They told him he would be taking a suppressant to ward off the effects of Amanda's pheromone, and yet... and yet he had dreamed of her every night since being in the house. In his mind, he had set a goal of asking her out on a date once they were finished with the nonsense experiment. As the hours had worn on, the date had become more important to him than any promotions that Mr. Moshida could offer. He thought about the two of them in a cinema foyer, queueing up to buy tickets to a film, sharing a large popcorn and Coke, laughing. Afterwards they would go to a bar, and a few gin and tonics later, they would call an Uber.

They would make love, and it would be delicate, and so special that neither of them would fall asleep at the end of it, but rather, they would stay up talking. And as the birds began to sing and the sky brightened, they would stand in front of the window, their naked bodies cocooned in a quilt, and watch the sunrise.

With a renewed sense of urgency, Claude pulled his top over his mouth and nose, raised his leg, and stomped the door. He felt the wood soften beneath his foot and thought that one more hard kick would do it. He reared back, the smoke blinding his eyes, and booted the door with everything he had. A gale of smoke blew inward, and he turned his face away as sparks and chips of doorframe littered the air.

One arm cradled his face, the other arm reaching into the wall of darkness beyond. She was alive, *alive*! He didn't know what would happen going forward, whether the company would step in and place them both under observation, but one thing was for sure. He would tell her that he loved her, because now it was the only thing that really mattered to him. He was in love with her, but not like the others. His love was pure, human. It was –

Amanda charged through the flaming threshold brandishing the broken bed slat. There were no survival tactics involved in her assault; she just ran forward with the pointy end facing outwards, hoping that her momentum was enough to cause a fatal blow. The wood found its home, and Amanda felt the odd resistance as the slat pierced flesh and muscle, scraping against her palm, splinters embedding in her skin. The force of the blow sent her sprawling, and soon she was rolling away from the door, the house a whirlpool before her very eyes. Her lungs felt as though they had shrivelled to raisins. The smoke coated her throat and ran all the way into her stomach. She lay there, powerless, every ounce of strength evaporating in the heat of the fire. But at least she had taken one of them down with her. That's all she really wanted to do anyway: go down with a fight.

Her head lolled to the side. Absently, she thought, In a million years I wouldn't have believed I died in a fire.

She relaxed, her muscles uncoiling. With the bedroom door open, the smoke had changed direction and Amanda saw a body lying on the landing. Her vision was bleary and when she blinked, it stung her eyes. She was going to die and, now that the adrenaline had fizzled away, that was perfectly fine. A warm, calm feeling embalmed her, soothing her pain, easing her mind, a rush of endorphins preparing her for death. Yes, this was alright. She could go now. She could just slip away.

She blinked again and tears rolled from her eyes. Her vision began to clear.

And that's when she saw Claude lying on his back with a piece of broken bed slat sticking out of his chest, just above his stomach. His mouth hung agape, his hands weakly flapping through the air, searching for the obtrusion. A spasm racked his body. Finally, his hands located the wood, but they were powerless to do anything.

Amanda went to him. His head turned toward her, his eyes wide and terrified. The blood pumping out of his chest looked dark and thick as treacle.

She knew immediately that she had stabbed him in the heart. She watched as he began to hiccup, blood bursting through his lips. His hand lay on the carpet, fish-belly pale and flecked with red freckles. His index finger twitched, and she reached out and clasped it.

"Oh no. Oh no, no, no. Oh, Claude I'm sorry," she said through smoky vocals. "I didn't... mean to... I thought you were one of them."

He gasped and his features rearranged his face into a mask of agony. The colour was tipping out of him before her very eyes.

Without thinking about it, she grabbed the slat protruding from his stomach, and yanked; she did not feel the same resistance on the way out as she had in. His eyes bulged from the pain, the cords standing out in his neck. A strangled groan slithered from his twisted mouth.

"It's going to be alright, Claude, OK? I just need to..." She had no idea what needed to be done. Even over the stink of smoke she could smell the tang of his blood, could feel the warmth of it over her hands. She did not want to look directly at the wound, but pressed her hand gently on it, hoping in vain that it would help staunch the blood flow.

Claude's skin became glossy with sweat. He tried to sit up, fell back down, his head thumping the carpet.

"Don't move. Don't move, please... oh god, please help me..." She looked up at the camera. "Damn you. Help me you bastards, he's dying!"

"They told me it wouldn't work on me," he said, frowning. For a second, a smile pulled at his now lavender lips. "I think they were wrong. They told me... wouldn't work..."

He grimaced, gasped, and tried to raise his head again. This time, he couldn't seem to manage it. Amanda stroked his forehead, leaving a red smear that mingled with the rivulets of his sweat running down the side of his face. Claude's lips murmured wordlessly and she bent her head to them, hoping to hear whatever he had to say.

All she caught – or thought she caught over the crackling blaze – was the word love, and then his head rolled away from her.

"Claude," she said, forcing herself to speak clearly. Drawing from some reserve of strength that she didn't know she had, she looked down into his face, hoping that his eyes would focus on her, but they never did.

Behind her, a large piece of the doorframe broke away and clattered to the floor. Ashes and sparks infested the air around her. She cradled Claude's face against her and began to cry.

"I'm so sorry," she whispered into his ear. "Forgive me. Please, please forgive me."

Then she heard the laughter.

CHAPTER 50

Amanda thought she had imagined the sound, that the trauma was making her hallucinate. The heat was almost unbearable, the black smog pooling ominously against the ceiling. Gently, she lay Claude's head back down on the carpet and got to her feet.

The laughter echoed out to her through the smoke; a wild, hyena cackle of madness. Amanda straightened, wiping the tears, all fear and sorrow singeing away with each step she took. She stumbled, righted herself, shook the dizziness off.

Sherry was crouched on all fours like a mangy dog, her remaining hair sticking up in burnt tufts on her blistered scalp. The laughter was coming from *her*.

"A man goes into the bakery," she choked out between chuckles. "He asks for a loaf of bread. The woman at the counter says… white or brown?" She looked up at Amanda, and the smile peeled away from her face. Her lips wriggled like worms, chewing over the words. "I don't know the punchline for that one. What… what did they do to us, Amanda? What… did… they…"

Amanda saw the axe, and Claude's lifeless face popped into her mind like a subliminal message. It should have been Sherry lying dead with a shard of wood in her stomach, not him. It was meant for her.

"I think I'm dying," Sherry said. "It hurts. Everything hurts."

"*Good*," Amanda said, the word sour in her mouth. "It's what you deserve."

"I know," she said, pitifully. Sluggishly, she baby-crawled over to the axe. Amanda didn't try to beat her to it. She just stood there, watching as Sherry fumbled for the axe handle, desperately trying to lift it from the ground. "End it for me, Amanda. I don't want to suffer any more."

Sherry's fingers finally curled around the handle, and she got to one knee.

"Do it for me, please," Sherry croaked, before coughing violently, her back quivering with the effort. She groaned and lifted the axe, presenting it to Amanda like a ceremonial sword. "I'd really like you to do it. It's mercy. Please."

Amanda saw Sherry's shape wobble and wave through the heat.

"Do it yourself," she said and stepped around her, her hand braced on the balcony's banister for support. She padded to the staircase, pausing at the top as her vision cut out for a couple of seconds, and then struggled down the first couple of steps.

Behind her, Sherry crawled toward the staircase after her. "It's all your fault," she growled. "All your fault. All your..."

Amanda looked back over her shoulder, saw Sherry perched and ready to pounce, her charred head bowed. She expected a new surge of energy to reanimate Sherry, for her to leap into action and charge her down the stairs. But there would be no final jump scare. Sherry fell onto her side, one limp arm outstretched toward Amanda as though appealing for a helping hand. Amanda waited a heartbeat longer, and after seeing no further movement in Sherry's body, continued on down the stairs.

She was halfway down when she saw Justin's body curled into a foetal ball, a slick puddle of blood pooling from his head. She did not spare it a second look. It was only her will to live that kept her on her feet at all. Each step across the vast reception area took immense concentration, as there was nothing to hold onto for support. It felt like she was floating, the roar of the fire rushing through her ears, though it was considerably cooler away from the proximity of the flames.

Somehow, she made it to the other side, her hands leaving sooty prints on the wallpaper as she palmed her way along. She thought about Claude's body up there on the landing and found herself wondering whether it would have caught fire by now. A feeble whine left her lips, and she tried to push the image away, but found she wasn't able to. She envisioned that first flame meeting his trouser cuff and then spreading up his leg.

"Stop," she said, or thought she said, pressing a hand to her booming skull.

The ground began to feel more solid beneath her when the grandfather clock came into view, as though the sight of it unlocked a reservoir of strength she never knew existed. Wheezing and spitting a gout of black phlegm, she located the panel that led to the passageway. She gave it a feeble push but felt no give. She leaned on it with her shoulder, lacking the energy for anything more forceful. The sound of the blaze travelled through the house in a hushed, almost soothing burr, offering all the incentive she needed. Her fingers crawled over the panel's surface and felt its fallacy; it stuck out past the other panels by a few millimetres, just enough for her to get her fingernails behind it and pull. The panel swung open, and the passageway's damp breath sighed over her.

She stepped inside the passageway, completely unafraid of the darkness that had seemed so sinister before. Her mind began stuttering as she remembered Claude's excited face the first time he showed her this secret, which really hadn't been a secret to him at all. He had been a mole for Midori, he had been in on the whole thing, facilitating the ruse, ensuring that they all played along. She thought about him on the landing again, his shirt catching fire and his lifeless arms unable to bat away the flames.

When she was halfway through the passageway, blinking at the light ahead, she heard something behind her. Her knees locked, feet becoming cinderblocks, her heart a pincushion of pain as the fear mounted her. She spun around and saw something obscuring the light at the open panel. A rusty hand grabbed hold of her throat and stole the scream that wanted to leap out.

Someone was entering the passageway behind her.

"S'il vous plait ne laissez pas mon amour," Wish said, and began moving rapidly and erratically toward her, feeling along the passageway walls like a spider.

CHAPTER 51

The shock turned Amanda's blood to cement. She wanted to run, but in that instant the sight of Wish clambering toward her stalled the fight-or-flight response. Wish muttered frantically in French, wheezing and grunting, and then proclaiming in English: "You set me free. My body was broken... You don't understand. You're the only reason I'm still here. I figured it out. My calling in life, Amanda, please, just stop and listen to me. You are my sister. Can't you feel it? I know you feel it!"

Finally, Amanda's engine turned over and all her senses came back online. She spun, dashed toward the ladder at the end of the passageway, the adrenaline flooding her system. Her hands found the ladder and she began to climb, scraping and banging her knees on the rungs. The fear made every follicle on her face tingle unbearably. When she neared the top, she reached out and pushed against the grille that covered the entrance. Her hand was met with resistance, but the grille did move, and so she pressed the crown of her head against it and pushed harder, finally dislodging it. She had just pushed the grille aside and made enough space to wriggle out when a jagged flare of pain ripped through her calf. Wish was biting her, her mouth locked around Amanda's leg like a pit bull.

Amanda howled as Wish's teeth sank deeper into her flesh. She could hear Wish grunting and snarling, shaking her head in a futile attempt to free Amanda's leg from her body. With her other foot, Amanda kicked down into Wish's face, once, twice, three times and then the bear trap released and Wish finally lost her purchase on the ladder, tumbling to the floor.

There was no time to acknowledge the pain or wonder how much of her calf Wish's teeth had claimed. She could feel the warm blood flowing down into her trainer but didn't let that gory little detail dissuade her from continuing up through the passageway exit. Rain spat down on her from a cigarette-smoke sky, and she sucked in a lungful of clean air, which detonated stars in her vision. The world trembled before her eyes, darkening around the edges. She shook her head to clear it but couldn't seem to lose the tunnel vision.

It was only when she heard Wish pulling herself back up the ladder that Amanda realized she was cornered in the courtyard. Any second now, the top of Wish's head would poke up through the square, and instinctively, Amanda tried to run for the grille. Her idea was to smash the grille on her head and press it down on the exit, ensuring that Wish couldn't rise up and enter the courtyard, but of course that didn't happen. As soon as Amanda put her weight down on her left leg, it gave out beneath her. Wish must've bitten through the tendons in her calf because Amanda went sprawling on the concrete, unable to support herself.

Then she saw it: the Queen Cage. It was the only option left.

Amanda clawed her way toward it, the strange metallic booth gleaming dully in the rain. Her hands met the cold metal shell, and she put all her weight down on her good leg in an attempt to stand back up. The effort pulled fresh torrents of sweat from her pores, and she felt the wound in her calf pulse like a heartbeat.

"Tu ne vas pas me quitter," Wish said, her voice oddly slurred, losing all its lyrical inflection.

Amanda pulled the cage door open, her mouth braced to scream, and slid inside the Queen Cage just as Wish got to her feet. The door clicked closed, sealing Amanda in and locking all sound out. There wasn't enough space to turn, or squat or bend;

she just had to stand, the leather upholstery holding her in place. She felt like a Barbie doll still in its box. Her rapid breath quickly misted the window, which was mere inches from her face. Still, she could see the confusion wash over Wish as she scanned the courtyard, her attention settling on the Queen Cage. Wish ran toward it, her ruined face filling the window.

"S'il vous plait ouvrir," Wish said, her upper lip swollen to the size of a slug. Blood streamed from both nostrils and drooled from her mouth. "Open it Amanda, please. I'm begging you. What about our music video? Ma sœur, please... let's just dance. Open it up, we can sing and dance. It doesn't matter. Nothing matters, just us, that's all."

Amanda barely heard the words, but flinched back into the leather, wondering whether Wish would find a way in. Amanda felt for a handle or something she could hold to prevent Wish getting the door open, but there was nothing. Wish's head swivelled as she took stock of the booth, trying to gain entry. She found the door's ridge and tried to pry it open, and when that failed, she returned to the window and slapped it with her palms.

"LET ME IN YOU FUCKING BITCH!"

Amanda shook her head. Wish's expression turned ugly, and she reared back and head-butted the window. The impact registered as a dull throb on the inside of the booth. She head-butted the window over and over, until her skin opened up and left red splotches on the glass.

"Why... won't you just... love me?" Wish asked breathlessly, or at least, that's what Amanda thought she said. It looked as though the constant battering had taken its toll on Wish, but just as Amanda thought she had given up, Wish went back at it, punching and clawing at the glass. When that didn't work, Wish brought her mouth to the window and began to bite. Her teeth scraped the glass leaving faint scratches, the friction creating a horrible squeak. She adjusted her jaw, sucked onto the glass, and tried again.

Then, she fell down abruptly and there was something else standing in her place: a man in what looked like riot gear, his face obscured by a gas mask. He raised one gloved hand and used it to wipe the window clean. Then, he simply stared at her.

Ding-dong. The chime rang inside the booth, jangling her nerves.

"Well done, Amanda. It's all over," the Overlord's voice said. "The rat has solved the maze and found the cheese. You can relax now."

"I want to go home," she said miserably. Her voice sounded flat and featureless in the soundproof booth.

"You will. Soon. But first, sleep," the Overlord replied.

Amanda was unconscious before she was even aware that gas was filling the Queen Cage.

CHAPTER 52

Black.

Then light. Blinding. Movement – she was floating, looking up at the white light. She was on her way to heaven.

"She's waking up." A man's voice. No, not heaven. Where I am? Still in that house? Oh god, please don't still be in that house. No, I made it out, didn't I? Climbed the walls and... the Queen Cage. Wish, biting the window, her teeth cracking in the gums.

She tried to sit up, couldn't. Something was pressing against her chest, keeping her in place. Through her blurry vision, she could just about make out the white walls and the faces of the people looking down on her.

An audience... just for me... is this... where... I give an encore?

Then she realized she wasn't floating. She was strapped down on a gurney, being pushed through... a hospital? Was that it? Yes, now she thought about it, she could feel something on her face, pressing down into her skin. It was a mask, but not like the surgical ones the people around her were wearing. It was an oxygen mask. But there was no more pain, and somewhere deep in the swampy catacombs of her mind, she supposed she had morphine to thank for that.

"Help Claude," she attempted to say, but her tongue felt like it was untethered from her mouth, lolling lazily. A vague sense of pain itched through her throat.

"Don't try to speak," another male voice commanded.

So, she didn't. She closed her eyes, and the faces disappeared.

Sometime later, she surfaced from the abyss, only to find that she was sitting up, but still restrained. A perfect circle of blinding white light shone directly into her eyes, burning through her corneas. A wisp of memory – the set of a music video – a dark studio, the heat of the spotlights trained directly on her, a wind machine blowing the hair away from her face.

Another memory. Bunny's voice. A pep talk in her office on the day that Amanda made her decision to sign with her. There's more to this game than just singing. It's a job – a tough fucking job, and it takes hard work. But if you're willing to trust me–

She groaned and called for help, but there was no response. Somewhere behind her, she could hear movement, and then a moment later, the figure of a man stood in front of the light. Backlit, the silhouette was nothing more than a distorted black shape. But beyond it, she sensed, or imagined, dozens more people; her audience, One Night with Amanda Pearson.

"How do you feel, Amanda?" Another voice, one she thought she recognized. It was the Overlord, there in the flesh. Even doped-up, she still had enough wits about her to feel a creepy tingle of déjà vu.

"Whuurrrrs Claauu?" the words gurgled in her throat, bringing that itchy pain back. Every inhalation caused fork prongs to scrape down her lungs.

"Shh, shh." His hand stroked her hair. "Just settle down. There's a good girl."

A brick sat in her stomach, and she thought that at any moment she would vomit it out. Her head was full of gravel, too heavy for her neck. Her eyelids were rusty iron shutters.

She tried to concentrate through the quicksand of her thoughts. The temptation to relax and give up the fight was overpowering. It was like a weight crushing down on her, forcing her into submission. Each time she thought she would relent, she saw Claude's face, twisted at the horror of his own imminent murder, his hands gingerly reaching for the wood protruding from his chest.

"Everything is fine, Amanda." His hand had settled on the crown of her head, his thumb tenderly rubbing droplets of sweat away from her forehead. "It's over. You've been such a treat to watch. Also, I suppose we owe you a round of applause. You are the first person in human history to complete a course of Honeycomb beyond twenty milligrams. What you have done in these past few days, the information you have provided us with, has been invaluable. Invaluable."

She felt him kiss her through the mask.

"Let's hear it for Amanda Pearson. The Queen Bee."

The uneven sound of clapping ricocheted around her head, but she had no idea what any of it meant. Through the fuzz, she became aware of more people surrounding her. They could be phantoms, some hallucination she'd conjured through the fugue, she just didn't know. It was making her crazy.

"...Be sick," she tried to say. She couldn't reach up to take the oxygen mask off her face, and nobody seemed interested in helping her. "Gonnabe sick..."

"What was it like to have that feeling back?" the Overlord asked. "To have people love you, willing to do anything to please you? How seductive is success, Amanda?"

"Nnnt..." She had wanted to say: Not real. None of it was real.

"One pill a day and everyone will be falling over their feet to say hello, to wish you a good morning, to offer you a seat on the tube, to take a picture with you. How amazing would it be to turn people's heads in the street again, Amanda? One pill a day and you wouldn't need to kill yourself in a studio or go on lengthy tours. You could have that feeling every minute of every day and not need to do a single thing, except swallow a small, harmless pill."

Somehow, through the riot of confusion and fear, she began to feel a low pulse of anger. She tried to lurch against the restraints, but the attempt was feeble, and after a few seconds of protest she slumped back, fireworks exploding in her head.

"Gnna k... gnna kill..."

"Don't talk, just rest." His thumb wiped away another bead of sweat.

"I'm... gonna... kill... you..."

"No," he said, turning away from her, losing interest. The light went out. "You're going to thank me."

Black.

CHAPTER 53

The phone was ringing, drilling through her dreams. Amanda sat up, the world an unrecognizable smear around her. She didn't know how long she had been asleep for, but her head felt as though it were stuffed with cotton, and her eyes sat heavy in their sockets. Opening her eyelids became a strict act of defiance. It felt like she was wading through sludge, her mind spinning like a ceiling fan.

The phone, bleating and vibrating, somewhere to her left. She opened her eyes and looked down to see her iPhone flashing and picked it up.

"Hello?"

"Don't tell me you aren't ready Amanda, for fuck's sake."

"Ready?" She spoke through a mouthful of marbles. Ready for what? She didn't even know where she was. The heaviness in her skull remained, but the confusion started to sift through the cracks. She was in her flat. Sitting on her sofa. Holding her phone. And… she was cold. She looked down, and her breath caught in her throat. She did not recognize the dress she was wearing, but from the look and feel of it, she knew it had to be extremely expensive.

"The limo driver is on his way to you now, so if you're wearing heels you might want to get a move on down those stairs because I know your lifts aren't working."

Amanda's eyes rolled down her shaved legs and settled on her feet. They were snug inside black patent shoes, and when she lifted her ankle, Amanda saw that the soles were blood red: Louboutin's.

"I'm ready…" she started to say, but her voice was thick and croaky. "Um… sorry, I've just woken up."

"I knew you'd fall asleep," the voice said through the receiver, but not unkindly. "You're getting so predictable, you know that? I hope you haven't been smoking marijuana young lady."

"No, no I haven't," she spluttered. Her thoughts were so soupy that she didn't have a clue what day it was let alone where this limo was supposed to be taking her. And then there was that other thing… "Um, this is going to sound like a stupid question but… who is this?"

"Oh my god, I've heard it all now. It's Bunny. Remember me now? Go and splash your face and liven up. You'll feel better soon."

"OK, I will." Amanda could hear herself speaking but wasn't conscious of doing so. "Um, where am I going?"

A pause on the other side of the phone. "Amanda, I want you to listen to me very carefully now. Have you taken something?"

"Taken… something?"

"Yes. You know what I mean."

"No. I've…" *I've been locked in a mansion for the past week and, yes, I was taking something that made everyone lose their minds. But that was… how long ago?* "I haven't taken anything."

"Alright, well don't panic. I'm sure once you get some fresh air, you'll be fine. Look, I don't want to get you worked up, but you know how important tonight is, don't you?"

"Yeah… yes," she lied.

"Because I had to call in favours from all over the place to get you these ten minutes on *Shannon Driver*."

The Shannon Driver Show? Is that what she was talking about? No, she couldn't be. That was the most watched show on terrestrial TV. What would she be doing on there?

"Thank god you're miming tonight. Look, don't fret. It's a good thing I booked this limo early. I'm gonna jump in a cab and get on my way over to you. You're just nervous, I know. Go and make a cup of instant and I'll be there in a few minutes."

"Sure, I'll do that."

"It'll be alright," Bunny said. "Tonight we start afresh. Amanda Pearson rises from the ashes to take over the world. Right?"

"Right," she repeated, touching her face, making sure that it was still there.

By the time Bunny arrived, wearing a cute Givenchy number, Amanda was beginning to feel human again. A residue of uncertainty lingered, but Bunny's enthusiastic smile went a long way towards alleviating her fears. Back in her wild days, Amanda had woken up in some strange places with no recollection of how she had got there, having to piece the memory of the evening together through social media and the messages on her phone. She felt a stab of panic, fearing that all her hard work of staying sober had been undone in a night (week?) of weakness. But she didn't have time to dwell on it, because Bunny was bundling her in a coat, and leading her to the stairwell.

In the limo, they cracked open a bottle of Perrier water, forgoing the champagne. Bunny did her usual routine of talking to Amanda while somehow keeping her attention glued to her phone, her thumb dextrously tapping out tweets, hashtagging the performance ahead.

Had it really all been a dream, a wildly vivid series of hallucinations? Had she relapsed, overdosed, and conjured the whole thing up on the brink of death? *Yes, that was it. A dream.*

Yet, as much as she had wanted to convince herself of this, her hand slipped down her leg. She touched her calf, felt a circle of raised flesh, the scar from Wish's love bite.

"Bunny?" Amanda said.

"Mmm?" Bunny didn't look up from her phone.

"What happened to them?"

"Happened to who, honey?"

"Claude and the others."

Bunny peeled her attention away from the screen, her brow unable to furrow in order to express her confusion. "Who?"

"Don't lie to me, Bunny. I remember everything."

Bunny opened her mouth to speak and then thought better of it. There was a sly gleam in her eyes. "Does it matter?" she asked. "You're at the top of the mountain again."

And with that, she returned her attention to her phone, and the pantomime resumed.

They pulled up at the guest entrance of the TV studio and were ushered through to the green room. A producer with a clipboard gave Amanda a rundown of the interview, checking to see what questions she was comfortable answering.

"I don't want to hear anything about her past," Bunny cut in, when the producer read a question that hinted at Amanda's newfound sobriety. "Nothing about drugs or YouTube. This is a fresh start for Amanda, so none of that shit, otherwise I'll come right on that stage and pull her off. You got it?"

"That's fine," the producer said. "We'll just cover the questions about her musical influences, what she likes to do when she's not writing and recording music."

And then it was off to makeup. She was powdered, sprayed, and had a dab of blush applied to her cheeks to give her a rosy little girl look. Bunny sat on the sofa behind her, still tweeting, snapping photos, and uploading them onto Instagram. She said something about a clip on TikTok blowing up, but Amanda didn't catch it. Then the producer bounded into the room, one finger pressed against her earphone as she listened to her instructions.

"OK Amanda, we're ready for you."

Amanda stood up. She appraised herself in the spotlight mirror. She looked like a star again.

Bunny admired her like a proud parent, almost welling up at the sight of Amanda. Careful not to disrupt the makeup, Bunny leaned in and gave her a light hug. "Before you go…" She went into her purse, removed a silver case about the size of a cigarette packet, and opened it. Inside it, sitting on black velvet, was a small, white pill. "Pop this on your tongue," Bunny said, holding the pill up on her index finger.

"I don't want to," Amanda said, rearing back. "No, Bunny, I don't want to. It's dangerous."

Bunny smiled. "It's harmless."

"It's not. I don't want…" But already she could feel herself weakening. She wanted to go on stage. She wanted to be loved.

"Honey, it's a balanced dose, don't worry. Everything is going to be peachy, just you watch." And with that, Bunny placed the pill on Amanda's tongue, and gave her a sip of Perrier to wash it down. Bunny hugged her again, and whispered, "The phoenix has risen. Go and knock them dead."

The producer led Amanda down a busy corridor, the walls decorated with the pictures of previous guests from *The Shannon Driver Show*. To think she was going to be part of that elite group was bewildering to her. It wouldn't quite sink in, even as she neared the studio curtains, on the other side of which was an audience, and cameras that would broadcast her to millions of people.

"Don't be nervous," the producer said as they waited for the announcement of Amanda's name. The producer rubbed Amanda's bare, goose-pimpled arm. "You're gonna be fine. I saw some of your rehearsal yesterday, my god, it was amazing. Just relax."

Amanda smiled and nodded. She couldn't remember yesterday.

"…*Please welcome, the lovely Amanda Pearson!*"

This was it. The beginning of her new life. The start of her redemption.

And to think that she had dreamt of this moment, fantasized about another chance to put her career back on track. They would love her just like how they had loved her on *Searching for a Star*. Everything was going to be OK. No, more than OK – perfect.

Because everyone loves a good comeback story.

CHAPTER 54

Amanda woke up with grass in her mouth. Her face was pressed against the damp earth and she could hear the wind howling around her, the chill nipping at her skin. She tried to push herself up, her hands clawing in the mud, but she couldn't seem to find the strength in her arms just yet. She rolled onto her side, the world jittery and unfocussed. There was a steady pounding in her temples, the drumbeat of a migraine that seemed to change tempo with the slightest movement of her head. When the ground stopped tilting and her vision reorganized, she made it to one knee, took a deep breath, and then attempted to stand. She wobbled, then felt a fresh wave of vertigo crash over her. Her legs buckled and she crumbled back down into the mud.

She was sitting alone in a tree-lined field. In the distance, there was an empty playground, the apparatus occupied by the wind. She could see a basketball court penned in by a mesh fence, and beyond that, the peak of Liston Place, the tower block she lived in.

Something touched her hand, wet and rough. Amanda's attention shot toward it, and lightning crackled in her skull for her troubles. There was a small dog, maybe a terrier – she wasn't sure – licking her fingers. She watched it curiously for a moment before attempting to get back to her feet.

"Pixie, come here," a woman's voice called, the slightest hint of fear tinging the words. "Pixie, get here *now*."

Amanda looked over at the woman. The woman would

not look back at her. Amanda once again attempted to stand, commanding her legs to obey. She got there, just about, but Pixie was still at her heels, sniffing the cuffs of her tracksuit bottoms.

"Pixie, you come over here right this instant!" the woman said, and then to Amanda, "What's the matter with you? Why're you sleeping in the park?" The woman, probably in her sixties, with thick glasses and a purple woollen hat, was staring at her accusingly. "It's six-thirty in the morning. What are you doing here?"

Amanda looked at her mud-streaked hands. She was about to answer when a bead of perspiration trickled from her armpit and rolled down the flank of her torso. She was sweating. Almost instantly, the woman's face softened, her eyes warming behind her magnifying glasses.

"Are you alright love? Has something happened to you?"

"No," Amanda said, taking a step back, hoping her legs would keep her upright.

"Are you sure? Because I live close by, and if you wanted to, it would be no bother for you to come back to my place and get cleaned up." The woman dropped her retractable dog leash to the grass, freeing Pixie to harass Amanda further. "I... I made a cake yesterday. I'm no Mary Berry," the woman said with a nervous titter, "but I could make you a cup of tea and... look after you?"

The woman started toward Amanda, her gloved fingers flexing at her sides.

"No thank you," Amanda said, turned, and started to hobble. It was as close to a run as she could manage at that point. Her hips ached, and the muscles in her legs felt like they had been battered with a meat tenderizer. Pixie began to yap and spring alongside her, but Amanda ignored the dog and continued to focus on the park gates further down the path.

From behind her, she heard the woman call out: "Please? Come back to mine. I'll get you cleaned up. You can have... some cake."

*

The courtyard outside her building, which was usually busy with teenagers or mums pushing their kids to the playground in their prams, was empty. A blanket of thick fog curled around her feet as they slapped the concrete, eager to be inside. She needed a shower, something to drink, and a long time to think.

She pressed the lift button almost out of habit. Nine times out of ten, it would give no reaction, but today the doors rumbled open. She got in, rode it up to her floor, and when the doors opened again, she paused. Rather than hurry into the hallway, she popped her head out and checked. She thought she might see Sherry standing there, or Arthur bumbling around. Or worse – that Claude would be waiting for her, unable to speak but wanting to know why she had killed him.

But there was nobody. Liston Place was still asleep, and that brought a tremendous amount of relief. Hurrying out of the lift and moving guiltily toward her flat, Amanda became conscious of every squeak her trainers made on the floor. She reached her door, and then an enormous feeling of horror fell on her. She didn't have any keys. She didn't have her bag or any of the stuff she had taken. She didn't... she touched her pocket. There was a soft jingle. She reached inside and removed her door keys. She had no idea how they were in her pocket, only that they were there, and she was thankful. Sliding the key home, she opened the door and stepped inside the silence of her flat. She didn't know what day it was, how long she had been away, or how she was going to deal with everything that had happened. The first thing she was going to do was take a shower, then she would call the police and see if they would listen to her story. They might think she was mad. Maybe she was. But if she kept telling the story then someone was bound to listen. Maybe not at first, but eventually. She would make noise, cause a fuss, be called a crackpot, a conspiracy theorist, but she could deal with that. Somehow, it would be easier than being called a washed-up singer, a one-hit wonder. A nothing. A nobody.

One day, she would get them back for what they had done to her, to Claude, to Arthur, to Sherry, Justin, Wish, the woman who had begged for help outside the conservatory, and god only knew how many others.

One day.

But first, a shower.

She bumbled through the living room when something caught her eye. On the coffee table, next to the collection of bills, was a large, square stack of money. She didn't need to count it to know it was a quarter of a million pounds, less her advance.

The sight of it sickened her. She wanted to pick the bundles up and throw them out the window; let the rest of the estate have a party on her. Then she saw something else on top of the money. It was a white card with black lettering printed on it. Amanda approached it with the same caution as she would an armed bomb. She picked the card up. The inscription read:

Nobody will believe you

Now it all made sense. There had been no comeback on *The Shannon Driver Show*. There was no pot of gold at the end of the rainbow. There was only a head full of nightmares.

Nobody will believe you

The third time she read the sentence, she began to laugh.

She laughed, and laughed, and laughed.

They were right. What was she going to do? Make a YouTube video about it?

Rochelle wasn't sure what woke her, only that she needed to get up. Through the cardboard-thin walls, she thought she could hear Amanda walking around in her flat, and then there was the burr of water from the direction of Amanda's bathroom. Rochelle pulled the quilt off her and got out of bed. Despite the cold in the evenings, she was wearing only bra and knickers, because that was the only way she was comfortable sleeping. Without stopping to put on more clothes, fuelled by an irrational sense of urgency, she crossed the bedroom and did something she had never done, or even contemplated doing before: she left the flat without taking Andre with her. The boy was asleep, but she hadn't checked to know for sure. The thought hadn't even crossed her mind because just then, she needed to go to Amanda. It was more important; she just didn't know why.

Someone was standing outside Amanda's flat. Sharon from a few doors down, half-asleep, a long t-shirt covering her upper body but leaving her naked lower half exposed. And next to her was the Indian man – a student who moved into number 85 a few weeks ago. He had his palm pressed against the door, but neither of them spoke or made any kind of move as Rochelle neared.

Rochelle was going to ask what they were both doing at Amanda's door, but didn't. Instead, she just stood there, staring at the door in silence.

A couple of minutes later, she heard another door open up further down the hallway. She didn't look around to see who it was. She could hear the footsteps as the person approached to join the queue outside Amanda's door.

Rochelle didn't care.

All she wanted was Amanda.

EPILOGUE

"Can't you shut her up? She's doing my fucking head in," Tim Barrett, who had worked security roles in some capacity or another his whole adult life, said. He was very big; built like a powerlifter with the face of a bulldog, as intimidating a man as you could hope to find. And, as his appearance would suggest, there were very few things that could send the frighteners up him.

The French woman didn't just bother him. She *frightened* him. He wasn't a man that believed in ghosts, but he thought there were some pretty fucked-up people in the world that believed that *they* were seeing ghosts. The French woman wasn't just haunted though, she was possessed, and her constant, single-minded ravings cooled his blood to ice.

"You know we can't give her anything," Tim's colleague, a veteran at the institute called Gary Winters, told him. They were on suicide watch, standing outside the cell, their attention locked on the woman to prevent her smashing her head against the wall or trying to bite off her own tongue. The straightjacket kept her from clawing at her face anymore (she had tried to pull out her eyes), but her legs remained free to kick and buck at the air.

"What is she saying anyway?" Tim asked, rolling his shoulders.

"Don't know. I don't speak French. I wouldn't worry about it though. She won't be able to keep this up for long. She'll blow her voice out again soon enough."

"I wish I could go in there and just shut her up," Tim said as the French woman released a horrendous scream and broke down into hysterical sobbing.

What they didn't know was that Wish wasn't speaking French at all. It was her accent, and their simple understanding of her background, that made them assume otherwise. She was in fact speaking gibberish. In another setting, a church of a certain denomination for example, they might have thought she was speaking in tongues.

Wish lay on her side, weeping, because she did not see the two guards blocking the doorway. She saw Amanda in a long dress, singing a song, just for her. To Wish, it was like hearing the voice of God, an out-of-body experience beyond the realm of the five senses. There was nothing else to do except weep, for she would never know beauty like this ever again.

And with that, Amanda took a bow, blew her a kiss, and disappeared.

ACKNOWLEDGEMENTS

First, a huge special thank-you to Simon Ward and Ella Chappell for their invaluable input, support, and enthusiasm.

Thank you to my wonderful agent, Laura Williams, who continues to guide and advise me.

A lot of people work on a book before it gets published; from editors, proofreaders, cover designers, sales reps, admin, interns, publicity and marketing people, and so on. I'd like to extend my thanks and appreciation to everyone at Datura/ Angry Robot for helping Honeycomb reach the hands of readers (but especially Caroline and Amy).

Last, but not least, thanks to Lorna W. and Theresa R.